THE
KEEPSAKE

By Julie Brooks

The Secrets of Bridgewater Bay
The Keepsake

THE
KEEPSAKE

JULIE BROOKS

REVIEW

First published in ebook in 2022
by HEADLINE REVIEW
An imprint of HEADLINE PUBLISHING GROUP

First published in Great Britain in this hardback edition in 2023
by HEADLINE REVIEW

1

Cataloguing in Publication Data is available from the British Library

ISBN Hardback 978 1 4722 7919 4
ISBN Trade Paperback 978 1 4722 7918 7

Typeset in Minion Pro by Avon DataSet Ltd, Alcester, Warwickshire

Printed and bound in Great Britain by Clays Ltd, Elcograf S.p.A.

Headline's policy is to use papers that are natural, renewable and recyclable
products and made from wood grown in well-managed forests and other
controlled sources. The logging and manufacturing processes are expected
to conform to the environmental regulations of the country of origin.

HEADLINE PUBLISHING GROUP
An Hachette UK Company
Carmelite House
50 Victoria Embankment
London EC4Y 0DZ

www.headline.co.uk
www.hachette.co.uk

For Ru and Kit

1

Somerset, England

2022

The last time Eliza celebrated a birthday where her name was spelled out in jellybeans, she was five years old and prone to squeals of joy. Yet here she was, thirty years later, slicing into a lopsided chocolate cake bedecked with a kaleidoscope of candy. Secretly, she suspected the cake was a symbol of all that her life had become, living in the same house, surrounded by a revolving parade of curios at the Cabinet of Wonders, and following in her parents' footsteps. She may as well have been five years old and marooned on a merry-go-round in her party dress.

'I'm loving the decorations, Jude,' she said, removing a single pink candle and cutting her aunt a generous slice.

'I've exceeded all expectations, if I do say so myself. You wouldn't know it came out of a packet!' Her aunt gave herself a pat on the back before adding, 'Now, how about pouring some of that champagne?'

Eliza did as she was told and they clinked glasses, their knees nuzzled by her schnauzer Bobby, who twirled from one to the other, moustaches twitching. No doubt more interested in cake than champagne.

'You really shouldn't have gone to so much trouble.'

'Well, I know what you're like, pet. If I didn't bother, you'd ignore your birthday completely.'

Eliza took another sip of champagne, patting Bobby absent-mindedly as she gazed at the cake. Her aunt was probably right; she would have ignored this milestone. But birthdays didn't hold the same appeal they once had, when every day glimmered with possibility. Of late, her days held only the patina of sameness. Work, eat, sleep, get up and work again. *And whose fault is that?* her inner voice sniped if she ever succumbed to even a modicum of self-pity. For as inner voices went, hers was largely devoid of sympathy.

'You really should get out more,' Jude said, raising her glass.

'I get out.'

'To estate sales, yes, but what about a bit of fun?'

'Estate sales are fun.'

'Sniffing through dusty tomes and rattling chipped crockery doesn't sound like much fun to me – and I'm a crusty old lady of seventy-five, not a gorgeous young woman in her prime.'

Eliza leaned over and gave her aunt a chocolatey peck. 'No one could call you crusty, darling, but I'll take the compliment. And stop feeding Bobby titbits under the table.'

'I didn't. I'm not. I am a mistress of restraint. Besides, he had a sausage in the kitchen while you were setting out the plates,' Jude said, exchanging a conspiratorial glance with Bobby.

'You're a sneaky old woman. And you,' Eliza said, gripping the dog's nose and leaning in close to better make her point, 'are a very disloyal dog.' Which only resulted in a wet tongue to the nose.

'Eww . . . that is disgusting.'

'I do have a nicer surprise for you, though.' Jude put aside her plate and glass to reach for a small package wrapped in Christmas paper that had been sitting on the side table beside her. Her aunt had never been one for convention. For Eliza's sixteenth birthday she had given her two tickets to an Oasis concert wrapped in what turned out to be a vintage Pucci scarf.

'Gimme . . .' Eliza held out her hand and waggled her fingers. One was never too old for presents.

The package fitted neatly into her hand; it was light in weight, with a firm exterior and a little give beneath. A manicure case or purse, perhaps. Knowing her aunt, it would be something personal. A jewellery case? She shook it gently, listening for a telltale rattle, but there was barely a whisper of sound.

She glanced over at her aunt, who was beaming like the Cheshire Cat. 'Give me a clue.'

'Hmm . . . I suppose you could say it's a . . . a pocketful of memories.'

'A photograph album?'

'No.'

'Some kind of hard drive?'

'Good God, no!'

'Give me another clue.'

'Not telling. You have to open it.'

Eliza slid a finger beneath the paper's edge and unfolded the wrapping. If anything, her aunt's smile grew even broader when the object inside was revealed: a small case formed from a thick envelope of faded red leather, scuffed, scratched, and marked with the remnants of past water damage.

'Is this what I think it is?'

Her aunt nodded. 'Probably. You're the expert on old things, pet.'

The sides of the case weren't sewn or joined together, and she turned it over to reveal a neat brass clasp. She tore her gaze from the gift to say, 'You shouldn't have. It's too much. I haven't come across one of these in ages.' Actually, two years earlier she had reluctantly passed on one that had been asking $400.

'Don't get too excited. It's just a little something I found when I was cleaning out some of Dad's old stuff. I thought you might like it.'

'I wonder where he got it? He and Gran weren't exactly collectors.'

'No, everything had to be new when your dad and I were kids.' Jude smiled at the memory. 'New and preferably shiny. I think it may have had something to do with living through the war and always making do. They rebelled as soon as they had the chance.'

'Well, they certainly didn't pass that trait on to *my* father. The only new things to appear in our house when I was a kid were underwear and socks. And he wasn't above picking up a pair of second-hand socks if he thought they had enough wear left in them.'

Her grandparents hadn't passed their love of the new and shiny on to Eliza either. She glanced down at the outfit she had chosen for this birthday tea at her aunt's cottage: high-waisted Romeo Gigli trousers in a black and white floral straight out of the nineties, a black rib-knitted top with a Peter Pan collar rescued from a sale bin in the high street, and vintage red velvet Dr Martens. Her brown hair was shorn to its usual one-inch crop, and she had completed the look with a lick of mascara, subtle wings lining her green eyes, and a cherry-pink lip, while an enormous retro crocheted bag perched on the sofa beside her.

'I think he may have had a special reason for keeping this,' her aunt said, a glint of mystery in her eyes behind their giant Limoncello-coloured lenses.

Intrigued by this hint, Eliza released the small clasp and opened the case to reveal the miniature book she expected to find. The pages were stitched into the leather cover, a tiny book incorporating a diary and ledger, small enough to fit into a lady's pocket or the palm of a hand. Plus, she knew it would contain a compendium of information both useful and trivial, with the added attraction of that year's fashion plates and engravings of great country estates or scenic vistas. She also noted that someone had written the date 1832 on the cover in a small neat hand, then added 1833 below.

What she held in her hand was a late-Georgian lady's pocket book. Who could tell what secrets it might hold? Her heart gave a skip as she turned to the flyleaf where the pocket book's original owner had inscribed: *Prudence Jane Merryfield, Somerset, 1st January, 1832.*

'Oh my God,' she gasped, 'where on earth did you find this?'

The owner's name was a shock, one she could never have imagined in her wildest dreams. To think she held in her hand an object once owned by the notorious Prudence Merryfield, possibly the most infamous of all former residents of their village. Prudence, her not-quite ancestor. Family, yet not family. Victim of perfidy and harbinger of disaster.

'I can hardly believe it's real.'

'I found it in an ancient hatbox buried deep in the attic. Full of Dad's old fishing magazines, the only thing he never let our mother throw out. She had an aversion for anything to do with the family history. Said it depressed her. I suppose he hid it from her on purpose. Maybe he was saving it for me, but of course I never thought to look through the boxes before.' Her voice faded, and Eliza caught a fleeting expression of sadness cross her face.

'You shouldn't be going up that ridiculous ladder at your age. And especially not alone.'

'They're stairs, not a ladder. And you are such a worrier.'

'And you, my darling, are . . . a wonder. If a somewhat careless one.' Eliza felt tears pricking her eyes and sniffed them back. 'Such a precious gift . . . and to think it once belonged to Prudence Merryfield.'

The name rippled from her tongue like a pebble tossed into a stream. Prudence Merryfield, long dead and gone, yet her existence still reverberated through the lives of generations of Eliza's family, the Ambroses. She double-checked the name written inside the flyleaf to make sure she hadn't imagined it. Yes, there it was in faded blue ink – Prudence Jane Merryfield – with the frontispiece on the facing page announcing the publication as *Peacock's Polite Repository or Pocket Companion*.

'It's in a pretty sorry state,' said her aunt, tucking one silver asymmetrical lock behind her ear as she bent to peer at the book. 'And some of the pages are missing from the middle.'

Eliza flipped through a few pages at random, opening the pocket book to one crammed with tiny words written in the same hand. She squinted as she deciphered one entry where the ink appeared darker, as if the pen had been pressed hard to the paper.

Monday: Father died. Sent for Norris. Weather inclement. Dined with Edward. Six courses.

The words were so polite, so devoid of emotion. And what a strange juxtaposition of events she had recorded. The weather had been given equal significance with her father's death. *Father died.* Those two dolorous words, with no mention of the diarist's feelings, yet dinner required all of five. And here too, in this first entry Eliza perused, was a reference to her own ancestor, Edward Ambrose – her great-great-something-or-other-grandfather – landowner, gentleman, neighbour and family friend to the Merryfields.

The diary felt warm in her hands, leather and paper – animal and vegetable. It was a custodian of memories, a keeper of secrets. What other surprises might this polite repository of a lady's daily life hold in store?

'This is too much. You must keep it,' she said, holding it out towards her aunt while simultaneously resisting the urge to clutch it to her chest. She was a keeper of old things, of people's pasts, of lives forgotten, and the pocket book seemed to promise – what exactly?

'Oh, it could just as well have come to your dad if he hadn't kicked the bucket before me. And I doubt I have too many years left,' Jude said, waving it away, 'so you might as well have it now. You'll be getting it one day, anyway.'

'You'd better plan on sticking around for a while yet. Where else is Bobby going to get his sausages?' Some might find Jude's reference to her father's death too casual, but for Eliza this very naturalness brought comfort. Every day, she was surrounded by reminders of her parents, in the store and the flat upstairs, yet she had no one to talk to about them. No one who would mention in passing her mother's fondness for daffodils or her father's pitiful way with a 9 iron.

'I'm not sure why my father buried it at the bottom of a box of stuff no one was ever likely to look through. Do you think he meant to hide it or save it?' Jude asked.

'He probably put it there so Gran wouldn't sell it to buy a new toaster.'

'And I wonder why Prudence added 1833 below the first date,' her aunt said, puzzling over the notation on the cover.

'Maybe she ran out of pages. Books were expensive, and people often reused them. Wrote in the margins, jotted things in the accounts pages, wrote vertically . . . they even bought them second hand and filled up the empty spaces.' Eliza answered her aunt automatically, but the date did ring a bell. No doubt the reason would come to her later.

'And some of the middle pages are missing. Torn out by the looks of it.'

'Just another missing piece in the great Merryfield puzzle,' Eliza sighed. After all, Prudence had set in train a chain of mysteries.

'Maybe you could solve it, love.'

'Solve what?'

'The Merryfield mystery,' her aunt said with an enquiring lift of the eyebrows.

Eliza laughed. 'That trail has almost certainly gone cold after nearly two hundred years.'

'But wouldn't it be nice to know the truth? I mean, for all us Ambroses, past, present and future? I, for one, think Edward got rather a raw deal. Tried and sentenced by rumour and innuendo, if not by a court of law. As if one of our ancestors could be a murderer!' her aunt said indignantly. 'Wouldn't it be nice to repair his reputation?'

'It's so long ago, and I've enough on my plate keeping the shop going.' Sometimes she felt like she was bashing her head against a brick wall trying to keep the doors open, albeit a wall with lovingly restored plaster and an intricate Georgian frieze. 'No, I'm no sleuth. Just a mere hunter-gatherer of bits and bobs.'

All the same, Prudence's words teased her, leaping out from the page like a portent. She scanned the words a few lines further down the open page.

Friday: Late breakfast. Strolled by river . . .

She recognised the word 'Edward' that followed, but what came next? She squinted, trying to decipher the minute old-fashioned script.

Edward proposed. Ruined mourning stockings.

That was odd. According to all reports, Prudence and Edward only became engaged later, after the events of . . . 1833. Not before.

Of course! 1833. She knew the date would come to her. That

was the year of Prudence's first disappearance – the year of the shipwreck.

'I remember the days when you planned to become an investigative journalist,' her aunt said, interrupting her thoughts. 'Remember when you were a girl, you had your own blog. And then after university you worked for that online magazine—'

'Girlish dream,' she said with a shrug. One that she had put aside after her father died and she returned home to help her mother. If she hadn't, the business her parents had built up over a lifetime most likely would have folded. So, instead of chasing stories for a living, she had begun collecting pieces of the past.

She was a keeper, not a seeker.

'That's the thing about dreams though, pet, they have a habit of recurring,' said her aunt, as she began gathering the tea things.

Not for Eliza. She couldn't afford dreams. She had a business to run. All the same, when her aunt disappeared to the kitchen, she found her fingers wandering automatically to the pocket book. She flipped up the leather flap once more and opened the book to the inside front cover where, as expected, she located a concertinaed pocket. For the pocket book wasn't only designed to fit inside a lady's pocket, it was itself a pocket. A place to store keepsakes. A receptacle for love letters, tickets, sentimental drawings, a lock of hair, a favourite poem. A secret.

She didn't expect to find anything, not after one hundred and ninety years. Nevertheless, she slipped the tips of her fingers inside the silk-lined cardboard pocket, hunting for any memento stowed there by a woman dead for nearly two centuries. At first, she noticed nothing but the smooth silk lining. Then she realised that her nails had touched the crisp texture of folded paper. Turning her hand the other way around, she pinched her thumb and forefinger to grasp the corner of the paper and drew it from

9

the pocket. She sat looking at it for a few breaths, while Bobby licked hopefully at the rug beneath the coffee table and Jude made clattering sounds with the dishwasher.

'What's that?' asked her aunt, returning from the kitchen.

'I don't know yet. I found it inside the pocket.'

The paper was flimsy, print clearly visible, if not legible, on its inner side. It had been folded in half then both ends folded in to make a second pocket: a pocket that cradled another hidden object. An object that was flat and shaped irregularly.

'Aren't you going to unfold it?'

Her eyes traced the shape of the unknown object through the thin leaf of paper.

'It looks like a pressed flower,' said her aunt.

Eliza wasn't sure why she hesitated. Perhaps she was savouring the suspense, like the moments before she opened a carton containing a job lot she had purchased at a garage sale. In those moments before its contents were disclosed, the carton might contain anything. It might be the bearer of treasure. Or perhaps she was merely afraid that in revealing the paper's secrets she would be drawn so far into the mystery of Prudence's disappearance that she wouldn't be able to ignore it. Well, there was only one way to find out.

She unfolded the yellowing paper carefully so that it lay flat upon the coffee table, revealing a brown flower that may once have been pink or red. The paper beneath bore the printed title 'Cabin Passenger's Contract Ticket', with the words 'Prudence Merryfield' inked in a faded blue hand below.

'It looks like a hibiscus,' Jude said, inspecting the long trumpet shape of the flower.

Gently sliding the desiccated flower on to a piece of discarded Christmas wrapping, Eliza read aloud the words inscribed upon the ticket.

The Keepsake

Cabin Passenger's Contract Ticket

Prudence Merryfield
Alexander and Company, East India Agents
Ship *Exmouth* of 650 Tons Register
To sail from the Port of London for Calcutta
On the Fifteenth day of July, 1832

What she held in her hand was evidence of Prudence's flight from London, the very beginning of her adventures, before events spiralled out of her control, transporting her to a tiny island in the South Seas and marooning her there.

2

Somerset, England

1832

The morning after her father's funeral, Prudence woke to the liberating thought that this was to be the first day of her new life. The thought slipped unbidden into her head before she could open her eyes, to be followed by a twinge of guilt when she recalled the events of the previous days. But since she was accustomed to guilt, and since her father had raised her to be pragmatic above all else, the feeling wasn't severe enough to quell such a heady idea. She was thirty-five years of age, accounted an old maid by anyone's reckoning, yet finally her life might begin.

Her maid interrupted this reverie by entering in a rustle of serviceable linen and drawing the curtains with such vigour that Prudence blinked against the sudden onslaught of light. Wills coughed discreetly, a plump shadow haloed by morning sunshine, and patted her neat white headdress.

'Is that a new cap, Wills?'

Wills was fond of caps, and that morning's fine example was made of linen net, embroidered with daisies and finished with a trim of oak leaf and acorns.

'Yes, miss.'

'It's very elegant.'

'Thank you, miss, I'm quite pleased with how it turned out.'

Prudence had always admired her maid's ability to take pride in her work without any protestations of false modesty. She could not say the same of herself. Not from false modesty, for she had small talent to be modest about, but for lack of handiwork in which to take pride. No matter how dutifully she laboured over embroidery and such, her hands quite simply refused to follow instructions. They appeared to have a mutinous streak.

As Wills busied herself setting out the mourning attire, Prudence withdrew a hand from beneath the bedclothes and considered it. It showed no visible signs of rough work or hardship and yet she would not have called it pleasing to the eye. It was shaped well enough, with long slim fingers and oval nails, yet sprinkled with unsightly freckles despite Wills' many and varied potions. The same might also be said of her face, splattered with tawny spots across nose and cheeks, an inevitable companion to her particular shade of red hair unless guarded against with vigilance. Perhaps that's what came of not having a mama to enforce the wearing of bonnets and gloves. A governess may only command so much.

'Your work is so intricate. My hands are good for nothing but snipping roses or managing a recalcitrant nag,' she said. Even so, the butler made a better job of arranging the roses.

'Nought but practice is needed, miss.'

This comment, however kindly intended, served only to remind Prudence of the many sorry examples of needlework littering the house.

'I dare say.' She flicked a glance at the ragged stitches embellishing an antimacassar draped over the back of a chair.

'Breakfast will be going cold,' Wills reminded her.

Breakfast was always served at nine at Westcott Hall, and her maid uttered these words with the hint of disapproval one tended to overlook in a maid of fifteen years' service. But Prudence was not to be deterred from her objective – not by her maid, and not on this first day of her new life. Now was as good a moment as any to begin a new regime.

'I believe I will breakfast in my room today,' she announced. 'In fact, unless we are to have guests, I believe I shall breakfast in my room hereafter.' She made this declaration with all the authority she could muster, given she was barely awake and dressed only in her chemise.

Wills glanced at the miniature portrait of Prudence's father that took pride of place upon the chiffonier, and wrinkled her nose. Another grander portrait of Sir Roderick looked down from the lofty heights above the fireplace in the library, flanked by more modest portraits of Prudence and her Merryfield grandmother. The master of the house usually stared out from this small silver frame with studied dignity. There were no curling locks or dandified neckcloths for him. However, today his image was veiled in black crêpe.

'Sir Roderick always insisted upon breakfast in the dining room,' Wills ventured through pursed lips.

And woe betide the person who arrived late for breakfast in Sir Roderick's house, for they would find in place of a crisp rasher and warm roll, a dry quarter of orange, or a crust of desiccated rye served upon an admonitory silver salver. The servants had their instructions, after all. Except her father had been gone these five days past. He could reprimand neither her tardiness, nor any other of her faults. On Monday he had risen at six o'clock as usual, breakfasted at nine, chastised her housekeeping at ten, complained of a headache at midday, and was dead by six that evening. He had been such a robust figure in life, fuelled by a thousand opinions, never suffering the vagaries of uncertainty, nor deterred by the imprecations of others. If she had not been the one to discover him, slumped over a copy of the *Gentleman's Magazine* in the drawing room, she would not credit it true.

Yet there it was. Her father was gone. And she was an

unmarried, orphaned daughter on the brink of middle age. Yesterday she had bid him farewell in a fashion befitting a man of his station and dignity. His corpse had been laid out in an elm coffin lined with silk crêpe, his body shrouded in superfine wool with his head resting upon a pillow of the same stuff. A velvet-draped hearse drawn by six horses adorned with black feathers and guided by a coachman dressed in the finest livery had transported him to the church. She had followed in one of six carriages ordered for the occasion, garbed in a gown of black bombazine with sleeves fashioned from a full yard of fabric each, and jet trimmings embellishing the bodice. Despite the concerns of her friend and neighbour, Edward Ambrose, she had remained dry-eyed throughout the service and wake that followed. It was the grandest occasion the neighbourhood had enjoyed for many a year and her father would have baulked at the extravagance, were he consulted.

But now he was gone, and she was mistress of Westcott Hall. She could break her fast at midday if she wished. A fact of which she could not remind Wills without seeming like a heartless, unnatural daughter.

And perhaps she was an unnatural daughter. Perhaps she was missing some element of womanly feeling that other women took for granted. She had not wept into her pillow through the night, nor required a gentleman's arm to support her through yesterday's proceedings. She had remained upright until the bitter end, despite a pounding head and galloping pulse. Yet she did not believe herself to be heartless. She had loved her father as dearly as any daughter might, despite such evidence to the contrary. She had waited upon his needs and deferred to his wishes for three decades, with little complaint. She had built her life about his. And without him, the house would surely ring like an empty bucket. It was only that at the age of five and thirty she could not help feeling suddenly, unexpectedly – free.

She was free to roam the Pennine Hills in a pair of stout boots or engage a bathing machine at Sidmouth to hazard the waves – an activity her father had always discouraged. She might even sail to far-off Calcutta without having to guard her pennies or her virtue, these two activities having been the key responsibilities of her life thus far. Without a husband or father to accommodate, her life would be limited only by her daring.

Of her first thirty-five years, little might be said other than they had been more akin to the notations in her pocket book than one of Miss Fanny Burney's novels. Indeed, if one were to peruse her *Pocket Repository* one would soon discover, alongside a precise accounting of expenditure upon theatre tickets, headdresses and the like, as detailed a record of daily pursuits as can be accommodated in a dozen or so words.

Monday: Father died. Sent for Norris. Weather inclement. Dined with Edward. Six courses.

Years later, long after the strange sequence of events that followed, she would recall the shock of that day. Those scant words jotted in her diary could not convey the truth that each of those six courses had lain like a lump of lard in her stomach while her father's corpse awaited the undertaker upstairs; nor that the rain drumming against the windows had seemed like a counterpoint to her throbbing head and thumping heart. She could not remember the days that had followed her mother's death, having been only five years of age, so she had no point of reference and no one she could ask. Upon her father's death, she could only wonder if this was how grief usually felt.

But by this morning, five days later, the heaviness had subsided somewhat, leaving a hollow with nothing obvious to fill it except, she was ashamed to admit, a quiet anger with the world. About what exactly she could not articulate. The anger pervaded her body like a low-grade fever that does not put one to bed yet infiltrates one's every waking activity. She was conscious that she needed to clear her head of its influence. Anger, although sometimes useful, is never held to be an attractive trait in a woman.

Wills was still fussing with the folds of bombazine, humming a soft dirge as she worked. Apparently, she had bitten her tongue and no further opinions regarding breakfast would issue forth from those lips. The humming, however, said it all. It would not do for Prudence to defend her wishes upon the matter of breakfast. Explaining only made matters worse. The last time she explained herself to the butler over a quite straightforward instruction regarding the placement of the joint at dinner, they had narrowly avoided mutiny in the dining room. The house followed a rhythm of her father and the butler's design. Breaking it would require time and determination if she did not wish to raise a tempest. A tempest she did not have the strength for this day. So, in thrall to the silent demands of routine, she sighed rather loudly, slid from the refuge of her bed, and allowed herself to be readied for the day to follow. Hopefully, there would yet be bacon.

Afterwards, it was a relief to escape a house festooned in black crêpe and step on to the terrace. It swept in a sward of grass towards a low stone wall and lavish plantings of rose and lavender. A statue of Mercury on his winged feet took flight at the lawn's centre, while further away the yew hedge – clipped to within an inch of its life for her father's funeral – marched across country with military precision. Beyond the terrace, the park stretched before her in a lush green cloak, with an avenue of ancient chestnut trees leading southwards towards the darker gleam of the river. While behind her, the house spanned the terrace in an elegant line of soft Ham stone seven bays wide, with mullioned windows, stately portico, and a vista of ancient oak trees rising above the lichen-etched roof. For all its sombre interior, the only clue that a house of mourning lay inside was a twist of black crêpe about the doorknob.

She set off across the terrace at a brisk pace, intending to escape the house if only for an hour, and walk off her second cup of hot chocolate. Wills never could be persuaded to allow for breakfast when lacing her corset. Sometimes she missed the more comfortable short stays of her youth, although she did not regret the passing of thin muslin gowns that did not flatter a more mature figure, especially one of diminutive stature and fond of chocolate. Nevertheless, it was almost summer and she stepped lightly; glad to be out of doors, breathing in the scent of freshly scythed grass, the sweet perfume of damask roses and the dusky aroma of lavender. It might have been any summer morning where she set off for her walk, leaving her father ensconced in the library with one or other of his friends or men of business.

'Prudence! You do walk with a purpose!'

She had reached as far as the avenue when she heard a voice hail her from a distance. She did not need to turn to know that it was her friend and neighbour, Edward Ambrose, and could not refrain from bristling somewhat. Could he not have left off his official condolence call for a day or two? She had seen him only yesterday. Could he not leave her to grieve, even a moment, in private? But Edward was nothing if not punctilious in his courtesies. In deference to her grief he had organised the printing of the memorial cards, and conferred with her father's solicitor, Norris, about the funeral so that she did not have to bother her head with the arrangements. He was known far and wide as a good neighbour and a true friend.

As he drew closer she noted that he looked quite spruce this morning, despite being garbed in deep mourning as a courtesy to her father. Since his wife's passing, three years earlier, his appearance had suffered somewhat. He wore his sandy hair without a lick of pomade and had never suffered the use of curling tongs, despite his late wife Alice's urgings. Presumably he had more pressing matters on his mind; without his wife to see to his neckcloths they were invariably greying and arranged with no care for fashion. Most days, he dispensed with a double waistcoat – even last month, on the occasion of the Whitmarshes' annual ball. And he had not ordered a new coat for at least two years.

But today he had donned what appeared to be a new black tailcoat with a velvet collar, and swapped his usual breeches for the more fashionable trousers. He wore a second waistcoat of purple figured silk, and his neckcloth was arranged in the latest style. Although Prudence was not fond of a long sideburn, she had to admit that Edward wore his rather well. They accentuated his strong chin and long straight nose and drew the eye upwards to his rather fine blue eyes so that you forgot his pale brows and lashes.

'Carp told me where to find you.'

She had long been aware it was impossible to escape Westcott Hall without the butler knowing her whereabouts and thus took this information in her stride.

'I hope you don't mind if I accompany you. I wouldn't want to intrude upon your grief,' he said, a trifle more hesitantly than his usual manner.

She wondered briefly what he would do if she said she did mind, and for a moment was tempted to do just that. But courtesy won out and she indicated her acceptance with a nod so that he fell in alongside, matching her swift pace with his long strides, her head bobbing at his shoulder level. Once or twice, as they headed towards the river, she felt his sleeve brush hers, but this was to be expected when they both wore the voluminous cut of the day, and she thought nothing of it. As luck would have it, Edward was not a romantic soul.

3

By the time they reached the river, a quarter mile distant, Prudence and Edward had exchanged precisely thirty-three words.

'I thought the funeral went off rather well yesterday.'

'Yes, thank you for your assistance, Edward.'

'We did your father proud.'

'Father was a proud man.'

'Have a care for that deer scat.'

The scat in question was a neat pile of shiny black fallow deer pellets. She sidestepped them neatly, thus saving her new kid half-boots from one more indignity, before they continued on in silence. Between two persons thrown so often into company, this paucity of conversation might be blamed upon the sombre nature of the occasion, but in truth it was characteristic of Prudence and Edward. Although they were neighbours and frequent visitors to one another's homes, he had always been more her father's friend. Younger than Sir Roderick by a good ten years, and older than Prudence by a similar number, he had married when she was not long out of the schoolroom. Despite the long years and myriad events since, she still blushed at the memory of the day he informed her of his forthcoming marriage, and the childishness of her response. Even now, at five and thirty, he still regarded her as a child, she sometimes thought, from the manner in which he sought her opinion at the dining table then demurred to her father's.

So it was with small surprise that they arrived at the river without further personal observations and certainly no outpouring of feeling or venturing of opinion upon recent sad events. Prudence was suffered to grieve quietly, while ruminating upon her future and enjoying a quiet stroll across the park. Edward likely weighed the merits of introducing willow to his lower fields or leaving them to sheep. Thus they walked in silent companionship, turning downstream of the river by unspoken agreement.

Although it was a river in name, if one were to happen upon it without prior acquaintance, one might take it for a mere stream or creek. For the majority of its course, the river was narrow and not above thigh deep. However, it flowed quite reliably for almost thirty miles, collecting rivulets and streams along its journey, before joining a wider, grander watercourse further downstream from the hall.

The river bordered the estates of both Westcott Hall and Edward's residence of Queens Knoll. The neighbouring families were intimate with its quirks for a good five miles, from the village watermill upstream that had tamed its waters for at least three centuries, to the ancient stone bridge that spanned its widest, deepest section downstream. And here, at the bottom of the Westcott home farm, it skipped nimbly along, its banks lined with a profusion of alder, before diverging to flow around a section of slightly higher ground to form an islet.

'Oh look, a tree has fallen,' she said, stirred from her reverie by the sight of an elderly alder lying across the river. As they drew closer she saw that its bark was rutted and crusted with lichen, its leaves yellowing and sparse when the leaves of those around it fluttered like a profusion of bright green coins. In falling it had formed a bridge across the river to the islet, its top branches now lying enmeshed in the reed bed.

'Not much good as firewood, but your father was planning a footbridge over yon stream in the lower pasture.' Edward considered the stricken tree with an eye for economy. 'It might serve for footings.'

Although unladylike, she could not refrain from rolling her eyes in silent sympathy with the tree. 'I suppose we could also set the tenants to carving clogs from the timber.'

For as long as she could remember this particular alder had stood with dignity upon the riverbank, its leaves sustaining caterpillars and moths, its catkins nourishing birds and bees, its roots providing a home to otters. It deserved to rest in peace. But Edward would reduce it to footings without taking even a moment to mourn its passing.

'I suspect they purchase their clogs,' he observed.

Prudence was a pragmatic soul but in her idle hours, like any other lady, she was not averse to reading a volume of verse or a novel. She always suspected that her neighbour did not have a poetic bone in his body, and now he had confirmed this. For Edward, every object or person had its use or purpose. It was only necessary to discover what that use might be and put them to it. She wondered what use he would put her to if asked. She possessed few useful talents, unlike his wife Alice, who had been a fount of housewifely knowledge, an excellent horsewoman, and always happy to play the pianoforte should her hosts wish to get up a ball. Although he never breathed a word of it, she suspected he missed her greatly, as did they all.

This day, something about his comment, inoffensive as it might have seemed at another time, contributed to the ripple effect of the previous few days' events and a lingering disappointment with her lack of resolve over the vexed question of breakfast. In short, she was in an ill mood. Most of her acquaintance would acknowledge that she was rarely in bad temper, a smile being her usual armour against unpleasantness, but today she was feeling uncharacteristically contrary.

Gathering the stiff folds of bombazine and a froth of petticoats in one hand, and taking a steadying hold upon a branch with the other, she stepped up on to the fallen log. She wavered there for a moment, the trunk being no more than a foot in diameter, but two decades of balls with oft-inept dance partners, rescued her. Once sure of her balance, she set out along the tree's length, dodging branches that sought to disarrange her hair at the least, or knock her from her perch at worst.

'Prudence, what are you doing?'

'I'm making use of this bridge with which nature has so kindly provided us,' she answered, turning to look back at him with what she hoped was an air of nonchalance, as if she was in the habit of balancing upon logs every other day.

'But you may fall – or worse.'

She wondered what might be worse than the indignity of a fall. A stab in the eye with a stray twig? A dousing in the river? Surely the water was barely waist deep.

'I am perfectly safe, Edward, and have always wished to explore this islet. Now may be my only chance.' Before the poor tree was chopped into pieces and put to better use. Before she was dried out and put upon a shelf.

Edward gazed up at her with one palm raised, as if he would curtail her foolishness with sleight of hand or silent command. When she ignored him, he stared down at his new trousers ruefully, rocked twice on his heels, before proceeding to consult his watch.

'It is one o'clock already. Luncheon will be waiting.'

'I'm sure it can wait a little longer,' she called over her shoulder, half expecting him to follow.

But Edward was made of sterner stuff than the romantic

young beaus who frequented the Bath assemblies, and maintained his ground firmly upon the river's bank. 'Be it on your head then,' he said with a shrug.

She shuffled forward, conscious of the water gushing beneath her feet, liberating her sleeve from a branch here, releasing her hair from a twig there, until she gained the island, her person only slightly the worse for wear. Aware of Edward watching her from the far bank, she intended to leap delicately from the log on to dry land, then stroll across the grass to a willow tree standing sentinel in the middle of the island. She would be the picture of an elegant adventuress. But upon reaching her destination she discovered that the island's fringe of reeds extended almost to its centre, where the lone willow crowned a knoll of coarse grass. The tip of the stricken alder lay embedded in the reeds, with the only way to reach the willow being to wade through bulrushes that appeared a good deal taller than they had from the other bank.

'It looks rather damp over there,' Edward called from the safety of dry land.

'It is only a few reeds,' she replied, silently cursing the man's habit of stating the obvious.

Well, she was here now and she could hardly return home without putting a toe to the waters – not if she wished to retain any semblance of superiority or independence of spirit. Besides, how was she to go adventuring further afield if she did not possess the gumption to get a trifle wet? She may as well grasp the nettle now. She took hold of a meagre branch and lowered one foot towards the reeds that guarded the island in a phalanx of feathery spikes. Then, closing her eyes, she took the plunge, wincing as her foot sank to the ankle, even as the other held to the log. Cold muddy water seeped into her boot, drowning the black silk of her mourning stocking. This sinking feeling was accompanied by a sinking of her spirits. Perhaps this hadn't been such a good idea, after all. She could hear the faint sound of her father's voice in her head, chiding that she was a silly chit to think she could prosper alone.

But Sir Roderick was dead and could chide no more. She was to be the arbiter of her own decisions from now on, for good or ill.

A crackle of movement nearby caused her eyes to fly open. She cried out in surprise, to witness a great white egret take off in a flap of angry croaking, its long black legs trailing. As startled as the bird, she wobbled precariously for an instant, almost falling from her perch. Then, taking a steadying breath, she dragged up one soggy black leg, together with her waterlogged dignity, and hauled herself back to the safety of the log. The island may as well have been a hundred yards distant. To gain the grassy knoll was beyond her.

She paused to regain her equilibrium before swivelling gingerly upon the tip of the tree and beginning her ignominious return. But before she could take a single step, she felt the tree shift and looked up to see Edward coming towards her, his arms outstretched as if he too would take flight.

'Edward! What are you doing?'

'I might say rescuing a damsel in distress but I'm hardly making a good job of it,' he said, teetering along the log.

'Go back! You will have us both from the tree and deposited in the river.'

'I should never have allowed you to embark upon such a foolhardy quest,' he muttered.

'It was never your place to stop me.' Her words were intended as a shout, but decades of drawing room decorum blunted them so that the rebuke emerged as a croak of dismay.

'But that's just it, Prudence. I would make it my place.'

'What on earth do you mean?' she asked, peering at him in surprise. Declarations were hardly Edward's stock-in-trade.

25

He opened his mouth to say more, running a hand through his hair so that it looked even more untended than usual, his customary genial expression marred by a worried frown. Her stomach lurched at the expression in his eyes, akin to that of her dog, Posy, when she waited to be taken in her mistress's arms.

'Oh no, pray do not say it. I do not want to know. It is . . . it is too late for that,' she protested.

She had seen that same look before, a dozen years ago or more, when the rector's son cornered her in the library while paying a morning call with his mother. On another regrettable occasion, the handsome Captain Harding mirrored the expression when he implored her mercy after one too many glasses of Madeira at the Bath Assembly. At the time she had attributed his ardour to the heat of the overcrowded ballroom and six hours of vigorous dancing. But Edward did not have that excuse. And he had never been a man given to rashness. Yet here he was, apparently embarked upon a mission, and nothing and no one, least of all Prudence, would prevent him accomplishing it.

He stopped halfway distant from the bank and dropped to one knee, hand clinging to a branch. His new trousers were forgotten in the heat of the moment.

'I promised your father that if anything happened to him I would see you safe.'

'I would be safer if you returned to the bank,' she said, with a frown that would have stopped a more astute man in his tracks. But he had set his jaw in a manner that suggested there would be no escape. What had got into him? He usually showed more interest in his hounds than in her.

As he opened his mouth to clear his throat, she was tempted to put her hands to her ears.

'Prudence. My dearest Prudence.'

'This really isn't necessary, Edward.'

'I have watched you blossom from an awkward girl into a . . .' He scanned the sky for the appropriate adjective.

'. . . a contrary spinster?'

'What?'

'You have watched me grow from an awkward girl into a contrary spinster.' How could she ever forget that awkward girl? She was imprinted upon her memory as indelibly as the words in her pocket book.

'That wasn't what I was about to say. I was about to say "a poised young woman".'

'Well that is debatable, since currently I am neither young nor particularly poised.'

'The point is,' he said, 'the point is . . . since Alice died I have been too much alone, and it has been your company, and that of your father, which has sustained me. I dare to hope that my company, if only in a small way, has brightened your life also.'

She batted away the thought that perhaps Edward should have married her father and said, 'You have been a great comfort to us both.'

'So for some time, I have wrestled with the idea of offering for you.'

'That is very considerate of you, Edward. I am flattered, naturally.'

'No, I m-mean . . . I have chosen my words ill. The reason I haven't offered for you before this is that I was reluctant to steal you away from your father. He has been a great friend to me and I know he depended upon you.'

'One could say that.'

'But now he is gone. You are alone and in need of a protector. Someone to love and watch over you.'

He wobbled momentarily, no doubt buffeted by the power of his emotions, before righting himself to stand, sturdily unaided, his chest and chin thrust forward. Her doughty protector. She did not wobble at all, despite the fact that she was poised on a log above a gushing stream. This was not the time for wavering. One weak moment and her future might be whisked away from her.

'Edward. *Dearest Edward*,' she began. 'For thirty-five years my father has loved and watched over me . . . the last thing I need is someone to take his place.'

She wondered briefly if he had not heard her above the gurgle of the river and the hum of insects, for he knelt expectantly, his serious brown eyes fixed upon hers.

'I would be your husband, Prudence, not your father,' he said eventually, in case she had not understood the full import of his words.

In the face of his conviction, emotion overcame all restraint and she spluttered, 'And I can manage quite adequately alone!'

'But no man . . . or woman is an island.'

'I beg to differ.'

'Your father loved and cared for you.' He cleared his throat. 'I love and care for you.'

'Yet to all intents and purposes, I have managed alone for thirty years.'

After the brief elation of speaking these words aloud, a shiver overtook her, suggesting that she should have been more tactful, more hesitant – more sensitive to her old friend's feelings. His face bore an expression of puzzled horror, most unlike his usual tepid politeness. Then again, the shiver may have been due to her waterlogged stocking.

Edward, meanwhile, was creaking to his feet. He brushed any remainder of indignity from his trousers, saying, 'Forgive me. I should have thought. You are still in the first throes of mourning.'

With those words, he retreated to the riverbank, alighted from the fallen alder in a bound and extended his arm to assist her to dismount. When she was once more upon solid ground he released her hand, nodded once and announced, 'I shall not speak of this matter again until you are more yourself.'

She prayed that day might never come. Or at least she thought she did.

Later that night, by the light of a lone candle, she penned a memorandum of the incident in her pocket book. A memorandum she would have cause to ponder many times in the course of the years to come.

Friday: Late breakfast. Strolled by river. Edward proposed marriage. Ruined mourning stockings.

4

Somerset, England

2022

Her aunt's house offered several inviting prospects for walks, and Bobby knew them all. There was the hedgerowed lane that meandered over an ancient stone bridge spanning the river, a folding landscape of fields ripe with lush grass or golden rapeseed, an ancient wood rising beyond the distant rooftops of Westcott Hall, and an avenue of elderly chestnuts that led to that decaying mansion. A veritable chocolate box full of fine prospects.

With a flick of the tail her dog set off across open pasture, taking a shortcut to the river, no doubt intent upon the scent of hare, vole or some other poor unsuspecting creature. Usually Eliza let him lead the way, content to amble along in his wake, but this afternoon she hesitated. Halting just outside her aunt's garden, she found her gaze tugged from Bobby's chosen route and drawn towards the pair of tall iron gates that guarded the entrance to the estate. The rusting curlicues of iron did not look particularly unusual – the gates propped shut, as they always were – but she was accustomed to seeing them secured with a chain and padlock. Now the chain was missing.

Gatehouse Lodge, her aunt's abode, had once been part of the original Merryfield estate. It was a remnant the Ambrose family had managed to retain after parting with Westcott Hall in the late 1970s, and it had come down to her aunt. Eliza's father had inherited a shop in the village that her parents subsequently sold and leased back after the 2009 recession. The original Ambrose house, Queens Knoll, had passed to a now distant branch of the Ambrose family and been sold off in the late nineteenth century. Gatehouse Lodge was the only remnant of two large estates that remained in Ambrose hands. Her aunt was its loving custodian.

Of course, Eliza could have accessed the drive to the hall at any time by climbing her aunt's back fence or clambering over the bordering hedgerows. However, the missing chain acted as an invitation, luring her to the gates and the weed-choked drive that led to the main house. She gave one of the gates a shove and when it refused to budge, exerted some effort to lift it free of the gravel and prop it wider open. She whistled for Bobby and a minute or so later, the pair set out along a lane shaded by two rows of elderly chestnut trees, gap-toothed where they had succumbed to time or disease.

At first, the trees and an ancient yew hedge beyond were tall enough to hide the house from view but as they drew closer its lichen-etched roof, dormer windows and chimneys appeared above the treetops, to be followed by glimpses of mellow honey-hued Ham stone. The house was bathed in late afternoon sun, giving it a soft glow, the sparkle of light on ancient glass imbuing it with energy so that one did not at first notice the decay. Then, as the drive rounded a bend, the entry at the side of the house came into full view in all its damaged glory.

'What do you think, Bob? Should we turn back?'

The dog answered with a short bark and trotted forwards, without a backward glance, his nose leading him to the broad step beneath a once stately portico of flaking stucco and columns with chipped pedestals.

'I guess that's a no then,' she said, ignoring a tingle at the thought of being caught trespassing. She was unpractised as a breaker of rules. But to be truthful, she didn't wish to turn back either. It had been years since she'd ventured all the way up the lane – long before the death of her parents. Not since the days when the house, although evincing only a vestige of its former glory, was still occupied. Despite her protestations to the contrary, Jude's gift had stirred her curiosity about Prudence, the mystery surrounding her life and death, and the empty house she had once called home.

Westcott Hall.

Following Bobby's lead, she stepped on to the portico to stand facing a panelled door that must have been imposing in its day, with its brass lion's head knocker and octagonal doorknob. Now it was in dire need of a lick of paint, and an ugly bolt and padlock had been installed to secure it. She stepped to the side, peering through one of the windows on either side of the door, but there was little to be seen inside the entrance except shadows. If she remembered correctly, a main receiving hall was situated to the left and a smaller room, which had probably once been presided over by the butler, led off to the right. Bobby was already nosing around under a pair of tall windows in the overgrown shrubbery to her left. Eliza decided it couldn't hurt to have a peek too.

She waded into a morass of unidentifiable plants, except for a straggling rose that made itself known by wrapping itself around her calf and digging in. She managed to prise it loose with only minor damage to skin and trousers, then leaned in to set her face to the dusty glass. Inside, the main hall was devoid of furniture and the mantle had been stripped from the fireplace; some of the floorboards were even missing, giving the room a sad look of neglect.

'I guess no one's home, Bob,' she muttered into the glass.

'Were you looking for someone, mate?' a voice growled from

the portico in a distinct Australian accent.

She sprang back in surprise, only to become entangled once more in thorns. 'Ouch! Where did you come from?'

'I might ask you the same thing. You're trespassing, mate.'

Ignoring him for the moment, she bent down to free herself, succeeding in prising loose the rose bush. And a piece of her trousers.

'Now look what you've made me do,' she muttered, looking up at the culprit for the first time. 'These are Romeo Gigli . . .'

'Whoever that is.'

'. . . and I'm not your mate.'

'No, I can see that now,' he said, inspecting her face, no doubt taking in the by-now-smudged eyeliner and lipstick. 'But you're still trespassing.'

She stomped free of the garden bed to join him on the portico, realising as she drew closer that he was younger than he sounded, only a lick of grey in the brown hair at his temples (that actually looked quite cute, come to think of it) and a fine web of lines at the corners of his hazel eyes.

'You sounded like my old headmaster,' she said, brushing dirt and leaves from her trouser legs.

'My father was a headmaster – and I've been told I'm a chip off the old block. Handy, if I ever need to sound authoritative.'

'And do you?'

'Hmm?'

'Need to sound authoritative?'

He shrugged, 'Well, if it helps . . .'

He was interrupted by a growl hailing from the garden bed on the other side of the portico, and Bobby scampered over with a yip to seek sanctuary behind her legs.

'Ruby!' the man shouted, and a red setter soon emerged from the bushes and grinned up at him hopefully. 'Sit, there's a good girl.'

The commotion under control, he turned back to Eliza. 'We had a break-in the other day, so Ruby and I aren't taking any chances. You're not thieves, are you? You and your canine friend here?'

He said it so matter-of-factly that she wasn't sure whether to take the question seriously or not. 'No, I'm an antique dealer. I have a store in the village. My aunt lives in the gatehouse cottage.'

'Ah yes . . . I've heard about you.'

'You have?'

'Single, turning thirty-five, pretty in a gamine way, MA in English, woeful cook, can be obstinate and short-tempered, kind, reliable, hardworking . . .'

As he continued to list the finer points of her character, Eliza found herself longing to curl into a ball. There were benefits to being a millipede.

'You've met my aunt then,' she sighed, looking down at her feet in embarrassment.

'She was kind enough to offer me a cup of tea yesterday, and dropped bits of information about her favourite niece into the conversation while feeding me scones with jam and cream.'

'Only niece.' Of course Jude had offered him tea. She offered everyone tea. But did she have to sugar it with intimate details of Eliza's private life? Sometimes she thought her aunt was so immersed in village life that she no longer differentiated between public and private, except when it applied to her. 'I'm so embarrassed. I don't know what she was thinking. She might as well have posted an ad spruiking my wares in the local paper.'

'I think she's proud of you.'

Eliza dared to look up from her boots, to find the stranger grinning at her.

'It's really not funny.'

'Oh, I think it's very funny actually. My day was quite boring until you came along.' He held out his hand. 'Daniel O'Neill, building contractor.'

'Eliza Ambrose, single woman in want of a partner. Apparently.' She took the proffered hand.

'I haven't met any Elizas recently.'

'Old family name. And it's not true, by the way.'

'What?'

'I'm too busy working to be looking for romance.'

'Point noted.'

'Not that I'm suggesting you're looking either.'

'No, too busy hammering to be looking for romance.'

He was still grinning but she found she didn't mind. Providing him with his daily dose of amusement wasn't so bad – at least she had made someone laugh.

'But you did seem to be looking for something, if peering through windows is any indication. Can I help?'

She considered his offer for a moment. She didn't need help because she wasn't really searching for anything. Then again, the house and the mystery surrounding its former owner dangled before her like a party treat on a bobbing string. She shoved the hand that had clasped his deep into the pocket of her anorak, groping for her aunt's gift – her newfound pocket companion. What harm could it do?

'Have you heard the story of Prudence Merryfield?' she asked. 'The Merryfields once owned Westcott Hall.'

'Until it passed to the Ambrose family,' he said, quirking an eyebrow in her direction.

'I see you've done your homework on the house's history.' She nodded in approval. 'And yes, there's a family connection, distant though it may be.'

It was his turn to nod.

'Well, my aunt and I happened to be discussing Prudence earlier today and I suppose I was curious to see the house again.

The chain was off, and it's been closed up for so long.' She didn't mention the gift of the pocket book or her aunt's suggestion that she play investigator.

'I've locked up for the day but I can show you around another time if you'd like. I'll be here quite a bit from now on.'

He held her eyes with his gaze as he made the suggestion. The hazel eyes were compelling but hard to read, and she wondered why he would go to the trouble of giving her a tour.

'You could? That would be . . . ah . . .' She hesitated, unsure what her answer should be. Even more uncertain about what she might like it to be.

'Great?' he finished for her.

She thought of the online orders always waiting to be packed. She thought of the new marketing campaign she had yet to design. The list of forthcoming estate sales she should research and attend. The constant need to clean and dust and polish. Not to mention keeping the shop doors open with only a part-time assistant. And yes, she decided, 'That would be great.'

In more ways than one, her inner voice prompted but was firmly silenced.

'I'll be here on Wednesday morning.'

'Wednesday would be great.'

'I'll see you then.'

A few minutes later, she was coaxing Bobby out from behind her legs with an encouraging pat, and setting off down the drive, enjoying the purposeful sound of gravel crunching beneath her boots. She ignored the urge to look back for the first two hundred yards, but by the time she reached the path that led to the old stables she could no longer resist. She turned her head, expecting Daniel to have returned to whatever he was doing before chasing off intruders, but he was still standing in the portico watching her walk away. Perhaps making sure she did indeed leave the property. She lifted a hand in farewell and he waved in return.

The house loomed behind him in the dusk as she resumed her walk down the lane, trying to banish all thoughts of Westcott Hall, its charming Australian contractor, and the enigmatic Prudence Merryfield.

She had work to do.

5

Somerset, England

1832

Bessie could tell the rector was angry from the manner in which he flew down the drive, his coat-tails flapping like a giant crow. His boots barely crunched the gravel in his haste. What she did not know was whether he was angry with her, or some other person not in evidence at that moment. People were frequently angry with Bessie, so it was a reasonable assumption. Except that a booted foot, a swift backhand or sharp words usually accompanied that anger. And there had been no sign of this yet from the rector.

Still, uncertain of his mood, she dawdled a good distance behind, leaving any anger free to roam without alighting in her vicinity. If there was one thing she knew with certainty, it was that anger of any description was best avoided. Dawdling also gave her leisure to contemplate the imposing vista of Westcott Hall receding into the distance over her shoulder, a dark forested hill towering behind its rooftops. She followed the rector down the drive and along the shady lane that led to the village where she had lived for most of her fourteen years. In all those years, today was the first time she had ventured inside the hall, and since it was unlikely she would ever visit again, she wanted to imprint its splendour upon her memory.

They had been greeted at a giant wooden door by a tall, unbending creature known as Carp, who was even more frightening than the gargoyles upon the roof of Mr Custard's church. His face was long, his mouth narrow, and winged by two deep creases that seemed to express his displeasure with the world in general and Bessie in particular. He had ushered them into an entry hall large and high enough to host a game of village cricket, and had proceeded to talk down to them from his great height. What transpired during that conversation had not pleased the rector at all, but whether she was at fault, the man called Carp, or some other person who remained unknown, she could not say with any certainty. The result, however, had been a swift exit from the hall and a trail of quiet muttering issuing from the rector as he flew down the drive.

By the time he halted abruptly and glanced behind him, the distance between the two exiles had stretched to twenty yards.

'There's no point dilly-dallying, girl. I had hoped to save you from the workhouse, but the hall was my last option. None of the farms hereabouts will take you.' His gaze scraped her person from the tip of her head to the bare feet peeping from beneath her ragged skirt, and she was conscious that she came up wanting. She put up a hand to tuck a strand of sooty hair behind her ear, noticing for the first time the half-moons of dirt encrusting her nails.

'You should have thought of that earlier,' he said, frowning at both hand and hair.

Earlier, Bessie had been too busy scouring the scrap of woodland on the outskirts of the village for mallow and mushrooms, to bother about her hair. And her hands, for want of easily accessible water – and, it must be said, a certain disinclination – were perennially filthy.

'Carp made up his mind after a single glance. That man has a heart of stone.' Mr Custard shook his head in displeasure.

She hoped he would not delay much longer. It was a fair walk to the next village where the parish workhouse was situated, and they would already miss dinner. If she were lucky, they might arrive in time for a crust of bread and cheese and a mug of beer before bed, which was more than she was accustomed to with her grammer and granfer – even more so, these last weeks.

The thought of her grandparents caused her to hiccup, which caused her eyes to fill, which led tears to spill over her cheekbones and dribble down her chin, leaving track marks through the grime.

'And blubbering serves no purpose. At least you will find a bed, such as it is, and a bite to eat at the workhouse. We can't have young girls sleeping under hedgerows. Not in my parish.' He frowned at her once more, as if holding her personally responsible, which she supposed she was, in a manner of speaking. Not for the death of her grandparents, for they had collapsed of the cholera a month before, but for sleeping under hedgerows after the landlord turned her out of her grandparents' cottage. Nevertheless, to Bessie's way of thinking, a hedgerow was a good deal safer than a barn or stable where any eager farmhand might discover her.

'Come along then,' said the rector, clicking his tongue and setting out once more for her prospective new home.

With a lingering glance at the wide stone expanse of Westcott Hall she followed after him, ignoring the stabbing of gravel beneath her bare feet while dreaming of a warm bowl of porridge with a slug of fresh cream.

They had been trudging along the lane for several more minutes when Bessie spied two figures gliding towards them in the distance. The figures were silhouetted against the afternoon sun like monstrous black shadows that filled the path ahead. At the sight, her heart began to rattle against her ribs as the thought occurred that they might be spectres. The spectres of her grandparents come to haunt her – angry that she dreamed of porridge and cream when they lay mouldering in their graves. Her grandparents had often regaled her with fireside tales of goblins, pixies and assorted spirits, so Bessie was not surprised that they might return in spectral form. In life they had been loving, if somewhat stern taskmasters – since it demanded the work of three to glean the barest living from their patch of garden and any intermittent employment – in death they were an unknown quantity.

Disinclined to risk retribution for the understandable sin of being hungry, she ducked behind the rector, hoping the oncoming shadows might not notice her behind his impressive waistline and dangling coat-tails.

'What are you doing there, girl?' he snapped, reaching around to snag her by the skirt and drag her forward. 'It's Miss Merryfield, the lady of Westcott Hall, and her neighbour, Mr Ambrose of Queens Knoll. You would know that if your grandparents had taken you to church as often as they should. Stand up straight and try not to look so . . . so slovenly.' He emphasised the last word with obvious distaste.

Bessie's relief that her grandparents were not come straight from Hell was tempered by the puzzle of how not to look slovenly when she did not know what 'slovenly' meant. Plus, there was the quandary of meeting the mistress of such a grand estate as Westcott Hall when she had never been introduced to such an eminent person before. She pulled back her shoulders and ran her hands through her hair to restore some order, before hiding the evidence of their griminess in the folds of her none-too-clean skirt. Cleanliness was next to godliness, according to Mr Custard's teaching. But so much of his preaching was beyond Bessie's ken that she tended to ignore it all.

'Perhaps we can convince her to take pity on a poor wretched orphan where that flint-hearted fiend would not. But not if you are skulking behind my coat-tails.'

As the pair loomed closer, the rector planted a broad smile upon his face in readiness. Bessie was surprised to see that the lady was almost as bedraggled as she was. One side of her face was adorned with hoops of shiny red curls, while matted tendrils of hair drooped forlornly against the other cheek. One sleeve must have caught on something sharp for it resembled a ragged wing, while her right boot was plastered in mud. Despite the lady's scowl, Bessie felt a mite better about the coming encounter, until she felt a jab to her side and looked up to see the rector blinking at her vigorously. At first she wondered if he had dust in his eyes, then she remembered his instructions earlier that day.

'If you chance to meet Miss Merryfield, do not forget to curtsy,' he had said. 'And remember she has lost her beloved father recently.'

Bessie dipped her knees obediently and tried to look sad, which wasn't difficult since she had no home and her only living relatives were dead. Sadness had become a perpetual state, but not one upon which she could afford to dwell, the gnawing of her belly being more pressing.

'Ah good afternoon, Miss Merryfield . . . Mr Ambrose. How fortunate to encounter you. We've just come from the hall.'

'Good afternoon, Mr Custard. How fortunate for us not to have missed you,' said the lady as the gentleman doffed his hat and nodded his greeting.

'May I present my young protégée, Bessie,' said the rector, with another furtive jab to her side.

'I be sorry for your loss, m'lady,' she said, head and knees dipping in unison this time.

'Thank you, Bessie, but since I am not your lady, Miss Merryfield will suffice.' The lady's words were accompanied by a smile that barely touched her lips before fading away.

Bessie did not blame her. The lady might be mistress of half the village, but she was an orphan too. She had lost her mother, her father, and given her advanced age, almost certainly her grandparents too. Bessie felt a few more tears well up for the lady, who was looking surprisingly dry-eyed. But she supposed a lady as elegant as Miss Merryfield could not allow herself to weep, even if she wanted.

'How can I be of service, Mr Custard? I did not expect to see you until Sunday, after you spoke so eloquently at my father's funeral. He would have been most gratified.'

'Indeed. It was my great pleasure. And forgive my intrusion at this unhappy time, but the matter is dire, at least for this poor child.'

Both the lady and gentleman now turned to inspect Bessie, possibly searching for direness.

'Her parents have been dead these ten years . . .' the rector began.

It was true that her mama had been taken by the influenza when Bessie was four, or so her grandparents had told her, but her father had taken himself off before she was born. Strictly speaking, he may not have been dead but Grammer had always instructed her to ignore that fact and say she was an orphan, if asked.

'. . . and now her grandparents have succumbed to the cholera. My curate found her sleeping under a hedgerow.' He sighed loudly and frowned so deeply that his eyebrows almost met.

Bessie dropped her eyes to the ground, trying to look as pitiful as possible without appearing simultaneously slovenly, since the rector had specifically forbidden it.

'The poor child—' began the lady.

She was interrupted by the man, who was almost as tall as the person known as Carp but a good deal more kindly looking, despite the fact that his waistcoat was the most alarming shade

43

of purple that Bessie had ever seen. 'I'm sure Miss Merryfield is sympathetic but I fail to see how she may help,' he said.

'Unless I can find someone to take the girl, she is headed for the workhouse, Mr Ambrose.'

'And have you discussed the girl's situation with Carp? I believe Sir Roderick entrusted him with the hiring of indoor staff.' The gentleman tapped one hand against the side of his thigh as he spoke. Bessie was always alert for such signs but in this instance the tapping seemed benign.

'We've just come from an interview with Mr Carp. Unfortunately, he did not take to the girl.'

Bessie risked a swift upward glance. The two men conversed over her head, as the lady stood by silently. The rector regarded the other gentleman with pursed lips while that gentleman nodded agreeably. His hands, now done with their tapping, were hooked into his waistcoat pockets. Meanwhile, the lady stood with her chin thrust forward like the village thatcher's old terrier, her lips parted as if about to snap at someone. Bessie drew back a pace. The terrier's bite was much worse than his bark and she once had the puncture marks on her shin to prove it.

Out of the corner of her eye, the lady must have caught her watching, for she swivelled to face her, saying, 'Do not trouble yourself, child, he has not taken to me either, and I have known him my entire life.'

This was too much for Bessie, whose eyes spilled over once more. Mindful of the rector's admonition, she tried to sniff the tears back, only succeeding in snorting like a hog at a trough. 'He said I be a sn-sn-snivelling guttersnipe,' she snuffled miserably.

'Never mind that, Bessie, Miss Merryfield ain't interested in the details.'

'Oh, but I assure you, Mr Custard, I'm most interested to hear the child's thoughts on the matter.' The lady inspected Bessie

44

with her head tilted to the side; a twist of red curls drifting across her cheek.

Unaccustomed to anyone being interested in her thoughts, and certainly not a lady as fine as the mistress of Westcott Hall, Bessie at first did not answer.

'Miss Merryfield wants to know what else Mr Carp said to you,' the rector prompted with a sharp look.

'He said them at hall might catch something from me.'

'Did he so? What else did he say?'

'He said he would not employ me if I be the last girl in Somerset.' Conscious that a string of mucus threatened to join the tears, she forgot herself for long enough to prise a dirt-encrusted hand from her skirt and wipe the offending slime from her nose.

The lady stared at Bessie's hand as if it were a creature she had not encountered before, but her eyes expressed mild interest rather than disgust. 'Carp's standards are somewhat more exacting than the rest of us,' she said, smiling for the first time.

Basking in that unexpected smile, Bessie forgot her tears, forgot the rector's warnings, the butler's cruel words, even forgot briefly the loss of her grandparents. She smiled in return. There was something comforting about the lady, something that harked back to a memory from long ago . . .

'Prudence! You cannot be thinking of—'

'Of employing her? Why certainly, Edward. She is in need of a position, and Westcott Hall is crawling with servants. One more can't hurt.' She seemed about to laugh but then thought better of it, clamping her lips together with a conspiratorial glance at Bessie.

'Carp won't be happy,' said the gentleman.

'Carp is never happy. That is what makes him such an excellent butler. He has made it his mission in life to be permanently dissatisfied.'

'But what shall you do with her? She's not fit for a housemaid, and I doubt your cook will have her anywhere near the kitchen.' It was the gentleman's turn to stare at Bessie with a concerned frown.

She scratched nervously at a scab on her arm.

'The poor child. She looks half-starved. But once you take her up, you cannot just forget about her, Prudence.'

The lady glanced from the scab to the man and back again. 'Something will be found for her. I have no doubt there is a person hiding beneath all that dirt. She just wants finding.'

The scab, successfully loosened, floated to the ground, leaving behind an island of pink skin with a bead of red at its fringe. Bessie lifted her arm to her mouth and licked it away, unaware of the expressions of horror upon the faces of her betters. The lady had saved her from the workhouse. Surely her future must be looking brighter. It certainly could not get any worse.

6

Somerset, England

2022

Later, Eliza would describe to Jude her feelings as she followed Daniel through the empty rooms of Westcott Hall as uncanny; as if tiny spiders crawled amongst the hairs of her arms, or that proverbial stranger trespassed upon her grave. But this was with the romance of hindsight and a healthy glass or two of Pinot Noir as her aunt gently quizzed her about the appointment with the handsome building contractor. At the time, she marked only the chill air, the creaking floorboards and a lingering odour of damp.

'Mind that rotten floorboard,' said Daniel, as her attention wandered to a bowed section of cornice in an acanthus pattern high above the main staircase.

'Noted,' she answered with a smile.

'Upstairs or down?'

Upstairs or down. The question teased her. So many rooms, so many unknowns. 'Upstairs first, I think.'

The bedrooms would be upstairs. She wanted to find Prudence's lair, the room where she had written the brief lines that encapsulated her life. *Saturday: Pot-au-feu for luncheon.* Where she wrote those small reminders to herself. *Must repair mother's locket.* Of tasks needing attention. *Order more watercolours.* Appointments to be kept. *Called on Lady Gwendolyn.*

Monies spent. *Flemish lace 10 shillings.* She wanted to picture the desk where Prudence had sat, perhaps placed before a window where she could gaze out over her heritage, the Merryfield estate.

These were the facts Eliza gleaned from her first deciphering of Prudence's pocket book in the spare hours she had managed since her last meeting with Daniel. But like this empty house, the words were devoid of furniture, bare walls without the decoration of emotion or context. Worse still, the story was only half told, with the middle pages loosed from their binding and the latter pages filled with a printed almanac.

As they climbed the stairs to the first floor, Eliza turned a professional eye to the barley-twist balustrade of the staircase. She had a mid-nineteenth-century tripod table with a barley-twist column in the shop at the moment, but here the entire balustrade was a forest of twisted mahogany spindles with fluted columns for newel posts. Daniel bent down to run a hand over one of them.

'A few splits here and there, and we've lost some spindles on the second floor, but the staircase is in remarkably good order. Luckily, the carpet saved the treads from the worst wear. Can't say the same for some of the other woodwork.'

She liked the way he stroked the timber, as if it were a living thing. 'There's been a house on the site since the thirteenth century, but we think Westcott Hall was built largely between 1715 and 1720,' she said. 'The staircase appears to be original.'

'According to Historic England's records the architect is unknown, and there are no plans we can find. But we have located some early drawings and paintings of the facade and the park.' He unfurled his body and turned to face her. 'I've been doing my homework,' he added with a grin.

She noticed how white his teeth were against his tan. Holiday in Ibiza or working outdoors?

'Dare I ask what that entails?' Everyone in the village had followed the progress of the planning application, some more favourably than others, so she was familiar with the plan to redevelop the old house as a country hotel.

'Plans for the restoration mainly,' he said, resuming the climb to the first floor. Clearly, he wasn't about to say more just yet.

At the top of the stairs he paused, eyeing her with a questioning look. The main bedrooms faced south, with a view out over the terrace towards the river; the lesser bedrooms faced north, with the nursery on the second floor under the dormer windows of the servants' quarters. But where would the daughter and ostensible mistress of the house have chosen for her quarters? She closed her eyes for a moment, trying to recall any clue she had garnered from her reading so far, but nothing came to mind. Prudence was parsimonious with detail.

'Communing with the spirits?'

'Huh?' she opened her eyes. 'No . . . far more humdrum than that. Trying to guess where Prudence's room might have been.'

'I may be able to help with that, I think.'

Veering to the left, he led her along a hallway of scuffed oak floorboards to a room at the end of the corridor where a tall door opened into a large sunlit chamber.

'After you,' he said, gesturing her onward with a flourish.

She stepped into the room, her eyes immediately drawn to the faded mauve-and-green-striped wallpaper that lined the walls. 'Is this Georgian?'

'I had a sneaky look beneath a loose section in one corner and found an earlier layer.'

'So this could be much later?' Disappointment punctured the tantalising thought that Prudence may have selected this very wallpaper.

'No, I'd say no later than late eighteenth or early nineteenth century. It's block printed.'

'Prudence's era then,' she said with a breath of relief. How had it survived so long?

'The funny thing is, we think this room may have been closed up for quite some time. It doesn't show the same degree of wear as the remainder of the house.'

Now that he said it, she noticed that unlike the floors in other parts of the house, the parquetry here still retained a faint sheen and the plaster cornices were largely intact. She stepped closer to inspect the wall in more detail, stretching out a tentative hand to explore the texture of the paper. Closer to, she saw that the stripes were actually panels of interwoven leaves and flowers, sheaves of what appeared to be lavender flowers alternating with trailing fernlike leaves.

'Lavender . . .'

The scent of lavender had hung in the air as Daniel let her into the house earlier. The garden beds encircling the terrace had been largely left to their own devices for decades, but apparently the lavender refused to be entirely subjugated by encroaching shrubs. There had been something in the pocket companion too, a reminder to *Cut lavender for Wedgwood*. Fashionable Georgian ladies liked to scent their houses using vases brimming with potpourri. Eliza had once sold a Jasperware potpourri vase to a woman from Sydney who planned to store her late dog's ashes in it. Lavender was definitely preferable.

'Come and take a look at this.' Daniel's voice emanated from a narrow doorway at the other end of the room.

Wrenching her attention away from the field of lavender, she followed him into a small, windowless room attached to the bedchamber, probably at one time a dressing room. The air here was even damper than the rest of the house, heavy with the chill of long disuse. And rather than wallpaper, the walls were lined from floor to ceiling with wood panelling, giving the room a gloomy atmosphere. On three walls the wood was dark with age, while the fourth wall appeared slightly lighter and not quite so ancient.

He bent to a squat in one corner of the room and pointed to a spot near the floor. She knelt on the floor next to him, hoping that the high-waisted Jean Paul Gautier sailor jeans she had picked up on eBay didn't protest. It was an odd feeling to be kneeling on the floor so close to a stranger in this cavernous old house, a house which had been peopled by none but ghosts for at least a decade. She supposed she should feel some trepidation, but oddly she felt perfectly safe.

'What do you see?' he asked.

She was close enough now to see the slight stubble on his chin and a faint scar at the corner of one eye. Those warm hazel eyes that peered far too intently into hers. She looked away, suppressing a shiver, and turned her attention to the panelling. Perhaps not so safe, for all that.

Her arm brushed his as she leaned closer to make out a word scratched in the wood panelling. The letters were etched deep into the timber by an inexpert hand, like a child's.

P-R-U-D-E-N-C-E

Seeing that name carved into the wood made the woman's presence almost palpable, a woman who had disappeared more than one hundred and eighty years earlier. Disappeared or died. Either way, her absence heralded the long slow decline in the prestige of the Ambrose family. At first, their reputation – for few wished to invite a reputed murderer to supper, and even fewer wished to marry his son – and in subsequent years, their wealth.

'It was Prudence's room then,' she murmured, conscious of his arm next to hers.

'Either that, or her mother's where she played as a child.'

Prudence must have been very young when her mother died; probably still in the nursery, by all accounts. Eliza always thought

51

herself unlucky not to have her own mother until at least middle age, but it could have been worse. She could have lost her before she really knew her. She could have scrabbled her way through her teens motherless. Who would she have rebelled against then? Who would she have blamed for her miseries? There was something comforting about having a mother to push back against. She missed that. Being able to flounce out of a room and know that you would be welcomed back.

Daniel's arm still touched hers, the only spot of warmth in this cold, dark room. Despite her intentions, she shivered in her light cotton jersey.

'Cold?'

'A little.'

'Let's get you downstairs where it's warmer.' He stood, reaching out a hand.

She took it, surprised that she did not refuse the offer as she usually would. Surprised too that their hands were almost of a size. His hand fitted hers like a glove. She did have rather large hands for a woman, often decorated with grazes and cuts from making minor furniture repairs, but his were of medium size for a man, with slim fingers, neatly trimmed nails and a narrow palm.

By the time they reached the library, the last room on their tour, it had been a full hour. It was such a sad room, scarred and forlorn where shelves had once lined the walls, devoid of the comfort of books and conversation where once it would have been the sanctuary for generations of Merryfields – and later, Ambroses. Standing shoulder to shoulder, they stood gazing through the French windows, which opened to a fine view of the overgrown sward that had once been lawn.

'This is the room where Prudence's father would have conducted his business affairs,' Daniel said. 'Not a bad spot to run things from.'

The room was large, yet he had placed himself a mere elbow's length away from her. She resisted the urge to take a step back. She couldn't help wondering why he had given her so much of his time, since he was no doubt busy.

'Why are we here?' The question emerged before she realised she was about to ask it. 'I mean . . . why did you offer me a tour?'

'Does there need to be a reason, Eliza?' He made a point of emphasising her name. 'Maybe I was showing you around simply because you were interested.' He didn't seem offended by her question, although she had to admit she had been quite rude. Just her usual bristling self when cornered, except she hadn't exactly been cornered.

'I suppose so,' she conceded, puzzled by her earlier reaction.

'Or maybe I felt like company.'

She supposed it could be quite lonely in this big empty house on your own all day. She supposed he might like company and wondered what other company he might be going home to.

'Anyway, maybe you can help me too. It's clear you know the history of the house. You have a family connection to it and you know the era. Maybe I can run a few ideas by you. I'm staying in the pub while I do some more research.'

'If you think I can help.' For a moment she considered mentioning the pocket book, with its minutiae of daily life at Westcott Hall, but he spoke again and the moment passed.

'It's a shame the house hasn't been maintained,' he said, 'but at least it's still standing.'

'The Ambrose luck seemed to run out with Prudence's disappearance,' she said. *Our luck* ran out, is what she meant. Her Ambrose forbears, who had sold the estate bit by bit to finance their woes. Sold or lost. Westcott Hall had become a burden rather than a boon with its reputation for secrets and rumours, of worse.

No wonder those ridiculous whispers of a curse still circulated in the village when there was nothing better to talk about at the pub. Fanned not a little by her aunt's love of a good story, and fondness for a glass or three of Chablis.

'I wonder what Prudence thought when she inherited the estate?' Daniel mused. 'She married Edward Ambrose later in life, several years after her father's death. I wonder if her father expected that she would manage the estate alone.'

'I don't think her father arranged matters exactly as she might have hoped or expected,' said Eliza.

After Jude had given her the polite repository, she'd found it relatively easy to access a copy of Sir Roderick Merryfield's will in the Somerset Archives. It was there for anyone who cared to look. But it was his daughter's words that had shocked her more than the dry legalese of Sir Roderick's last will and testament, the words Prudence had written on that day less than a week after her father's death, the day she discovered the contents of his will. The words in her diary were so clotted with ink they were barely legible.

Saturday: Pot-au-feu for luncheon. Father willed away inheritance. Betrayed by Edward.

Prudence's anger was gouged into the page.

7

Somerset, England

1832

They awaited Mr Norris's arrival in the library. Although neither she nor Edward had referred to his surprising offer since that awkward conversation by the river, it lingered in the once-comfortable silences between them. With luncheon finished, they had no salmon or pot-au-feu to occupy them, so his proposal was almost a physical presence in the room. Nevertheless, she was determined not to let it distract her from the forthcoming meeting with her father's solicitor.

The library at Westcott Hall was the most elegant room in the house, replete with a set of horsehair-padded easy chairs upholstered in raspberry silk damask; numerous side tables ensured the port always lay within reach; and several towers of handsome, leather-bound volumes were displayed upon carved mahogany shelves. Despite her father's careful oversight of household expenditure, he never stinted when it came to his masculine comforts. She hazarded a glance at his portrait above the fireplace, now shrouded in black crêpe. Alongside his portrait, her own painted image stared back at her. The artist had ignored her freckles, giving her a translucent complexion, and she wore the fashionable white muslin gown of her youth, her mother's gold locket nestling against her collarbone.

'Perhaps you'd be more relaxed seated?' Edward indicated the chair at his side. Fashioned of delicate rosewood curlicues with a cane seat, the bishop had once come to grief upon a similar chair after a hearty eight-course dinner.

'I assure you I can survive a meeting with my father's solicitor without resorting to the smelling salts.'

She took up a position facing away from the French windows, not wishing to be distracted from the business that would secure her future far more satisfyingly than any talent for the pianoforte, or indeed any fortunate symmetry of features. Her father had not instructed her in the ways of business, as he may have done with a son, but she had garnered some useful morsels by listening to his conversation over the dining table with his associates. Her hearing was particularly acute when it came to the subject of matrimony, her ears pricking up at the mention of jointures, coverture and pin money. So much so that when, on the occasion of her twenty-first birthday, her father presented her with a copy of Mrs Taylor's *Practical Hints to Young Females on the Duties of a Wife, a Mother and a Mistress of a Young Family* (no doubt conscious that she had no mama to advise her in such matters), the book's contents only bolstered that knowledge.

This knowledge had also doused any feelings she may have harboured for a certain dashing baronet, a distant relative of her mother's. Marriage was not to be entered into lightly if she wished to retain any independence of person, fortune, or indeed thought. Thankfully, neither had Sir Roderick appeared eager to deliver her into a husband's care, content to keep her at Westcott Hall as companion and hostess rather than part with the considerable dowry a prospective suitor would expect.

'I do not desire to give some fortune-hunting rogue a petticoat hold on my fortune,' he was fond of saying when any of his associates enquired after her marriage prospects.

Out of curiosity she had once asked if he did not desire

grandchildren. To which he replied, 'What do I care for posterity when I am dead and gone?' She wondered at the time if pragmatism precipitated his answer or whether the loss of her mother had drained all desire for further progeny from his heart.

The redoubtable Mr Norris began their meeting with a lengthy preamble, replete with much coughing and clearing of the throat, his speech bloated with vowels and swallowed consonants. It flowed like a river bobbing with words such as 'preamble', 'covenant' and 'trust'. Now and then, Edward flicked a glance in her direction, a look of concern in those familiar blue eyes, but she thought nothing of it. If anything, her heart softened towards him. Perhaps he had spoken the truth yesterday by the riverbank. Perhaps in offering for her he really did have her interests at heart, mistaken though he might be as to their nature.

Later, she would realise that she had been lulled into complacency by the interminable nature of Norris's speech. She didn't comprehend what would have been plain to a more astute listener. It had been there in the furtive glances the two men sent each other. Yet, unsuspecting, she hadn't seen it at the time. In her naivety, she hadn't recognised this perfidy for what it was. Only Norris's repeated mention of the sum 'five hundred pounds' finally succeeded in prodding her awake.

Surely her father's estate was worth far more than five hundred pounds?

"'. . . bequeathed the entirety of my estate, lodged in the hands of her trustees in trust, for her sole and separate use, from which she is to be paid a sum of five hundred pounds per annum from the income of the estate, until such time as she should marry. Upon said marriage, the husband shall have a life interest in the assets and income of the estate and the sole management thereof in trade, apart from a sum of five hundred pounds per annum from the income of the estate, which is to be paid to her for her sole and separate use. Upon the husband's death—'"

'I beg your pardon, Mr Norris, what are you saying? Am I not to have the entirety of my father's estate?' she asked, interrupting the river of words. 'Is there another beneficiary?' To her chagrin, her voice jumped an octave upon these last words so that they emerged as a shrill tweet.

Norris looked up from his sheaf of papers, extending his considerable chins as if he longed to run a finger beneath a too-tight collar. He didn't answer immediately. Perhaps he hoped that her interjection would be fleeting and could be safely ignored. Or perhaps he imagined she might be quelled by silence. However, she was not to be deterred, for there was too much at stake.

'Am I not to receive my father's *entire* estate?' she repeated, fixing him with a glare.

Finally, beneath her intense gaze, he cleared his throat and sighed. A heaving sound redolent of discomfort, whether from the pain of his duty or lingering après luncheon dyspepsia, she could not say.

'In a manner of speaking.'

'In a manner of speaking, yes or no, sir?' The man clearly had a torturous relationship with words. The meaningful ones must be sifted from the straw like wheat from chaff.

'Yes . . .' he began, casting a placatory glance in her direction, '. . . and no. Suffice to say that Sir Roderick has placed your inheritance in trust as a separate estate, to be managed by a trustee.'

'I'm not sure I understand.'

'In short, you will not have the managing of his estate. That is to be handled by a trustee appointed by Sir Roderick. The capital is to be managed by the trustee, as is all household expenditure. You are to receive an income of some five hundred pounds per annum to accommodate your personal expenses,' he explained, looking to Edward as if for reinforcement.

'But surely my father's estate shall have an income of more than five hundred pounds?'

'Indeed, I believe the sum to be more in the vicinity of three thousand pounds.'

'Then what is to happen to the other two thousand five hundred pounds?' She could subtract five hundred from three thousand as well as any tradesman. She eyed the solicitor sternly, but by now he was searching his papers for happier news and did not meet her eye.

'Er . . . some of it shall pay for the management of this household.' Again he looked to Edward, brown eyes meeting blue in silent communion. Even so, she did not predict the extent of the looming perfidy.

'And the remainder?'

'Shall be retained and invested by the trust for your future use or that of your future husband . . . Five hundred pounds is a very nice sum, Miss Merryfield. Why, a family could live quite comfortably upon that sum. Although I cannot say it would extend to the keeping of a carriage.'

'They could live more happily upon a sum of three thousand pounds. But that is beside the point. I do not understand why my father would do this.'

The solicitor sighed once more. 'It is a matter of coverture, dear lady. As you know, once a woman marries, she comes under her husband's protection. She becomes one with her husband. All that she owns becomes his to order as he sees fit. She cannot enter into any financial arrangements, for example, nor bequeath property in a will . . .' He paused to take a sustaining breath.

'Usually a trust of this nature is established in anticipation of a marriage, to protect the interests of the prospective wife, but since a marriage was not . . . erm . . . contemplated when your father drafted this will, and he wasn't in the first flush of youth, he sought in his usual prudent manner to protect your interests in the event of his demise.'

'By giving them to someone else?'

'No, not giving . . . no, not at all. Entrusting. A completely different situation altogether, I hasten to say. Now, in the event you should marry, your inheritance will be outside of your husband's ownership. He will have the use of the income in his lifetime only. Upon his death the estate shall pass to your children. Only if you should die without issue shall the estate pass to your husband upon your death.'

'But I do not intend to marry.'

'Then the estate shall pass to a distant cousin of your father, or his male descendants, upon your death.'

Despite her unspoken promise to herself to remain calm, she felt her anger swell. Like a rogue wave it threatened to swamp all restraint. She had shielded her heart for this? She had guarded her person and her fortune for this? To have her future stolen as surely as if she had married the first shiny suitor who happened along. Why would her father betray her thus? She had thought he was indifferent to the fate of his fortune upon his death. Indifferent to . . . she did not trust herself to finish the thought. Instead, she turned once more to his agent and mouthpiece.

'And what paragon of righteousness has my father deemed worthy as trustee?' she asked, already dreading the long years ahead where she must beg her money from one of her father's ancient cronies, forever bargaining for her independence.

'Why . . . your friend and neighbour, Mr Ambrose. That is why I begged his attendance.' Norris beamed from Edward to Prudence, as if he would sway her to his viewpoint with good will alone. Edward, meanwhile, was diligently studying the carpet, his hands fiddling with his pocket watch.

So . . . she was doubly betrayed.

'You would own me twice over, Edward?' she asked.

'Own you? What do you mean?' he said, looking up at last. Given his betrayal, he regarded her with an almost comical air of puzzlement.

'Well, once as my trustee and twice as my husband?'

'Th-th-that was not my intent at all. Your father enjoined me to protect your interests. I th-thought that you would be pleased by my offer.' He blinked at her.

'Pleased? Why should I be pleased?'

'G-given past . . . erm . . . events . . .' He trailed off.

'Past events?'

'Once, I was under the impression an offer from me would not be unwelcome to you,' he mumbled, and she could almost see the sandy-haired boy he had once been. She would not be taken in by this air of innocence.

'In another distant age, perhaps. When I was little more than a child given to romantic notions of love and marriage,' she said, 'and you were about to marry elsewhere.'

Thankfully, his marriage to Alice had scuttled any further delusions of that nature. And now Prudence was a woman of middling years, yet he appeared to believe that she nursed an unrequited affection for him extending two decades. The conceit of the man!

She clutched at her mother's locket, the only thing that had brought her comfort all those years ago when she had sobbed into her pillow for the very last time.

'I sought only to offer you the protection of a husband's love.'

'I assure you that Money secures a woman's future, not Love,' she said, twisting the fine gold chain around her hand.

Edward blinked, as if unsure he had heard correctly. 'Everyone is in need of love, Prudence.'

'I've done without it thus far. I don't see why that need change now I am an orphan.'

For a moment she wondered if her words were true, if she had ever known love. Except that she did feel a flush of warmth whenever she thought of her mother. Rocking her. Tending small hurts. Whispering words of comfort. Yet it was so long ago.

Norris cleared his throat, but before he could speak Carp appeared at the open door accompanied by a young woman in neat but plain dress. The butler came to a halt on the garland of flowers that formed a herbaceous border about the carpet. He indicated the young woman with a flick of his eyes.

'Forgive the intrusion, Miss Merryfield, but I have Miss . . . er . . . Pike for you. I thought you may wish to speak with her while Mr Ambrose is here.'

Prudence took a breath to calm her rising anger. She did not recognise the visitor as someone of her acquaintance, yet both girl and butler regarded her expectantly. And although she always chose her friends for their conversation and amiability rather than their fortune, she had to admit that Miss Pike's dress was somewhat poorer than her usual acquaintance, being devoid of pleats, lace, embroidery, or indeed any embellishment. And rather than a pair of fashionable half-boots, or delicate kid slippers, her feet were shod in rush slippers.

Yet there was something familiar about the tendrils of strawberry hair peeking from beneath her cap. Something about the wide-set green eyes that watched her from beneath sandy lashes. Some familiarity about the small lips, parted as if about to launch into . . . a lullaby.

Lavender's blue, dilly, dilly, lavender's green.
When I am king, dilly, dilly, you shall be queen . . .

The tune drifted into her mind, bringing with it a flash of memory. How extraordinary. Some little thing about the girl reminded her of her mother.

'I wondered what you would have me do with her.'

Prudence reached automatically for the locket resting at her breast. Captured for eternity by the miniaturist's art, her mother's face was the last thing she saw every night and the first thing she saw every morning; the hair cascading like sunset, the face a pearly oval, the lips a dew-kissed rosebud, forever young and beautiful. Younger than Prudence by a decade, and with each passing year the gap between them widening. She had given her daughter life but had not lived long enough to know her, nor for Prudence to know her mother.

Carp cleared his throat. 'What would you have me do with her, Miss Merryfield? I presume, since you directed me to employ her, that you have something in mind.'

'Do with her?'

'With Bessie,' said Edward, smiling in the girl's direction. 'The child we met with Custard. Coming along the road. How are you, Bessie?'

'Good, if it please your . . . your lordship,' said the girl, attempting a rather wobbly curtsy.

Of course. How remiss of her to forget the orphan girl so quickly, and how noble of Edward to remember. Her heart and mind had been buzzing with so many other matters: Edward's unexpected offer; Norris's arrival; her father's betrayal; and not least her own equivocal feelings about these events. She was all turned about.

She saw now that the girl regarding her shyly was the very same orphan they had met coming along the lane with the rector only yesterday, although with the dirt washed from her face and hair, and some decent clothes, she looked a different creature. Strange, how she had caused Prudence to think of her mother. Red hair was not so unusual, after all. She was graced with it herself.

'Do what you usually do with new staff, Carp. Find her a position to suit her talents,' she said.

'So far I have been unable to discern any.'

'Well, put her in the kitchen then. Cook can always use another pair of hands.' She waved a hand in the general direction of the servants' realm.

'Cook says she will be more trouble than use, getting underfoot, not knowing her knees from her elbows.' The butler's face was as expressive as stone.

From the corner of her eye, she noticed the girl staring up at her portrait above the fireplace in wonder. Perhaps the child had never seen a proper portrait. Perhaps her life had been bare of all art and comforts. And now she had lost her grandparents too.

'I have given the rector my word. So we must find something . . . anything. Anything you deem appropriate.'

'Of course, miss,' he nodded. 'I shall find something suitable.'

Once he had departed with the girl, she glanced over to find Edward frowning. She lifted an eyebrow in his direction but would not give him the satisfaction of enquiring as to his opinions. He could keep his admonitions *and* his proposals to himself. She could not leave the child marooned under a hedgerow. Nor could she suffer her to be shipped off to the workhouse. All kinds of dangers lurked for a girl stranded alone in the world.

Carp would find something.

'Once you take her up, Prudence, you cannot simply drop her again, you know,' he said, hands clasped behind his back. How had she never noticed how sanctimonious he had become?

'Perhaps you would prefer to order my household yourself, since my father has appointed you keeper of the purse strings. Since he didn't trust me to order my own life.'

Norris's chins wobbled as he shook his head in earnest. 'I'm confident your father made these arrangements out of love for you, Miss Merryfield, not as punishment.'

She was still clasping the locket, feeling cool crystal and metal beneath her palm. Seemingly of its own volition, that hand now wrenched at the twisted links of the delicate chain so that the locket broke away to dangle forlornly about her wrist.

'Now look what you've made me do,' she whispered angrily to everyone and no one. 'I've broken my mother's locket.'

She closed her eyes, shutting out both Norris's surfeit of chins and Edward's blue-eyed gaze, to conjure the halo of red hair and the gentle smile that shone from the miniature painting in the locket. That love shone for her alone. Her mother wouldn't have willed her away. Of this she was certain.

'God save me from a father's love,' she pronounced, as she turned with a swish of skirts and stomped towards the door. 'Good day, gentlemen.'

And God save her from a husband's love too, she thought, as she headed for the sanctuary of her bedchamber. Once there, she took a seat at her desk beneath the window, seeking solace in the comfort of her pocket book.

Saturday: Pot-au-feu for luncheon. Father willed away inheritance. Betrayed by Edward.

Although her hand shook as she etched the words into the paper, her mind was clearer than ever. No matter what her father or her erstwhile suitor intended, whether conspiracy or not, she would not let them rule her. Somehow, she would find a way to chart her own course and be her own woman. She alone would determine what her life was to be. And that would be whatever she was brave enough to make it.

She blotted the words and was about to close the book when she remembered: *Must repair mother's locket.*

She could not bear to lose this fragile connection to the woman she had lost thirty years before. Thoughts of her mother calmed her shaking hand and angry thoughts. Her mother would watch over her. With a steadier hand, she sketched a tiny version of the oval frame in the margin, a chain of unbroken links encircling the page. Her mother would be her guiding star.

8

Somerset, England

2022

An unwelcome pile of paperwork awaited Eliza's attention beneath a delicate Baccarat millefiori paperweight that had been a favourite of her mother's. The glass orb bloomed with a 'thousand flowers', belying the terrifying stack of bills it held in check. Her mother always said, 'Beauty is in the eye of the beholder, so a little Baccarat atop the bills can't hurt.' And Eliza continued the tradition, dutifully printing out the invoices and propping them under glass. She never tired of its intricate beauty. Her practical side also appreciated the fact that it would probably fetch at least a thousand pounds if she were desperate.

Her desk faced a small window that gave on to the showroom from the office. From here she could keep an eye on the store when alone. Although the stock was ever changing, her desk was the same one she had played beneath as a child; an eighteenth-century Welsh oak dining table in a rustic three-plank design. Its surface was littered with papers, a touring atlas of the UK, and several curios awaiting minor repairs. In the middle of this organised chaos sat her laptop and, beside it, the pocket book tempted her with its contents. Looking at it, she wondered what she would write in twelve words or fewer to describe her day. Like Prudence, would she stick to facts?

Wednesday: Porridge for lunch. Toured Hall with Aussie builder. Located Prudence's bedroom.

Or would she confess her deepest, darkest secrets?

Wednesday: Pantry bare again. Hall haunted by scarily hot builder. Must visit Tesco.

Her aunt had urged her to investigate Prudence's story; to discover, once and for all, what part, if any, Edward Ambrose had played in her disappearance. But even if Eliza somehow found the time to begin that research, even if she were to dust off her journalistic skills, chances were her efforts would be fruitless. If the authorities hadn't solved the mystery at the time, what hope did she have almost two hundred years later?

Still, the pocket book called to her. Prudence's voice whispered across the centuries like that of a long-absent friend. She reached a hand across the desk, drawn by its lure. The faded red leather was worn with use at the corners. The front cover was scratched and buffeted by who knew what calamities. And creeping across the surface like a tide mark in the sand was the evidence of past water damage. Almost of its own volition, her hand opened the book and began idly turning pages. She had read through the entries once already, but since then she had found Sir Roderick Merryfield's will and discovered Edward Ambrose's trusteeship of the estate. She also knew from the pocket book that Edward had proposed to Prudence before she purchased the ticket to Calcutta. These facts shed a different light on the following remark from June.

Friday: Must escape. Trip to Sidmouth. Dip in ocean. Edward followed me.

Perhaps her escape wasn't a simple pleasure trip to Sidmouth, as Eliza had thought upon first reading. Perhaps it was the formation of a plan to escape Edward Ambrose. Much as she didn't want to believe that one of her ancestors held sinister, possibly murderous, intentions towards Prudence – it now appeared possible.

What harm could another quick look do? Flipping open her laptop, she opened the browser and logged into The British Newspaper Archive. 'Let's start at the beginning,' she muttered, as she typed in the following search terms: 'Prudence Merryfield disappearance 1833'. Then she sat back and waited for the search fairy to work its magic. The catalogue of articles that materialised was a roll-call of newspapers from across Britain, most no longer extant. Scrolling down the page, she selected an article from London-based masthead *The Globe*, dated 7 August 1833, and began reading.

LOSS OF THE *KANGAROO*

The arrival of the *Amity* from Sydney, New South Wales, into Liverpool, on Wednesday has brought further news of the missing merchant vessel the *Kangaroo*.

A barque of some 300 tons, she departed Singapore in January, en route for Sydney via the Feejee Islands, where she planned to take on a cargo of bêche-de-mer. She took on provisions and cargo at the port of Makassar, but as of the *Amity*'s departure, she was yet to arrive in Sydney.

Grave fears are held for the safety of crew and vessel. In addition to the ship's master, Captain James Weller, and a crew of 14, it is believed that the ship also carried two female passengers, a Miss Prudence Merryfield, late of Somerset, and her maid.

Miss Merryfield is believed to have departed England the previous year in what was intended as a pleasure voyage. The trustee of her estate, Mr Edward Ambrose, requests us to make public his desire for any information as to her route or current whereabouts. Any news of the fate of the *Kangaroo* will be gratefully received.

So Prudence must have sailed from Calcutta to Singapore, which would have been a fledgling English settlement at that time, and then taken passage to Sydney. The question was – why did she leave England in the first place? What would induce a single woman in possession of a good fortune to leave the luxury of Westcott Hall and travel to the other side of the world? Why would she brave the discomforts and dangers of that voyage? A poor and marginalised woman might seek a better life. And the wife of a farmer or tradesman might hope to build wealth upon the land. But Prudence was already an heiress. What need did she have of land grants and sheep farms? No, it was either adventure that called her – a risky but not unknown business for a woman in the 1830s – or she was running from danger.

Eliza might never discover exactly when or why Prudence embarked upon her onward voyage from Singapore, as a wad of pages had been torn from the middle of the pocket book. The diary entries ended before she arrived in Calcutta. But perhaps she could find further clues if she read between the lines, searching for a motive amongst the writer's sparse recounting of events. Well, she could if she had the time. Inclination alone wasn't reason enough to put aside the tasks at hand when she had a responsibility to keep the store afloat. More than a responsibility – a solemn promise.

Through the window the store spread out before her like the Cabinet of Wonders her parents had named it. She may have inherited the store, but in the last two years she had made it her own. Each piece of furniture, each decorative object, each article of clothing had been lovingly chosen by her own hand. Some quality about each had called to her, be it the colour, texture or shape, or quirkiness that appealed. Sometimes the allure was simply a mystery.

She arranged each object as part of a story that might never be told but nevertheless existed in her imagination. Each piece was incorporated into a living tableau: an art deco table set for two with a romantic sixties cocktail dress draped over the back of a chair; a Georgian four-poster bed layered with vintage brocade cushions and pristine Victorian nightwear; a rustic Welsh dresser filled with early twentieth-century stoneware and antique Chinese ceramics. She hoped these living tableaux would appeal, but the characters who may have sat at that table, slept in that bed, worked in that kitchen, lived only in her imagination.

She sighed, relinquishing the idea of investigating the pocket book further today, and reached instead for an envelope sitting atop the morning's mail. She slit open the envelope with a bone-handled letter opener and withdrew a single sheet emblazoned with the letterhead of her rental agent. A letter she had been waiting on for the last month.

'*Dear Ms Ambrose . . .*' she read.

The letter began in the usual manner, before dealing her such a blow that she almost forgot to breathe. When she finally remembered, it was as if the wind had been literally knocked from her sails and she had to take a giant gulp of air to replenish it. Then she rested her head upon her arms on the desk, the weight of her head too great a burden to bear. Maybe if she pressed her nose to the warm timber and cradled her ears with her arms she could hide from the knowledge, if only for a few moments. But the words were already seared into her brain.

'*Dear Ms Ambrose . . . etc., etc. . . . . in reply to your application to renew your lease, please find enclosed a "Section 25 notice: to oppose a new tenancy".*'

Surely it couldn't be true? Not after her years of hard work and her parents' labour of decades. *Oppose a new tenancy.* In other words – evict her.

In the midst of her distress the bell rang, heralding the first customer of the day. Pulling herself together as best she could, she summoned a welcoming smile and headed for the showroom. The man had his back to her. He was tallish, with a navy jacket clothing his broad shoulders and a sprinkle of grey in his neatly trimmed, dark brown hair. The jacket was casual but she suspected Burberry. Not short of a quid then. He was inspecting a Georgian-era side table in the Chippendale style that she had picked up at a recent estate sale. She was particularly pleased with its brass axe-head handles and escutcheon plates, and the fretted brackets beneath the tabletop.

'Good morning, it's lovely, isn't it? Solid mahogany, we think circa 1780.'

'Yes, quite lovely,' he said, turning to her with a smile, revealing both the Burberry monogram on his jacket and a familiar face, albeit one that was today wearing a pair of black-rimmed glasses.

'Daniel, how nice to see you,' she replied, trying valiantly not to let her smile slip. A visitor was the last thing she needed. She would have to offer him tea after he had been so generous with his time the other day. She would have to sit opposite him in the cramped space of her office, knees almost touching as they sipped tea and talked of history while she held back the floodgates of panic.

'Careful that smile doesn't get stuck permanently.'

'What?' For some reason, seeing him here in her shop in the midst of her disarray was triggering an irresistible urge to sob. She felt her mouth twitch, heading downwards as tears threatened. Tears she was determined to resist.

'Just joking. Really. Nothing wrong with professional poise. I could certainly do with a bit more . . . obviously.'

'Professional p-p-p- . . .' she said, swiping an arm across her face to banish the recalcitrant tears, '. . . p-poise?'

'I can come back later. I was just passing and dropped in to have a peek.'

'No. Please stay,' she said, sniffing for good measure. 'I'll make tea. Just give me a m-m-m—'

'Where are the tea things? I'll make it.'

Five minutes later, she was back in her office, sitting in the wreckage of her parents' life work, cradling a cup of tea in a Staffordshire Old Inns series mug (how did he know it was her favourite?) and trying to concentrate on the conversation. Unfortunately, her eyes had other ideas, drifting repeatedly to the open letter on her desk, even as she endeavoured to keep them politely focused upon her guest.

'From what I've seen so far your showroom is lovely.'

'Thank you. I'm aiming for eclectic, yet cohesive. As if you were entering the rooms of someone's house. Someone with excellent taste, naturally.'

'Well, you clearly have good taste. Do you have a background in interior design?'

'No, journalism actually. I kind of fell into this.'

'Part-time work at uni that got under your skin?'

'No. Family business. I inherited the store from my parents.'

There was a lull in the conversation, as if he was waiting for her to say more, while she was having difficulty finding any words at all. The only words that occurred to her were 'lease', 'tenancy' and 'oppose'.

'I'm sorry for your loss, Eliza,' Daniel said, before the silence could grow too uncomfortable. His chin dipped towards the hands cradling his mug, but his eyes tilted upwards to her face. 'Was it recent?'

She cleared her throat and blinked, turning to gaze out over the showroom so that she didn't have to meet his gaze. Furniture was safer; it demanded little of her except dusting and beeswax. None of this hankering after connection and revelation – even of the superficial variety.

'My father died of a stroke eight years ago. Mum died of a massive heart attack in 2020. They were both seventy when they passed.' Her parents hadn't been exactly young when she was born but they had been so full of life, so full of plans. And now all their plans for the store, all the plans she had made with her mother, would come to nothing. 'What about you?' she asked, to stem any further courtesies or sympathies. 'Did you fall into building, or was it a lifelong ambition?'

'Ha, well, there's a story. I'm from Sydney originally. Took a year or two off after doing science at uni to go travelling. Started work on a building site in Bristol. Fell in love with the trade. Studied building part-time. Then fell in love with a girl and ended up staying.'

'What happened to the girl?' She tensed in anticipation of his answer.

'Oh, the usual. Married . . . grew apart . . . divorced. I think we probably just met too young.'

She itched to ask more about this girl who had won and then lost his heart, but resisted the urge.

'Do you miss Sydney?'

'Sure. I go back every year. I probably would have returned permanently but . . . well, I've built up a good clientele. Keeps me busy. I'll probably go home one day.' He shrugged, then placed his mug on the shelf beside him and looked at her thoughtfully for a few moments. 'The thing is, Eliza, I've been thinking.'

'I can see that,' she smiled, more a twitch of the lips really. 'You have this little frown thingy happening when you're deep in thought.'

'Do I? Well, the thing is, I wondered whether you'd be interested in helping me source suitable pieces for the hall. I don't think it's much of a secret that my clients are redeveloping it as a hotel. The plans have already been through the council and the work should start later this year. As well as the architect, I'll be working with an interior designer, but the client has asked me to help source some of the furniture locally, especially if we can find pieces that have a story to tell.'

She considered him for a few seconds, not sure that she'd heard correctly. She had been commissioned to source furniture and artefacts for clients before, of course, but only for private houses. Nothing as grand as the hall. And nothing as public as a hotel.

'Won't your designers want to use their own contacts?'

'Ah . . . well . . . I have some influence there. The designers will be sourcing all the new furniture, but I've done a lot of work for these particular clients and they've asked me to see what I can find in the way of antiques. Plus, I've taken a minor financial interest in the project. Anyway, it takes a lot of furniture to fill a building that size. And I thought, since you know the area, you might be able to help. What do you think?'

What did she think? What *did* she think? She thought she would be a fool not to leap at the opportunity. But then there was the letter. She might not even be in business in six months.

'It will be a lengthy timeline, if that's a concern.'

She took a deep breath, her eyes drawn to the letter.

'That was a big sigh,' he said, following the direction of her eyes.

'Normally I'd jump at an offer like that,' she said, 'but . . . I may not be here much longer. I may not even be in business in six months.'

He raised his eyebrows in a silent question.

'I've just received a Section 25 notice to quit.' She nodded towards the offending letter. 'My landlord wants to occupy the premises.'

'Ah, I see. Well, the landlord will have to offer compensation, and you can find new premises. I've noticed a few "To Lease" signs since I've been in the area.' He said the words so mildly, so matter-of-factly, as if losing your home and business was an everyday occurrence. Perhaps, in his line of work, it was an everyday occurrence.

'You don't understand . . .' she began, her treacherous voice faltering.

'Help me understand.' The frown thingy was back between his eyebrows, giving him the expression of a concerned librarian.

'I can't lose the store.'

'Uh-huh. I suppose it's been in the family a long time.'

'We used to own the premises.'

'That's a shame. And I know moving can seem daunting, but it's quite doable. I should know. I've done it plenty of times, both home and business. You might even find something better.'

'It's not just that. You see, my mother . . . my mother . . .'

She could picture her mother so clearly, it might have been yesterday, the paramedics in their fluorescent orange jackets lifting her carefully on to the trolley and strapping her in. She had folded her arms casually at her waist, belying the pain in her chest and the difficulty she faced breathing. She was smiling beneath the clear plastic of her oxygen mask. Soft white hair spread upon the pillow like a halo about her head. Eliza and Jude had followed the paramedics as they wheeled the trolley through the clutter of the shop and out on to the street. And as they were about to hoist her into the open rear of the ambulance, her mother had lifted a hand and beckoned Eliza closer.

'Mind the shop when I'm gone, love,' she had said, her voice barely audible, her lips hardly moving beneath the mask.

'I will, Mum.'

'And don't forget to water the plants.'

'I won't.'

And those were the last words her mother ever spoke to her. She was dead before the ambulance could arrive at Accident and Emergency, an inconceivable seven minutes and forty seconds later.

'I can't lose the store,' she murmured to this strange man from the other side of the world who had arrived on her doorstep, unannounced and uninvited. 'I promised my mother.'

She might be able to break a promise to a mother who was still living – for there was always the prospect of forgiveness – but a dead mother was unwavering in her demand for love and loyalty.

9

Somerset, England
1832

Bessie didn't bother to stifle her yawn since, for once, no one was looking over her shoulder waiting to scold. She had lost count of the fireplaces she had emptied and scoured that morning. The number had gone beyond the count of her fingers and into the province of her toes if she dared remove her shoes to count. She had raked and swept and brushed until her back groaned. Then rubbed and shined and polished until her arms ached. She had begun before dawn with the massive range in the kitchen, then the drawing and dining rooms, the library with her mistress staring down from above the fireplace, then the servants' quarters while they took a quick slurp of oatmeal. Lastly, she had tackled the lady's chamber while she breakfasted downstairs.

Yesterday, Mr Carp had instructed her in the correct manner of setting a fire but she couldn't remember whether he had said three pieces of charcoal or four was the correct number to set the fire burning brightly. She had solved this problem quite cleverly, however, by setting half the fireplaces with three pieces and half with four. So, if he decided to count the charcoal remaining in the bucket she could only be half wrong.

But now her knees were throbbing from kneeling on cold stone hearths, and when she wiped her nose with the cloth Cook had pinned to her dress for that purpose, it came away smeared with black. She knew that the lady liked to take a long walk after breakfast, although why she walked when she had a carriage and horses to spare, Bessie could not fathom. She also knew that the lady's maid, Miss Wills, was in the habit of visiting the stables – and the stable master – during her mistress's excursions. So what harm would it do if Bessie took a few moments for herself in the lady's room? No one else was likely to enter until the upper housemaid came to dust all the pretty things after she finished with sweeping and polishing downstairs.

Leaving her brushes and buckets to fend for themselves, Bessie made a circuit of the room searching for the most likely spot where she would leave no sign of soot to betray her. She decided upon the lady's dressing room, a room lined with wood panelling and the only place bare of rugs and draperies. She settled in one corner as far as possible from the dressing table littered with objects whose use was a mystery to her but whose daintiness suggested certain danger. Curling into a ball on the floor next to a chair that concealed the chamber pot, she closed her eyes. As she drifted off to sleep, enclosed in this cosy den of wood, she breathed in the warm aroma of timber, the lingering floral scent of the lady's clothing, and the comforting stink of stale urine.

'We shall leave first thing in the morning. Tell Bobbett to have the carriage ready. I shall take an early breakfast and we shall leave at nine.'

'Should I also send a message to Queens Knoll for Mr Ambrose?'

'Mr Ambrose? What business is it of his what time I take breakfast?'

'I thought only that you might wish to inform him of your travel plans.'

'What business of his are my plans?'

'None, of course, miss.'

'And neither is it your business to think, Wills, other than of gowns and petticoats and so forth . . .'

Bessie floundered, emerging from an exhausted stupor, roused by what she thought at first was the screech of a barn owl outside her granmer's cottage but soon realised was actually her mistress in full flight.

'. . . I shall do all the thinking on my plans. Not Mr Ambrose. Nor Mr Norris, nor Carp, nor Bobbett, nor . . . nor . . . any other gentleman of my acquaintance.'

The screeching tapered off into a grumble of names before petering out into a loud sigh. Bessie made her body as small as possible, hoping no one would have urgent need of the dressing room. Clearly, something had set a cat amongst the pigeons and the lady was very upset. If she screeched at Miss Wills over her plans for breakfast, how might she greet the surprise discovery of a sooty housemaid hiding in her dressing room? Bessie did not want to find out.

'Now, Wills . . .' another loud sigh, 'I'm sorry if I seem a little harsh. The last weeks have been very trying to say the least. Let's say no more about this matter, and instead turn our thoughts to packing.'

'Yes, miss.'

'I shall wear my blue carriage dress for travelling, of course. And my blue pelisse, should the weather turn. We'll take the pink organza for evening with the India silk shawl and ivory satin gloves. And the printed cotton and the yellow silk for day, I think.'

'Yes, miss.'

Wills sounded unperturbed by her mistress's outburst but Bessie knew she would need to stay out of the senior maid's orbit for at least the rest of the day or she would cop it for sure. The other woman never said a bad word about her mistress in Bessie's presence but she complained to the upper housemaid about Miss Merryfield's 'whims and nonsense' regularly, about her unconcern for the hard work of others.

'You may select suitable gloves and shawls for day and the appropriate sleeve pads for each gown. And . . . oh . . . bonnets. I cannot bear to think about bonnets.'

'Of course. Will you be riding?'

'No. But I shall be bathing . . . in the sea.'

'Then I shall pack extra shifts.'

'And for yourself as well, for I may have need of you.'

The lady's words were followed by a small yelp that caused Bessie to huddle further into her corner. 'Me? But I daren't! I cannot swim.'

'That is the point of learning.'

'But I will catch a fever.'

'Nonsense! The seawater is quite bracing.'

'Begging your pardon, Miss Merryfield, but me mam says cold water lets in disease.'

'Well, I cannot force you, though it be for your own good,' the lady said in a clipped voice, and the light tread of slippers that followed warned she was headed towards the dressing room.

Bessie had a single moment to panic before she would be discovered. She used that moment to scramble across the floor to the chair, upon her knees. When the lady appeared in the doorway of the dressing room she had no need to feign surprise, for her terror did the job for her, widening her eyes and setting her heart to thumping so hard she was certain the lady must hear.

Her mistress appeared almost as surprised as she was, taking a step back and exclaiming, 'Oh! It's Bessie, isn't it? What on earth are you doing in here, child?'

'Emptying chamber pot, milady.'

'On your knees?'

'Didn't want to spill it, milady.'

'While I commend your attention to detail, perhaps you could stand next time, Bessie?'

'Yes, milady.'

'Miss. Yes, miss.' She stared at Bessie for a few seconds as she removed a half-full pot from the chair and attempted to stand while clutching it, all without spilling a drop. Then the lady raised her eyebrows, saying, 'I suppose I shall have to wait until you return then, shall I?'

'M-m-miss?'

'The . . . ah . . . pot.' She nodded towards Bessie's burden.

'Oh . . . sorry, miss.' Trembling now, the contents in even greater danger of slopping over the bowl, Bessie returned the pot to the chair and began backing away from the room. How could she be so stupid?

'You can return in a few minutes. Oh, and do you swim by any chance? You look like a girl who has spent time out of doors,' the mistress said, sweeping a glance from the top of Bessie's head to her toes.

Having a particular aversion to water, Bessie had silently agreed with Wills' opinion on bathing in cold seawater. Her grammer would have been horrified at the idea too. Then again, Bessie had never been to the seaside. She had never been further than the next village.

'Yes, miss,' she said firmly. 'I be a good swimmer.'

'Well then, you may accompany me to the seaside too. I may have need of a strong girl to fetch and carry for me while bathing. And I'm sure the sun and sand will do us all no end of good. Won't it, Wills?'

'Yes, Miss Merryfield. No end of good, to be sure.'

Later, in the hallway outside her mistress's chamber, Bessie waited to deliver a brimming pot of urine to the cesspit behind the stables. Her breath came as quick as a cat in a sack. The lady was to take her to the seaside. She would ride in a carriage all the way to a place called Sidmouth, be subjected to the angry stares of the lady's maid – who wasn't at all happy at the prospect, she could tell – and the puzzling whims of her new mistress. She would visit the sea for the very first time, feel the sand beneath her feet and dip her toes in salty water. It would be a world unlike anything she had known in her life.

Now, if only she could learn to swim before tomorrow.

10

Devon, England

1832

Wills trudged along the beach towards her, kicking up sand. The hem of her skirt was damp and salt-stained, and she did not appear at all happy. Beyond her, in the east, Peak Hill glowered beneath looming clouds but her maid's demeanour was darker than any cumulonimbus. In her severe black gown and sturdy boots, she was a dour sight amongst the vibrant schools of pleasure seekers promenading along the esplanade in their sprigged cottons. Wills' only concession to seaside dress was an embroidered pelerine in white cambric that she had tucked into her belt, and a braided straw bonnet ordered directly from Mrs Sherborne in Bath.

The beach was peppered with bathing machines, available for hire, and fishermen's boats hauled up on to the sand waiting to put to sea. As Wills navigated around them, her distaste was confirmed in a pursing of lips and indrawn chin. The seaside was decidedly not her natural element, nor was she happy about the presence of 'the urchin', as she had taken to calling Bessie. Prudence surmised that including 'the urchin' in their little excursion was an affront to her maid's sense of propriety and the proper order of the world, but Wills would never say as much. No, her protests were never audible. Nor did she speak any unkind word to Bessie in Prudence's presence, but her uncharacteristic and exaggerated efforts to please, her frequent references to the talents of 'the urchin' told their own story. Wills was displeased.

'What have you discovered?' Prudence asked, fixing a smile to her face as her maid drew near.

'A Mrs Barrett operates the bathing contraptions for ladies,' Wills said, her mouth proving almost fish-shaped now. 'One shilling and sixpence a time! Highway robbery, if you ask me.'

'Does that include the services of a dipper?'

'I believe that is an extra sixpence, miss. A good thing you'll only be paying for the two. Although, perhaps you could dispense with the dipper . . . since the urchin is such a fine swimmer.' She cast a sideways glance at Bessie, who had barely spoken a word throughout the entire journey from the hall. 'She can keep a hold of you in the sea, miss.'

Before Prudence could respond to this suggestion, Bessie squeaked out, 'I baint so fine a swimmer as that. Not to keep the lady afloat. And I never been swimmin' in the sea in all me life.'

As she said this she took several steps backwards, disappearing somewhere behind Prudence's skirts. Did the poor child think she was about to be tossed to the waves?

'It's all right, Bessie. I think we can afford the sixpence for a dipper. But I would feel safer for having you at my other side . . . if you can see your way clear to venture into the waves.'

'Yes, miss.'

'And Wills, you may await us in safety upon the shore.'

It was settled then. Despite her employee's inclination towards mutiny, Prudence would make her first foray into the ocean.

A short while later, she stood in the bathing machine garbed only in a linen shift and drawers. After helping her disrobe, Bessie hung her dress, petticoats and pockets from a hook at the rear of the machine, and placed her corset, bonnet and stockings upon a stool. Although it was clear from her hesitation that the child had never unlaced a lady's corset before, she had nimble fingers and learned quickly. All that remained to remove was her mother's locket with its new-mended chain. Over the years it had become her talisman and she would not risk losing it. If it were to disappear beneath the waves it would be as if she had lost her mother all over again.

She took a last look at the locket before venturing into the sea. A tiny version of her mother stared out at her, face pale and bright as a new moon, with a cloud of cascading auburn curls, sparkling eyes and a smile playing about delicate rosebud lips. She knew the artist would have enhanced her mother's features, but even so, Prudence took pleasure in her beauty. This tiny portrait was all that she had of her, for she had died before her father could commission a proper portrait of his young wife. This and a few fragments of memory.

She closed her eyes, trying to summon her mother's voice. Had it been low and melodious, or sweet and high? It was so long ago and difficult to recall. During those last months of her illness, her mother had seemed to fade before her eyes, becoming even thinner and paler until her daughter feared she might disappear altogether. Years later, she realised that her mother's decline was due to the effects of consumption but at the time she remembered asking her father if the fairies were coming to steal her mother away. In response to which he ordered her nurse to stop telling her bedtime stories.

Now, all she could remember of her mother's voice was a handful of words from that last visit to the sickroom, for these she had carried with her every day for the ensuing thirty years.

'Promise me you will look after your father, my big girl. For he will be lost without me.'

What could a five year old say to this? Other than a tearful, 'I promise, Mama.' After all, she was her mother's big girl, and her father needed her. So she had kept her promise. She had stayed by her father's side for the next thirty years, keeping his house, keeping him company and ordering her life to the rhythm of his days. In truth, she could not attest whether this diligence was by chance or design. Nevertheless, it was a promise kept. Now, with his death, she was released.

Removing the locket from around her neck, she handed it to Bessie with the instruction to place it in one of the embroidered pockets that were ordinarily tied about her waist beneath her gown. Then she took the last tentative steps to the open doorway and stood staring out at the waves. The man who hauled the bathing machines out to sea had departed with his horse, leaving them alone apart from the distant white sails of pleasure boats tacking across the bay. Closer to, the sea chopped about the sturdy figure of Mrs Owen, the dipper, frothing white at her waist and lapping almost at the doorstep of the bathing machine.

'Come along then, Bessie. Time to dip a toe in the waters.'

When the girl did not immediately answer, Prudence glanced behind to see that she was still fully clothed, hugging her arms about the dun wool of her dress.

'You will have to remove your dress, for Wills has not packed a change of clothes for you. Only a change of shift.'

'Water be deep, miss.'

'Mrs Owen is standing but waist deep.'

'Yes, miss.'

Head bowed, the girl proceeded to unlace her bodice, fingers suddenly fumbling and clumsy where before they had been deft and quick. Beneath the bodice she wore a long-sleeved shift of white cotton and a single petticoat, which she stepped out of gingerly. Whereas Prudence's chemise was gathered at the neck, with a band beneath the breasts and delicate embroidery of white flowers, the maid's was a mere sack with sleeves. She pulled the garment close about her body, ankles and shins protruding beneath in their bony paleness.

'Thee can jump, or I can drop the stairs for thee,' Mrs Owen called above the swishing, crooning sound of the sea.

'Stairs please, Mrs Owen.' Despite her confident assertion regarding the water's depth, Prudence wasn't about to risk sinking into a hole in the sand, or worse.

The stairs in place, she descended slowly, testing the water at each step, holding her breath at the sudden lash of cold stinging her legs and inching up her chemise. Reaching the last step, she extended a foot, searching blindly for the sandy floor. But before she could touch the bottom, Mrs Owen grabbed her by one arm, pulled her from the stairs and flung her bodily into the cold clutches of the ocean. Caught unawares, her head sank below the waves and her mouth and nose were inundated with what felt like a gallon of salty water. She surfaced sputtering, her feet finding the bottom, and turned to face the dipper indignantly.

'Sorry, miss. Sudden like, that be best way to larn thee. Lean back now,' the dipper said, slipping an arm behind Prudence's waist and encouraging her to lower her body into the water once more. 'I got thee.'

With the strong arm of Mrs Owen beneath her, and the promise of another arm should she need it, Prudence settled back, girded by the bracing chill of gently swelling waves. She stretched out her legs and arms, surprised to find that she did not immediately sink. Instead, she bobbed upon the water, her chemise floating free about her while seagulls dipped and soared above. As she grew accustomed to the cold she relaxed further, relishing the feeling of lightness, her limbs unencumbered except for the fine linen of her undergarments. She did not at first notice that Mrs Owen had removed her supporting arm, so that when the woman spoke she started in surprise.

'Now, miss, turn thee over and paddle.'

She attempted to comply, wallowing gracelessly and spitting water from her mouth in a most unladylike manner.

'Paddle with thy arms and legs. Like a dog or a horse.'

Prudence was grateful when the dipper resumed her hold, giving her the confidence to strike out with arms and legs in the manner of a hound tracking prey across a river.

'I do believe I'm swimming,' she spluttered happily several minutes later, when the dipper finally removed her arm once more.

'I believe thee are, miss.'

'Perhaps you could assist the girl now. What say you, Bessie?' Pausing in her exertions for a moment, she allowed her feet to touch bottom and looked towards the stairs of the bathing machine where her maid stood shivering and white-knuckled. 'It's much the same as the river or the village pond, I warrant, only salty.'

'The sea be so great. I cannot see to other side.'

'No, I dare say you can't see all the way to France.'

'It might carry me away,' Bessie stated, her eyes fixed on the horizon.

'Mrs Owen won't let it, will you?'

'No, I be holdin' tight to the girl,' said the dipper, smiling encouragingly as she waded over to the stairs.

'What say you?' asked Prudence, realising that the answer was writ plain as the fear on Bessie's face. But before she had a chance to relent and allow the girl to retreat to the safety of the machine's interior, the matter was taken out of her hands.

The dipper grasped the frightened girl by the forearm and hauled her mercilessly into the water. She hit the waves with a shriek, churning the water with thrashing arms and legs. She splashed and flailed so fiercely that Prudence feared she might drown, though the water was but waist deep. Her terror was as palpable as it was mysterious. Prudence revelled in the feeling of floating free, buoyed by the saltwater and the bobbing waves, the closest thing to flying she could imagine. Why then was the child so terrified? Especially since she claimed to be a practised swimmer—

But there was no time to waste in puzzling further over the matter as Mrs Owen hastened to the girl's side to hold her shoulders firm and calm her struggling limbs. Meanwhile, Prudence attempted to quiet her shrieks with soothing words, all the while pondering how she had managed to procure such a troublesome child to her service and wondering how she might be rid of her. At the same time, she couldn't help feeling responsible for this flame-haired, none-too-clean urchin who had landed on her doorstep at the behest of the rector. Why she felt this way she could not say. After all, she wasn't personally responsible for the parish poor. At Westcott Hall they always paid their poor rate and church tithes faithfully. So why, then, did she feel a chafing guilt at the thought of ridding herself of this whirling, squalling wretch?

The girl's shrieks finally subsided to a low whine as the dipper succeeded in propping her upright. There she cowered, shivering in her sodden shift, the wet fabric revealing a painfully thin frame, the flaming hair now a dark cap plastered to her scalp.

'Come along, Bessie, no need to cry any more. We shall have you out of the water and dry in no time,' said Prudence, her voice quaking through chattering teeth, her limbs shaking with cold.

And then she would work out what to do about her new maid.

11

By the time the bathing machine was once more beached, the clouds had made good on their bluff, and a cold wind had sprung up from the west. All the sedan chairs had been requisitioned by other refugees from the sudden deluge, leaving nothing for it but to make a dash for their lodgings. Prudence had taken rooms in a terrace overlooking the Fortfield, in a pretty white building with an iron balcony and a fine aspect to the sea. In good weather it was a short stroll to the waterfront. In bad weather it might as well have been France.

So, when they finally arrived at the entrance to their lodgings after toiling across the muddy waterfront mall and wading through the dripping grass of the Fortfield, Prudence was almost as wet as she had been while swimming in the sea, despite Wills' futile efforts with the parasol. Her skirts were rimed with a wide brown stain, her corded silk boots were reminiscent of a pony's shanks, and rain had turned her *coiffure à la Chinoise* to a sodden mop. She could not wait to submit herself to her maid's ministrations with warm water and towels. But when Wills opened the front door and let her into the hall, who should she discover seated on the love seat in the landlady's parlour but her former friend, current neighbour and, she feared, future nemesis . . . Edward Ambrose.

'Prudence, there you are!' he said, leaping to his feet at her appearance. 'You look like a wet foxhound.'

'And you are the whipper-in, I suppose.'

At his crestfallen expression she experienced a moment of remorse, but only a moment, for he followed up this unorthodox greeting by remarking, 'What on earth possessed you to visit the seaside without telling anyone? We have all been quite concerned.'

To which 'we' did he refer, she wondered. The 'we' of her staff, whose sole business was her welfare, not her whereabouts. Or the 'we' of himself, appointed by her father as executor of her estate – not her person.

'You seem to have found me without a deal of trouble, since I arrived only yesterday.'

'Apparently, your stable master acquired some intelligence as to your destination,' he said, averting his eyes.

'Oh, did he so?' She flicked her maid an interrogative glance. Wills and Bessie were the only ones privy to her destination, other than the coachman. She had kept the exact details of her destination close, knowing that Carp could be relied upon to report her business to their neighbour at Queens Knoll. And Edward was the last person she wished to inform.

Wills schooled her face to a picture of innocence but Prudence had suspected for some time that there was more between her maid and the stable master than the woman had thought fit to confide. On more than one occasion she had returned early from her walk, called for her maid, only to observe her from the window hurrying along the path from the direction of the stables. She need hardly consult the horse master on a recipe for lip salve or a health-giving elixir. Little wonder, then, the parade of new caps and collars her maid had taken to wearing of late.

'Is there something you wanted to tell me?' she asked Wills, with a lift of one brow, and was rewarded with an expression of injured innocence in return.

'Miss?'

'Something about your friendship with Bobbett perhaps?'

'There be nothing untoward in it, miss.'

'No one would blame you for being fond of him. Bobbett is a fine figure of a man and a valued member of staff.'

The mutinous look in her maid's eyes softened for the first time since they had embarked upon this apparently ill-fated journey to the seaside. 'He has asked for my hand,' she replied.

While she had voiced no dissent about her mistress's expedition, Prudence knew that Wills was none too pleased from the outset. The addition of Bessie to their small party had only added to her displeasure. No wonder she was reluctant to be whisked away to the seaside when marriage was in the wind.

'I suppose congratulations are in order.'

'I haven't given him my answer, miss.' Not yet, but her smile was answer enough.

'Well, I hope you'll not be leaving me. I'm sure we can find suitable accommodation for you both on the estate,' she said, turning to Edward. 'That is, if Mr Ambrose pleases, since he seems to be the arbiter and orderer of my estate now.'

'Yes, of course, I shall ask the estate manager to look into it.' Edward had been waiting awkwardly throughout this conversation and seemed relieved to have the matter concluded. 'Perhaps Miss Wills and Bessie might be permitted to go up and change?' he asked, glancing at the two maids with a particular smile for the younger.

He was right. Prudence had forgotten their current state of dress in her umbrage at Edward's appearance. Righteous anger had a way of inducing single-mindedness. She now saw that the girl was shivering so hard her teeth chattered, and her ordinarily neat-as-a-pin lady's maid was looking uncharacteristically bedraggled.

'You may take Bessie up to change, Wills,' she said, putting both maids out of their various miseries. 'I'll be up directly.'

Once they had disappeared upstairs to the suite of rooms on the first floor, she turned to Edward. 'Are you required to vet all my movements, now that you are appointed trustee?'

'What? No, of course not. Only . . . I was concerned for your well-being.'

Her well-being, or her wealth, she could not help but wonder.

'So that is why you stoop to snooping with the servants.'

Her umbrage was in full flight now and Edward was momentarily taken aback, so that he looked everywhere except at her for inspiration. His damp trouser legs caught his particular attention.

'I seek to be your protector, Prudence, not your gaoler,' he said at last.

'The two appear one and the same to me.'

'If only . . .'

'If only what, Edward?'

'If only you . . .' But the words seemed to be stuck to his tongue.

'What?'

'If only you had come at the invitation of friends, I would have no qualms.' He stared at her face as if searching for some sign of . . . what? Acquiescence?

'I am a woman of five and thirty years, Edward. One might think I could take my chances in the wilds of Sidmouth,' she said, crooking her mouth to one side.

'There are unseen dangers, even in the most benign of locations,' he insisted, frowning. Whether at her intransigence or the unspecified dangers of the seaside, she could not be sure.

'I haven't ventured out of my depth, you may rest assured.'

93

'There are rakes in the garb of gentlemen and cads dressed as lords . . .'

And here she thought they were speaking of the watery depths and its inhabitants. Not Sidmouth society.

'. . . whose sport it is to prey upon innocent young women.'

Not so young, and not such easy prey.

'Edward, I have five and thirty years under my bonnet. I've met my share of fortune hunters and pleasure seekers and managed to escape unscathed.' She held his eyes, pausing to allow her words to sink in, to watch his face register her rejection. And perhaps her suspicion.

'In future, I prefer to take care of myself. So, unless there is some other matter you wish to discuss, I should like to change out of these wet clothes before I catch my death of cold.'

'Of course, of course, I shall call on you tomorrow. And Prudence . . . I have only ever had your interests at heart.'

She could barely restrain herself from applauding as he retrieved his hat from the hallstand and bowed himself out through the door. After he was gone, she remained motionless in the hall for several minutes. So intense were her feelings that she noticed neither her shivering nor the muddy water dripping on to the parquetry. Inside, she seethed with silent rage. Was this to be her life for the next thirty years? Her movements scrutinised at every turn. Her expenditure examined. Her life managed. She had thought she was done with that. She had thought her life was to be her own now. Instead, through Edward, her father controlled her future from the grave.

'Why, Father?' she murmured aloud. 'Did I not serve you well? Did I not keep my promise to Mama?'

Yet perhaps it was a scheme devised between her father and Edward. Perhaps once her father no longer needed her as his helpmeet he thought to relinquish her to his friend. During all those cosy chats in the library when she thought they were discussing the latest advances in science or the most efficacious treatment for scrapie in sheep, had they actually been plotting how to govern her? And what better way to do it than by stealing away her choices, to coerce her into marrying Edward.

Well, she would be bullied no longer. She would be caged no longer. She would defy them both. Even if it meant leaving Westcott Hall in Edward's clutches. At least she would be free of him. And that is what she wanted, wasn't it? To no longer see that look of concern in his dark blue eyes. To never again have him take her arm in his solid grip to assist her in negotiating a puddle or a steep incline. Never to see his face across the dining table, or sit knee to knee with him in church. To be free of Edward Ambrose, once and for all, even if it meant sailing to the other side of the world to escape his reach.

Friday: Must escape. Trip to Sidmouth. Dip in ocean. Edward followed me.

12

Somerset, England

2022

Any sunny Sunday after closing would find Eliza lounging in her aunt's garden sipping wine and munching pizza. The weekend following the arrival of 'the letter' was no exception. Despite Eliza's inclination to wallow like a hog in the mire of her own misery, Jude would have none of it. The garden was her pride and joy. Not through any particular attention to the neatness of its edges, or the regularity of its pruning, but the sheer pleasure she took in it. And although Eliza knew for a fact that she devoted several hours each week to weeding and feeding her babies, she preferred to leave them largely to their own devices. As a result, the garden had grown wilder with each passing year until only a small gravelled terrace and a narrow winding path catered to inhabitants of the human variety.

'I still say the Napoletana would have gone better with the Pinot Gris than the chicken tikka pizza,' Jude observed, as they enjoyed the last of a warm summer evening on her terrace.

'No, the chicken tikka is just right. Napoletana is definitely made for red,' Eliza said, taking a large bite of pizza to prove her point.

So when the back gate squeaked and Daniel suddenly appeared with a hearty, 'Good evening, ladies,' her mouth was so full of chicken and cheese that she had to chew a full ten seconds before answering.

'Daniel . . . hi. I didn't know you were coming.' She would have changed out of her habitual après work uniform of black leggings and tie-dyed T-shirt if she had. Although why she should care what he thought, she couldn't explain, even to herself. After all, they barely knew each other.

'Jude invited me to drop in any time I was passing. I noticed your car and thought, "Daniel, now's your chance to catch two intriguing women with one stone."'

'A little charm goes a long way with me, pet.' Jude patted the empty chair between them and headed for the kitchen door, no doubt to fetch another glass, while sneakily leaving her niece alone with an eligible male. Given her proclivity for matchmaking (she was arguably an accessory to three village marriages), Eliza often wondered why her aunt had never married. She had asked her once and been met with the enigmatic response, 'It takes two to tango, not three.' Further questioning only elicited vague references to 'rats' and 'weasels'. Rodents weren't her aunt's favourite mammals.

'What about you?' Daniel asked, turning to Eliza with a smile. 'Is it working?'

She wasn't sure about his charm – she was usually immune to such bedazzlements – but his smile was certainly doing something.

'We'll have to wait and see.'

'Ah, I admire a cautious woman.' He slid into the chair and eased it closer to the wrought-iron table, almost grazing her knee with his. Why did men always have to spread? She wasn't sure whether it was the two glasses of Pinot Gris, or his inviting smile, but she issued herself a stern instruction not to touch.

'Which reminds me, have you thought any more about my suggestion?'

'Suggestion?' she mimicked, although she knew very well which suggestion.

'About sourcing furniture for the hall.'

Of course she had thought about it. She had thought about it every idle moment during the last week when she should have been thinking about how to keep the shop afloat. His offer was tempting. It spoke to both her love of the past and her ancestral connection with the Ambrose name. And there was little doubt she could use the money. Except she would have to work closely with Daniel O'Neill – and intuition told her that could be dangerous.

Before she had a chance to answer, Jude returned with an empty wine glass, another plate and a tattered accordion file, which she deposited on the table with a flourish.

'I've been meaning to hunt these out for you. Pour us all a glass, will you, pet?' she said, motioning to Eliza as she opened the file with a flourish. 'The spoils – or should I say the toils? – of being chair of the local history society. We beg people to send us their photos and they take us at our word. Then we have to find time to place and date them. Not to mention scanning and uploading them to the website.' She shot Eliza an admonishing look.

'I know. I know. I keep promising to help out.'

'Anyway, Daniel, I know there are some pictures of the hall in here that you may not have seen. I thought we could have a poke around, see what we can find.'

'Jude, you're a wonder.'

'I keep telling my niece that, but she's yet to be convinced.'

'That's not true!' Eliza exclaimed. 'I'm reminded every Sunday that you're a veritable force of nature.'

Jude reached into a bulging compartment and withdrew several manila envelopes, placing them on the table between Daniel and Eliza.

'You'll see that the name of the donor, the date and any other information about the contents are written on the envelopes. So don't mix them up. This lot are all connected with Westcott Hall.'

Despite her hesitation about becoming involved with Daniel's project (or the man himself), Eliza's fingers itched to open an envelope. 'Do you want to do the honours?' she asked – quite graciously, she thought.

'Sure.' He slid the contents from the top envelope and picked up the first photograph, an exterior shot of the hall in faded sepia. When he flipped it over they found that a previous owner had kindly noted the date in pencil – 1897.

'Well, the garden has certainly run wild in the last one hundred and twenty years,' she remarked, noting the estate's once-clipped hedges, neat lawns and well-tended garden beds.

'I like a bit of wildness,' Daniel said, a hint of laughter in his voice.

She flicked him a questioning glance but he was studying the scene earnestly. They sifted through other photographs of the hall's exterior taken at various points throughout the last two centuries, Daniel examining them with a practised eye.

'These are great, thanks, Jude. I've seen several of them before but there are a few new ones. Do you think it would be okay if I took copies for reference during the refurbishment?'

'I don't think the owners would mind, so long as you're not publishing them. They've been provided for future study. The next few envelopes are mostly interior shots, taken at various social functions over the years. A lot of them have people in them and they're not always of the best quality. Family snaps and that sort of thing.'

'They might still provide some inspiration for the interiors,' he said, turning to Eliza with an enquiring expression, 'and help us in sourcing the furniture and artwork.'

The first envelope produced snapshots of a cocktail party held sometime during the 1970s, judging by the miniskirts, platform boots and the faded quality of the colour prints. Another held more recent photographs of a Christmas party from the early nineties, in one of which she spotted a younger Jude in a plunging silver jersey wrap dress and Santa hat.

'Looking sexy, Jude,' Eliza said teasingly.

'I thought so. Although, in hindsight, maybe a bit too much cleavage.'

'You can never have too much cleavage, in my opinion. I'm just waiting for that open shirt, gold chain look to return for men,' Daniel said.

Eliza couldn't help picturing him with an unbuttoned shirt. Would he be hairy or smooth?

They sifted through a small envelope containing tiny black and white photographs taken at some point in the 1960s. They were quite eclectic, as if the photographer wanted to capture all the rooms that held any special meaning or memories before saying goodbye to them forever. There were close-ups of drapery-framed views, magnificent fireplaces, lofty Georgian wardrobes and lamp-lit reading nooks.

'Lucky last,' announced Daniel, holding aloft the final envelope, a serious brown cardboard sheath with a metal butterfly clasp. 'Eliza?'

She took the proffered envelope and opened the clasp, sliding out a series of eight-by-ten, glossy black and white photographs that clung together as if they hadn't been examined since they were first deposited in the envelope many years ago.

'They're all shots of the same room,' she said, as she separated one from the other and set the first two on a cleared space beside the pizza box.

'It looks like that small sitting room on the first floor,' Daniel said, leaning in closer so that she caught a whiff of cologne, overlaid with the tang of white wine and curried cheese. 'Judging by the old radio, it might be the 1930s.'

'Look at the walls,' Eliza breathed out, 'they're covered in framed sketches. Just a sec, I have a loupe in my bag.' She rummaged in her bag for a few seconds, before producing the steel loupe she used to inspect maker's marks and jewellery. With its aid, what she discovered hanging on the walls of the cosy sitting room from the 1930s was a series of watercolours depicting beaches, canoes and thatched open-sided houses, all sheltering beneath the towering fronds of coconut palms.

'They look like sketches of a tropical island,' she said, turning to her aunt with a surprised smile.

'Prudence's work you think?' Jude asked. 'We know she was shipwrecked in the South Pacific.'

Her mouth suddenly dry, Eliza could find no words to respond, and simply nodded as she scanned the walls of the room with her loupe. Prudence's life stared back at her, she was certain, encapsulated in a series of tiny rectangles within rectangles. To think she might be looking at this long-dead woman's memories, captured in paint.

Meanwhile, Jude was staring at another photograph from the pile. 'Look at this,' she said, pointing to one of the artefacts behind the glass doors of a mahogany display cabinet. 'I wonder what it is.'

Eliza tore her gaze from a watercolour showing two girls in grass skirts, their hair shorn on one side and a long curl twisting over the opposite shoulder, as they paddled a canoe towards a distant island floating on the horizon. She bent her loupe to study the photograph Jude held instead.

'It's some kind of woven mat, I think. We could probably discover its origins with a bit of research,' she said, but she was still thinking about the sketch of the two girls. Despite the naive style and a certain dreamlike quality about the picture, the artist had captured the energy of the canoe skimming across water and the animation of the paddlers. Almost as if she had once joined

101

those two young women as they paddled across that faraway lagoon towards a humpbacked islet. How disconcerting it would have been for a conventional Georgian woman to be stranded in such a strange place, thousands of miles from home. How frightening it must have been, knowing she might never return.

Yet Prudence hadn't been a conventional Georgian gentlewoman. She had set sail on a voyage to distant shores. Eliza recalled the words she had inscribed in the pocket book in her own hand: *Must escape.* Then a week or so later: *Passage arranged . . . To Calcutta and beyond!*

And she did escape – journeying far beyond Calcutta – to an island in the middle of the Pacific Ocean. She could hardly have travelled further from her grand mansion in the Somerset countryside if she had taken a rocket to the moon. But did she find paradise or privation on that island? The sensationalist newspapers of the day described Prudence's sojourn in Samoa as 'perilous' – a poor stricken woman alone in the wilderness.

'If Prudence painted these sketches, she can't have been so very traumatised by her sojourn in Samoa.' She raised her eye from the loupe to consider her aunt and Daniel.

'They look almost nostalgic,' Daniel said. 'I'd want to go there.'

The artist had imbued the sketches with details that were quite intimate. Flowers in a girl's hair, a woman wading in the shallows, a child throwing something upon a beach. Nothing like the sensationalist narrative Eliza had once read, when she'd first become intrigued by the life of her notorious not-quite ancestor, which purported to portray the 'Shipwreck, Sufferings and Miraculous Escape of Miss Prudence Merryfield'.

'I wonder how we could find out what happened to the sketches?' she murmured.

'I might be able to help there,' Daniel said, looking up from a photograph that captured two paintings of a neat village and a row of beached canoes. 'The previous owners of Westcott Hall handed over decades of records of furniture and artwork sales with the sale documents. We might be able to hunt down the information in some of the receipts or auction catalogues. Or do I sense a wavering?'

'Wavering on what?' asked Jude, and Eliza could almost see her ears twitching. 'If you're referring to my niece, she never wavers. She's as stalwart as the Tower of London.'

Detecting a hint of reproof in her aunt's tone, Eliza glanced up but found nothing but blatant curiosity in those crinkling, warm brown eyes.

Daniel took a sip of his wine before saying, 'I've been trying to convince her to help me source furnishings for the hotel but she says she'll be too busy searching for new premises for her store. I haven't given up, though.'

'Whoa! What's that?' Jude held two fluttering hands to her heart. 'I've not heard a whisper of any of this.'

'It's nothing, Jude. I'll explain later,' Eliza said, trying to head her off. She had meant to tell her, she really had. Why, then, had she kept this nugget of information from her aunt? *Because you were afraid she would talk you into it,* her inner voice answered. *And then where would you be?*

Daniel mouthed a silent, 'Sorry,' in Eliza's direction, before adding, 'I'd really appreciate your help. You never know, if we track down the sketches, we might be able to convince the owners to part with some of them.'

He was studying her as intently as she had studied the picture of the two Samoan girls in their canoe, surrounded by the paraphernalia of that 1930s sitting room in a grand English manor. She couldn't work out why he was so keen to have her work with him. She wasn't deluded enough to believe that he couldn't find someone else qualified to help him search out furnishings for the new hotel. Nor was she vain enough to think he was seeking an excuse to secure her company – much as she might *like* to think so. She might not have room in her life for love but it was nice to contemplate, all the same. Like watching reruns of *Love Actually*. It bore little resemblance to real life, and you knew exactly how it turned out, but that didn't stop you tuning in for a quick look when it turned up on TV every Christmas.

'You already have a good feel for the house and its history,' he added, zeroing in on her indecision.

Perhaps it was as simple as that. He wanted her because he wouldn't have to waste time getting someone else up to speed on the background. He was right; she did have a feel for the house and its history. And, she was discovering, a compelling curiosity about its most famous, most elusive, most mysterious former resident. Prudence Merryfield. Prudence, who had embarked upon a voyage to the other side of the globe without a male protector; who was shipwrecked in a storm in the south seas; washed up alone on a deserted island and sojourned for a year in a Samoan village. Who was rescued and returned to England; only to disappear five years later; presumed dead under circumstances that to date had never been properly resolved.

The pocket book had piqued Eliza's interest. But the sketches . . . the sketches called to her, reaching out across time. Daring her to investigate Prudence's life. Distracting her from her true responsibilities.

'What do you say? Partners in crime?'

He held out his hand, palm turned slightly up, as if to suggest he held no threat. And despite intuition warning her that he might very well prove a threat to her peace of mind, if nothing else, she clasped his hand and shook it.

'Partners.'

13

London, England

1832

It needed little but a carpet bag and a hooded cape for Miss Merryfield to be the very picture of a runaway or a thief. In the first place, she had declined her host's offer of a carriage for that morning's business. (Although Bessie knew for a fact – since the pot boy had boasted of it – that the family had recently acquired a fancy new carriage, called a 'landau', where the roof could be folded back to suit the weather and allow the occupants to show off their finery.) In the second place, she had informed Miss Wills that she was not to accompany them on their errand, since she was needed to repair a tear in the green silk, a tear that had not been there when Bessie put away the gown the evening before.

Thirdly, throughout their journey from the house on Berkeley Square to their destination, the lady kept twisting her neck at a most uncomfortable angle to see out of the window of the hackney coach. And when the vehicle finally came to a halt, setting them down outside a vast building in a hectic part of London, she would not alight until she had cast a careful eye up and down the street. A person might think she was hiding from someone. But who that someone might be Bessie could not hazard a guess.

She had thought Sidmouth was grand, but London was like a

dream, and a terrifying one at that. Perhaps this was the reason for her mistress's furtive behaviour; she was as frightened as Bessie by the clamour of the city, although she had not known her to be frightened of anything before. She knew her mistress was no thief, and only a fool would run away from the riches of Westcott Hall, but she was certainly acting in a strange manner.

After the previous night's rain, the street was churned to mud so that Bessie was glad she wore her wooden clogs rather than the shoes the lady had given her for their journey to London. She had never owned a pair of leather shoes and these had once belonged to Miss Merryfield so they must be of the best quality. The toe, heel and sole were of black leather but the sides were purple cotton and so pretty that she feared to wear them outside. Especially since they were a trifle large and in danger of falling off. She had a new dress too, of blue cotton with tiny white flowers, which the lady had told her to wear this morning for they were 'embarked upon an important mission' and she must look her best.

'There it is, Bessie, the East India House. The home of one of England's oldest, most infamous companies,' Miss Merryfield said as she stepped gingerly on to the street.

Foot traffic bustled up and down the roadway, while several important-looking gents in long-tailed coats congregated in twos and threes outside the entrance of this famous house with its soaring columns and tiers of windows lining the facade that fronted on to the street. Narrow lanes sprouted at intervals along the way, and the smell of soot and garbage wafted about the noisy crush of carriages and people.

'We have reached our destination,' the lady added, turning purposefully towards a row of buildings that loomed over the street.

'We have, miss?'

'Do you see? Here are the offices of Mr Alexander.' She

pointed towards a row of shops, an expectant look upon her face.

Bessie directed her gaze towards the buildings indicated, but since she could make neither head nor tail of the words printed on the muddle of signs posted outside the shops and doorways, her eyes swept on. They meandered off into the distance, alighting upon the unusual sight of a dark-visaged man wearing a feathered white turban on his head. He conversed with a gentleman whose hair dangled down his back in a single long braid. She had never seen a man wearing a turban before – only spinsters and old ladies – and supposed he must be a Turk.

'Do you not see, Bessie? It is the same as the advertisement.'

Her employer pulled from her reticule the small book she always kept about her person and opened it to a page with some words printed in tiny black writing. Bessie tore her gaze from the more compelling sight of the foreigners in their fancy dress and considered the note.

'Yes, miss,' she said. She didn't like to admit that she couldn't read, since Miss Wills read her Bible daily and Mr Carp scoured the newspaper from cover to cover before delivering it to his employer, since it was his duty to stay informed of any important happenings in the world that might impact upon the family. But Bessie knew nothing except the first letter of her name. 'B' for Bessie. At least, that is what Miss Wills had told her.

'You cannot read, Bessie?' Miss Merryfield asked, glancing at her with a frown so severe that Bessie hoped she wasn't about to lose her position. Mr Custard had said nothing about reading, only washing her hands and face and keeping her nose clean. She considered lying about her lack, but since the lie would be discovered easily, she decided upon the truth.

'No, miss. Me granfer didn't believe in reading.' There was a dame school in the village, but her grandparents had been too poor to send her – and her grammer said the dame could read no better than her, anyway.

'I see. Well, perhaps it's time you learned.'

'I don't think me brain be big enough for reading, miss.'

'Nonsense! Everyone's brain is big enough for reading. It is only a matter of applying it . . .' She paused for a moment, before continuing in a hushed voice, 'Can you keep a secret, Bessie?'

Bessie had kept many a secret in her fourteen years. She kept secret the mystery of her father's absence. She kept secret the hares her granfer was accustomed to trap in the Merryfield woods. She kept secret her grammer's cordial recipe that she inherited from her grandmother and sold as a remedy for everything from stomach gripe to teething pain. And she kept secret, even from her grandparents, the dreams that came to her on certain nights . . . of water filling her mouth and a pressure on her shoulders that pushed her down, down . . .

'Well, girl?'

'Yes, miss. I be good at keeping secrets.'

'So then . . . we are arrived at the offices of Alexander and Company. Agents for –' the lady pointed to the words written in her pocket book and continued by reading aloud from it – '"negotiating passages to India and the Colonies. Plans of every ship, with prices of the several cabins, may be seen at one view, and passages engaged on terms infinitely more favourable than can be done by direct applications."'

'Now . . . what do you think of that?'

What did she think of that? She thought it had nothing to do with her – and nothing to do with her mistress, either, that she could see. But Miss Merryfield was proving herself to be a rather odd fish, prone to strange whims and fancies, such as swimming in the sea and looking up the names of India agents in her pocket book. Who was Bessie to say what might or might not be important to her?

'It be very good, miss,' she said with a nod.

'Yes, I thought so too. Very good indeed.'

*

Standing outside a shiny black door with an impressive brass handle, Prudence heaved an audible sigh of relief. She had got this far without sight or sound of Edward Ambrose or any of his known lackeys. Her friend Mrs Fitzpatrick had obliged her by issuing an invitation to stay with her in London for several days, giving Edward no justifiable excuse for accompanying her. She had rather cleverly dispensed with the services of Wills that morning without arousing her suspicions. That left her with the obliging, if rather inept, attendance of young Bessie, who could be relied upon to ask no questions and offer few opinions.

She turned the handle, cautioning the girl not to jiggle so, and stepped inside. A dozen or so men were seated at rows of desks huddled together in a large room, lit only by a few gas lamps and the thin light filtering through two slim windows. She blinked, allowing her eyes to adjust to the dimness, and cleared her throat. At the sound of such a feminine *ahem* a dozen pairs of eyes swung in her direction, and a short compact man of indeterminate age rose to greet her.

'Good morning to you, madam. John Abercrombie at your service. How may I be of assistance?'

She drew in a breath, as if the fug of sweat, ink and cigar smoke could fortify her purpose, and said, 'I wish to procure passage to Calcutta and . . . and the Colonies.'

'For yourself and your husband?'

'For myself.'

She had prepared herself to present arguments, to defeat any protest that a lady did not travel without the protection of a male relative, but Mr Abercrombie only smiled and opened a great ledger resting upon the counter.

'We should be delighted to arrange passage for you, Mrs . . . ?'

'Miss. Miss Prudence Merryfield.'

'Indeed, Miss Merryfield, I have had the honour of organising the voyages of many a young lady travelling alone. Some were joining a fiancé abroad. Others were undertaking a pleasure voyage. And not a few were taking up employment in the Colonies as governesses and the like,' he said, taking up his pen with a flourish.

'Well, that is good to know, I'm sure.'

'Yes, Alexander and Company would be pleased to arrange *all* matters pertaining to your voyage, if you so wish.'

'There are other matters?'

'Why there is the outfitting of the cabin, the collection and transportation of luggage, the arrangement for letters of credit in Calcutta and beyond, should you so wish.'

'I see. Of course.'

'And we would not wish to see a lady subjected to the insult and inconvenience of an ill-equipped and poorly provisioned second- or third-rate ship, would we?'

'No. We would not.'

'For a lady, a stern cabin on the poop deck of a first-rate ship is a necessity. Outfitted with the latest ship's sofa in rosewood or mahogany. An easy chair, washstand, chest of drawers, perhaps a wardrobe.' Here he raised his eyebrows and summoned a smile, as if to suggest he was intimate with the needs of ladies. 'A few select provisions, to supplement the ship's dining table, perhaps?'

'Yes, perhaps. And do you have anything suitable to prevent water damage to say . . . a book?' she asked, conscious of the pocket book in her reticule. She would not wish to subject it to the vagaries of the ocean without protection.

'A length of oilcloth will suffice,' he said. 'And will miss be requiring further passage, beyond Calcutta?'

'Yes, yes, I should think so.' Indeed . . . why not sail on? 'To Singapore, perhaps, and on to . . .' Where did one go from Singapore?

'To Shanghai? Or perhaps you have acquaintance in Sydney?

Here at Alexander and Company we can assist with planning a voyage around the entire globe. Should you so wish.' The man's eagerness was palpable in his twitching pen.

Why not sail to the ends of the earth? Why not choose an adventurous life? She did not have to bow to her father's dictates or Edward's protection. She had her allowance, paid annually. She had her mother's jewellery, secreted in a hatbox at the bottom of a trunk in her room. Surely that would be enough to fund a journey across the oceans? And she could return when she wished.

'And what would be the fare for a stern cabin on the poop deck of a first-rate ship to Calcutta, Mr Abercrombie?'

'Ah, well . . . that would depend upon the ship and the route. Whether by sea around the Cape of Good Hope, or overland to Egypt and then via sea to Bombay. The former is slower but far more comfortable, especially for a lady such as yourself.'

'Yes, I should like to be comfortable,' she said, for talk of Egypt conjured images of camels.

'As it happens, there are several ships departing in the coming weeks. The *Exmouth*, an excellent ship of some seven hundred and fifty tons with superior accommodations for passengers, for example. Or the *Moira*, a teak ship of seven hundred tons with splendid accommodations. A cabin on either ship could be had for a modest sum in the vicinity of one hundred and fifty to one hundred and sixty pounds for a single berth, or two hundred pounds should you wish your maid to accompany you. Plus, of course, the cost of furnishing the cabin, arranging transportation of luggage . . .'

As Mr Abercrombie continued to enumerate the various costs associated with the journey, Prudence turned to consider the girl standing mutely at her side. Her burnished hair was neatly brushed and braided, her feet shod in rather muddy wooden clogs, her thin frame garbed in a dress of blue floral. The girl was a far cry from the barefoot urchin she had rescued on the day following her father's funeral – at least upon the surface. Although her skills as a lady's maid left much to be desired, the man was right. She would need a maid to accompany her – for even an adventuress has standards to maintain – and clearly Wills could no longer be trusted to keep her secrets. Nor, she suspected, would she wish to travel to the far reaches of the globe and be parted from Bobbett. No, Prudence would have to find someone else to accompany her to the ends of the earth.

Someone young enough to heed the call of adventure. Someone who would be loyal to the woman who had saved her from the workhouse. Someone with no ties to bind her and few other options.

Someone like . . .

'Bessie, I believe we will have plenty of time to teach you the rudiments of reading in the coming weeks. What do you think of that?'

'If you say so, miss. I be pleased.'

'Well, that's settled then,' she said, turning to the accommodating Mr Abercrombie. 'Passage for two to Calcutta, please. The *Exmouth* should do nicely.'

Later that night, she would write in her pocket book with a feeling of lightness for the first time since her father's death. With the purchase of the ticket a great weight had been lifted from her shoulders. Soon she would be free to fly away. And once she had flown the coop, she and only she would decide when and if to return.

Thursday: Errand accomplished. Passage arranged. Provisions organised. To Calcutta and beyond!

14

Samoa

1833

Lupelele put a hand to her brow, shading her eyes from the dazzle of sun glinting off water. Her cousins, Fata and Tuna, were about to launch their canoe, intent on venturing out beyond the reef. The canoe was beached above the high-tide mark, alongside the other small dugouts, while the longer atu canoes and the large double-hulled travelling canoe were housed beneath a thatched shelter. The boys each grabbed one boom of the outrigger and slid the craft over the sand into the lapping waters of the lagoon. Fata paused to scoop up a dead jellyfish and toss it at his brother, but once Tuna retaliated with a desiccated fish and a few choice words, they launched the canoe into the shallows.

She grinned at the froth of white water foaming about the canoe as they dug their paddles into the water. They struck out, brown arms flashing, and whooping as they gathered speed. Her cousins might think they were the fastest creatures on water, but their paddles still kicked up more water than a breaching whale. She poked her stick into the sand and turned to the tall girl who dawdled at her side. She had intended to point out how her cousins might improve their technique, but one look at the wistful expression on her friend's face stopped her in her tracks. To'oa was gazing at the canoe as if she was somewhere else entirely.

Lupe nudged her friend to get her attention. 'We could paddle faster than the boys if we were allowed to leave the lagoon.'

To'oa wrenched her attention away from the boys gliding across the lagoon and blinked at her friend. 'What did you say, Lupe?'

'I said that we could paddle fast too – if we were allowed to do more than play around in the lagoon. Fata is only a year older than me, and he can fish in the open sea.'

'What did you want to play?' To'oa asked, still with the faraway look in her eyes.

'What's wrong with you today? You're not even listening.'

To'oa sighed, her gaze following the boys as they paddled parallel to the beach, a stone's throw from shore, skimming over the clear pale waters, as they followed two older boys who were heading for a narrow pass through the reef to the darker waters of the open sea. 'I was thinking that I might not be here in the village much longer,' she said. 'Sometimes I wish I could stay here with my family and you forever.'

'You know they won't let either of us marry a boy from our village. And besides, your family will have bigger fish in mind for you.'

Lupelele's father was a matai, the head of her extended family and a man of rank. But her friend's father was chief of the entire village, and To'oa was the taupou, the ceremonial maiden. She was descended from a long line of chiefs on both sides of her family. Alongside her father, she greeted every important visitor to the village and participated in all the official ceremonies. Her father would expect her marriage to connect their family to a high-ranking family in another village. The women of the family were already producing many fine mats to offer in return for the elaborate gifts of canoes, tools and animals they would expect to receive from the son of a prominent chief – or an orator, at the very least.

'It doesn't hurt to dream,' said To'oa, gazing out over the water wistfully.

'At least you can come back home after you've given your husband a child, if you don't like him.' Lupe tried to cheer her friend up, but sometimes she too wished she didn't have to leave home. Sometimes, when she saw how sad her father had become since her mother died, she wished she didn't have to marry at all.

'Well, we'd better get started.' Hefting her stick on to one shoulder, To'oa turned in the direction of the tidal pools and coral beds spread out below the headland of their small bay, where they planned to gather fish and shellfish in the shallow waters of the lagoon.

Today the ocean was relatively calm, small waves breaking upon the reef encircling the island that was home to her village and others like it. Neat, orderly villages fringed the entire coastline, with well-kept paths winding between them, while others sat high on the mountainside in the rainforest. Yes, the gods were smiling today, Lupe thought, but when the wind sprang up, those innocent-looking waves could turn into killers, smashing unwary voyagers on to the sharp beds of coral below.

Outside the lagoon she could see the humped back of the islet shaped like a crab, its pincers enclosing a tiny lagoon on the lee side, and beyond the shadowy outline of another small island. The boys were probably heading for the fishing waters between the reef and the islands. Their mother, her Aunt Masina, might not like it, but with their father dead from the sickness that had also taken Lupe's mother, her cousins considered themselves to be men. They weren't content to fish in the lagoon any more. They wanted to live up to the prowess of the legendary brothers for whom they were named; the long-ago brothers who freed Samoa from the rule of the Tongan king. They conveniently forgot that those same brothers came to blows in the end, leaving a third brother to become high chief of all Samoa in their stead.

115

But Fata and Tuna did not have a third brother. Not yet, anyway – and not ever, if Lupe had her way. She did not want her widowed father to partner his dead brother's wife, as half the village expected. No one could take her mother's place.

'Lupe!' Tuna's voice carried across the lagoon. 'Lupe! What fish would you like for dinner?'

'Whatever you want to cook, Tuna,' she said. Boys and men had all the fun jobs in the village – well, except, of course, for farming. She did not envy them the digging and harvesting of taro. They climbed the coconut palms, fished from canoes and cooked the family meals in the earth ovens. The women and girls spent their days foraging in the lagoon and preparing hibiscus bark to make siapo cloth, or plaiting pandanus leaves to make mats. She just knew she could paddle more swiftly than her cousins, given the chance. She could probably spear more fish too. She longed to leave the shallow waters of the lagoon behind and discover for herself what lay beneath the ocean outside the reef.

'Congratulations on your paddling!' she called, trying to be polite when she longed to say something rude. Her aunt had already scolded her once today for her impudence.

'You must be strong to paddle out beyond the reef,' Fata said with a laugh. 'It takes strong arms to handle the currents.'

'You need a pair like this!' Tuna rested his paddle for a moment and crooked an arm, the better to show off his muscles.

'You're right, bro. Otherwise you'll capsize.'

'I'm strong,' Lupe called, but the onshore breeze muffled her voice so that it did not carry to the boys cruising towards the reef. 'I'm tall and strong.'

'Come on, Lupe.' To'oa tugged gently at the leaves of the skirt that girded her from waist to knees. 'Forget about paddling canoes and spearing fish.'

Lupe turned her head away from the canoe, the shadow of the reef and the green hump of the island, and focused upon the shoreline. 'We'll probably find more shellfish, anyway,' she muttered to herself.

And it almost worked. She almost convinced herself not to mind that she was stuck here in the shallows while her cousins ventured out to sea. But then she heard their laughter drift across the lagoon as they picked up their pace. She watched the sea froth and foam about the canoe as their lean arms worked to haul them over the water towards the reef, and she stopped in her tracks. It was too much. She knew she could paddle faster than her cousins. She knew she could spear fish from the canoe, if she had the chance; she had watched her father spearing fish in the lagoon often enough.

She turned and began striding back the way she had come, the plaited bark of her sandals making slapping noises on the hard sand. Usually she went barefoot, but coral and bare feet were not friends.

'But what about gathering shellfish?' To'oa asked, hurrying after her.

'There'll be more fish out on the reef.'

Lupe had huffed halfway down the beach to the village before she realised her friend wasn't following. Maybe To'oa wasn't as excited by the prospect of paddling out to the reef as she was.

'Aren't you coming?' she called out with a puzzled frown.

'You know we're not allowed to paddle out beyond the lagoon. And only men fish with spears.'

Lupe shrugged. 'We're not allowed to do a lot of things, but that doesn't stop me.' Her aunt scolded her regularly for taking out her father's small dugout or for not showing enough respect to her elders. And if it wasn't enough that Masina scolded as her aunt, she also chastised Lupe in her role as leader of the aualuma, the society of adolescent girls and unmarried women.

'And you know I'm not allowed to leave the village alone,' To'oa said.

'You won't be alone. You'll be with me. And we won't be gone for long.'

'I don't think you count.'

'Come on, To'oa, don't be a baby! The boys have all the fun. We won't go far, just to the outer ledge of the reef.'

'My mother told me not to stay in the sun for long, either.'

As the village maiden, To'oa was supposed to keep the fair skin of someone who stayed inside all day. But that also meant not having much fun.

'Do you always do what you're told?' Lupe asked.

'Yes. Pretty much. You know that.'

'Just this once.' Lupe dropped to the sand, careless of the dead jellyfish squished beneath her knee, and summoned her most pathetic face. 'Please, please come with me, oh great lady. Please, please, honour this humble commoner with your presence.'

'You are such an idiot.'

'Does that mean you'll come?'

'All right,' her friend sighed, 'but promise we won't paddle too far.'

'Never.' Lupe grinned and beckoned with her chin. 'Let's get the canoe.'

Every household in the village had at least one canoe, and the village also owned a large, double-hulled canoe with a mat sail for longer voyages. Lupe's father owned a small dugout canoe he had carved himself, shaping and hollowing the log of a breadfruit tree with his stone adze. But their āiga also owned a larger canoe, the va'a alo, that was used when venturing beyond the lagoon to fish for atu. Such craft were lighter and faster than a dugout, being made of fine planks laced together. They needed to be fast to catch the swift-swimming atu as they hunted schools of smaller fish in the open sea.

She remembered the time when a team of skilled carpenters had been invited from a nearby village to construct the va'a alo at a cost of many fine mats. The large canoe had taken several weeks to build. The carpenters, their wives and children, had all been hosted by Lupe's āiga while they shaped the planks to an admirable thinness, lashed them to the keel and caulked the hull with a gum made from breadfruit. Afterwards, the canoe was decorated with intricate carvings and rows of white shells. It was so beautiful, it seemed a shame to get it wet.

She looked longingly at her father's va'a alo, but women were forbidden to touch it, and even she dared not break that taboo.

'You take the fore boom and I'll take the aft,' she said to her friend, grasping one boom of the outrigger on the small dugout. Her father paddled this smaller canoe alone, but it was large enough for two girls. Once upon a time, Lupe's mother had taught her to paddle the lagoon in it. But that was before the sickness came and spirited her mother away, along with Fata and Tuna's father and too many of their neighbours.

They slid the small craft across the sand into the shallows, the hull scraping over shell grit and ropes of drying seaweed. Once the canoe was properly afloat, To'oa climbed aboard, being careful not to rock it. The outrigger could easily flip up and toss them into the water if they were not careful. Lupe followed, seating herself aft. Then each girl took up one of the large, leaf-shaped blades and began to paddle. It took a moment or two to find their rhythm, but it was not long before the dugout was skimming across the ocean, chasing the boys who had almost reached the narrow passage that led through the reef and out into open water. If To'oa worried that she was disobeying village custom and the edicts of her mother, she kept her qualms to herself for the sake of her friend. As for Lupe, she had no qualms. All she wanted was to be noticed: by her cousins, her āiga and her village. And that was definitely not the Samoan way.

15

Singapore

1833

'Well, Bessie, that's the last we shall see of Singapore,' Prudence remarked, her voice competing to be heard above the slap of oars and the cries of boatmen. She watched the town retreat as they were rowed downriver towards the harbour where their ship lay at anchor. Ranks of buildings crowded shoulder to shoulder along the riverbank, with shops and godowns on the ground floor and living quarters above. In her month-long sojourn in the town, she had visited several of these premises with her host – a mercantile connection of friends she had met in Calcutta – discovering for herself the cornucopia of goods housed within their walls.

She had marvelled at the riches of tortoiseshell, pearl and ivory, of ambergris and gold dust guarded by these treasure houses. Of precious woods such as ebony, camphor and sandalwood; of the finest Souchong, Congou and Bohea teas; the rivers of fine silk and batik from the East, sturdy cotton and wool from the West. She had admired the prized vessels of tin, gold and porcelain; scented sacks of nutmeg, cloves, pepper, cassia and turmeric; the exotic flavours of bird's nest, shark's fin, bêche-de-mer, and an improbably named ingredient known as 'fish maw'.

All these goods mingled in the warehouses of this town where the nations of East and West came to trade. So much so that Prudence could purchase almost anything her heart desired, from Swedish steel to a hogshead of British ale (should she be so inclined), or the oddly named 'dragon's blood', a dark red resin that was said to be an aid to digestion. At the urging of her host, she had purchased a ready supply as preventative against the dysentery that plagued even the most hale and hearty of travellers.

In the distance, a hilltop fort watched over the busy river traffic, where small craft jostled for position alongside the quay, while further upriver the stream was dotted with the palm-thatched houses of Malay fishermen rising on stilts from the water. She had grown accustomed to the sight of these fishermen plying river and coast in colourful boats with high prows and ribbed sails. The men were usually garbed in a single length of cloth wrapped ingeniously about their waists and another circling their heads. Their wives and daughters wrapped a similar cloth beneath their arms, knotting it in such a way as to preserve their modesty. She wondered at the skill involved in such a mode of dressing. She doubted she would ever attain the knack of it, and wondered idly whether Bessie could be induced to learn the art.

As they left the river behind, the entire town was spread before them, her countrymen having chosen to settle the flat land adjacent to the coast. Open water lay ahead, and soon she would leave the tropics behind for the cooler climes of Sydney town. A flotilla of vessels in a multitude of shapes and sizes waited in the harbour, from the towering hulls and mighty sails of the East Indiamen to the batten-rigged Chinese junks and Malay proas that plied the South Seas, plus the many smaller craft that traded amongst the neighbouring islands of Sumatra, Java and Borneo. Singapore, she had learned, was a merchant's paradise.

'Well, we shall soon be on our way to Sydney,' she said, a short while later, as their boatmen drew up alongside the *Kangaroo*, a barque of some 300 tons that would ferry them on the next leg of their adventure to Sydney. What they would find when they arrived remained an enigma. Thus far she had discovered that travellers' tales were all very well but the true nature of a destination lay in the eyes that beheld it. And each person's eyes clothed the world in a different hue. The deep green valleys and rugged mountains of St Helena, where she had visited the tomb of the notorious Bonaparte; the beauty of Cape Town, overlooked by the lofty Table Mountain, where their ship had been escorted by a flock of Cape pigeons two miles in breadth; the two months in Calcutta where she had tasted food so hot it scorched the roof of her mouth; and now Singapore . . . each port wore a cloak of many colours. Each was a strange hybrid of their native peoples, the canny merchants who exploited their riches, and the foreign adventurers who sampled their delights. And now she was one of them. An adventurer. Who would have thought it, a year earlier?

Prudence Merryfield. Lady Adventuress.

A man might not deem her so, for unlike the heroes of most adventure tales, she sought neither to conquer nor to name. Not a single mountain, not a lone river, not an empty space upon a map. It was her own self she wished to discover. The terra incognita of the interior.

'It says here, miss, that pepper has been doing very little in Penang this week,' Bessie announced, interrupting her reverie. '"We have heard of sales of small parcels at six-sixty cash, and since the arrival of several pr-pr-proa –' she hesitated over the word – 'from Delhi, of further sales at six and a half cash."'

'What *are* you reading?'

'*Singapore Free Press*, miss. It be very informative.'

'I don't doubt, but the price of pepper in Penang will be of little use to us in Sydney, I fear. Once we're settled in our cabin I shall look out a pamphlet I obtained in Calcutta. *Practical Hints for Settlers to our Australian Colonies.* I have it in my trunk.'

Of course, Bessie would know this, having packed that trunk. Perhaps she had even perused it already. The girl was becoming a proficient reader, given the extent of free time they had had on their three-month voyage from London to Calcutta. Time enough to learn her ABCs and a lot more besides. Maid and mistress had both learned, of course. They had discovered the dreadful tedium of a long sea voyage, and the dangers and unpredictability of the ocean. Flat and immobile one hour, wild and tumultuous the next, where the ship pitched from mountain to valley and waves crashed over the forecastle of the *Exmouth* as if she were a paper boat. Where Prudence, unaccustomed to dressing herself, had learned to clean up another's vomit, lest she live with the stench for days.

'Are we settling then, miss? In Australia?'

The girl perked up, fixing those wide eyes on Prudence's similarly green but world-weary ones. Perhaps she searched there for some clue to their future. Perhaps she tired of all this travel, the novelty worn to a nub by the privations of sailing ships and unruly weather. Prudence sympathised with her desire to settle, to put down roots and make a home. She imagined that Bessie's grandparents' hold on their cottage had been tenuous at best. But travel was the only sure way Prudence would stay free of Edward's clutches. News travelled fast in a mercantile world. Even now, he might have procured agents in the East India Company to search for her. Try to lure her back. Or worse. Who knew what mischief he might make if thwarted in his plans?

'We are on a pleasure cruise, Bessie,' she said, somewhat optimistically. 'What need we to settle when we have the entire Pacific Ocean before us?'

'But ocean be very big, miss. What if we become lost?'

'We must trust in the captain to know where he is going.'

She had embarked upon her adventures on impulse, giving

little thought to the reality of traipsing halfway around the globe. Her father would have put it down to a surfeit of self-will – a most unseemly quality in a young woman of good family – and promptly quashed it. But impulse had become mettle, and mettle had become habit. She enjoyed being a Lady Adventuress. She did not wish to be lured back to the comforts of hearth and home. She did not wish to settle. And she vowed not to be returned against her will.

If Prudence was dismayed by her first sight of the cabin they were to share for their voyage to Sydney, she tried not to show it. She had not expected carpets and curtains but the accommodations upon the *Exmouth* had led her to expect a certain degree of comfort. Upon being shown to their cabin aboard the *Kangaroo* it became apparent that a first-class cabin upon a 750-ton East Indiaman sailing the clipper route from Europe to the Far East rose to a higher standard than that upon a second-rate barque plying the South Seas. But if she had learned one thing during her months of being a fledgling Lady Adventuress, it was to make the best of things. And that is what she proceeded to do, notwithstanding the unfortunate dimensions of their new abode.

Their furnishings were already installed, the very same which had outfitted their cabin upon the voyages to Calcutta and from Calcutta to Singapore. Her rosewood ship's sofa and Bessie's iron camp bed were looking somewhat the worse for wear after their travels, as were the table, washstand and chest of drawers. But her trunk was in place; the mattresses were only slightly salt-stained; and her chest of wine was fortuitously intact.

'The chintz and cushions are in the sea chest, miss,' said Bessie, as she set about unpacking, 'along with the looking-glass and linen.'

Their passage included all victuals, but after her experience of previous voyages, Prudence wasn't taking any chances. She had secured supplies of tea and coffee, bacon, eggs (which she had learned to pack in wood ash to preserve them), rice, sugar, butter, salt cod and a quantity of ship's biscuits. She had also learned, to her dismay, that the washerwoman aboard was generally a sailor and not so particular in the matter of whiteness as the laundry maid at Westcott Hall. Consequently, she had arranged for an Indian tailor to make up a good number of extra shifts, drawers and petticoats for both herself and Bessie.

'And I packed your hair powder, knitting and Cologne water in the trunk,' added Bessie, head and shoulders deep in the open sea chest, while her rear almost collided with the washstand. The cabin was tiny indeed. 'Do you think, miss, that Mr Ambrose's correspondence might catch up with us in Sydney?'

'Mr Ambrose? Why do you ask, Bessie?'

'Well, we be gone so long, he –' she gave a small shrug, from deep within her chest – 'may be worried for thee . . . for you.'

'Oh, I doubt we would call it worry.'

'But anyone may see he holds thee in high regard.'

'Some may call it that.' Others might call it holding her to ransom. Certainly that is how she had felt in those weeks following her father's death. As if, in longing for independence, she had instead been held captive to her father's whim and her neighbour's fancy.

'I seen the way he looked at thee, beggin' thy pardon, miss,' Bessie persisted.

She appeared so young in the light flickering upon her face from the hanging lamp and the tiny window to the sea. Her face was a heart of freckled gold, wreathed in a cloud of red. As she knelt in the cramped cabin, the curved timber walls enclosing her like a womb, she appeared small and vulnerable, her growth stunted by years of hunger. She was thin, but not so thin as she had been that day, nine months earlier, when Prudence and Edward had come upon a barefoot urchin on the lane leading to

125

the hall. Prudence recalled that she had felt compelled to take her in, and Edward had chided her that she could not take the girl up only to forget about her later. Could she ever have guessed that the two of them, woman and child (for all her worldly ways, Bessie was very much still a child), would embark upon such an adventure together? Now, even if Prudence wanted, she could not leave her behind. Even if Bessie begged her. For what would become of a fifteen-year-old maid, alone at the ends of the earth? Bessie had become her charge, as much as she was Bessie's.

'How did he look at me?'

'Like he wanted thee for his own.'

She had never noticed Edward looking her way with desire, nor with the tiniest glimmer of romantic interest. Although, once upon a time, she would have welcomed such a token of interest from him. Before his marriage, she could have mastered the art of papier mâché, she had shredded so many love letters written to him in secret. For even a motherless girl knows that letters from a fifteen-year-old girl, not yet out in society, to a twenty-five-year-old man are beyond the pale, no matter how love-struck. Especially when he barely acknowledges her existence.

Well, not until that God-awful day. The day he remarked idly over the pea soup that he would be getting married to one Miss Alice Pemberton come the spring. Prudence had been so distressed that she sprayed her mouthful of soup over the damask tablecloth and promptly dissolved into tears. Both Edward and her father were so surprised that neither of them thought to console her with the offer of a handkerchief, although Edward did enquire whether the soup was too salty for her taste, while her father directed Carp to bring a fresh bowl.

'But you were to marry me!' she had sobbed, astonishment robbing her of all good sense and propriety.

These words had stunned the two men afresh, her father blinking as if she were a new species of beetle he had discovered, while Edward sat open-mouthed, his tongue working to find a suitable response.

'My dear Miss Prudence,' he had said finally, above the wracking of her sobs, 'you are as precious to me as a sister but . . .'

Naturally, she had not heard what followed that 'but', for her tears reached a crescendo and she gasped, 'But I am not your sister!' before pushing back from the table with such force that she knocked the tureen from Carp's gloved hands, sending hot soup spilling down the front of her sprigged cotton afternoon dress.

Yes, that day was scalded into her memory long after the redness on her thigh had faded. For a six-month after, she made it her business to be indisposed whenever Edward came to dine, even if it meant going hungry to bed. And for nigh on three years, despite shedding copious tears over the doomed love of Princess Charlotte and her German prince, and reading every novel of Miss Selina Davenport's that she could lay hands upon, she could not look him in the eye.

Looking back upon her younger self, she saw that she had indulged this romantic wallowing immoderately, long past an age where such fantasies may be forgiven. Why, she must have read Mr Huish's memoir of her Royal Highness Charlotte Augusta at least three times, while dreaming of what might have been. All the while hiding her enmity towards the new Mrs Edward Ambrose behind a mask of amity. She saw now that her later impatience with Edward may have stemmed from this girlish bedazzlement.

Still, that did not absolve him of his duplicity.

'Wants me or my fortune?' she said to Bessie, reassured that any feelings Edward might have for her were protective at best, pecuniary at worst. Certainly, he could not love her. Had never loved her. He had made that plain, two decades ago. And people did not turn about so, did they?

'Mr Ambrose be a fine, upstanding gent, miss,' the girl persisted.

'How can you tell?' How could this slip of a girl tell when Prudence could not?

'He be kind to me, miss. He asked after my health whenever he saw me at hall. He gave my grandparents work at harvest when some wouldn't. And does he not have a fortune of his own?'

Not a fortune no, but a sizeable estate, which added to that of her father's created a fortune. Her fortune . . .

If it were possible to dismiss a maid in a room the size of a wardrobe, she would have done so. But in the confines of the ship's cabin, she did the best she could. Sometimes, a lady just needed to be alone with her thoughts, to quell them into submission at the very least.

'I think I shall write in my pocket book now, Bessie, if you can lay hands upon pen and ink.'

Friday: Farewell to Singapore. Set sail for Sydney. Grand adventures ahead.

16

Hampshire, England

2022

All the way to the New Forest, Eliza was conscious of her hands playing with the battered auctioneer's catalogue resting on her lap. Straightening dog-eared pages, smoothing a bent cover, keeping her hands occupied so that she would not reach for her phone to check her messages, or needlessly fluff up her hair. She was conscious of a jittery nervousness swirling in her stomach, setting her hands to fiddling and her feet to shuffling restlessly upon the floor of Daniel's pickup. She didn't know what had got into her. Wasn't sure whether these jitters were due to their current mission, the call she was awaiting from her solicitor . . . or this unnerving proximity to Daniel.

Or all three of the above.

'Do you need a rest stop?'

'What?'

'You're jigging about a bit. I thought you might need a quick pit stop.'

'Oh, no, no, I'm good. Just keen to reach Mr Hobbs's house and finally see Prudence's watercolours in real life. We were so lucky to find the auctioneer's catalogue amongst the hall's records.'

She glanced down at the plain black font announcing the sale of *Property from the Collection of the Late Mr Winston Ambrose at Westcott Hall, Somerset, 10th June 1979.* Winston being her great-grandfather, and the 'Collection' being the last of the art and furniture from Westcott Hall, before the estate was sold out of the family forever. Someone, possibly one of the beneficiaries of Winston's estate (or quite possibly a fairy godmother) had thought to jot down the price received for each lot, the buyer, and in several cases a phone number. As luck would have it, the fairy godmother had written the phone number of one Harold Hobbs, resident of Hampshire, alongside a listing for 'The Merryfield Watercolours: Including six sketches depicting Regency and Georgian domestic life and nine sketches of the Isles of Samoa, by Mrs Prudence Ambrose, née Merryfield'.

'Are you sure that's the only thing bothering you? You've been looking very jumpy for the last half-hour.'

'Well, I'm waiting on a call from my solicitor,' she admitted with a sigh. 'She's been trying to negotiate with my landlord's reps to see if they're open to some other arrangement.'

'Such as?'

'Such as letting me stay.' In other words, begging.

'Good luck with that,' he replied, but his expression said she was deluding herself.

'I know, it's probably wishful thinking but . . .'

'Eliza . . . there's something I've been meaning to tell you.'

'Hmm?'

'I . . . um . . .'

'Yes?' she asked, when he failed to finish his thought.

'I . . . um . . . I like what you're wearing today. Nice shoes.'

Normally, on a workday scouring estate sales or country fairs, she would be dressed at her most prosaic. Black cords, blue jeans, something hardy that did not show dirt and did not draw attention. But today she was celebrating this gorgeous summer day amongst the leafy green haven of the New Forest, and the close proximity of her almost as gorgeous (let's be real – *just as gorgeous*) new client by donning a vintage Emilio Pucci long-sleeved shift in a leaf pattern, paired with platform Jacquemus sandals. She was feeling stylish and – dare she say it? – pretty gorgeous herself.

'Oh, thanks,' she said with a smile, the compliment soothing her nerves where stern self-talk had failed miserably.

They emerged from the forest canopy, whereupon the paved lane they were driving along dwindled to a gravel drive, then dribbled to a halt outside a thatched cottage by the banks of a minor river. Of course, Mr Harold Hobbs, purchaser of the Merryfield water-colours, would reside in such an estate agent's idyll. She glanced across at Daniel, who had switched off the engine and was smiling at her, his hand upon the door handle.

'Ready?' he asked.

'Can't wait.'

'Don't be disappointed if he no longer owns them.'

'And don't you be disappointed if he has no interest in parting with them.'

Mr Hobbs turned out to be the farthest thing from a pernickety old collector they could imagine. About the height of a twelve-year-old boy, with a thick brush of white hair, round wire-rimmed spectacles and the frame of a featherweight boxer, he ushered them through the cottage to a stone terrace overlooking the river and produced several tall glasses brimming with a frosty liquid.

'Cheers!' he said, clinking glasses. 'So nice to have visitors. The neighbours are all in Spain, or somewhere or other, and the Airbnb people have descended upon us.'

Expecting lemonade, Eliza took a gulp, realising to her delight that the drink was laced with white rum. 'L-l-lovely. Just what I needed.'

'Mojito. Learned to love them in Cuba during . . . well, never mind.'

'Mmm, I can see why,' Daniel said, taking a second sip.

'Now, you said on the phone, Miss Ambrose . . .'

'Eliza, please.'

'. . . that you were trying to trace the contents of the upstairs sitting room from Westcott Hall.'

'Yes . . . as I said, Daniel and I are researching the interiors and, if possible, purchasing suitable artworks or furniture for the hotel that is being developed on the site. Luckily for us, we found your details written on an old auctioneer's catalogue.'

'Do you mind telling me the name of your grandfather?' he asked, pulling a little black notebook from the pocket of his jacket.

'My grandfather? My Ambrose grandfather?' she asked, not a little surprised at his question.

He nodded. 'If you don't mind.'

'George.'

'Ah, the elder son.' He made a note in his book, before continuing, 'For the family tree, my dear. I've gone as far back as the sixteen hundreds, but I'm missing some of the present generation.' At her puzzled look he added, 'My mother, Elizabeth, was an Ambrose. A cousin of your grandfather.'

'So you would be my Aunt Jude's second cousin?'

'Yes, that's right. I believe I may have met her once at a garden party at the hall when we were children, sometime in the fifties or early sixties. Before they sold the lot off – when old Winston was still terrifying the grandchildren.'

'So that's why you purchased a collection of amateur nineteenth-century watercolours?' Daniel asked.

'That and a certain notoriety of Prudence's. To be plain, she was no Diana Sperling. Well, apart from some of the Samoan works she completed after her return from the South Seas. They

132

have a certain lively quality about them. The earlier works,' he grimaced, 'are quite drab. But you can see for yourself once we've finished our tipple.'

Of course, Eliza was familiar with Diana Sperling's landscapes and depictions of Regency life. She remembered a particularly charming watercolour they had once had in the store: a lively rendition of a lady and her maid slaughtering flies in the drawing room. The details she included in her sketches were a wonderful insight into daily life in Regency England. She had been hoping Prudence's watercolours might provide similar clues to her life and adventures. Somehow, Jude's nagging about solving the mystery of Prudence's disappearance was morphing into a quest to uncover the mystery of her life and adventures.

Once they finished their mojitos, Harold led them back through the cosy sitting room, with its mock Tudor architecture, to a sunny room bathed in southern light that looked out over the river. One wall was lined with shelves, the books arranged in military precision, with ranks of travel tomes, political works and spy thrillers.

Daniel was prompted to comment, 'I see you're a keen traveller.'

'Once upon a time. Travel was unavoidable in my line of work, but I rarely travel far these days. I expect it would take a national emergency to lure me out of retirement,' he said with a chuckle.

'What line of work?' asked Daniel.

'Oh, the civil service. Not as exciting as your work, hunting down the past and all that. In retirement I've made the past my business too.'

Eliza was conscious of the conversation between the two men, even while she was inextricably lured towards the further corners of Harold's study. There was a wall of French windows opening on to the terrace, but it became apparent that the two remaining walls were devoted to paintings and sketches of Westcott Hall, Queens Knoll and the watercolours of Prudence Merryfield.

'There are so many,' she breathed, her excitement mounting. She was still unsure why she was here in the sitting room of this newly unearthed cousin. And why exactly she had accepted Daniel's mission, against her better judgement, when she had a more pressing matter to solve, facing the threat of the imminent loss of her home and place of business. She really needed to maintain her perspective and not let curiosity take over. 'We couldn't tell from the photographs Jude had.'

'There are a couple of sketchbooks as well. One survived from her girlhood – lots of drawings of puppies and horses – and another she must have completed from memory after her return from Samoa.'

'Do you mind if we take some detailed photographs?' asked Daniel, getting down to practicalities.

'Not at all, I wanted to save them as a record for posterity. Who knows, one day, someone may even solve the mystery of Prudence's second disappearance?' he said, glancing at Eliza over the top of his spectacles. 'There were several artefacts too. A beautiful shell headdress, a length of *siapo* and a fine mat.'

'*Siapo*?' she asked, unfamiliar with the word.

'Mmm, a Samoan textile of pounded bark.'

'May we see the artefacts – that is, if you still have them?'

'Oh no. Repatriated them, my dear. Through a fellow I know at the Foreign Office. Better for them to return home to Samoa. They'll be cared for more professionally in a museum too.'

He must have read Eliza's disappointment in her face, for he added, 'But I have a photographic record, if that's of use. I'll look them out for you later.'

'Oh, wonderful.' She stepped closer to this private family gallery, scanning the dizzying array of paintings and sketches lining the walls.

A few of Prudence's watercolours were English rural scenes; one of a woman hurrying through the woods with something clutched in her hand was quite stilted. But it was the Samoan works that snared her eye: the round and oval houses with their high domed roofs of thatched leaves and their open sides; the neatly swept paths winding through villages; the children playing games upon the beach; the fishermen paddling their canoes across the lagoon; and the young girl with the lopsided haircut and the animated gestures who was depicted in painting after painting, sometimes trailed by what appeared to be a chicken. There was such energy about her movements, as if the artist's brush was trying to capture the wind.

'I think I can guess the answer,' Daniel was saying to Harold, 'but we'd love to purchase some . . . any of these works, if you felt inclined. We're hoping to tell some of the house's history through its interiors.'

'I couldn't bear to part with them,' Harold replied with a shake of his head. 'In a way, Prudence has inveigled her way into the Ambrose family tree, despite the fact that none of us are descended from her. The family's fortunes certainly changed with her demise. Not that I'm complaining.'

'I understand. I wouldn't part with them either, if I were you.'

'But,' he continued, with a perky lift of his brows, 'I'm happy for you to reproduce them.'

'Actually, that's a fantastic idea,' she heard Daniel say. 'And once we're up and running, we could make the reproductions available to our guests – with a royalty payable to you, of course.'

Daniel and Harold continued to discuss the possibilities of reproducing the watercolours, but Eliza was no longer paying attention. She had locked eyes with a flame-haired young woman in a gown of faded yellow that billowed in the wind. She leaned against a ship's rail, her hair fighting valiantly to be free of its pins, while behind her the sea stretched in an azure sheet to the horizon and the cloudless sky was dotted with wheeling gulls. One hand was raised, gesturing towards a distant smudge of what may have been land. The other battled to preserve her modesty.

'Is it a self-portrait?' she asked, turning to her host. 'The only other portrait I've seen wasn't taken from life but we know that Prudence had red hair.'

'No. There's a notation on the rear of the painting that reads simply, "Bessie 1833". I believe Bessie was the maid who accompanied her on her voyages. Like all of the Samoan and South Seas works, Prudence painted them from memory upon her return. Any works she may have completed during her journey were lost with the ship.'

Eliza stared into the eyes of the young woman who had travelled halfway around the world in service to her mistress, and wondered if she had gone willingly or because she had no other choice. She could not get a sense of it from the sketch; the eyes were mere specks of colour, the cheeks pink from the wind and the sun, the mouth striving to smile in the face of the elements.

And what did this young maid think of her mistress, a woman who had abandoned convention to journey unescorted across the oceans? In leaving England, was Prudence running away from something or running towards something? More particularly, was she running from Edward Ambrose? Her pocket book implied so, with her talk of escape. Perhaps Edward had threatened her. Eliza didn't like to think that her great-great-something-or-other-grandfather was a stalker. An abuser. A wife killer. She didn't want to believe it, except such stories were perennial.

No. Eliza most certainly did not want to believe it. Prudence had simply embarked upon a journey of discovery. She had journeyed far to learn about other places and, in so doing, discover herself. Or perhaps in another setting, far from the confines of an English drawing room, she could become someone else. Eliza drew in a breath. Despite her loose Pucci shift and open-toed sandals, she suddenly felt constricted, as if a giant hand had grabbed her around the middle and squeezed. She felt hemmed in by walls she had created for herself. Unlike Prudence, her life had become narrow, crowded with objects instead of people or places. Her feet never ventured far and always returned to the same location.

She closed her eyes, squeezing back tears. *Breathe*, she commanded silently. *Breathe.*

'Eliza?' She felt the light touch of Daniel's hand upon her arm. 'Are you okay? You've gone kind of white.'

When she didn't answer immediately, he swept his hand over her arm and along her shoulder to cup her cheek. She was conscious of his fingers resting gently upon her cheekbone, the heel of his palm cradling her chin. Strange, how his hand fitted her face perfectly, just as it had matched her own hand. She couldn't remember any man cupping her face in such a manner, not a single boyfriend or lover. There had been none of the intimacy of kindness.

Only her mother had ever stroked her cheek when she cried over some injury, large or small, as a child. She closed her eyes, suspended for a moment in the texture of his palm and the feather-light touch of his fingertips, until he slid his hand over her cheek, breaking the spell and releasing her. Did she imagine that brief caress of his finger as it drifted across her lips?

'Eliza?'

'I'm fine,' she answered, blinking open her eyes and taking a half-step back from him. 'I was just wondering why Prudence left England in the first place.'

'I see. I thought it might be something more personal.'

'No, nothing personal.'

'The account of her journey published later was pure speculation,' said Harold, apparently noticing nothing of import between the two of them. 'She never spoke publicly of her voyage, that we know of.'

No, there was nothing personal between her and Daniel. She needed to remember that. 'If I had the missing pages of her pocket book I might be able to answer that question,' she said, trying to get the discussion back on track. 'Her diary entries end before she reached Calcutta.'

Both men started, eyes widening. She only realised her slip when it was too late.

'What pocket book?' Daniel asked. She had already discovered he was nothing if not forthright.

'Jude gave me an ancient pocket book for my birthday that she found amongst some magazines of her father's. It was Prudence's, for the year 1832. The year she disappeared that first time.'

'You haven't mentioned it.' Daniel's voice was carefully neutral. Except she knew already that neutral was not his natural element.

'No. I've been meaning to,' she said, with a shrug that was so adamantly nonchalant that even Harold's ears pricked up, his chin raised, his nose almost twitching with curiosity. 'So far I haven't found anything in it that would help with the interiors of the hotel.'

'Hmm, a pocket book you say. Now, that is interesting,' Harold said, glancing from one to the other.

She thought of the pocket book nestled in the depths of the Delvaux bag slung over her arm, for without knowing why, she had taken to carrying the little book about with her. Nor did she know why she had failed to mention its existence. There had been several moments in her previous encounters with Daniel when she had actually bitten her lip to stop herself. It was as if she wanted to keep that tiny bit of Prudence all to herself. Perhaps it was the link to the past, her Ambrose family's past, which she hadn't been ready to share. She hadn't been ready to trust him with it. *With her.*

With her, Prudence, or with her, Eliza? that annoying inner voice of hers nudged.

'I wonder what happened to the missing pages,' Harold mused.

'I suppose they were lost at sea. The existing pages are water-stained. I can show you one day, if you'd like,' she said, feeling like a child unwilling to share her shiny new birthday gift. 'If you'd like me . . . us . . . to come again.'

'Capital,' said Harold, rubbing his hands together. 'Next time, I'll try out my caipirinha recipe on you.'

She glanced over at Daniel to see that he was smiling, a wide-mouthed grin that crinkled the corners of his eyes – eyes that looked Harold's way, not hers.

'Oh, and by the way, my dear, if you don't mind me asking, do you have siblings? For the family tree, you understand.'

'No. There's only me.'

17

South Pacific

1833

The sea was behaving itself this morning, extending to the horizon in an endless pane of deep blue. Except the sea was a law unto itself, as her granfer used to say, and Bessie knew not to trust it. Like a cat, it could turn on you in an instant. Soft and friendly one moment, circling your shins and lifting its chin for a scratch, and the next hissing and scratching and arching its back in displeasure. No, the sea was a creature that would not be tamed, no matter how shipshape the deck or canny the captain.

She grasped the rail in a steely grip with one hand, while battling the flyaway skirts of her dress with the other. It was the yellow gown with the white collar that Miss Merryfield had a tailor alter for her use in Calcutta, a gown that her mistress no longer wore. It was the prettiest dress Bessie had ever owned but it did show the dirt something terrible.

'You can let go of the rail now,' Miss Merryfield called to her from behind her easel.

But Bessie's grip did not falter. It was all very well for her employer to be free and easy, since there was always someone to look out for her: a sailor, a servant, or a gentleman like Mr Ambrose. Bessie knew that holding on was imperative. Life might be stolen from you in a blink of the Lord's eye. One morning, her grandparents had been chivvying her to 'hurry thee along, girl' fetching water from the village well, and the next they were cold as two pebbles, nestled side by side on a riverbed. Oh no, letting go was the quickest way to disaster. That is why, despite the urgings of her mistress to release the ship's rail, she held on, white-knuckled. (That and a certain stubbornness that had kept her alive all this while.)

Since the first wild storm on their voyage to Calcutta, when the waves rolled so high they swamped the forecastle, and the ship rolled so violently the jib boom ran beneath the water, she spent as little time on deck as could be managed. And when she did surface, at the urgings of her mistress, to bathe in the soupy saltwater, or fetch and carry her paints and parasol, she lurched from hatch, to mast, to rigging, to rail. For you never knew when the sea might turn on you.

None of that seemed to bother her mistress. There she was now, perched upon a three-legged stool, her paints propped atop a barrel, her easel inching this way and that across the deck if she did not hold it still with one hand, while she painted with the other. For lack of other amenable subjects she was painting Bessie. From what Bessie could tell the mistress was yet to master her brush. But what did she know of painting and such? That young sailor, Williams, must appreciate her mistress's talents. He had been hovering in their vicinity for at least a quarter-hour, smiling at Bessie and grinning foolishly at Miss Merryfield's easel.

'It's quite calm, don't you think, Williams?' her mistress said. 'I think Bessie can safely release the rail and gesture to the horizon with one hand. The other . . . the other can . . . float free. I shall capture her like an albatross sailing across the sky.'

Bessie did not feel like floating on air – or water, for that matter. No, definitely not water. She felt like returning below deck and tidying their cabin. Creating order out of the chaos Miss Merryfield left in her wake. The gentry expected their belongings to be in their rightful places, no matter where they last left them. And in a way, tidying was soothing. For if every-thing was in its rightful place, then you knew how to be going on in the world. If everything was slip-sliding around, then anything might happen. If she had known of the existence of waves taller than a house and winds that howled louder than church bells, she would never have joined the mistress on her adventures, no matter how much she cajoled or chastised (both of which tactics Miss Merryfield had employed to get Bessie on board).

But that wasn't true, was it? That was a trick she played with her mind as she heaved up her guts in the worst of the weather, pretending she had said no, and was still brushing out hearths and emptying chamber pots at the hall. She would never have said no, for what was the alternative? As soon as the mistress had run away on her adventures, Carp would have had Bessie out the door and bedded down at the workhouse, as quickly as you could say pease porridge. And her sufferings on-board hadn't all been for nothing. Her lady had looked out for her, in her way. She had complained to the captain if the sailors got too free by word or deed. She had nursed Bessie through a fever in Calcutta. She had taken her in hand and shown her how to be maidservant to a lady. And she had kept her promise and taught Bessie to read. So that when they arrived in Sydney, well, perhaps . . . perhaps there might be a kindly employer searching for a girl like her. A girl with a strong right arm and a quick wit; a girl who could milk a goat, sew a decent seam, arrange a lady's hair, or even read aloud from *Practical Hints for Settlers to our Australian Colonies*.

She would bundle up her wages and her belongings and be gone. And if she sometimes wavered, thinking that she might remain in service to the woman who had, in her own way, been kind and even caring, she pushed the thought away. No, when the ship berthed in Sydney she, Bessie, would never set foot on a ship again – either for love or money, or indeed the whims of her betters.

The child was impossible. No matter how Prudence cajoled, she could not convince her to let go of the ship's rail. Could she not see that the ocean was as flat as a Banbury cake? Yet she held on as if the Roaring Forties might come careening around the corner and blow her away. Prudence had hoped to inject more movement into her sketches by painting upon the ship's deck but the sailors simply would not stay in one place long enough for her to capture them, and Bessie was refusing to cooperate. She had tried her hand at elephants in Calcutta and monkeys in Singapore, the former emerging as big grey cows with flapping ears and a trunk, the latter like wizened furry children. For all her hours of practice since setting out upon this voyage, there was little observable improvement in her skill thus far.

She was about to admit defeat and pack up her easel and paints when the wind freshened, setting the sails to snapping and the blocks to jangling against the masts. It swooped in out of nowhere, scooped up Bessie's skirts and set them to flapping about her legs like a ship in full sail. Caught by surprise, the girl released the rail to flail at her flyaway skirts, as her hair fought to escape its pins. The sight was so unexpected that Prudence could not help laughing.

'The wind is picking up, Miss Merryfield. Might be wise to pack up for the day.' The captain appeared at her elbow in the midst of her laughter at Bessie's battle, so that she did not at first realise he was there.

'I was thinking the same, Captain Weller.'

'And Williams, haven't you work to do rather than ogling your betters?'

'Aye, Captain,' Bessie's young admirer said as he scooted out of the captain's orbit.

It would certainly be safer to retreat below deck as the captain advised, yet there was something about the quickening breeze and skipping waves that tempted her to hoist up her hem, cast off her stays and throw her great sleeves to the winds. She had grown accustomed to the heat of these tropical climes, learning to loosen her stays to accommodate the humidity, but when the weather turned wild she found a certain freedom, even exhilaration, in its turbulence. She had come to revel in the unexpected.

'We could be in for a bit of weather the next while.'

For now the sky overhead was empty of cloud but she had learned not to be so quick to judge the weather. 'Might that not hasten our passage to Sydney town?' she asked. Bessie, for one, would be pleased to arrive on dry land in good speed.

'Ah . . . well . . . I've decided upon a small change of course. We had word from the *Orion*, the brig we passed yesterday, of a commercial opportunity.'

Yesterday, the *Orion* had passed them at a distance of several hundred yards, yet Prudence did not find this comment strange. As a seasoned adventuress, she was used to the practice of communicating with passing ships via a series of flags. And she was also aware that as a passenger aboard a vessel that dealt mainly in mercantile freight, she was deemed less lucrative cargo than many another. She could only hope that this detour would not take them too far off their course.

'May I ask where we are headed?'

'The Feejee Islands, dear lady, where I hope to take up a load of bêche-de-mer to fill an empty corner of the hold. The trade is lucrative in China, where we're headed after Sydney.'

144

Her hosts in Singapore had urged her to try a soup made of the dried and smoked flesh of this cucumber-like sea creature that was such a delicacy in China. But she could not see what all the fuss was about, the texture being quite rubbery and unpleasant to her taste.

'I have heard little of Feejee. Do the British have a settlement there?'

'I would not call it a settlement, but various British and American merchants have established outposts to process the creatures. There was once a good trade in sandalwood to be had, though the wood is all but gone now.'

'And are the local residents of a friendly disposition?' From what she had heard, the oceanic peoples could be quite hostile to Europeans, not to mention each other.

'There have been beachcombers and deserters washed up on Feejee shores since the turn of the century. Some have found homes there; a few have been murdered over the sandalwood. But mostly the natives seem to be at war with each other. Though not so hostile to us as the savages of the Navigator Isles.' He shook his head at some remembered depredation or other by the denizens of these other islands. 'We shall sail quite near them on our course for Feejee but will not make landing.'

'The Navigator Isles? I've heard little of them either.'

'Bougainville named the archipelago for the skill of the canoeists he encountered as he sailed along its shores.'

'And have you dropped anchor at these Navigator Isles then, Captain?'

'No call to, dear lady. A few whaling captains anchor there, to take on supplies and water, but since the Dutch first sailed the coast a century or more ago, apart from those few whalers most avoid those islands. Especially given La Pérouse's account of his voyage.'

'What did Captain La Pérouse have to say of them?'

'He described the men as the tallest and most robust he had met in the South Seas. Ferocious warriors covered in tattoos from waist to knees. The women are almost as tall, I believe, and equally fierce. At one cove he sent out several longboats to replenish his water supply and his men were attacked. In their previous encounters the natives had presented the captain with all kinds of fruit and fowl as gifts, and the French had reciprocated with gifts of iron and beads. At this landing all had seemed peaceable too, until the savages set upon the sailors with stones and clubs. Eleven of La Pérouse's men were massacred.'

'And did they not fight back?' she asked in surprise, since the French were not known for their timidity. She could not imagine them accepting such losses with impunity. Guns most certainly would have been produced.

'I could not say,' the captain shrugged.

Once, she would have blanched in fear at the thought of such fearsome natives. But she had met people of many hues and customs upon her travels and found them obliging, for the most part; eager to sell their wares and be of service for a suitable fee. Few seemed threatened by a European lady in her cumbersome dress; her only weapon a silk parasol. Perhaps there had been some misunderstanding between the French and the natives of these Navigator Isles. Or perhaps they were as fierce and unpredictable as Captain La Pérouse had described. In any case, she would not be venturing there, so it was merely a matter of idle curiosity. Nothing for her to be concerned about.

'Best get below, Miss Merryfield ... Miss Pike,' said the captain, pointing to the west where a bank of dark clouds loomed upon the horizon. 'Looks like a storm is brewing.'

Indeed the wind had garnered momentum, so that Bessie abandoned all pretence of posing and frowned in Prudence's direction. She could not say she blamed the girl.

'Should we be worried, Captain?' she asked, thinking of those

146

unending days confined to their cabin during the squalls and storms of their passage from England to Calcutta.

'Nay, dear lady. We navigated the labyrinth of the Torres Strait successfully. The vast reaches of the Pacific should give us little trouble. We shall batten down the hatches, if need be, and the *Kangaroo* will see us safely to the Feejees.'

18

Samoa

1833

Even a small child could have pointed out the location of the reef near Lupe's village, for a barrier of foaming white water marked where the shelf of rock and coral fringed the lagoon. In the dry season, when the sky was untroubled by clouds, the lagoon shimmered a translucent turquoise, while beyond the reef the ocean swelled deep blue. But come the rainy season, when the fishermen were perpetually on guard against the knock-down winds that could descend upon the island from four directions at once, the ocean roiled an angry grey and even the shallow waters of the lagoon were choppy and unpredictable.

But today the morning sun had a bite to it and there wasn't a cloud in the sky as Lupe and To'oa paddled towards the reef, trailing after the boys who headed for the passage leading to the open sea. Most of the time the girls' arms moved in a synchronised dance as the canoe skimmed across the glassy surface, sand and coral clearly visible on the sea floor a body's length below. A few times they missed their rhythm, and there was a momentary wobble when a large creature glided beneath the hull, but it turned out to be nothing more predatory than a large turtle. Its mottled brown shell appeared dark and shadowy when glimpsed out of the corner of one eye but as it surfaced on the other side

148

of the canoe they saw clearly its pale yellow underside, pointy beak and flippers. It considered them for a moment, its beak seeming to sniff in their direction, before ducking under the water once more to continue its journey across the lagoon, probably heading for the sponge garden on a nearby coral bed. These hawk-billed turtles liked to feed on the large sponges that grew there, while the green turtles preferred to graze on the sea grass waving gently in the current.

Lupe's mother had once told her that turtles were sacred because they were known to save stranded fishermen from drowning, and Lupe believed that. They had a gentle look about them, a look of kindness. She liked to watch the mother turtles sometimes, sneaking from her mat late at night after the other girls were asleep to watch them nest on a nearby beach. Night after night in the dry season they would crawl up the beach past the high-tide mark, almost to the coconut palms, to lay their eggs in holes scraped in the sand with their flippers. In the sea they swam swiftly and gracefully through the water but on land they were slow and cumbersome. She wondered at the way they made themselves so vulnerable in those moments. She could stand right beside a mother turtle as she laboured to dig her nest and drop her precious eggs into the hole, and she would take little notice, so intent was she upon her toil. So urgent was her mission. Luckily, since only the high chief was permitted to eat of their flesh, not too many were taken.

Not too many mothers were lost.

'Can you see where the passage through the reef is, Lupe?' her friend's voice jolted her from her study of the turtle.

'We'll just follow the boys.'

'The boys have passed through the reef and are out in the open sea.'

Lupe looked to the west, where a narrow finger of land jutted into the lagoon, and beyond, where the green shadow of an island interrupted the horizon. She knew the easiest passage through the reef lay not far from that fingertip, but Fata and Tuna had already paddled a good way towards the island, and the older boys were mere dots in the distance.

'It doesn't matter. Keep paddling. The passage is just over there,' she said, pointing vaguely towards the area at the tip of the cape where the reef almost touched the land. Here the water boiled and foamed about the rocks.

'Maybe this isn't such a good idea.'

'I know where it is,' said Lupe. 'It's not far now.' She dug her paddle deep into the water on her right side, with its blade flush to the hull, so the canoe veered towards the place where she knew the passage must be. As the more experienced paddler of the two, she had assumed the stern position and responsibility for steering. But perhaps she dipped her paddle a little too ferociously for the outrigger began lifting off the water, threatening to tip the small craft over.

'Lupe!' To'oa shouted in warning.

The outrigger hovered an arm's length above the surface now, tipping the girls to the right – almost far enough for seawater to lap over the side of the canoe. Lupe leaned to the left, hoping her weight would counter the outrigger's lift, as did To'oa. When she felt it settling upon the surface, she set her blade to paddling once more.

'Don't be such a baby,' she laughed, when the canoe was righted. 'Paddling is hot work. I could do with a swim.'

'Maybe for you, but if I come home with my skirt soaked, my mother will know I've been doing something I shouldn't. I'm not supposed to wear the ie tōga outside the house.' To'oa bent her head to check the mat that covered her to the knees, the shells of her many necklaces dangling. Whereas Lupe's skirt was made of long grassy leaves braided together around her waist and designed to be thrown aside and remade each day, To'oa wore a mat so soft that it had taken her mother many months to plait. Her friend always looked especially pretty in her tall, feathered headdress and her necklaces of shell when she led the other women in the dancing at parties and celebrations.

All the women of the village turned their hand to making fine mats, as well as the siapo cloth pounded from the bark of the paper mulberry, but To'oa's mother's designs were the most beautiful, her mats the softest, and Lupe's Aunt Masina's designs were almost as fine. Lupe didn't know how her aunt had the patience. Making siapo was a painstaking process of beating the bark of the paper mulberry to a pulp, drying it in the sun and then fixing the strips together with arrowroot. Making a fine mat meant soaking pandanus leaves in boiling water, bleaching them in the sun before splitting them into thin strips for plaiting. Both gave Lupe callouses.

'Don't worry, I won't let us capsize,' she promised her friend.

To'oa snorted doubtfully but continued paddling, and soon they were picking up speed, skimming smoothly over the glassy waters of the lagoon. Yet, as they drew closer to the reef, the white water marking its location began to look less like gentle ripples and rather a lot like breakers. The roaring was rapidly becoming a bit too insistent to ignore.

'I think the swell is picking up,' To'oa said, unhelpfully.

'Stop panicking and keep paddling,' Lupe admonished, but her words did not emerge as confidently as she could have wished, especially when they were half drowned by the crash of waves. Both girls could swim like fish, but that didn't mean they relished the prospect of being tumbled unceremoniously on to hard rocks or scraping their bare skin over sharp coral. Not to mention any damage they might inflict upon her father's canoe or To'oa's precious mat.

'Paddle as fast as you can, and I'll steer straight for the passage.'

She could see it there, couldn't she, a narrow ribbon of calm between rolling white waves? She had to, for her friend had taken her at her word and was paddling furiously, the muscles of her back straining to pull the small craft forward. For her part, Lupe alternated between paddling and steering, trying to keep the canoe headed straight for the gap through the reef that would take them out into the open sea. Trying to avoid the boiling water, jagged rocks and sharp coral. Then all at once they were there, slipping through the reef to the rhythm of her breath, the splashing paddles, the skimming outrigger and the crashing waves. She didn't know which sounded louder: her panting or the pounding ocean.

'Keep going,' she urged.

'I'm going, I'm going.'

And then they were through, the breakers falling harmlessly behind them as they shot through the gap and out into the open sea.

'The boys make it look so easy,' panted To'oa as she slackened her pace.

'They've had more practice. Next time, it will be easier.'

Her friend stopped paddling and turned to give her a look.

'What?' Lupe said with a shrug.

'The next time I sail beyond the reef, I will be in my father's double-hulled canoe with ten men paddling and a fine mat sail lifting in the breeze. The next time, I will be welcoming important visitors, to the sound of the ceremonial conch, not trying to out-paddle your cousins.'

'But you have to admit, it's fun with just the two of us.' Lupe grinned, and poked her friend in the shoulder with her paddle.

'Maybe.' To'oa poked her back. 'What do we do now? I have to be back soon.'

'Let's see if we can spot some fish along the reef slope.'

'Maybe we should go back now.'

But Lupe was no longer listening. She was already guiding the canoe parallel to the reef, staying far enough away not to get caught up in the breaking waves, yet close enough to study the wall of rock and coral spilling out from the lagoon. Despite the swell, the water was clear enough to see the sandy bottom far below, too far to tell exactly how deep, but she knew that if she stood on To'oa's shoulders, still her head wouldn't touch the surface. The reef terrace sloped up from the sand in a jumble of rocks and a litter of dead coral, the slope dissected by channels and grooves, creating perfect hiding places for disgruntled eels. Large plates of coral, as wide as the span of her arms, were spread out over shelves of rock, with bushes of branching coral dotted amongst them. Tiny particles of sand and seaweed stirred up by the swelling current drifted in these deeper reaches.

Closer to the surface, the water sparkled a clear swirling turquoise, with boulders of bright green coral and the oscillating pink and cream fronds of soft coral clustering along the reef slope. And darting amongst them was a myriad of fish in all shapes, sizes and colours: blue and green lalafi, with their stripes and jutting jaws; fuga'usi with their rainbow hues and parrot-like pouts; bright orange malau with their big eyes and fanlike fins. And then she saw it, a flash of yellow-green as long as her arm, darting out from behind the branches of a bright turquoise coral that was growing on one of the reef spurs. Its long dorsal fin rippled like a sail through the water. A masi masi – her father's favourite.

'What are you doing?'

She did not have time to answer as she retrieved her father's spear from the bottom of the canoe and stood, determined not to wobble. Wading in the shallow waters of the lagoon or picking her way around the tidal flats, she was handy with her long stick, but a canoe made for a far more precarious platform. Not that she would admit this to anyone – not even her best friend – for she was Lupe the risk taker, Lupe the troublemaker, Lupe who did not care what scrapes she fell into.

She steadied herself by placing one foot slightly ahead of the other, and concentrated on following the masi masi with her eyes, hoping it would not be startled by the shadow of the canoe and dive deeper, out of reach of her spear.

'You're rocking the boat,' To'oa hissed.

'Keep us steady.' She drew her brows together fiercely, so that she bore a strong resemblance to her father when he was deep in thought, trusting that To'oa would wield her paddle to stop them drifting towards the breakers.

'It's not a good idea, Lupe. You know we're not supposed to fish with spears.'

'If my cousins can do it, how hard can it be?'

The masi masi did not seem too bothered by the almost stationary canoe, intent on tastier fare; an orange striped sumu nosing amongst a clump of coral. The masi masi hovered out of the sumu's line of sight, a sinuous yellow streak beneath the canoe's outrigger. Lupe beckoned with crooked fingers for her friend to edge them closer to her prey, and raised the arm holding the spear.

'We're getting too close to the reef terrace,' To'oa warned, her voice teetering at the edge of panic.

'Hold her still,' Lupe hissed, bending towards the stern of the canoe, predicting the direction the masi masi would take when it pounced. And pounce it did, shooting in a flash of silvery yellow beneath the canoe's hull. She swivelled her torso to the other side of the canoe, leaning out as far as she dared, and pitched the spear into the sea with all her might. For a fraction of a heartbeat she dared to think she had sunk the spear into its side, and her lips twitched at the thought of her father's delight when she returned with such a prize, enough to feed half the āiga. But a twitch was all she managed, for rather than the satisfactory writhing of a struggling fish at the end of her spear, her spear dived into nothing but water, its momentum somehow carrying her with it so that she toppled forward. Her body weight tilted the canoe, causing the outrigger to sail up into the air and over, capsizing the small craft and tossing both girls into the water.

She surfaced to find To'oa glaring at her across the hull of the upside-down vessel. She avoided her stare by swimming for the paddles, which were in danger of floating out to sea unless prompt action was taken. By the time she reached them, her friend's tirade was already in full flow.

'. . . asked you not to . . . told you . . . drifting towards the reef . . . now look . . .'

The words were swallowed by the waves washing on to the reef, the muffling of sound as she moved through the water, and her own inclination not to hear sentiments that echoed her own. Why did she always leap before she looked? Why hadn't she heeded her friend's warning?

The paddles safely in hand, she took a breath and turned back to find the canoe drifting dangerously close to the reef.

'To'oa! Stop shouting and start kicking!' she urged, before swimming for the canoe as fast as she could. She swam alongside her friend, grabbing hold of the outrigger with her free hand and kicking furiously.

There was no breath for further recriminations as they manoeuvred the craft away from the reef terrace and set about righting it. Releasing the paddles temporarily, Lupe clambered on to the hull. To'oa took up her position at the outrigger, ready to push the float upwards while kicking her legs hard. Lupe's job was to use her body weight to haul the hull upright at the same time.

'Ready?' she asked.

'Go!' To'oa shouted, pushing up with all her might.

As the canoe tilted, Lupe heaved backwards, letting out a sigh of relief when the hull rolled upright once more. She gathered the paddles floating nearby and tossed them into the canoe, then held it steady as her friend climbed aboard. She followed after, slithering into the small craft as nimbly as possible to avoid another ducking.

In silent concord they set their paddles to the water and began paddling back the way they had come, To'oa once more in the bow and Lupe in the rear. She did not dare speak for fear of angering her friend further. But once they had steered the dugout through the passage in the reef, To'oa let loose anyway. Luckily, there was an onshore wind, whisking away the harshest of her comments so that Lupe caught only fragments of sound.

'. . . stupid . . . selfish . . . careless . . .'

Even so, by the time they beached the canoe in the shallows near the village, she had the general idea. Except this was no time for grovelling. They had to get the canoe out of the water and up the beach before the boys returned. For if her cousins spotted her friend clad in the soggy mess that had once been a delicate mat, they would know what had happened. And Lupe would never hear the end of it.

'Let's get the canoe up the beach, and then you can go home and change. I'll make it up to you, I promise,' she said to the back of her friend's head.

She received nothing but a grunt in response.

Lupe unfurled herself from the canoe and stepped lightly into the gentle waves lapping on to the sand. The sun was high in the sky, its rays bouncing off the shallow waters of the lagoon in a sparkle of light. Blinded for a moment, she put a hand up to shade her eyes, so that she could better make out a figure approaching them from the foreshore. She hoped it wasn't anyone from her āiga, for they would almost certainly inform her father. Her eyes shaded, she recognised the tall, muscular form of the woman walking towards her, and her hopes were crushed. The woman was clad in an ordinary workaday leaf skirt, with garlands of hibiscus and shells looped about her neck, her hair shorn all over in a symbol of her widowhood, and her expression was far from welcoming.

'Tālofa lava, Masina,' Lupe said, hoping that her aunt had only just arrived on the beach.

'You should call me Mother, for as your aunt and the leader of the aualuma, I am as a mother to you. You know this, Lupelele.'

So said her uncle's widow, the woman who was always telling her what to do, always poking her nose where she wasn't wanted or needed, who lay in wait to catch her niece in each new transgression. The woman Lupe sought to escape at every opportunity.

'So ... I see you have ventured somewhere you shouldn't again.'

The woman who sought to take her mother's place. As if anyone could ever take her mother's place.

'Just foraging for shellfish in the lagoon, Ma— ... Mother.'

Her aunt quelled her impudence with a look. 'I see no shellfish. And where are your nets and baskets?'

Floating out towards the horizon by now, with her father's spear. They had been lucky to rescue the paddles.

'An unlucky event,' she answered with a shrug.

'And you, To'oa, I expected better of you. You have ruined all your mother's fine handiwork.' Her aunt frowned at the soggy, not-so-fine mat that hung damply about To'oa's hips. 'So much work wasted.'

'I'm sorry, Masina. It will be good as new once it's dry. Our canoe capsized and ...' her friend tried to explain.

But Masina was having none of it. 'And where *exactly* did it capsize? Remember, you can be seen from the beach.'

'Out beyond the reef ... but only a little.'

'You are supposed to stay *inside* the lagoon. All kinds of dangers lurk beyond the reef for untried girls.'

'We meant no harm, Masina.' To'oa bowed her head.

'You had better go to your mother's fale and explain to her what you have done. I will speak of this further at the aualuma fale, later. Run along now. *I* will help Lupe return her father's canoe to where it belongs.'

She shooed To'oa towards the thatched fales and lawns of the village, before turning to her niece and remarking with a stern look, 'I remember when your father made this canoe. So many weeks of back-breaking work. Searching for just the right breadfruit tree, cutting it down, swimming it all the way to the village, hollowing out the log, shaping the hull, constructing the outrigger.'

'I know . . . Mother.'

'For many years, he has fished from it. For many years, it has repaid his time and labour.'

'I know this.'

'How disappointed he would be if it were lost through the foolhardy actions of his prideful daughter. Especially when he is slowly beginning to recover from his grief.'

'I'm sorry, it was an accident.' Lupe hung her head, when all she wanted to do was glare at her aunt. But that would compound her disgrace with rudeness.

'It was no accident that you took your father's canoe out beyond the reef where you had no business doing so. And you fished from that canoe when you had no business doing so. It was pride and disobedience. And for that you shall be confined to the fale to plait sleeping mats and mend curtains until I can trust you outside the house.'

As her aunt spoke, Lupe felt herself shrinking. Growing smaller and smaller with each utterance, until she wished she could withdraw into her shell like the creatures that inhabited the rocky ledges of the lagoon. She would tuck herself inside and close the door to the world. Then no one could tell her what to do. No one could bother her. Then she would be alone and no one would ever leave her again.

Then she would be safe.

19

Hampshire, England

2022

The weather was too nice to sit inside a low-ceilinged pub, no matter how rustic its charm. Luckily, they managed to score a table in the garden, settling on to opposite benches with a bottle of New Zealand Sauvignon Blanc between them and menus in hand. Pots of petunias bloomed by an ancient timber door, while a row of narrow upper-storey windows peeked out from the whitewashed building's helmet of thatch. Eliza looked down to see that a black and tan dog, which had welcomed them to the pub earlier, was now sitting by her feet waiting for her attention. But for the moment that attention was divided equally between the menu and the man sitting opposite her. Doggie would have to wait.

The fat chips on another diner's plate looked tempting and she was just deciding between the cauliflower and red pepper curry with pilau or the salmon with hollandaise and tarragon sauce (maybe they could get chips to share), when she felt something cold and wet against her shin.

'I think I've made a friend,' she said, reaching down to scratch the dog behind the ears.

'I think you've made more than one friend,' Daniel said.

'You do?'

'Harold was quite taken.'

'You think so?' she asked, not a little disappointed to realise that he hadn't been referring to himself.

'He's not the only one.' His smile was as tempting as any glass of wine.

'No?'

'No. You have a legion of fans. Not just old men and puppy dogs.'

'That's a relief.'

'There are young blokes too. I swear that bartender gave you the once over.'

'What about a youngish bloke with a three-day stubble?'

'Oh, that guy with the crappy old ute and Blundstones? He's your biggest fan.' He was still grinning as he said this but his eyes were suddenly serious.

'Is he? I thought he was all business.'

'He was . . . he—'

Before he could finish what he had been about to say, two things happened: her phone rang; and the dog decided to get serious by standing on its hind legs and placing his forepaws on her lap, his claws scratching her thighs in the process.

'Ow! Get down, you little rogue,' she said, prising his claws from her Pucci shift, before scooping him out from under the table and depositing him at a safe distance, with a pat. 'Stay,' she added without much hope. Then, checking her phone, she cast an apologetic glance in Daniel's direction, saying, 'Sorry, I have to take this. My solicitor.'

'I'll order for us at the bar.'

'Salmon,' she mouthed as she hit the green button, her heart buoyed by possibly misplaced hope.

Five minutes later, she hung up, the buoyancy turned to ballast. The landlord was willing to negotiate on compensation but refused to budge on renewing the lease. They were sorry for any inconvenience caused to Miss Ambrose but wanted to move home and business into the premises, having purchased the property years earlier with this intention. They expected her to relocate by the end of December when the lease expired.

'I'm sorry, Eliza,' her solicitor said, 'but they're within their rights, and were we to take them to court I doubt we'd win. Best to negotiate on the compensation front.'

After she hung up she sat staring into space for a moment or two, one hand idly patting the dog while the other clenched her glass so tightly it was a wonder it didn't break. She needed to compose herself before Daniel returned. The last thing she needed was sympathy, for that might shatter any remaining composure. Clutching her handbag, she swung her legs over the bench and crunched across the gravel terrace to find a more secluded spot in the garden. She rounded a bend out of sight of the other diners and came to rest beneath an oak tree facing away from the dining terrace.

She knew she had been pinning her hopes upon a thin possibility, but that didn't make the failure any easier to accept. She had made her mother a promise and she had broken that promise. She couldn't even tell her she was sorry. She couldn't tell her anything. She couldn't tell her that the shop was empty without her. Nor that she missed her. Nor that she loved her. She couldn't even tell her goodbye.

And the worst betrayal was that if she were truly honest, she wasn't sure that she wanted to keep the shop going. Until now, she hadn't allowed that possibility. But in these last weeks, she had found a greater enjoyment in the brief hours of tracking down clues to Prudence's life and disappearance than the shop had provided in months. She wasn't about to tell Jude, but her aunt's suggestion of a book had infiltrated Eliza's thinking. She had begun transcribing the diary entries from the pocket book, collating notes on the documents she unearthed, the historic photographs she collected – and now she could include descriptions of Prudence's watercolours.

Then there was her work with Daniel, tracking down furniture for a refurbished Westcott Hall. No, the work and her research weren't the actual betrayal – it was her enjoyment of them. She should have been reserving her energies and investing them in keeping the shop going. She might have to relocate but that would be a lesser evil than letting the business go altogether. Relocation was an evil for which she could be forgiven. For which she might eventually forgive herself. But how could she forgive herself if she abandoned her parents' life's work?

'Eliza?'

Daniel had a knack for sneaking up on her when she wasn't prepared, for honing in on her vulnerable moments, that was *really* annoying. And who let him get under her skin? Who let him get within arm's length? She didn't usually let anyone but her aunt rummage about beneath the surface. And even Jude was only allowed the tiniest peek. Well, it wouldn't do. He needed to be put back where he belonged, beyond reach of her arms or her heart.

She brushed away a tear and turned to face him, as bright-faced as could be managed in the midst of an existential crisis. 'Just finding a bit of privacy for my phone call,' she said, avoiding those twin wells of hazel. Best not to fall in. Lust, that is, not love. She hadn't been thinking of love. No, that definitely wasn't on the menu.

'I'm guessing the news wasn't what you were hoping for.'

'No.'

'You know, moving the store mightn't be all bad. I noticed a "For Lease" sign on a nice little shop in town. Sound structure, good condition, in a block with a homewares store, a bookshop and a popular café. You'd get more foot traffic.'

163

'But Bobby doesn't want to move,' she hiccupped.

'I know.' He placed his hand on her arm just above her elbow, and squeezed reassuringly.

What was it with this man? Everything was so physical with him. So . . . so comforting. She didn't need comfort, she needed . . . she needed to be left alone to wallow in her misery. That's how she usually solved her problems. Wallow for a bit. Chastise self for wallowing. Then pick self up and get on with it.

So she should have known better. She should have pulled away. Should have made it clear, in no uncertain terms, that she didn't need his comfort or advice. That she didn't need him. Full stop. But she didn't. Instead, she clasped his free arm in the same place, just above the elbow. Then she slid her hand up that arm, feeling the hardness of his biceps beneath his jumper, and looped her fingers around his neck. And then she pulled herself towards him.

Later, she wouldn't remember whether he bent his head to find her mouth, or she raised her head to find his. But she did remember the tang of Sauvignon Blanc on his lips and the hum that vibrated through her body as they found each other. She remembered her quick intake of breath as she looked into his eyes and the sensation of his arms encircling her, pulling her even closer so that the entire length of her body dissolved into him. She closed her eyes, all thoughts of shops and antiques and Prudence evaporating as she was caught in a whirlpool of desire so dizzying that when he pulled away she floundered, almost swooning at the knees like a nineteenth-century heroine in a melodrama. If it weren't so humiliating it would have been comical.

'I'm sorry, Eliza. I shouldn't have done that. It was unprofessional.'

'I thought I'd done that,' she blurted.

'Well, let's just say we both did that. And it was unprofessional of us both.'

'Yep. Very unprofessional. Don't know what we were thinking.'

'Must have been the sunshine, the wine . . .'

'Not to mention the mojitos.' She joined him in dousing the flames. 'Will never happen again.'

'Pinky promise?' he said, holding up his little finger.

What else could a red-blooded straight man do when a woman threw herself at him except kiss her back and then regret the future complications almost immediately? But like a gentleman he was trying to save her face.

'Pinky promise,' she agreed, hooking his finger with hers as she tried to calm her breathing. Then she brushed away the invisible creases in her silk dress and turned in the direction of their table, hoping her salmon would have miraculously appeared. Then she could focus on the fish rather than the man.

What had she been thinking? Kissing a man who was essentially her client, albeit during an existential crisis. A man who'd made it clear that theirs was a business relationship. Was she bonkers?

Yes, said her inner voice, *and what is wrong with a bit of bonkers now and then?*

Everything. Everything was wrong with bonkers.

Is that what had happened to Prudence? She had set out on a voyage to the far reaches of the globe – alone, except for her young maid. Had she gone bonkers? That would explain every-thing. A momentary madness leading her to abandon a privileged life in England for the dangers of the open sea and the foreign lands to which she travelled. Had it been a mad whim that spirited her away? Not once, but twice?

Prudence had been eccentric enough to run away once. Perhaps she had run away twice. Perhaps her husband hadn't murdered her, as the reports of the day suggested. As the Ambrose curse suggested.

Eliza was suddenly conscious of the weight of her handbag where she carried Prudence's pocket book. Her ancestor's diary entries were so cryptic. And many of the pages were missing. But Eliza could not forget the last entry in the pocket book. It must have been written on that first voyage, for there was no mention of what happened after the ship docked in Calcutta. If there ever had been, they were ripped from the spine. As were the mystery pages from 1833, the year she was cast away. No, these words had been written on the *Exmouth* before Prudence was anywhere near the Pacific Ocean.

Wednesday: Ship tossed by storm. Bessie and I beset by most unladylike ailment. Am I mad?

Was Prudence mad? That's what was once said of all women who didn't conform.
Locked up. Put away. Disappeared. Silenced.
Is that what happened to Prudence?
Or did she choose her own ending?

20

South Pacific

1833

The dark of the early hours with the ship rolling like a country dance wasn't the most propitious time to seek out the chamber pot, but a lady's needs must be obeyed. Prudence had been confined to her sofa or tied to a chair for two days, the captain deeming the movement of the ship too savage for a woman to hazard the saloon or the poop deck. And although a sailor was tasked with scrubbing the cabin with chloride of lime twice weekly, the smell of vomit emanating from the corner where the slop bucket lived would have turned her stomach had there been contents left to turn. The chamber pot, lodged alongside it, added to the unpleasant fug.

The cabin was scant yards square but the distance from her sofa to that noxious corner was daunting, even for an adventuress accustomed to the privations of shipboard life. With no candle allowed and storm clouds obscuring the night sky, the portholes and skylight were dark, sound and memory her only guides to navigating the cabin. Anything not battened down was liable to roll or slide underfoot as the ship pitched in the heavy seas.

She swung her legs over the side of the sofa and stood holding the wooden arm as the deck teetered beneath her. She was fully dressed in a gown of India cotton that she'd had made up in Calcutta, a white chemise (rather the worse for wear from being washed in saltwater) and petticoats with her pockets tied beneath. The mate might knock upon their door at any moment and it wouldn't do to be found in a state of undress. Unfortunately, her skirts wrapped about her legs as she lurched across the cabin so that she cried out in surprise and not a little pain when she bumped her shins against Bessie's camp bed. Judging by the intermittent moans issuing from the girl's lips, poor Bessie lay wakeful upon her trundle. Prudence felt a modicum of guilt for dragging her upon this voyage but it was soon mislaid in the depths of her own misery.

After several more misadventures, her nose found the noisome corner and she proceeded to wrangle her skirts to squat over the pot. She was just congratulating herself upon completing her mission when there was a fierce roar and the ship gave a great shudder as it rolled to port, bowling pail and pot aside and knocking Prudence from her feet. She heard Bessie scream and felt herself thrown across the cabin as a great gush of water flooded through the skylight. As the ship slowly righted, the water continued to pour in so that it was almost up to her elbows as she steadied herself on all fours. She tried to scramble upright, but her legs became entangled in her soaked skirts and the threat of further lurching sent her back to her knees.

'Bessie, how do you fare?'

'I be dying, miss. God be punishing me for my sins.'

'You're not dying.' At least, not yet. 'And if God is punishing you, then we are all equally sinners.'

'I cannot escape fate, miss. It be my fate to drown.'

Hearing this, Prudence abandoned all thought of clambering to her feet and crawled on hands and knees, through the foul-smelling water, towards the sound of the girl's voice. The sea pouring through the skylight had lessened somewhat but she could also feel water flowing underneath the cabin door.

'It's not your fate, Bessie. We must be brave and resolute,' she said, as she reached the girl's side. 'I'm only sorry that I've brought you to this state of affairs.'

'You don't understand, miss. I should be drowned long ago but I be saved. And now God be taking his due.'

'Nonsense! God doesn't take young girls as his due,' Prudence said, before realising that Bessie needed reassurance rather than logic. 'It will be all right. We must wait for word from the captain. He will see us through the storm. I shall sit here and hold your hand until someone comes. We must let the crew do God's work.'

They sat in silence, hands clasped, the girl squeezing hers each time the ship pitched or rolled, while outside the tempest raged. For all she had survived the harshest of educations – her life – Bessie was hardly more than a child. And in the blackness of night, with the waves roaring and the wind howling, she clung to Prudence as she might once have clung to her mother. Whimpering, as the ship was tossed like a leaf in a whirlpool. And Prudence clung to her, overcome by the realisation that Bessie was only here at her whim; that she had dragged the girl across three oceans and now she might die. Bessie was young enough to be Prudence's child. But she had been born into poverty, whereas Prudence's child – the child she would most probably never have – would be born into privilege.

Loosening her left hand from Bessie's grasp, she replaced it with her right. Then she slid her arm around the girl's shoulders and pulled her into an embrace. 'Don't cry. I'll stay with you. I won't let you drown.'

They stayed that way for some time, before a knock sounded at the door and one of the crew entered, a lantern held high.

'Captain ordered me below to see how ye be faring,' he said, his lantern finding them in the dank cabin. For all his tanned and reddened features, the boy was hardly older than Bessie. Eighteen or nineteen years old at most, the son of a seafaring father from Cardiff.

'I don't mind admitting we are perilous afraid, Williams.'

The boy nodded. 'The sea is running mountainous high, miss, and the wind is blowing a hurricane. Ye cannot see more than a ship's length. Captain has ordered the sails close-reefed and the men are pumping something fierce below.'

'We've had water bucketing through the skylight and under the door. Is the hatch to the poop deck leaking?'

'Aye, we lost part of the bulwark and the hatches are all leaking after that last great roll to port. Best stay put. Captain will see us through.'

'Are we near land then?'

'The wind has blown us off course, miss. Captain says the Navigator Isles be somewhere to the north. The Feejees somewhere to the south. Both too far to swim.'

He tipped his hat, which through some strange turn of fate had managed to keep a hold of his head, and began backing into the passageway between their cabin and that belonging to the only other passenger, a merchant by the name of Curry.

'Before you go, Williams, may I ask about the boats?'

'The boats, miss?' he said, his eyes shadowed in the lantern light.

'Yes, the boats.'

'Captain has ordered them readied but it shall not come to that.'

Prudence doubted they could get a boat over the side, in any case, in this weather. Only as a last desperate act.

'Well, I best be getting on,' he coughed. 'Captain says to check on Mr Curry and then go below and check the stores. Evening, Miss Merryfield, Miss Bessie,' he said, looking particularly in Bessie's direction.

Despite the lad's reassurances, Prudence was taking chances with neither fate nor the sea. She vowed to be as prepared as any adventurer to take to the boats, if need arose.

'Is ship going down then?' asked Bessie, her hand tightening about Prudence's.

'Not at all. It is surely a precaution.' She said the words as merrily as could be managed in the midst of a hurricane. But best to take a few precautions. 'Let us fill our pockets with a few necessities, should we need to leave our cabin in a hurry.'

Pulling her hand from the girl's as gently as possible, given her death-grip, she stumbled in the direction of their chest of drawers where she kept her most important possessions to hand. She opened the drawer and felt amongst its contents. Her hand closed about the familiar contours of her pocket book, wrapped in oilcloth to protect it from spray when she took it on deck. The pocket book safely in hand, she continued searching with the other hand, finding first her pencil, then the bone-handled penknife amongst her pens, inks, watercolours and brushes, and lastly a spare pair of pockets. For a moment her hand hovered over the box of watercolours but even a fool knew they would prove a liability rather than an asset should she have to abandon ship.

With a sigh, she set these necessities upon the chest and unwrapped the oilcloth, refolding it to enclose the pencil. Then she navigated her way back across the dank and slippery floor to Bessie's side.

'Bessie, do we have any ship's biscuit to hand?' It was dreadful stuff but she had put in a store for emergencies.

'It be in chest with cod, tea, coffee and other supplies, miss.'

Prudence could feel the child shivering in the dark, from fear more than cold, for despite the driving rain it was as hot and humid a night as any she had known in Somerset.

'Then we shall tie a pair of my pockets about your waist and fill them with biscuit and perhaps a little salt cod. In the unfortunate event we must take to the sea in boats, the good Lord will provide us with loaves and fishes,' she said with a smile in her voice.

'Or biscuits and fishes,' said Bessie, her shivering abating enough so that she could lift her skirts for Prudence to help her tie the pockets around her waist above her petticoats. Then they both proceeded to fill their pockets, Bessie with biscuits and salt cod wrapped in waxed paper, Prudence with pocket book, pencil and penknife. Should they be forced to abandon ship for the boats, at least she could look up the baronets of England or the fare of a waterman in London. Such information was bound to be helpful.

Briefly, she considered placing her mother's locket in one of her pockets but decided it would be safer around her neck where it belonged. Safer and more reassuring, if it came to that. There was a certain superstitious comfort in having her mother nestled against her skin. Watching over her.

They sat in the dark as the storm raged and the ship reeled, with no further word from above or below. Nor did they hear anything from Mr Curry across the passageway. Perhaps he deemed it safest to remain in his cabin, or perhaps the captain had enlisted his help. But when Bessie began shivering violently once more, Prudence decided that action was required.

'Gather our cloaks and bonnets, Bessie.' She released the girl's hand and patted her on the shoulder. Giving her a task might help take her mind off their predicament. 'I shall investigate the passageway.'

Trusting Bessie to find their belongings in the dark, she waded through six inches of water in the direction of the door, her hands spread before her as a bulwark against mishap. Reaching the bulkhead, she felt for the door and upon finding it, lifted the latch to step into the passage. The first thing she noticed was the open hatch to the poop deck where water and faint light streamed in. The second thing she noticed, despite the all-pervasive smell of salt air and seawater, was the scent of smoke. She lifted her nose to the wind that coursed through the open hatch, but it wasn't emanating from above. No, the smoke was coming from below. Down on the lower decks where the cargo and supplies were stored. Where the whale oil and gunpowder, rum, tar and rope were housed.

'Bessie!' she shouted. 'Bessie!'

At the sound of her urgency, Bessie materialised at her side, Prudence's cloak draped over one arm and her bonnet dangling from its ribbons in one hand. 'What is it, miss?'

'We must venture above. Now!'

She did not give the girl a chance to question this order, for she could not risk mutiny. Not with so much at stake. Quickly donning cloak and bonnet, she took Bessie by the hand and waded towards the ladder, wondering how the fire had started and why none of the crew had come to warn them. Fire, she had been warned repeatedly, was perilous aboard ship. Had the boy, Williams, dropped his lantern as the ship was tortured by the heaving waves? There was no time to ponder the reasons when their lives might be at stake.

'You go first,' she said, when they reached the ladder. That way there would be no escape, no returning to the false comfort of the cabin.

'I cannot go out there. Sea will take me.'

'You must, or I shall beat you, you wicked girl!' she said, shoving her in the back to make her point.

Bessie complied with a whimper, placing first one foot and then the other upon the rungs of the ladder and slowly ascending. Prudence followed behind, holding her sodden skirts high. There was no one behind to catch her if she fell, no one to come to her rescue. As she emerged from the hatch behind Bessie, she was

173

almost blown from her feet by the buffeting gale. Their cloaks whipped at the air like loose sails and the weight of her dress pulled her down even as the wind ripped the bonnet from her head. And above the howling wind, the shouts of sailors, and the creak and groan of ship's timbers, she heard the panicked bleating of sheep and the crazed squawking of fowl that were housed upon the main deck.

From where they cowered by the aft hatch she could just make out that the main hatch was also open. Clouds of smoke issued from it, billowing upwards into the storm. She could hear few sailors moving about on deck; most would be below, fighting the flames. Others would be manning the pumps. Those she could hear were lurching towards the boats as someone cried out from the direction of the bow. 'Out boats!' The cry echoed along the deck. 'Out boats!'

How could they launch the boats in such wild seas? Even Prudence could see that the tackle could break with the force of the gale and drop the boat into the turbulent water below. Or the waves could dash the lowered boat against the ship's hull, breaking it up or filling it with water before the crew could row it free of the ship. In such wild and broken seas, the boats were indeed an act of desperation.

'What shall we do, miss?' Bessie huddled against her, her voice little more than a mouse's squeak in the storm.

'I don't know,' Prudence answered without thinking. But the girl needed certainty or she might crumble. 'We shall ready ourselves to board the boats,' she said with as much authority as she could muster, although what that might entail, or how it might be managed, she could not imagine. They would have to trust the judgement of the captain and the expertise of the crew, a crew that seemed to have forgotten them. 'Perhaps we might do better holding to the bulwark on the starboard side,' she said, for she thought she spied a great gap in the port side where the bulwark had been broken away. 'Let us try to make our way there, Bessie.'

But when she tried to move she found that the child had planted her feet and would not budge. She was almost of a height with Prudence now and too heavy a burden to drag, even if she did not fight back.

Rain and spray lashed Prudence's face, filling her eyes with saltwater as the men struggled to ready the boats on either side of the ship. She could hear other sailors emerging from the main and forward hatches. Perhaps the open hatches had done their work, the incoming water having put out the flames. The ship was wallowing in the heavy seas, pitched about by wave and wind, and sinking lower by the minute.

'We cannot stay here,' she shouted into the wind.

The only answer she received was muffled sobbing.

The men were already clambering into the boats when Williams hailed them from the main hatch. 'Miss Merryfield, Miss Bessie, wait there. I'll come and get thee.'

'Lower away!' came the signal, the words battered by the wind as the ship's bow began descending into the ocean. Prudence wondered for the first time if these would be her final minutes on this earth. She sent up a silent prayer to commend her soul into God's keeping, then set about taking matters into her own hands.

She watched as the tackle on the starboard side was unhooked and the boat was lowered into the sea. On the port side, the last of the men were climbing into the other boat. So, to port it must be.

'We must get to the port side! Move, you great lump of a girl. I shall set Carp on to you if you do not move this instant. You wicked, wicked girl!' she screamed, and slapped the child across the face with her open hand, then dug her claws into Bessie's upper arm and pulled with all her strength. For a second it seemed as if she might resist, but a lifetime of obedience won out and she allowed Prudence to drag her towards the remaining boat, as the deck tilted beneath their feet. Prudence could feel the ship sliding into the abyss as she staggered towards their only hope. All around them barrels were sliding across the deck. Animals had broken free of their pens and were scrambling upon the slippery deck. The hen coops were adrift, many of the hens appearing drowned from the waves that battered them. The cacophony of the storm, the panicked cries of animals and men were deafening, but despite the din Prudence was conscious of the frantic beating of her heart and the terror that threatened to overcome her.

She took hold of the main mast with one hand, her other locked on to Bessie's arm. They were still several yards from the port-side boat when the ship shuddered, her timbers groaning, and the tackle gave a great snap, so that the boat broke free, spilling its crew into the waves below. Stunned by this development, Prudence could only stop and watch as the boat swung madly in the air. She could vaguely hear Williams calling to them but his voice seemed far away. In that moment, she realised that if they waited for Williams or the boats, it would be too late. They must depend upon themselves alone.

'Take off your cloak and dress, Bessie. They will drag you under,' she ordered as she whipped the cloak from Bessie's shoulders before beginning to remove her own clothes. The cloak came easily, but her fingers fumbled upon the fastenings of her dress, a simple gown of blue India cotton, sprinkled with tiny white roses. The sleeves were shorter and narrower than her usual attire, but it fastened at the back with an interminable row of hooks and eyes. She got halfway before reaching her arms up behind her back and tearing the remainder free. She stumbled free of the dress, then loosened the ties of both petticoats and stepped out.

'Bessie, take off your dress. We must abandon ship! It's the only way.'

But the child did not budge. Nor did she answer. She merely held on to the mast for grim death, the yellow dress clinging to her wetly, her hair glued to her cheeks by the rain.

Prudence was about to bend down and release the ties of her leather slippers when the ship lurched, wrenching her from her feet. She heard herself scream as her body began sliding down the deck. As she scrambled to grab on to something – anything – her hands found the wooden bars of a hen coop, and she held on for her life as barrels rolled past her, and the ship continued its inexorable dive into the sea. She chanced a glance behind her, to see that Bessie still clung to the mast.

The ship groaned again as it listed to port, sending the hen coop careening towards the bulwark. She closed her eyes, sure now that she would meet her end smashed against the ship's timbers or buried in a watery grave. But something in her, some primeval instinct for survival, kept her hands locked around the bars of the cage as it careened through the gap in the bulwark and out over the water, to hit the valley between two mountainous waves and sink beneath the sea.

21

She remembered Miss Merryfield cradling her while water lapped at their feet. She remembered her mistress's soothing words as the water crept past their ankles to their shins; the cabin tipping sideways like an overburdened barrow and the lady crying out as she fell to the deck. She remembered stuffing her pockets with ship's biscuit wrapped in waxed paper and that boy, the one who had barely sprouted whiskers, knocking upon their door at the height of the storm. And finally, Bessie remembered being dragged coughing down a watery passage smelling of soot, and being shoved up a ladder by her mistress.

Or did she?

Surely it couldn't be true? For one thing, Miss Merryfield had never been known to either hug or shove her. She was much too grand to indulge in such vulgar displays. For another, if it were true, then God must have decided to punish Bessie by sending her to Hell. Although, that had always been on the cards, for nobody gives up what was once theirs without a fight, not even the good Lord. And she had escaped him once already.

The only other explanation she could see was that she still slept and the wind and water were all a dream. A nightmare. Like those other dreams that haunted her sleep since she was a wee girl. The ones where her mouth filled with water and her skirt belled out to float like a giant lily pad about her waist. That must be it. She wasn't really standing on a tilting deck lashed by rain and wind, with the ship tossed about by waves as big as mountains. She hadn't just witnessed her mistress strip down to her chemise for all the sailors to see. And she wasn't really stranded on a ship in the middle of the ocean in a hurricane. Soon she would wake in her own little bed in the attic at Westcott Hall.

But when she opened her eyes, she found herself clinging white-knuckled to a mast, the thunder of God's wrath booming in her ears. She knew all about God's wrath, for Mr Custard had talked of it. And this must surely be what he meant, this roaring maelstrom of chaos. In any case, it was all the same to Bessie. Whether she was caught in a dream or a waking nightmare, she wasn't about to let go of the mast. No matter how hard the lady slapped or chided her. No, she might be unschooled, she might be an orphan but she wasn't a fool. She wasn't about to abandon a three-masted barque for a tiny boat crammed to the gunwales with rowdy sailors and only a pair of oars to get them anywhere. She might be an ignorant village girl from Somerset but even she could see that if the ship's boat wasn't dashed to splinters against the hull it would be drowned in the mountainous waves.

Just as one minute a wee girl could be hugging her ma's legs, enveloped in the warmth of woollen skirts, and the next she might be taken by the hand – her ma's familiar chafed hand – and led down the riverbank into the water. She might have her eyes covered by her ma's other hand as the river took them both. Swept from her feet, her hand wrenched away as her ma waded into the deepest part of the river. The heavy stones in her ma's pockets and the wet wool of her petticoats and skirts dragging her to the deep, dark bottom of the river, where only eels and fish and dead people swam. While her child, her terrified,

179

bewildered daughter, thrashed in the freezing river, calling out for her . . .

Until an old man, with a face as worn as old sacking and eyes that crinkled at the corners, pulled her from the water by the only bit of her he could catch – her pigtail – and handed her like a drowning puppy to an old woman.

That dream. She would not go back there. Not ever.

Bessie wasn't stupid enough to be fooled a second time. She wouldn't be lured into the cold dark waters of death again. Not this time. No matter how loudly God or her mistress stormed.

Later, long after the *Kangaroo* lay at the bottom of the ocean and her crew were either dead or gone, all Prudence would recall of the ship's last moments was the flight of the hen coop and a last flash of Bessie's stricken face, before her mouth, nose and eyes filled with saltwater. In that moment, she must have been dragged under by the suction of the sinking vessel, for she surfaced spluttering, gasping for air, with her hands no longer gripping the bars of the hen coop. Terrified, she kicked and paddled, as the dipper had once taught her on that single, happy excursion to the seaside at Sidmouth. All around her the waves rolled in peaks and valleys and she rolled with them, floundering to stay afloat. For despite the almost tepid waters of this tropical sea, she knew she would not be able to keep it up for long.

In the dark of the moonless night she could see little further than a few yards in front of her. But she could hear. Oh, she could hear. She could hear the muffled shouts of men and the roar of the storm. She could hear their cries of fear and the lashing rain pelting the waves.

'Help! Help me!' she cried out. But even to her own ears, her cry sounded feeble, drowned by wind and rain.

A sheep floated by. And another. One dead, one thrashing about like her. And then she heard the faint, plaintive cluck of what could only be a chicken. She turned about in the water, peering into the gloom while struggling not to go under. Not far behind her, she made out the vague outline of a hen coop bobbing on the waves. Her hen coop, she presumed. At the outset of their voyage the coop had housed at least two dozen chickens but most had met their ends on the mess table. Now only one sorry-looking hen perched atop its roof. She could not see any others. The hen coop might once more prove her saviour, if she could only manage to reach it. Already, she was tiring at the unaccustomed movement of her arms and legs, sinking lower with each passing minute.

She took a deep breath, trying not to swallow the salty water, and struck out towards the unlikely boat. Arm over arm, one leg then the other, as hard and fast as she could manage. Yet, although she expended great effort, her reward was pitiful in the giant swell. The coop appeared barely closer but Prudence was not to be thwarted. She had not survived thus far to falter now. She renewed her efforts, thrashing through the waves, her legs beating at the water as if in punishment for the sinking of the *Kangaroo*, the loss of Bessie and any number of the ship's crew. Inch by inch, she crawled closer to the bobbing coop, urged on by the clucking of its solitary survivor until, finally, with heavy legs dragging her down, she grasped a bar of the cage and held on for dear life.

Resting for a moment, buoyed by the coop, she waited for her breathing to slow. Inside the cage, drifting and bumping about, was a clump of dead hens. They must have drowned when the coop hit the water, or before that, when waves crashed upon the deck. The lone survivor had somehow escaped, squeezing between the wooden bars. Or perhaps it had been freed from another damaged coop and sought the only refuge it knew. Now it perched atop the coop, its feathers bedraggled, clucking pitifully.

Nevertheless, she did not fancy spending her last hours with a load of dead chickens. She would have to find a way of getting rid of them, all but her noisy friend. She fumbled for a latch and, finally finding one, opened the hatch door. Then she reached in as far as she could, pulled out as many dead hens as she could grasp and consigned them to the watery depths. When she had finished, she replaced the latch and took a few moments to catch her breath, watched by her fellow survivor. Then, with a last surge of energy, she reached her arms over the roof, levered the coop down and, with the weight of her body and a last kick, she hauled herself aboard. With a bit more luck and a prayer, she hoped that she would not capsize her unlikely craft, or cause it to sink. And for the first time in her life she was glad of her diminutive stature.

At some point in the night Prudence must have fallen asleep, for she woke to weak sunlight and a stiff breeze ruffling her hair. She became conscious of a dull throb to her temples, lips that were pasted together, and a mouth tasting of nothing but salt. She swallowed but could barely summon enough moisture to wet her parched throat. Her hands ached from hours grasping the edges of the coop on its wild ride through the storm. In the night her coop had bumped and jostled flotsam from the wreck, some of which turned out to be the corpses of drowned sailors, so Prudence became reluctant to lift her head and look around.

However, corpses or no, the storm had finally blown itself out and she needed to take stock of her situation. The hen coop rocked on a moderate swell, while the lone hen remained perched alongside her. It appeared to be asleep, legs tucked beneath its body, head nestled between its wings, not worrying for its future. Perhaps if Prudence buried her head in her arms and returned to sleep, when she awoke all would be well. Except, of course, it wouldn't. She would still be bobbing on a hen coop in her chemise somewhere in the Pacific Ocean, and Bessie would still be dead.

Pale-faced, terrified Bessie. For the first time Prudence could remember since she was a child, tears welled, mingling with the salt spray on her cheeks. She must postpone thoughts of Bessie and corpses until later. There would be time enough for guilt and recrimination if she were lucky enough to survive. For survive she was determined to do, she had proved that to herself already.

Forcing herself to action, she pushed up on to her knees and sat back on her heels to consider her situation. She was facing into an early morning sun that peered through banks of low cloud. The rain had worn itself out for the moment. She turned to the south where she believed the Feejee Islands lay. Finding nothing there but the specks of distant seabirds, she swivelled to the west where a barrel and what appeared to be a ship's spar bobbed upon the waves about fifty yards from her raft. With her hopes sinking, she turned northwards.

And there it was. Land. A curve of white sand and green coastline with a mountainous interior, spread before her in the distance. She felt a surge of hope, gasping so loudly that her companion raised her head, ruffled her feathers and stood up with an indignant cluck. There might be people there. There were people everywhere on this earth, weren't there? At least so it seemed. Everywhere that the Englishman ventured, there were people. She remembered her conversation with the captain about the Navigator Isles, with their fierce reputation, and wondered if this land might prove to be one of them. But whether its residents turned out to be fierce or welcoming – whether they greeted her with spears or tea – Prudence had little choice. The nearest land must be her objective.

The wind had shifted in the night and was blowing from the south-east, by her amateurish reckonings. Yet the coast was so far away, too far to swim, and her raft looked to be sailing straight past. Her only other hope was two humpbacked islets rising from the sea between her and the larger landmass. Steep forested hillsides dropped down to shores where waves pounded rocks. Not an inviting prospect. However, the alternative was not to be contemplated. Drifting alone without food or water on a flimsy raft in the vast expanse of the Pacific Ocean, her only hope of rescue a ship happening by – well, that was a fool's dream. No, the wind and currents appeared to be taking her in almost the right direction. Perhaps if she were to enter the water once more she could propel the raft towards one of the islets.

'What do you think, Madame Hen?'

Madame Hen cocked her head to one side and blinked.

'Yes, I think so too.' She would deal with the rocks, and the islands' incumbents, when and if she arrived. *If* being the principle word.

Conscious of the weight of the pockets tied around her waist, she considered what to do with them. Fashioned of linen, and embroidered by her own hand with vines and flowers (not very successfully, she must admit), the pockets now contained all her worldly possessions. Her pocket book and pencil were wrapped in oilcloth and stowed in one pocket, while the other held a small penknife. Briefly, she regretted the ship's biscuit and salt cod lost with Bessie at the bottom of the ocean, but having decided to postpone thoughts of the dear child until later, she would not dwell upon the biscuit either. Well, the pockets would be an added weight in the water. Plus, she was not sure how well the oilcloth would withstand a prolonged ducking. Better to remove them from about her waist, tie their strings to a bar of the coop, leave them atop the raft and hope for the best.

Having dealt with the pockets, she inched towards the edge of the coop and sat with her legs dangling over the side. Her legs were pale, even whiter than her face, which Wills had taken such great pains to protect. Strange, how she rarely considered her legs. They were part of her and yet perpetually hidden from the world. A brief glimpse as her maid slipped a chemise over her head to exchange it for another, a sliver of ankle as she clambered over a stile or mounted a horse. Nannies, governesses, one and all, had discouraged her from regarding herself naked. Yet now, it was these same limbs, naked beneath a flimsy shift, which must save her life.

She slid into the sea with a gentle splash, immediately feeling the choppiness of the waves. Taking hold of a bar in each hand, lest the coop escape her, she let her body stretch out upon the surface of the water. Then, with the most powerful kick she could manage, she set out towards the islets. As she swam, pushing her raft before her, the breeze whipped the waves against her face, filling her mouth with saltwater she had to spit out, and making her eyes sting. Every so often, she paused to check her heading, taking the opportunity to catch her breath. She refused to contemplate what might swim below her, what dangerous sea creatures might lurk below the surface. Only fear and inertia lay in that way of thinking.

As she swam, her legs grew progressively more tired, although the distance to the islets shrank ever so slowly. Once, her long country walks and regular excursions on horseback had given her a certain ladylike vigour but being confined to ship had weakened her. At one point, her heartbeat positively raced when she spotted a group of sleek grey shapes swimming nearby, slipping in and out of the waves. She halted and was about to struggle back aboard her raft for fear of sharks or other fierce denizens of the deep, when one of the creatures erupted into the air in a spinning, twisting leap, before diving back into the sea. She realised that the creatures were dolphins and meant her no harm. The second and then third acrobat soon followed the first, as if the pod was joined in an exuberant dance.

Time passed in a blur of salt spray and tired muscles. Only the height of the sun in the sky gave a clue to how long she had been paddling – perhaps two hours or more. But she was drawing closer, the current and her own unrelenting efforts pulling her towards the two islets. From the little she could discern at sea level, rocks girdled both, but the waves seemed to pound the larger island with less force. And the shore of the smaller islet appeared to be riddled with shallow caves and rocky protuberances. After resting for a few minutes, she set out once more, kicking with what was probably the last of her resources towards the larger islet.

As she drew closer, it became apparent that the rocks facing her were too steep to climb, even if she could avoid being dashed upon them. Her hopes sank and she briefly contemplated hauling herself aboard the raft with the last of her strength and subjecting herself to the whims of fate.

'What should we do, Madame Hen?' she asked, her mouth dry, her throat parched, despite the constant stream of incoming seawater. But Madame Hen did not deign to answer.

'I see. Well, it appears our fates lie in my hands then.'

She could not debate long, for the sea would surely snatch her up and cast her on to the rocks, if she gave in to the tide.

'We only see one corner of the islet. I suppose there may yet be safe harbour around the point.' There may be, but would Prudence have the stamina to resist the waves that were pulling her towards the rocks?

She must. Or it would be the end for both her and Madame Hen.

Redoubling her efforts, she kicked away from the rocks and set a course around the corner of the little island, hoping to find sanctuary. The current fought against her every stroke, but Prudence's will was not so easily resisted. She could not allow herself to be dragged closer, for then there would be no escape. She and her raft would be dashed against the rocks or sucked beneath the surface of the waves. Then everything she had endured would be for nothing. Bessie's death would be for nothing. With no one to remember her, she would be forgotten; her poor short life erased, as if it had never been.

Briefly, Prudence also considered abandoning the additional burden of the hen coop. But it provided buoyancy when she might otherwise sink. It was her only protection in the vast expanse of the ocean.

With every ounce of remaining strength, she propelled the coop adjacent to the islet's shore. Kick by kick, until finally she saw beyond the point of the islet. Beyond the wall of rocks, to a narrow strip of white sand that beckoned her like a welcome mat to sanctuary. With her heart clamouring for rest, and her legs weaker than a newborn foal's, she allowed herself a moment to catch her breath before riding the swell towards the beach.

'We made it, Madame Hen! We are saved!' she gasped, as her feet touched the sandy bottom of a shallow cove at last.

They were saved, her stoic feathered friend and herself. At least, for now.

But not Bessie. Prudence had not saved her maid. To her shame, she had let the girl drown. She should have compelled her to remove her clothes. Dragged her over the side, despite her panic. In her short life, Bessie had grown accustomed to self-reliance. But a child does not always know best. Sometimes an adult has to take charge. Prudence had been content to order Bessie when it suited her own needs, but when it came time for her to step forward and take responsibility, she had failed. Now she would never be able to make amends. She would have to live with the consequences of her inaction, all her remaining days.

Days that might be numbered, if she continued to dwell on what could not be undone. So for the present, she must put aside the past and concentrate on the future.

No doubt the past would return to haunt her soon enough. It always did.

22

Somerset, England

2022

'You're looking wistful, pet,' Jude announced as she entered the shop to the sound of a tinkling bell. 'It's a lovely day. Fancy a walk in your lunch break?'

Bobby had a remarkable facility with human language, for a dog. He could pick out the word 'walk', for example, from an entire Shakespearean soliloquy. So on hearing Jude's invitation, his ears pricked up and he began barking, bouncing from his usual resting place behind the counter to greet his second-favourite human in the world.

'Hi, Jude. Just doing a virtual stocktake. You know, trying to fix a picture of the store in my memory before it disappears forever.'

Eliza surveyed the shop floor as she spoke, her eyes lingering on her latest tableau atop a nineteenth-century French elm and fruitwood dresser. She had picked up a set of wonderful old hat blocks on pewter stands at a recent estate sale and coupled them with a framed 1854 map of the Malay Archipelago by John Tallis, two top hats in excellent condition and an Edwardian gentleman's travelling case. It might very well be one of her last displays.

'You're sounding very melodramatic this morning,' Jude said, placing her bag on a handy milking stool and bending to give Bobby a pat.

Just for a second, Eliza wished she were getting a pat from her aunt too. She wouldn't even object to a pat on the head, although a shoulder rub would be nicer.

'I'm feeling very melodramatic. I feel as if a villain is hiding behind that hand-painted canvas screen, twirling his moustaches. Any minute, he'll leap out and foreclose on the heroine's property and she'll be left sobbing and homeless.'

'No joy from your landlord then?'

'No. And the whole thing is so impersonal. I hate it. Everything is done through solicitors and agents.'

'Probably for the best, love. Sobbing all over a stranger might not help matters.'

'I never sob. When did you last see me sob?' she said, crossing her fingers behind her back at this demonstrable falsehood. Her only defence was that Jude hadn't been there to see her teary-eyed moment of weakness in front of Daniel on 'the Day of the Letter', nor her inexplicable behaviour at the pub on 'the Day of the Phone Call', as she had come to think of them.

'A few tears can be cathartic, I always say.'

'Well, I find them debilitating.'

Just then the bell tinkled again, causing both women to look to the shop door where Jan, their local postwoman, entered, leaving her trolley outside in the entrance.

'I thought I'd hand this one to you rather than slipping it under the door,' she said, passing Eliza a large pea-green envelope with a fancy printed return address in the top left-hand corner.

'How's the sciatica, Jan?' asked Jude.

Eliza was convinced that her aunt knew everyone living or working within a ten-mile radius. She kept expecting to be proved wrong, but so far her theory had proved unshakeable.

'That physio you recommended has got me moving again.'

The two older women turned to Eliza, staring pointedly at the envelope.

'Odd colour for an envelope,' said Jude.

'I prefer it to those black ones people are using for greetings cards, these days,' said Jan. 'Not very cheerful.'

'All right, all right, I'll open it.'

Eliza retreated to her office to grab a letter opener, Bobby following hopefully. He hadn't forgotten about the 'walk', even if the women had. When she returned, Jan had her foot up on the counter and was reaching hopefully towards her toes.

'Ah, sorry, Eliza,' she said, replacing her leg on the floor. 'Just demonstrating the hamstring stretch the physio set me.'

'No problem. What are counters for?' she replied with a smile.

She slit open the envelope – having already ascertained that it was from Harold Hobbs, owner of that prodigious collection of Prudence memorabilia – and withdrew a sheet of paper that had been folded over several times. She unfolded the paper and laid it upon the counter to reveal a poster showing an intricate web of names and dates.

'It looks like a family tree,' said Jan.

'It looks like *our* family tree,' said Jude expectantly.

'How exciting . . . well, I'd better be off,' Jan announced, her curiosity sated, 'before someone makes off with the trolley.'

Once she was gone, Eliza and Jude settled their elbows on the counter to consider the family tree. Eliza began her study with her own name. It was situated towards the bottom of the page, a single short line extending above it to her parents. They were, in turn, connected to her aunt horizontally, and above them to her grandfather, George, who was connected to his wife, Frances, and his brother, Edward. And above and beside them was woven a whole retinue of interconnected souls, extending back in time to the 1600s.

Eliza was connected to this web by that single thread only. She had no other lines, joining her to partner, sibling or child.

'Here we are,' said Jude, tapping at her name and Eliza's with her forefinger. 'And here's your newfound friend and relation, Harold Hobbs. No progeny either, I see.'

'He told me he was too busy working for the foreign office to have time for a family. I wondered if he might not have been a spy.'

'Really? MI5 or some such? Did he look . . . secretive?'

'Not really. Rather ordinary, in fact,' said Eliza, picturing the nondescript Harold, with his bonhomie and his mojitos, ensconced in the midst of the New Forest.

'I believe they like them ordinary.'

Harold appeared at the bottom of his line of descent, belonging to the same generation as Jude. And like Jude, he had no recorded children. His grandfather, Charles, had been brother to Jude's grandfather (Eliza's great-grandfather), Winston, and their sister, Elizabeth. Drawn irresistibly to this map of her family, Eliza traced along the branches with her finger, following the trail of her forebears to a point in the 1830s where she expected to find Prudence, first wife to Edward Ambrose and the last of the Merryfields. A woman with no issue, no child to link her to the future. She too was out on a limb, all alone.

Prudence Merryfield (1797 – ?)

That nine-point Cambria question mark symbolised the mystery that had haunted Eliza's family for seven generations. Prudence's disappearance heralded the slow decline of the Ambroses. It was as if the speculation that surrounded her vanishing sapped the lifeblood of the family. Cursing its descendants. Instead of multiplying, they remained few. Their wealth dissipated. Eliza didn't mind about the wealth so much, it was the loss of family that hurt.

And that question mark still tantalised her. How and when

had Prudence died? Had Edward been responsible for her death, disposing of her body somewhere in the grounds, as legend had suggested, where it had remained undiscovered for almost two centuries? With Prudence out of the way he would have been free to marry and beget a dynasty, albeit a short-lived one.

Then again, Eliza remembered the watercolours lining the walls of cousin Harold's study. The ones depicting the island of Samoa were lively. The palm fronds shimmered pale green in the sunlight; the houses were arranged like a storybook village around a central lawn. The people were all engaged in activity: fishing, swimming, cooking, even dancing, in what would have been a hot, tropical climate. The colours were pretty yet muted, the whole scene permeated with an atmosphere of longing. Perhaps when Prudence disappeared for that second time, she went of her own accord, escaping her life in Somerset to travel the world once more. She hadn't been murdered by persons unknown. She may even have returned to Samoa.

Whatever happened to her, that tiny question mark nagged, like a puzzle Eliza could not ignore.

'It's getting a bit thin, isn't it?' said Jude, interrupting her thoughts.

'Hmm, what is?'

'The old family tree. Needs some new blood.' Her aunt gave her a gentle nudge in the ribs. 'Daniel seems keen.'

'Oh my God, Jude. You're incorrigible! Why don't you just hang a sign around my neck saying "available". Daniel and I are working together. That's all. He's not interested in me romantically.'

The man had made that abundantly clear. It was only her heartbeat that had quickened at their kiss; only her legs that had wobbled in a most unbusinesslike manner at his touch. He was immune. Indifferent. Professional. No, she would stick to furniture – and Prudence – for the moment. Love could wait.

She needed to solve the problem of her store. She also needed to discover what had happened to her not-quite ancestor. There, beside Prudence on the family tree, was Edward Ambrose – and at his other side, his third wife, Eliza's great-great-something-or-other-grandmother.

'Anyway,' she added, determined to quell any more of her aunt's hints, '*you* never saw fit to add to the tree, did you?'

She could have bitten her tongue when she saw regret shadow her aunt's face.

'No, pet, I let disappointment turn me from that path. I made the village my family instead. But you don't have to do the same,' Jude said, her voice croaky.

'I'm sorry, darling Jude. I shouldn't have said that.'

'Not to worry,' Jude said after a moment. 'Things have a way of sorting themselves out.' She waved her hand in the air as if she were coaxing fate in her preferred direction.

'I hope so.'

'Well, what do you say to a walk? I know I have at least one vote in favour.' Her aunt regarded her with a thoughtful smile.

'Why are you looking at me like that? As if I'm one of your lost causes?' Eliza asked.

'Not lost, pet. Only waylaid,' Jude murmured.

Eliza was about to fire off a retort but the words didn't come. Was her aunt right? Had she lost her way? Is that why her feelings about the store had become so ambivalent recently? The question ricocheted like a pinball pinging through her thoughts. Is that why she had stopped looking for even a part-time lover? Let alone a forever partner. Because she didn't know where she was headed any more?

'Don't worry,' Jude said, enveloping her in a hug. 'You'll find your path again.'

Would she, though? Eliza wasn't so sure.

*

That night, while Bobby chased rabbits in his sleep on the rug at her feet, Eliza sat at her kitchen table with a bulging folder of clippings, printouts and photographs spread before her. She had always been tactile, drawn to texture, form and touch. Shuffling and rearranging paper helped her think.

She placed Harold's family tree on the table and began fanning out other documents and images around it: various historical renderings of Westcott Hall; the photographs Daniel had taken of Prudence's watercolours; clippings from newspapers of the day, variously reporting the wreck of the *Kangaroo*, the fate of its crew, Prudence's rescue and return to England, followed by her ensuing notoriety and subsequent second disappearance.

There was an historic 1834 pamphlet entitled *Narrative of the Shipwreck, Privations and Miraculous Rescue of Miss Prudence Merryfield*, which Eliza had purchased on eBay for $48; a copy of a newspaper report into the second disappearance sourced through the newspaper archives; and a sensational news article from 1838 speculating on what may have befallen Prudence. And in the middle of these documents, at the very centre of the mystery, Eliza placed the pocket book with its missing pages.

'What happened to you, Prudence?' she whispered, staring at the pocket book.

At some point, Prudence had written the year 1833 under the original year of the pocket book of 1832. And then, someone had ripped out the middle pages, removing the last months of the diary together with the section which, in other *Peacock's Polite Repositories* Eliza had seen, held the account-keeping pages. That left only such useful information as the almanac and a list of empire dignitaries. Presumably, those missing pages might give a more accurate account of Prudence's adventure. But since Eliza didn't possess the missing pages, she would have to make do with what she did have.

She flicked through the tattered pages of the *Narrative*, her eyes scanning the story she knew so well, hoping inspiration would strike. The account was undeniably embroidered. Written by one C. D. Prendergast, a supposed 'associate' of the ship's first mate, its language was extravagant and highly coloured. The portrayal of the Samoans was condescending, with the usual racist nineteenth-century overtones. And it depicted Prudence as a hapless, helpless spinster cast adrift in a hostile world. Yet it did contain the basic facts of the sinking of the *Kangaroo*, the marooning of Prudence on a tiny island off the coast of Samoa's main island, the voyage by boat of the ship's surviving crew and her maid, Bessie Pike, to the island of Tutuila. It also told of the arrival of Edward Ambrose in Samoa to 'rescue' Prudence and return her to England.

Something about the *Narrative* nagged at her.

Picking up the pocket book, she turned to the diary section. The leaves of the book were ever so slightly warped, the print sometimes blurred, as if it had met with a dousing at some stage and then had its pages dried in the sun. Had this little leather-bound book, small enough to fit in her hand, accompanied Prudence on her sojourn on that island? Had it been marooned with her? Eliza would probably never know for certain, but instinct told her so.

She turned the pages for January, February, March, April, May, her hands so gentle as to almost caress the paper. And then, in the second week of June, a name leaped out at her.

Thursday: Returned from seaside. Wills most put out with Bessie. Edward at luncheon again. Five courses.

Bessie.

Of course! Bessie replaced Wills in the diary entries once Prudence departed England. Bessie replaced Wills as Prudence's maid – a young woman known as Bessie Pike.

Elizabeth Pike.

Eliza shuffled the papers once more, searching for the family tree amongst the other documents. Finding it, she ran her eyes over the paper to the higher branches of the tree until she found what she was looking for. Nestled on the same branch as her ancestor Edward Ambrose and his first wife, the enigmatic Prudence, was her great-great-something-or-other-grandmother. Elizabeth Pike. Prudence's maid Bessie was Eliza's ancestor. At some point after Prudence disappeared, she and Edward had married.

And that hinted at a whole other story.

The rule of thumb for proceeding with criminal charges was motive, means and opportunity. If Edward, as husband, and Bessie, as lady's maid, both lived in close proximity with Prudence, then opportunity to do her harm would have presented itself regularly. And in a large house with extensive outbuildings and parkland, means must also have been to hand. Motive, then, was key. And what better motive than a romantic association between Edward and Bessie?

Prudence disappeared in 1838. According to the family tree, Edward and Elizabeth did not wed until 1845. Seven years would allow for his previous wife to be declared legally dead, and also plenty of time for suspicion to become less acute. The new bride was still young enough to bear children. And with the passage of time and the proclivity of families to bury their dirty linen, future generations need never know that Elizabeth Pike had once worked as lady's maid to Prudence Merryfield.

'Well, Bobby, that sets a cat amongst the pigeons, doesn't it? Now we have two potential murderers in the family tree.' Perhaps even a conspiracy. That is, if Prudence did not simply disappear of her own volition. That remained a possibility.

Eliza shifted her attention back to the photographs taken in Harold's study. There was a rather clumsy sketch of a woman in early Victorian dress hastening through woodland; a picture of a man and a woman riding across parkland; and a drawing room scene of two women at their embroidery. But it was the Samoan studies that captured her attention the most. The village in these watercolours was certainly appealing, with its open-sided houses, neat paths and swaying palms. In one sketch, a family sat upon woven mats under a domed roof eating dinner: a man, a woman, a girl on the verge of adolescence, and two teenage boys. In another sketch, the same girl waded through thigh-deep water with a friend, long sticks in hand, two small islands floating upon the distant horizon. In all the paintings, sky and sea shimmered like jewels. Light danced softly through trees. A haze of nostalgia and yearning drifted over each scene.

Or Eliza was making way too much of an amateur artist's style.

And then there was the sketch inscribed with Bessie's name. That bright copper hair and yellow gown gusting in the wind. A sturdy ship's rail painted a dark umber. Azure sky dotted with gulls. Midnight-blue ocean stretching to the horizon. There was nothing limpid or misty about this portrait. Bessie battled the wind. She fought the elements.

One thing was certain. Both Prudence and Bessie had proved themselves to be survivors. They travelled across the world, one woman and a teenage girl. They endured shipwreck in a wild storm in the South Pacific. Separated and possibly fearing each other dead, they survived being stranded in a strange land far from home. Both found their way back to England. Then one woman disappeared again.

Forever.

Was she murdered? Or did she choose her destiny?

23

South Pacific

1833

'You must come now, Bessie.'

Someone was talking to her. Not her mistress, who had ordered her to fling herself into the ocean, but a deeper voice that coaxed like a mother to her babe.

'We must away. Afore we drown,' cooed the voice, almost obliterated by the roar around them.

Bessie knew the voice only teased, for drowning was inevitable now. All she could do was hold to the mizzenmast for these last precious minutes. Water slashed at her face and hands, needling her skin and pummelling her body through the cloak. The sea had already taken half the crew, snatching their boat before it could be lowered and hurling it into the waves. She did not want to die that way. She had resisted her mistress's urgings. The *Kangaroo* was about to go down, she could see that. But why hasten her death just to please her mistress?

Despite the slashing rain, she felt an arm enfold her, reaching around her shoulders to whip away her cloak, Miss Merryfield's cast-off cloak of dark green wool. She shivered at its loss as the world tilted beneath her feet. Opening her eyes to the stinging rain, she watched that world sliding away. Goats, chickens, barrels. A hen coop. A half-naked woman in nought but her chemise. All sliding down the deck of the ship to their death. Only Bessie's arms, encircling the mast, prevented her from joining them. Soon the ship would drag her into the sea too.

'Come now, Bessie. I have you.'

The voice spoke again through the tumult around her. She thought it was that boy, Williams, the one with the kindly manner, but she dare not turn to look. If she let go of the mast, the only solid thing in the world, she would be lost.

'No,' she heard herself whimper. 'Go away.'

It was not to be. Hands that belonged to the voice wrenched her arms loose from the mast. She tried to resist, reaching out for her anchor, except the hands were stronger than expected, hands accustomed to hauling ropes and painting tar. Too forceful to be resisted, they dragged her from mast to rigging, to ship's rail.

'I can hold you aloft in the sea but you must be shed of the gown and petticoats or they will drag you to the bottom.'

She felt him press her against the bulwark. Then a wrench as her dress, her beautiful yellow dress, was torn from collar to waist, popping open hooks and eyes all the way down the front of the bodice. Another wrench, as he dragged the gown to her feet. Then her petticoats followed. She tried to cover her body, bare but for her shift, but to no avail. Then, as she huddled cowering against the rail, those same hands shoved her over the bulwark to tumble backwards through rain, wind and salt air.

Pain lashed her body as she hit the water and the waves closed over her head. She sank beneath the surface as water shot up her nose and stung her eyes with salt. She should have known this was coming. She should have known you could escape your doom but once. She had told Miss Merryfield it was her time.

And Bessie almost believed her own words. Almost believed those fears she had carried as long as she could remember. Except a tiny flame, an instinct for self-preservation and a hunger for air that would not be denied, urged her to kick upwards. She scrabbled at the water, fighting to reach the surface, emerging long seconds later, gasping and swallowing seawater. Lost in a valley amidst mountainous waves, she struggled not to be sucked under again. She did not want to be taken, no matter how she had sinned, how her mother had sinned.

She did not want to die.

A hand grabbed her arm. Perhaps the same hand as earlier but she could not tell in the darkness, immersed as she was in this frightening expanse of sea. She only knew that a head and shoulders swam alongside her and a voice inside her head urged her to follow. And she did, as best she could, working her legs and allowing herself to be half towed along as she and the boy fought to be free of the ship before it was lost beneath the waves. It creaked and clanked, and bellowed and groaned as it met its death knell. She did not need to be a fine lady with her books or a captain with his charts to know that as the ship sank into the ocean it would pull anything in its path down with it. And that included Bessie.

She was awake now and she did not have to let it take her. The man she called 'Granfer' had saved her once when she was too small to save herself. Now he was gone and she must do the rescuing. The flame flickered within her, forcing her onwards, when she might have given up, so that she made slow headway up one watery slope and down into a trough. Up another slope and down into—

A boat. She heard men shouting before she made out the dim shape of it looming out of the storm. She felt the boy's hand urging her onwards, even as the ship and the storm tried to hold her back.

'Give me your hand, lass,' rasped a voice from the boat.

She reached up with her free hand, water filling her mouth as she stretched shoulder and arm out of the waves. Her other arm was freed as the man in the boat clasped her wrist and hauled her into the boat, almost wrenching her arm from its socket. She was aware of voices raised above the noise of the storm, and the boat tilting as her companion was brought to safety too. Then, lying on the hard wet planks of the ship's cutter, she curled into a ball, closed her eyes and pretended it had all been just another bad dream.

It was thirst that roused Prudence. She came to her senses lying on her side with her cheek, shoulder, hip and thigh creating a sinuous hollow in the sand. The rhythmic swish of the sea sounded in her ears. Seagulls called to one another somewhere high above, and a breeze played across her bare limbs. She could feel the tightness of salt drying on her skin and the sting of hot sun on her face. Her mouth felt as if it were filled with sand and her head with rocks. None of this was pleasant, but it was her gritty mouth, parched throat and pounding head that roused her.

Struggling to her knees, she willed her legs to stand, for they ached more than they would after a long ride. Then, with one hand shading her eyes from the midday sun, she surveyed her surroundings. The sea spread to the horizon, white caps dotting a shifting sheet of blue, with the green islet she had passed in the early hours the only other landmass in sight. The small island on which she was stranded ascended to a forest-covered ridge several hundred feet tall. She was standing on a narrow stretch of sand guarded by rocky shelves and cliffs at either end of the beach. Coconut palms ruffled in the breeze along the shore, and through the palms she could see a forest of tallish trees with slender trunks topped by lush green foliage. Which was all very picturesque, except she saw no sign of her immediate need – a stream. Still, she had survived a storm, a veritable maelstrom. Such a deluge must have resulted in pools of fresh water. She would just have to find them, and sooner rather than later.

She was about to set off in search of just such a pool when she remembered two things: the pockets – containing her sole possessions in the world in which she now found herself – and Madame Chicken. The pockets, she was relieved to see, were still sitting atop the hen coop a few paces up the beach, but Madame Chicken was nowhere to be seen. To her surprise, the discovery almost brought a tear to her eye. And for no discernible reason she was suddenly flooded with an overwhelming sense of loss. As if everything and everyone in the world had been stolen from her. Even a chicken. As far as she knew she was the sole survivor of the *Kangaroo*, about to brave who knew what dangers. So even a chicken would be welcome company, if not security.

She thrust the feeling aside, to contemplate another day. Loss would not kill her. Thirst certainly would. Concave rocks suggested themselves as the most likely source of fresh water, so she set off along the beach towards a shelf of rock jutting into the sea below the cliffs. She had lost her shoes during the night and picked her way along the beach, feeling each sharp shell fragment and pebble protruding from the sand. Drifts of seaweed, greying coconut husks and the carcasses of various crustaceans littered the beach. And amongst this detritus, washed up on the beach – not unlike herself – she encountered flotsam from the wreckage of the *Kangaroo*: a cask, several planks of wood, the remnants of what appeared to be bedding. She bent to inspect the stencilled marks upon the cask, hoping it might contain something of use – even a keg of rum would be welcome in her present situation – only to discover the staved-in bottom.

Disappointed, she resumed her trudge up the beach, trying to ignore the blood oozing from a cut beneath her foot and the burning sun upon her bare neck and shoulders. She would have to find something to bind her feet later. Upon reaching the end of the beach, she picked her way over the rocks, skirting tidal pools encrusted with several kinds of shellfish, to seek out those rocks beyond the reach of the tide, where she hoped to find rainwater. Finally, at the foot of soaring cliffs, she knelt before a large concave rock in which a pool of water had collected. She scooped up a few mouthfuls and swallowed greedily, half expecting to spit it out again. But the water was sweet. Sweeter to her parched lips than the most expensive bottle of Château d'Yquem.

She drank her fill, then sat back against the rock and pondered what to do next. There was no precedent in any of her previous experience or education for the situation in which she now found herself. Her father's library held numerous instructional works: such useful tomes as *The Honours of the Table* with its instructions on the art of carving a joint and directions for going to market, plus several other manuals for the edification of young women. But this knowledge was of small use in her current circumstances. Nor did her *Polite Repository* – which in the normal course of events she could rely upon for such essential information as its table of weights and measures, its guide to places of general resort in London and Westminster, or its full list of the baronets of England – suggest any course of action. Even the scant knowledge she had garnered in conversation with Bobbett about the care and feeding of horses, or with Edward about animal husbandry, was of little efficacy when marooned in the middle of an ocean.

Prudence was quite alone in her predicament.

Unless, of course, she wasn't.

By luck, or God's good grace, she had been washed ashore on an island. A tiny island, to be sure, but that did not mean it was uninhabited. Perhaps the thing to do now was to discover whether she had neighbours. Neighbours who might be prevailed upon to furnish her with some form of garment, for she could not in all modesty continue in her flimsy cotton chemise, especially as ragged as it had become during the privations of the previous night. And more urgently perhaps, they might provide her with sustenance and shelter. If such kind neighbours could be discovered, she would do her utmost to repay their kindness.

Yes, that was the thing to do. She would climb to the highest point of this island and search for signs of habitation. But first, she would avail herself of several of the shellfish she had spied clinging to rocks in the tidal pools. She might not have the appropriate condiments or cream sauces to hand but at least she had her penknife. The creatures could not be so far different to an oyster or a scallop, could they? And hunger gnawed loudly and importunately at her stomach.

Late afternoon found Prudence sitting under the shade of a coconut palm, the sand around her littered with the cast-off remnants of a scant meal, contemplating the remains with dismay. Her efforts at food gathering had taken most of the afternoon, yet she was still ravenously hungry – and sorely wounded. She had torn a strip from the hem of her chemise and wound it around a deep cut on her left hand where she had stabbed herself trying to prise a particularly stubborn shellfish from a rock pool. The fact that it clung like a limpet to the rock suggested that it might indeed have been one. After that misadventure, she restricted herself to gathering a creature that more closely resembled an oyster and tasted largely of saltwater. None of this boded well for the future.

She flinched as a thud sounded behind her, but upon turning was relieved to see that the culprit was merely a falling coconut, not a dangerous creature about to pounce upon its prey. The sight of the fallen coconut lifted her spirits somewhat, for it reminded her of the delicious coconut dishes, both sweet and savoury, that she had tasted in Singapore and at the port of Makassar. She could also fill the emptied shell with fresh water.

The Keepsake

A coconut might be just the thing, if she could find a way to crack one open. Perhaps the rocks might provide an answer.

She picked up the fallen coconut and carried it down the beach towards the tidal pools, wading through shallows to avoid the worst of the broken shells that lay in wait for her poor feet. Her legs protested at each step, still aching from her exertions of the night before, coupled with her efforts at food gathering. Her arms were pink from the sun and she dared not contemplate what the sting of her nose and cheeks might suggest. Rest in the shade of the coconut palms tempted her, but soon it would be too dark to collect more food and water. She must make the most of the remaining daylight.

Upon reaching the tidal pools once more, she searched for a suitable flat shelf of rock and set about the business of opening the coconut. Its shell was a daunting barrier but hunger was a powerful motivation. She raised her arms above her head, closed her eyes, and cast the coconut to the rocks with as much force as she could muster. But when she opened her eyes, hoping to find the coconut dashed to pieces upon the ground, she was disappointed to see that it was still intact. In fact, after smashing the coconut to the ground numerous further times, her arms protesting in pain, the coconut remained in one piece, and Prudence could barely hold back her tears.

How was she to survive alone on this slab of rock if she could not feed herself? The island bristled with coconut palms. Its shores were encrusted with shellfish. Yet if Prudence could not avail herself of them, they may as well not exist. The coconut lay at her feet, battered but impenetrable. She hung her head, arms dangling at her sides, palms stinging from the rough surface of the fruit. The ragged shift barely covered her body; it was torn, and stained with salt and droplets of blood from the cut to her hand. Tears rolled down her face, to mingle with the salt crusted on her cheeks. She had failed. Just as she had failed in her desire to become a woman of independent means. As she had failed in her bid to manage her own affairs, or attain her freedom. As she had failed to save Bessie.

Stripped of her fine gowns and estate, of her laundry maid and gardener, of her coachmen and her cook, it was evident that Prudence was incapable of taking care of herself or indeed any other soul. She had few accomplishments and fewer skills.

She was a person of consequence to no one. Not even herself.

Sunday: Cast adrift on island. Bessie lost. Oysters au naturel. Starvation threatens. Losing hope.

24

Samoa

1833

Lupelele was sweeping the paths surrounding the fale where her father lived. Where she had lived before her mother died and she moved to the aualuma of girls and single women. It was nearing the end of the rainy season that lasted almost half the year, and the paths were wet and littered with debris. Two days ago, the rain had been so heavy they heard it coming several minutes before it arrived, striking the plate-like leaves of the breadfruit trees in a noisy deluge. Everyone had leaped into action: gathering all the cloth spread out to dry in the sun; securing the food baskets out of the rain; bringing the tame pigeons inside; paddling the canoes in from the lagoon and lashing them down near the houses. Sometimes the storms were so severe that the winds seemed to come from every direction at once, tearing roofs from buildings and destroying crops. This time, they were lucky.

This time, the storm's centre had been further out to sea so most of the buildings were still standing. But the winds had destroyed much of the breadfruit crop and blown down several ageing coconut palms. They had also damaged several houses and strewn tree branches and palm fronds from one end of the village to the other, all leading to a great deal of cleaning up. Lupe's arms were tired from sweeping, while her ears were sore from listening to her aunt giving her never-ending instructions.

Some of the men were still at work repairing the damage to the coconut leaf roofs or tidying the gardens, while the older women mended the plaited blinds that were rolled down at night. Masina had tasked her sons Fata and Tuna with putting the garden to rights and clearing the lawn of strewn branches and other debris, while Lupe laid the sleeping mats in the sun to dry and swept the paths and terraces around their family fales. By now, most of the other children were swimming, catching waves in the lagoon or playing wrestling games on the beach. Meanwhile, she and her cousins were still shackled to their allotted tasks.

'She's gone!' Fata shouted, sinking to the grass beside her.

Lupe pricked up her ears and turned to watch Masina striding towards the gardens on the outskirts of the village – no doubt in search of Lupe's father. There the taro leaves grew on tall stems that sprouted waist high from a single bulbous edible root, and the banana trees hung with tall clusters of fruit as heavy as a small child. Along with the ocean and the coconut palms, the taro gardens and breadfruit trees provided the main foodstuffs of the village.

'I thought she'd never leave,' she said, as Masina disappeared through the breadfruit trees. She threw back her head and stretched her arms behind her back.

'Let's go before she changes her mind and makes us rebuild the whole village,' Tuna said, turning to his brother and cousin with a mischievous look.

Lupe needed no further encouragement. 'Race you to the point!' she called into the wind, as she took off in the direction of the beach without waiting for a reply. She was fast but so were her cousins. Much as she disliked admitting it, they were taller and stronger and she needed every advantage she could get to outrun them.

She ran past a group of boys engaged in a tag-team wrestling match, spurred on by their friends. A few of her youngest cousins were playing in the shallows with toy canoes made from leaves, while out in the lagoon the older girls and boys were surfing waves churned up by the storm swell. Lupe ignored them all, content to feel the warm breeze ruffling her hair and the long leafy streamers of her skirt trailing in her wake as she sprinted towards the point at the other end of the beach. Behind her she could hear the squeak of sand as her cousins inched closer with every breath, and she pumped her arms harder, urging her legs onwards.

Fata and Tuna were nudging her heels by the time she spotted several strange objects, most unlike the usual refuse washed up on the beach after a storm. Her cousins noticed them too, slowing their pace so that all three came to a halt a short distance from the storm-wracked refuse.

'What's that?' Fata asked, pointing to a wooden object washed up at the tideline amongst the leathery ribbons of seaweed and the scattered driftwood.

'It looks like a pigeon cage.' It reminded her of the cages in which the chiefs kept their tame pigeons, only much larger. It was big enough to house an entire flock of pigeons.

'Look at these!' said Tuna. A few strides further along, several other strange wooden objects lay half sunk in the wet sand. Shaped like coconuts, except flat at both ends, they seemed to be constructed of planks like the large canoes the men used for hunting atu. Tuna drew back his foot and kicked the smallest one, only to discover with a yelp that it was either solid or filled with something heavy.

'Owww!' he cried, hopping about on his uninjured foot. 'Why didn't you warn me?'

'How could I know?' laughed Fata, bumping his brother with his hip so that he fell to the sand. 'You're the one who kicked it. Why didn't you pick it up and test it first?'

Lupe left her cousins to the bickering that would inevitably turn into a wrestling match, and opted to inspect a patch of bright yellow drifting in the lagoon. It floated in the shallows like a length of siapo, only rather than the reds and browns of fine bark cloth it was the yellow of a pua flower. She waded into the water, her feet tripping lightly along the sandy bottom of the lagoon. The sound of her cousins' bickering and the squawk of seabirds merged with the distant crash of waves upon the reef as she waded towards the mysterious object. On drawing closer, she saw that the patch of yellow was indeed a kind of textile, like nothing she had ever seen before. And dotted upon the yellow background was a field of tiny blue flowers. She gathered the waterlogged fabric towards her and returned to the beach where Fata and Tuna were rolling, oblivious, in the sand.

She draped the fabric against her shoulder and let it fall dripping to the ground around her bare feet. It appeared to be a garment of some kind, but much longer than the skirts worn by the men and women of her village. In fact, it was so long that it would have covered a grown woman from shoulders to ankles. And attached to it were two other lengths of fabric that looked like they were meant to cover the arms. It was the strangest garment that Lupe had ever seen.

Although it was wet, it wasn't damaged by its ducking, as siapo would have been, so she decided to wring out the water and try it on. She began at the end that seemed to be the neck opening and worked her way towards the feet, squeezing as much water as she could from the soaked garment. Then she held the garment level with her knees and stepped into it, trying not to let the wet material stick to her body. She hauled it up to her shoulders and squirmed her arms into the bulky coverings. It was unpleasantly heavy with the weight of water and the voluminous length of the fabric. Even if it were dry, how could a person run, jump or climb in such a garment? How could they work in the garden, build a house or paddle a canoe in such a silly piece of clothing? But perhaps it was not designed for ordinary wear. Perhaps it was the ceremonial garment of a chief or a village maiden from a land far away.

Or perhaps it was a garment worn by the papālagi.

The sound of smothered laughter interrupted her thoughts and she turned to see her cousins whispering to each other.

'She looks like a giant banana,' Fata was sniggering quietly to his brother.

He would not be rude enough to say this to her face, since it would break all rules of politeness between the women and men of the family.

'Or a giant yellow sea cucumber,' Tuna replied, smothering a laugh unsuccessfully.

'What was that, cousin?' she called.

'Oh, nothing. Only where did you find that thing, Lupe?' Fata asked, widening his eyes innocently when he realised she had been listening to them.

'It was washed up in the storm. Perhaps it came from the same place as those other things,' she said, nodding towards the unusual flotsam scattered along the beach.

'Perhaps it came from the papālagi,' said Tuna. 'Perhaps a pālagi canoe was wrecked in the storm.'

Lupe had been wondering the very same thing. The only pālagi man they knew had been cast up on their shores the year her mother died. Washed up on the beach like the strange yellow garment. But that man had worn nothing but a brown, two-legged covering. Unlike the men of Samoa, he had no tattoos upon his lower body, only the leg coverings. His face was red from the sun, but beneath their coverings his legs were as pale as sand.

It was said that he had swum to the village from a giant pālagi canoe, sailing past the island out beyond the reef, for a canoe so large could not enter the lagoon. He had stayed in their guest fale for a time, learning a few words of their language, helping with the fishing, and contributing greatly to the eating. But then one day he was gone and he did not return. Lupe heard tell he had gone to Apia, where it was said there were other papālagi. But mostly she thought no more about it, for that was the year of the great sickness, the sickness that had taken her mother, her uncle and many other villagers.

'Those papālagi are strange. So it may be so,' Fata said. 'I've heard tell they bring news of a powerful god.'

The people of her village had met only that single pale-skinned runaway, but the papālagi visited other villages in their enormous ocean-going canoes – not always happily – and the Samoans had heard rumours of their existence from the Tongans, long before they arrived in their islands.

Lupe picked up the long yellow skirt and flung it around, flicking droplets of water at her cousins.

'I want to try it,' Tuna said.

'I'm sorry, cousin, you know you can't touch any of my clothes.'

'But is it yours, Lupe, or a thing that belongs to the papālagi?'

Fata had a point, but she was not in a mood to listen. Listening was not one of her strong points.

'It's mine because I found it!' she said, forgetting politeness in the urgency of retaining possession of the garment. She skipped out of her cousin's way, just in case he abandoned politeness too and lunged for the hem of the yellow skirt.

'But if we ask nicely, you must give it to us,' Fata said. He gazed at her with his broad smile, as if the thing he asked was quite reasonable.

'I don't want to.'

It was hers. Gifts might be their custom, but her cousins could ask nicely as many times as they liked and still she would not give it to them. She had waded into the sea and rescued it from the storm. If she gave it to her cousins, she might never get it back. But if she did not take immediate action, they might decide to call in reinforcements – and reinforcements usually meant her aunt.

Lupe took off. She picked up the heavy yellow skirts that dragged around her legs and headed for a small dugout canoe she spotted beached in the wet sand by the shore. Despite her intentions, her progress was more of a clumsy lurch than a sprint. Behind her she could hear her cousins' laughter. With luck they would forget about the yellow dress, forget about her. In any case, by the time they remembered, she would be out on the water, out of sight and mind. Well, she would be, if she could just manage to push the canoe into the water without tangling her legs in the long yellow skirt first.

With her feet sinking in wet sand, the strange garment clinging to her body and wrapping itself around her legs, she struggled to heave the small outrigger across the sand and into the water. She tripped over once, then picked herself up and forged ahead, breathing a sigh of relief when she felt the canoe lift from the sand to float freely in the shallows.

She was just about to slide it further into the lagoon when she sensed ripples, as if someone waded into the water behind her, and heard a voice that sent tingles down her spine.

'Lupelele! Where do you think you are going? And what is that you're wearing?'

She wanted to shut her ears, to close her eyes and wish she were far away. She wanted to pretend that she had not heard her aunt speak at all.

'Do not ignore me, girl.'

She turned to face her aunt, keeping hold of the canoe with one hand as it bobbed in the shallows. There was something about Masina that refused to be ignored. Or perhaps, the truth was that Lupe did not yet have the courage to ignore her, for that would mean defying custom, defying her whole village.

'I'm going for a paddle . . . Mother,' she said, lowering her eyes to stare at the water lapping about her aunt's knees.

'You are *not* going for a paddle. If you are finished sweeping, you can help me set the aualuma to rights,' she said, drawing her brows together fiercely. 'And what is that ugly thing you're wearing?'

Masina's feet were partly sunk in the sand, and wavering in the watery light. They appeared enormous. Lupe wondered that she had never noticed this before.

'It belongs to no one. I found it floating in the lagoon. Perhaps it was lost from a pālagi canoe in the storm.'

'You must throw that thing away. It will bring sickness. Just as the pālagi runaway brought sickness to our village,' said Masina, her voice rising, her eyes glaring.

'It is just a piece of cloth.'

'It is an aitu thing. An aitu has touched it with sickness like the sickness that killed your mother and my husband. The sickness that killed so many of our people.'

As Masina's voice grew louder, her face seemed to grow in size too, her mouth opening wider, and her eyes swelling, until her face almost matched her giant feet.

'It's been floating in the sea since the storm. How can it be touched with sickness?'

'Aitu aren't bothered by the sea, girl.'

'But I found it,' said Lupe, her voice almost a whisper, a not-quite whimper.

'And I say you must throw it away.'

Slowly, Lupe lifted her free arm to her shoulder and took hold of the yellow dress at the neck. She could feel the fineness of the cloth through her fingertips. All she had to do was pull it down over her shoulders and arms and let it fall to the water about her knees. Yet her hand stalled, frozen in place at her neck, and her legs began shifting backwards of their own volition, pushing the canoe along beside her.

'Take that aitu thing off, Lupelele.'

The water lapped at her thighs now. The yellow dress wafted about her legs.

'It will bring the aitu to our village.' Her aunt glared at her, as if she could halt her niece in her tracks by will alone. Usually, she could.

But this time was different, and before Lupe knew what she was about to do, she was clambering aboard the canoe, an action that proved more an ungainly roll in the yellow dress. Then she was away, gliding at speed across the lagoon, the small craft heading of its own volition towards the horizon, never mind her paddle dipping and pulling her through the water. She caught the faint sound of her cousins calling to her from the beach, and the angry shouts of her aunt, but she ignored them. Just as she ignored the voice in her head that warned of consequences when she returned. Of what her father would say when he learned that she had paddled outside the lagoon alone again. Of all the adults of their āiga chastising her for disobeying her aunt and causing no end of trouble. Condemning her for risking the ire of an aitu.

Lupe ignored them all. Let them call to her. Let them search for her. She would go where no one would find her. She would paddle out to the small green islands that soared from the open ocean beyond the lagoon. She would go where she would be alone. Where there was no one to tease her or tell her what to do. No one to bother her with pointless rules. She would go where no one would find her. Then her cousins and her aunt would be sorry. Then they would regret the way they had treated her.

What she would do when she got there she would worry about later.

25

Somerset, England
2022

Dogs are eternal opportunists. Drop a morsel of food beneath the table and they materialise from nowhere to vacuum it up. Leave a freshly baked cake on the coffee table and they decimate it while your teabag is still dangling. Or put on your coat for a trip to the supermarket and they are panting at the door before you have the thing buttoned. Bobby was no exception. Eliza had arranged to meet Daniel at the hall to discuss acquisitions for the hotel foyer, but when she arrived she found his pickup parked near the back entrance and no sign of the man himself. While she checked her phone for a message, her canine friend took the opportunity to scamper off into the woods.

'Hey, come back here!' she called after him.

Of course, Bobby merely answered with a flick of his tail, as if to say, 'Hurry up,' and continued with his mission.

'Oh, for heaven's sake!' Succumbing to the inevitable, she grabbed her satchel and lead from the car, and followed.

Despite hard times, the woods remained part of the estate. In centuries past, they had been more extensive, yet even now they covered an area of several acres. They extended beyond the main house in a gentle upward slope that Bobby now covered in a canter. Sometime in the mid-twentieth century swathes of the original broadleaf forest had been cut down for timber and replaced with conifers, but pockets of earlier woodland remained further inside, and this is where Bobby appeared to be headed. Eliza called him again, to no avail, resigning herself to a late afternoon walk, whether she wished it or not.

She followed the narrow trail that led from the house at a brisk walk, trying to keep Bobby's receding tail in sight. At first, the path led through a stand of conifers, moss carpeting the ground beneath, but as she ventured further into the woods the conifers gave way to a mixture of hazel coppice, ash, alder and the occasional oak. She paused for a moment to admire a patch of late-flowering, white star-like wild garlic, before catching her sleeve on a low-hanging hawthorn branch, heavy with red fruit, in her haste to catch up with her disappearing dog.

A stream meandered through the woods towards the river, and she caught its tinkling sound off to her right, but she didn't stop. There was a badger sett in the woods and although she hoped Bobby wouldn't be stupid enough to investigate, she wouldn't have put money on it. Sometimes his curiosity got the better of him. As if to justify her fears, he uttered a short yip and set off at a canter over the rise further ahead. Eliza quickened her pace to a jog, wishing she had a lasso in place of a leash.

She came to a halt atop the rise, her gaze captured by the sight of Bobby galloping downhill through the leaf litter towards Daniel's dog, Ruby. The man himself stood beside a coppice of ash, late afternoon sun filtering through the trees and bathing him in a mellow light. He was gazing towards a wide hollow in the ground a short distance away. In profile, his face and hair were etched with a silvery corona, giving him a thoughtful, dreamlike quality. So far in their blossoming friendship she had managed to resist his physical allure – well, apart from that one brief moment of madness at the pub – but this stillness, this attitude of introspection, tugged at her in a new way. There was a calmness about him that drew her to him despite all intentions to the contrary. What to do about a kind and calm man? A man a woman could trust – and a sexy one at that. Kind and sexy might just prove an irresistible combination.

She caught her breath at this thought and he turned, as if hearing the whisper of sound that emerged. But it was Bobby he heard, with his forelegs now set to the ground, bowing down before Ruby, readying for a romp.

'Bobby! Where's Eliza?' He leaned down to tousle the dog's ears before lifting his eyes to the ridge where she stood, hand to her chest, holding on to her heart. He raised a hand in greeting, calling out, 'Am I running late? Sorry. Ruby and I lost track of time on our walk.'

'No problem,' she replied, her words belying the fact that she faced a very big problem indeed, if her racing pulse was anything to judge by. A problem of the heart with all its unpredictable, untameable longings. Daniel had made his feelings clear on the nature of their friendship that day at the pub. She would do well to remember that. She should have listened to her first instincts when he asked her to work with him on furnishing the hall. Why had she been stupid enough to agree?

Because you were lusting after him even then, her inner voice taunted. *And now, you've progressed from lust to—*

'What do you think this is?' Daniel asked, thankfully interrupting her before she could finish *that* scary thought. He indicated the hollow with a nod of his head. The depression was shaped like a bowl, possibly twenty-five feet in diameter and six or seven feet deep. Like other sections of woodland, it was covered in low-growing plants: grasses, ferns, snowdrops and what appeared to be an unfortunate clump of nettle. But clearly it wasn't a natural depression.

'Aliens, maybe?' he said with a grin. 'It's not a cornfield but . . .'

'It's a bell pit. Or what's left of one.'

'Some kind of mining then?'

'Coal. There was once a small seam quite close to the surface here. As far as I know it was never mined commercially, but people have dug for their own use over the centuries. Since at least the Middle Ages. Possibly the Romans.' She shrugged as she answered, trying to throw off other more worrying fixations. He looked so – delectable.

He returned to his study of the pit as she descended the slope towards him.

'Were the pits filled in for safety reasons?' he asked as she reached him.

'Sometimes. And sometimes the disused pits were used to dump the rubble from newer diggings. But in this case, it looks like the pit collapsed. The miners used to dig a narrow entry shaft, then widen it out into a kind of circular gallery beneath. They didn't use any supports or props, so the bells couldn't be dug too deep or too wide. When they exhausted the coal in their pit they simply dug another one nearby. There's a shaft fenced off a little further along the trail that hasn't collapsed yet.'

'Is there? And we probably don't know when this one subsided either, do we?'

'I suppose not. As far as I know they haven't been worked since sometime in the late eighteenth century. Probably around the same time as the enclosures were happening, when anything profitable was fenced off from the rabble,' she said lightly, trying to keep her thoughts focused firmly on geology when all she wanted to do was drink in the sight of him. Why was he so intent on a geological interrogation when her thoughts were leaning in another direction entirely?

'Are you thinking of a history trail for the hotel?' she said, to distract from the persistent fluttering that was muddling her thoughts.

'I wasn't but it's not a bad idea . . . my brilliant Eliza.' He smiled at her in a way that struck right to the heart. *His Eliza.*

'Thanks.'

'A self-guided history and nature trail maybe, where guests can stretch their legs, enjoy the fresh air and learn something about the local area. I'll suggest it to the other partners.'

'Prudence liked to walk in the woods,' she said, her hand straying unconsciously to her satchel where the pocket book lay snugly buried.

Daniel noted the movement. 'Did you get that straight from the source?' he said with a nod towards her satchel.

She sighed, thinking that perhaps it might be time to share the pocket book with him. After all, what harm could it do? It was only an object, albeit an object that meant something to her even if she wasn't sure how to explain what that might be. So in answer to his question she fumbled with the buckle of her capacious Maison Margiela men's satchel, to retrieve the tiny book from amongst the jumble inside. The danger of being prepared for any and every situation was a bag so overflowing with pens, notebook, wallet, phone, dust cloth, loupe, sunglasses, plasters, hand wipes, tissues, aspirin, lip balm, gloves, scarf, keys, power bank, earbuds, Swiss army knife, and emergency snack . . . that you could never find anything. She wished she was one of those minimal women who floated through life with nothing but a phone and keys, but the prospect terrified her.

Finally, she produced the pocket book with a flourish, opening it to flip through the pages and find the relevant entries where Prudence had mentioned the woods. As she studied the faded two-hundred-year-old words, Daniel stood next to her, looking over her shoulder. She became all too conscious of his shoulder brushing hers, his cheek mere inches away. She caught the soft sound of his breath, in and out, and forced herself to concentrate.

'Here we are: Friday, 20th January. "Snowfall in woods. Forgot gloves. Edward lent his. Stayed for dinner. Five courses."'

'So Edward Ambrose sometimes walked with her in the woods?'

'It appears so. Here's another one: Wednesday, 15th February. "Snowdrops blooming in woods. Edward remarked on beauty. Surprised he noticed."'

Now that Eliza thought about it, Edward was mentioned a great deal more often than one might have expected for a man whose suit she had rejected. The pocket book was dated 1832, long before the pair married. Yet he appeared to be a frequent visitor to the hall at this time. Although whether he was visiting Sir Roderick or Prudence wasn't clear from the diary entries. Perhaps Sir Roderick and her Ambrose ancestor had been cooking up more than a five-course dinner.

'You know, the woods are fairly isolated from the house,' Daniel said.

'I suppose so. Quiet. Private.'

And possibly romantic, if you were so inclined. Which Eliza definitely wasn't.

'You wouldn't hear much from the house, would you?' he said.

'I suppose not.'

'And those pits . . . they're fairly deep.'

'I suppose so.' *Tick tock.* Was she thinking what he was thinking?

'If someone fell . . . or was pushed . . . into a disused pit—'

'He or she might never be found.' She finished the thought for him.

There was silence for several seconds, before Daniel placed a hand on her arm in a friendly gesture, saying, 'Especially if the hall's new owner subsequently had that disused pit filled with rubble. For reasons of safety, of course.'

Despite her resolve, she shivered at his touch. Glancing down, she saw that the hairs on the offending arm were standing on end.

'Are you cold?'

'No.' She wished that she could retract the words as soon as she said them. She didn't want him to guess the true reason why she shivered at his touch. She couldn't bear further humiliation. 'Just underdressed. I grabbed the lead but no cardigan.'

'Here, room enough for two. I'll warm you up,' he said, opening his lumber jacket to share its warmth with her. And despite all her misgivings, she was propelled, shivering, into his arms.

'What's wrong?' he murmured into her hair, as he wrapped the jacket about her.

Why did he have to be so kind when all she wanted was to feel nothing for him?

'I don't know,' she said, her words muffled by his chest. Of course that wasn't true.

'You looked worried. Prudence isn't about to jump out of that pit and haunt us, you know.'

Probably not. Although, in truth, Prudence Merryfield's fate had haunted Eliza's family for centuries. And now it was haunting Eliza too. She should never have embarked upon this pointless quest to uncover a centuries-old mystery. It was taking over her life when she needed to focus on the future, not the past. She had almost succeeded in recovering her equilibrium after the last difficult years. She didn't need ancient events taking over. And yet . . .

'What if she's buried somewhere in these woods?' she murmured.

'Could be.'

Lying alone at the bottom of a pit. Dead. Without children or husband to mourn her passing. Murdered by a man who had vowed to love and honour her. She felt Daniel wrap her more firmly in his jacket and she tried not to lean against him, she really did. But the urge was too strong. And as she relaxed her whole body against the length of him, she breathed a sigh of something like relief. To her great surprise, being held by him felt like coming home.

'It's okay, you know,' he said. 'Even if Edward did murder Prudence, there's nothing to be done about it now.' He crooned the words into her hair. With her face smothered against the soft cotton of his T-shirt under his jacket, she almost giggled. He thought she was worried about having a murderer for an ancestor, when the reality was so much closer to home.

'I know,' she murmured.

She looked up, searching his face for clues. Surely she must be more than a chum for him to hold her like this. She couldn't be permanently friend-zoned, could she? Except, he wasn't taking advantage of their close proximity, just behaving as if he were a human blanket. Perhaps he was simply more tactile than most men she knew. After all, some people were huggers, just usually not Eliza. She hadn't even hugged her mother on that last day when she was taken away in the ambulance. If she had known what was to happen, she would have hugged her so hard the paramedics would have needed to prise her arms loose with a crowbar.

'And having a villain in the family isn't so bad,' he continued. 'I have a convict in mine. Transported for seven years for stealing a sheep. It's a point of pride in Australia.'

'I suppose that does have a certain earthy glamour to it.'

Except murdering your wealthy wife to marry your maid didn't have quite the same ring of social justice about it.

'But by trying to get to the bottom of Prudence's disappearance,' she explained, 'I was hoping to vindicate my ancestors, not convict them.'

'It's true, a bell pit might be an excellent hiding spot for a body,' he said, 'but there are plenty of other possible explanations for Prudence's disappearance. Who knows? Maybe she did a Robert Louis Stevenson and retired to the South Seas.'

'Have you been? To Samoa?' She closed her eyes as an image of him with a deep tan, sun-streaked hair and bare chest teased her thoughts.

'Not to Samoa, no. But I've visited Fiji, the Cook Islands and Vanuatu. You'd love the islands, Eliza. Beautiful one day, paradise the next. Isn't that what they say?'

'But they're so far away.' Especially for a woman who never went anywhere that didn't involve work.

'That's half the fun.'

Not if you were all at sea on a tall ship like Prudence, at the mercy of the elements for months at a time. Not if you were shipwrecked and stranded on an island half a world away from home. Unable to speak the language. Unprepared for life on an island. Confused and alone. Would Prudence really have returned to Samoa? It seemed unlikely. Yet the world could be an unlikely place and a person could just as easily lose their moorings in a small village in the middle of Somerset.

'I think I'm warm enough now.'

Daniel relaxed his hold upon her, leaving an arm draped around her shoulders like a buddy. She found herself mourning the loss. As if she was a child in need of comfort.

Or a woman in need of love.

So why would Prudence abandon her home and a husband who loved and cherished her? Far more likely that she never left Westcott Hall.

At least, not alive.

26

Samoa

1833

Prudence may have gained her sea legs but in the process she appeared to have lost her sure-footedness. The ridge she aimed for seemed to grow further away the higher she climbed. At first, she trekked through a tangle of trees with broad leaves and light green flowers, the trees growing so closely together that the branches interlocked overhead. When she stopped to catch her breath and looked up, the twisting branches and filigree of leaves formed a canopy of green lace. And although she admired the forest's beauty, the view was rather spoiled by the noxious smell of bird droppings. Hundreds of large white birds with bright red legs congregated amongst the trees, emitting an alarming array of squawks and an equally alarming volume of droppings.

As she climbed even higher, she escaped the noisy birds and the trees became taller, the trunks thicker and the undergrowth trickier. The branches were equally hazardous as she ducked beneath and skirted around, scratching her bare arms numerous times while trying to avoid them. Once, she caught a glimpse of a beautiful bluish-grey bird with rust-coloured wings and a powerful hooked beak. It was feeding on orange fruits, but flew off in a flurry when it heard her noisy approach.

So by the time she gained the ridge, she was panting, her arms and feet smeared with blood. Nevertheless, she exhaled with a sense of accomplishment. What would Wills say if she could see her now in her torn and tattered chemise? Prudence's embroidery skills might be poor and her talent for the pianoforte negligible, but she was on her way to becoming – who was she becoming? In what seemed a lifetime ago now, she had thought to become a woman of independent spirit and means. An adventuress. A traveller. In order to do so, she had prevailed against the opposition of her trustee – and, no doubt, the disapproval of most of her acquaintance. Now circumstances had set her upon an unexpected path, at the mercy of the elements and of fate. Her journey was no longer an adventure. It was a calamity; a calamity that had caused the death of a young woman under her protection.

She reached the top of the ridge, at last, but could not see her way through the forest to gain a clear view of her situation. So she set off along the ridge in a northerly direction, hoping that the forest might give way to thinner scrub close to the rocky cliffs she had noticed earlier. Once again, it was hard going, but Prudence was determined. So far, she had seen no signs of habitation on her little island, but she vowed not to despair. With luck she would sight a neat village in a sandy bay on the further side of the island, one with friendly, welcoming inhabitants, plentiful gardens ripe with fruit, and perhaps a pig or two. She refused to contemplate the idea that the inhabitants might be hostile. For the time being, she refused to dwell on her fate at all. She had survived a shipwreck, a perilous voyage aboard a chicken coop, and a night spent alone with nothing but a penknife to sustain her. If only she could acquire some shoes she would surely survive.

By the time she broke through the trees to a patch of low scrub, with glittering blue sea to the horizon, the sun was high in the sky and she had wounds too many to count. But she was free of the forest and as she turned to survey her surroundings she was pleased to see that there was, indeed, a small sandy bay on the westward shore of 'her' islet, as she had come to think of it. And beyond that little cove was a stretch of water separating it from a larger landmass. She was close enough to note that the coast of that other landmass was bordered by clear green-blue water that gave way to a deeper blue ocean. It was also encircled by a lagoon, it seemed. And on the shores of that lagoon she made out the tassels of coconut groves, and through the coconut palms what looked like a scattering of doll-like houses set amongst emerald lawns.

A village.

A village too far away to be reached. For without her trusty chicken coop she could not swim that distance. And she was not desperate enough to float her trusty coop around the treacherous rocks on the other side of her islet to reach it. Nor did she have the strength to haul the coop over the ridge to the little cove below. She would have to reconsider.

With her hopes dashed, she turned her back upon the village, sighed and set herself down upon a craggy rock that faced out over the cliffs to the far horizon. The sound of high-pitched chattering reached her from below. Rising to her feet once more, she stepped closer to the cliff's edge to find out what the fuss was about. Several small grey birds nested on ledges scattered across the cliff face. She had noticed the same birds yesterday, dipping and wheeling above the sea as they fished for their dinner. However, now they were engaged in raucous argument with a lone brown hen. Her hen.

'Madame Hen!' she exclaimed at the sight of her former shipmate. 'How on earth did you find your way down there?'

At the sound of her voice the chicken set to clucking piteously, perched as it was on a narrow ledge, perhaps fifteen or at most twenty feet below the cliff top.

'Well, I don't know what you expect me to do about it.'

Madame Hen renewed her clucking with gusto, accompanying her protests with an urgent flapping of wings.

'You cannot expect me to climb down there, madame. A lady is not a mountain goat, after all.'

But Madame Hen would not take no for an answer. In fact, Madame was an importunate bird indeed, interrupting her conversation with Prudence to lunge, pecking at her neighbours.

'Careful, you may fall!' she cried, stretching out her arms futilely as the hen hopped, flapping into the air, her brief flight only succeeding in bringing her a little closer to Prudence upon the same narrow ledge. There she perched, blinking up expectantly.

'I suppose it's only a matter of a few feet,' Prudence mused, unconvinced. 'And there look to be footholds.' Footholds, and a sheer drop of some two hundred feet to the rocks below. 'I suppose I could manage such a distance.'

She lowered herself to the ground and dangled her legs over the lip of the cliff. 'It's a good thing I'm not afraid of heights.'

Good, or foolish, depending upon one's point of view. It was rather a long way down, to be sure. But the hen was her sole remaining companion, her fellow castaway. For all Prudence knew, she and Madame might be the only survivors of the wreck. The ship's other boat may have sunk and taken the entire crew with it, for after those first panic-stricken shouts she had heard no more during her long night at sea aboard the chicken coop. Heard no more of Bessie either, driven to the bottom of the ocean aboard the sinking wreck. Poor, terrified Bessie, clinging to the mizzenmast in her rain-drenched yellow dress. Her hair draped like seaweed about her face. Prudence should have ripped her hands from the mast and forced her to abandon ship. She should have seen the girl into the waves before she looked to save herself.

Madame Hen was still gazing up at her, clucking piteously.

'If I must,' she sighed.

228

With her hands gripping the cliff edge, she felt below for a foothold. Then, finding the shape of a nook worn into the cliff, she placed her weight on that searching foot and turned to face the rock so that she could more easily descend. Once she had secured her position, she resumed the process, searching for another foothold, then using her previous foothold as a hand-hold. In this manner, using nooks, crannies and small shrubs that grew from the rock, she descended the cliff face towards the stranded hen. That is, until her very last foothold slipped from beneath her in a hail of loose stones and deposited her on Madame's ledge in a most unladylike fashion. Her arrival on that narrow ledge set Madame to even more frantic clucking, so that Prudence leaned down with one hand to snatch the demanding bird by the neck and set it upon her left shoulder, where it immediately dug in its claws as if it would never let go.

She stayed in that position to catch her breath, her tattered shift flapping about her legs in the breeze, while ruing the foolhardiness that had led her to play at heroics. She was no female Robinson Crusoe. She was no Lemuel Gulliver. She was an old-maid habituée of Bath assemblies and morning calls, not shipwrecks and deserted islands. What had she been thinking when she set out on this foolhardy quest for freedom? What had led her to think that she was equal to the hardships of a true adventurer? She hadn't the fortitude of the lady castaways in the novels she had devoured as a girl. She was no Hannah Hewit, cast away alone on an island in the South Seas. She was no Zélie in the desert. Her accomplishments were few, her fortitude untested.

Perhaps her father had been correct to set Edward above her as trustee of her estate and her person. She had lost Bessie to her hubris and now she might have brought about her own demise too. For if the drop to the rocks below had appeared perilously high a short time before, the climb from her perch to

Julie Brooks

the cliff top – which had appeared achievable earlier – now seemed unattainable. She craned her neck to stare upwards, conscious of her companion's feathery heartbeat pressed close to her ear. The last of her footholds had disappeared. And the other crevices she had used on her descent weren't visible from this angle. Above her, all she could see was sheer cliff face and cloudless blue sky. She dare not look below, for the sound of crashing waves told her all she needed to know.

'How have we come to this?' she lamented, quivering, to her friend.

To which Madame Hen replied with a swift peck to her ear. 'Cluck, cluck, cluck.'

27

Before Lupe knew it, she was almost upon the reef. Her thoughts were swirling so violently that she paid little attention to her direction. Only the crash of breaking surf warned of approaching danger. Paddling furiously, she narrowly avoided running her canoe on to the reef, steering instead towards the passage that led from the lagoon to the open sea. She did not look back. Somewhere behind her Masina would be simmering at her disobedience, but that was nothing unusual. Nothing about Lupe pleased her aunt.

Since her mother had died, her aunt hovered over her like a fui'a bird, screeching at her, chasing her away from anything that resembled fun, and generally making her life miserable. Once she had reached puberty and shifted into the fale of the aualuma where her aunt ruled, Lupe could never escape her. Whenever she turned around, there she was. She suspected that, not content with ordering her about, Masina wished to move into her father's fale and take over her mother's house altogether. The thought of her aunt settling into her mother's house with her fine mats and her baskets set Lupe to paddling even faster.

Ahead of her, the forest-draped outline of a small island

loomed large. Shaped like a crab with claws pincering the ocean, the islet was edged by a fringing reef. Soaring cliffs rose from the sea for much of its shoreline, but as she drew closer she made out the curve of a beach on the near side. Since her āiga shared ownership of the islet, her father sometimes visited to gather coconuts and hunt for the tasty coconut crabs that lived there. She also knew there was an abundance of shellfish and bird eggs, so she would not go hungry. If she were lucky, neither her aunt nor her father would think to look for her here. At least, not for a while. Sooner or later, someone from the village would visit the island. Her father would probably begin his search further along the lagoon, perhaps enquiring at nearby villages. In the meantime, Masina would have plenty of time to worry about Lupe's welfare, to think of all the horrible misadventures that could befall her. To be sorry she had been so unkind, sorry that she had thought to take Lupe's mother's place.

As she left behind the turquoise waters of the lagoon and the rainbow corals of the reef for the dark blue of deeper waters, a pod of mumua skipped across the ocean some distance away. One playful member surprised her by surfacing a few lengths from her canoe, and whistling at her. While further afield she watched the silvery forms of malolo gliding above the waves, no doubt escaping predators below. The beauty of the flying fish skimming the waves helped distract her from any thoughts of predators lurking beneath her canoe, or what might happen if she were to capsize. Alone, far from her village, on a day when no one was out fishing and everyone was clearing up after the storm, was not a good day to have to swim home. Especially when her arms were growing tired from the unaccustomed distance she had paddled. For one brief moment, she even wondered whether striking out alone on such a day had been a wise idea. But she put that thought behind her, along with all thoughts of her aunt, her cousins, even her father, and held tight to her anger. Anger was the one antidote she had found for fear – or grief.

Luckily, the tide was high as she approached the small island, since there appeared to be no channel through the fringing reef. The water was slightly choppy, but nothing she couldn't handle. She glided over the reef and entered the lagoon, but before she could beach her canoe and camouflage it in the shadows of the coconut palms her eyes were drawn to an unusual sight on the cliff top at the northern end of the beach. A pale human-sized shape wavered high up on a ledge, fluttering like the feathers on a bird's wing in the light breeze. Lupe's paddle stilled in the water and the canoe bobbed aimlessly as she tried to make sense of the vision. She blinked salt spray from her eyes, thinking to clear the apparition from her sight. Her first thought was that the events of the morning had been more exhausting than she realised and her imagination was playing tricks on her. Except, when she opened her eyes, the apparition was still there, teetering on the ledge, one thin white arm snatching wildly at the air.

Her second, more horrifying thought, was that her aunt had been right. That Lupe had stirred up the anger of an aitu by wearing the yellow dress. And now it had come to possess her. For what else could it be? The shape was too pale to be a Samoan, too tall to be a bird. And it appeared to be haloed by a cloud of long red hair. Could it be the dreaded Telesā, subject of so many fearful tales? Her heart beat faster than a log drum as she debated whether she should turn back. Return to the village with her head hanging low and words of regret upon her lips? The idea raised the hair on her arms. Yet surely a renegade aitu was more to be feared than Masina, especially an angry one that wanted its dress returned.

As the current dragged her canoe closer to shore she noticed that perched upon the aitu's shoulder was a bird, a bird that looked surprisingly like a chicken. A brown chicken. She had heard many tales of the doings of aitu in her life: causing floods as punishment for bad behaviour, biting those who offended them and making them sick, entering people's bodies through their armpits and possessing their souls. But not a single tale made mention of a chicken.

Clearly, whoever or whatever the mysterious figure atop the cliff was, it hadn't descended from the heavens in order to possess her soul. Either it was gathering gull eggs, or it was stuck there. Neither of which was very clever, in Lupe's opinion.

Madame's feathers were ruffled and Prudence's fingers were raw from clinging to the rock face. Each breath of wind threatened to blow them from their perch. Yet Prudence remained frozen to the spot, afraid to venture up or down. If only she had wings, proper wings that could lift her to safety. Madame's wings were for display alone. Through the vagaries of fate, her companion had been set free of her cage, yet thus far freedom had brought only further calamity. It appeared they both had much to learn about their new environment.

The ledge to which she clung petered out a body's length and a half further along the cliff face. If she were to risk sliding along that length she could perhaps find another pathway to the top. But that would require releasing her hands – and, like claws of iron, they refused to let go. She glared at them, as if it was their fault she was in this predicament. Once upon a time, she had lamented the freckles that marred the smooth paleness of her skin. Now sunburn, scratches and torn nails obliterated those freckles and her poor hands had developed a will of their own

'At least you've proved useful at something,' she said aloud, 'even if only to cling to a cliff on an uninhabited island in the middle of the South Seas.'

As if in answer, Madame began an agitated clucking, her claws digging painfully into Prudence's bare shoulder.

'I'm trying.'

Except trying would not gain their freedom. Only action would suffice. She had found the strength of will required to defy Edward, her deceased father and English society. She had found the courage to cross the seas. Surely she could summon the gumption necessary to venture a few steps in order to secure her survival. Even if those steps were vertical. There was no other choice.

Inching her face and body away from the rock, she twisted her head over her free shoulder to peer upwards, searching for footholds further along the cliff, only to catch her breath at the vision that materialised above. A figure appeared at the lip of the cliff, draped in folds of yellow. The fabric clung damply to the figure's legs, just as it had the last time she saw that same garment, when its folds were drowned by the lashing waters of storm and sea. Prudence was afraid to let her eyes follow a path upwards. Afraid of what she would find. Yet also afraid of what she might not find. Was chance at work here? By some miracle of fate or human endurance, had Bessie survived the shipwreck to make her way to the same island as Prudence? Or was this an apparition in the guise of her young maid?

Or perhaps her mind was playing tricks on her.

For several seconds she clung to the rock face, unwilling to look further than the apparition's knees. The former possibility brought a flood of hope. To have Bessie returned to her, returned to life. She did not want to see that hope cruelly dashed. Mired in indecision, trapped between hope and despair, she was jolted out of immobility when the apparition spoke.

'Tālofa.'

Prudence's shoulders sagged, and with them her hopes. The word was incomprehensible. And the voice bore no resemblance to Bessie's. Yet neither did it sound ghostly. She looked up, her gaze travelling from yellow-clad legs and torso to arrive at a young girl's pleasant brown face looking down at her curiously. The face, framed by thick brown hair shorn to a cap of short curls, could not be reconciled with the yellow dress. Last seen in a typhoon aboard the *Kangaroo*. A further cascade of syllables issued from the girl's mouth, none of which made any sense to Prudence, who was trying not to imagine how the girl came to be wearing Bessie's dress. For if her mind followed that line of thought, it might end up somewhere she did not want to venture.

The girl was not about to leave her to her thoughts, however. She began gesturing with an open hand, indicating that Prudence must move further along the ledge. Then she began pointing to a spot an arm's length above. All the while, the girl averted her gaze, as if she was an unappealing or indeed frightening sight. Prudence knew that she did not present the prettiest of pictures, sunburned, bleeding and half naked as she was, but exceptions could be made under the circumstances, surely.

Nonetheless, she obeyed the girl's directions, for this might be her last hope. She inched her way along the ledge, nose to rock, freezing each time she heard a clatter of pebbles. Her hands tried to find purchase on the cliff face, scrabbling claw-like for the tiniest protuberance (in those moments she forgave Madame for the desperate grip upon her shoulder), at other times glued to the rock as if she were a gecko. With her heart flapping like a trapped bird, she finally arrived at a spot that met with the girl's approval. And indeed, there was a small hole in the rock just above her knee, and other visible pockmarks ascending at intervals. If only she could summon the courage necessary to make use of them.

More sounds from above signalled that her guide was becoming impatient.

'I suppose it is now or never,' Prudence sighed aloud. No other help appeared imminent. She would have to save herself, and Madame, of course. Besides, if she remained on the ledge much longer, her fingers would turn numb and the question would be settled for her in a conclusive and presumably fatal manner. Having reasoned thus, she set forth.

One step. One hand.

Followed by another hand and a further step.

Ascending the cliff inch by inch, each wobble causing a flurry of clucking from Madame, each success bringing unintelligible but encouraging words from above.

In this manner, she gained the top. Her poor, scarred hand was grasped in a smooth brown one as she was hauled over the lip of the cliff, to lie flat on her stomach. Whereupon her fellow castaway immediately abandoned ship and took to pecking for insects beneath a meagre shrub several yards distant.

'How do you do, Mademoiselle?' she muttered hopefully into the dirt. '*Parlez-vous Anglais?*'

The figure was too solid for an aitu. Not that Lupe had ever met one of these spirits, but if she had, she felt certain there would be some otherworldly quality to them. This one's arms were covered in scrapes and bruises and there were bloody cuts upon its feet. No, this one was far too clumsy to be a spirit, and not very clever either, by the look of it.

She squatted near the prone figure, an arm's length between them, curiosity warring with caution. Masina's words echoed in her head. 'It is an aitu thing. An aitu has touched it with sickness.' While Lupe did not believe this being was from the spirit world, neither did she want to risk danger to her village. But she could not leave it here; it was clearly too stupid to survive alone. What other explanation could there be for getting stuck on the cliff like that? The words it spoke sounded familiar too, at least the sound and rhythm if not the meaning. Except, what to make of the long, tangled red hair? She had never seen the like.

There was a rustle and the being rolled on to its back in an ungainly movement, settling the matter once and for all, for beneath the torn white garment two soft pink mounds protruded. And the face was clearly human and female too, if Lupe was any judge. This wasn't an aitu, this was a pālagi, she was sure of it. Like the man who had lived in their village for a time – only this one was a woman. Lupe had heard no tales of female papālagi visiting Samoa, yet now one had washed up on the shore of this tiny island – Lupe's proposed hideaway. Perhaps, like the yellow dress, she too had fallen from a pālagi canoe.

Seeing the woman's red face, she wondered again if her aunt was right and the sickness that had scourged their village was an aitu thing brought by the pālagi runaway who had lived in their village. But from the woman's clear-eyed, curious stare, she did not appear to be feverish. And although her arms and face were an angry pink, her garment had ridden up, exposing white legs. Apparently, she did not have enough sense to protect her white skin from the sun.

The woman coughed and Lupe realised that she had been staring. She averted her gaze hastily. The woman was her elder and thus staring was most impolite. Elder or not, the question was, what to do with her. She could not leave her on the island, for clearly she did not know how to look after herself. If Lupe hadn't come along, she would probably be lying dead on the rocks at the bottom of the cliff. The polite thing to do would be to take her home to the village, where she would be welcomed as a guest. Then again, she should probably inform the chief and the various matai first. They might not be happy that she took this decision upon herself. More likely, they definitely would not be happy.

While she debated the best course of action, the woman had risen to her feet. She stood somewhat shakily, more strange words issuing from her mouth, with a distressed expression on her face. Lupe saw that the other woman was a full hand shorter than her, shorter than a thirteen-year-old girl. That decided it. She would have to take her back to the village in the canoe, for how could she leave a hapless creature like this to fend for herself? Someone needed to take her in hand or she wouldn't last long alone on this tiny island with her tame chicken. Perhaps the papālagi tamed chickens as the chiefs tamed pigeons.

Lupe smiled to herself. To'oa would be surprised when she paddled up to the beach with a pālagi on board. Tuna and Fata would most likely be envious that they hadn't discovered her. And her aunt would be livid.

'Lupelele,' she said to the woman, patting her heart.

The pālagi woman was silent for a moment, perhaps taking time to understand Lupe's meaning. Then she tapped her chest in return. 'Prudence,' she said, or something like that, as Lupe caught a hint of a smile peeking through the cracked and flaking lips.

How dangerous could this bruised and sunburned stranger be?

If Lupe returned with this woman aboard her canoe she would be the talk of the entire village. She would be at the centre of things, drawing attention to herself in a most un-Samoan way.

In other words, she would be in big trouble.

Nothing so unusual then.

28

Somerset, England

2022

'I wonder why Winston gifted the portrait of Prudence to the county. He could have sold it or bequeathed it to one of his children,' Eliza mused aloud as she and Jude purchased their photo licences at the Somerset Heritage Centre reception in Taunton.

'Perhaps he thought it was cursed.'

Eliza turned to her aunt in surprise, checking to see if she was serious. 'I didn't think you believed in that stuff.'

'I don't. But he may have. I mean . . . Winston was born at the end of the nineteenth century. He lived his entire life in the shadow of the family's decline. Getting rid of the portrait may have seemed like a good idea. Cathartic. Wiping the slate clean for generations to come.'

The Ambroses didn't have a monopoly on murderous ancestors, of course. There were numerous prominent families whose wealth had been built upon the scaffolding of the dead. The problem for Eliza's family was the mystery that surrounded Prudence's disappearance. It was the mystery that drove the curse.

'Now you've got me believing in curses,' she muttered.

'A good curse makes for an excellent story,' Jude said with a wink.

And a good story perpetuated a curse. The curse lived on through repeated retellings, so that ensuing generations saw the story of their lives through the haze of its glamour. Is that what she had been doing? Living her life as if she were cursed – or would be cursed, if she were to break her vow to her mother? Is that why she was so stuck?

'Well, no need to bother about that now,' her aunt added, when Eliza did not rise to her bait. 'Onward to the portrait!'

This wasn't Eliza's first visit to the heritage centre. Over the years, she had visited the county archives to research the provenance of prospective acquisitions. She had also explored the family papers at one time or another, usually when she was feeling particularly lost or disconnected. After her father died, she had been a regular visitor for a while. The Ambrose family papers had been deposited in the archives by Eliza's great-grandfather, Winston, the very same Ambrose who had donated the portrait of Prudence and sold Westcott Hall.

But today they were visiting the Museum Reserve Collection, before booking time in the archive search room. In one of her middle-of-the-night moments of inspiration, Jude had recalled an exhibition held at the Museum of Somerset some years previously, featuring portraits of prominent Somerset personalities of the eighteenth and nineteenth centuries. In the light of Prudence's notoriety, her portrait had been included. Jude insisted that a viewing was essential to Eliza's ongoing investigation into her ancestor's disappearance – not to mention the fact that she enjoyed any outing that included lunch.

In honour of the visit, and to pay due homage to the portrait, Eliza wore a sleeveless, knee-length Giorgio Armani dress, circa 2000. It was an empire-line style reminiscent of Prudence's Regency-era portrait, in lilac silk with a scoop neckline and pintuck detail. Except rather than kid gloves and half-boots Eliza wore it with white canvas tennis shoes and had accessorised it with a transparent plastic tote. Apart from the 'shocking' length, Prudence would have approved, she was sure.

Of course, she had seen portraits of Prudence before, reproduced in various historical accounts. One awkward rendering, printed in the exploitative *Narrative*, showed her clad in a grass skirt, a portrait that could not have been taken from life. In anticipation of the visit, Eliza had checked out the Somerset portrait in their online catalogue, where she found a modest digital reproduction of Mrs Prudence Ambrose née Merryfield (*Artist: unknown, Date: c1815–25, Medium: oil on canvas, Measurements: H 77.5 x W 64 cm, Acquisition: gift of Mr Winston Ambrose 1975*) that could not capture the detail or the mood of an original portrait. She hoped the original might shed light on the character of this enigmatic woman who had somehow wormed her way into Eliza's life.

Ten minutes after checking in, they found themselves being shown to a vast, neat storage space lined with rows of shelving, cabinets and racks that formed a maze of corridors in an Aladdin's cave of artworks. After a brief introduction from one of the collections officers, they were led to the row where Prudence's portrait had found a home – an unglamorous one, at that. Eliza couldn't help feeling disappointed that her first meeting with Prudence was so prosaic. There was little mystery and not a glimmer of glamour about the white trellised racks crammed with paintings and maps.

The unknown artist had posed Prudence in an empire-line, white muslin gown with a ruffled décolletage and a blue satin ribbon tied beneath the bust. Her skin was milky, almost translucent; auburn ringlets framed a heart-shaped face in semi-profile. She appeared to be staring at something off to one side, her small neat lips curved in a half-smile. In the painting Prudence looked to be perhaps twenty years of age or thereabouts – a slip of a girl. Her unlined, untested face gave no hint of the adventures and misadventures that would follow. Eliza noted the gold chain hanging around her neck and the oval locket of gold curlicues framing a miniature portrait. Given the late eighteenth-century design, the miniature would most likely have been painted with watercolours upon ivory and enclosed by a crystal cover. It might even have encased a lock of hair behind the portrait too.

Peering closer, Eliza saw that, like Prudence, the young woman in the miniature portrait also had red hair, cascading over her shoulders in ringlets. A wisp of white fichu concealed her décolletage. Her initial disappointment at the portrait's setting was succeeded by a jolt of surprise that coursed like static electricity through her body.

'I think that's the locket Prudence sketched in the pocket book, the one that belonged to her mother. She talks about having it repaired,' she said to her aunt.

Even now, that very pocket book rested amongst the jumble of 'essentials' visible in Eliza's transparent tote. She had taken to carrying the book everywhere. It had become like an anchor, although what it anchored her to she wasn't quite sure.

As if by silent agreement, both women now took a step back from the display rack, to regard the painting and its neighbours on either side. Jude with her arms crossed, Eliza with a hand on her chin. They looked at each other and sighed.

'Well, I didn't expect this, did you?'

'No. The exhibition certainly didn't include *that* painting,' Jude said. 'I would have remembered, if it had.'

'*That* painting' was one hanging alongside Prudence. Another portrait of a young woman with red hair, a white gown exposing her shoulders, the tight sleeves decorated with ruffles and blue satin bows. Unlike Prudence and her mother in the miniature, her ringlets were orderly and centre-parted, sitting just above her shoulders. A painting such as this wouldn't ordinarily be a cause for surprise, since the warehouse was lined with paintings.

Except, in this case, the subject of the portrait wore an identical locket to Prudence. And at the bottom of the frame an engraved, rectangular gold plaque read: *Mrs Elizabeth Ambrose née Pike, 1846.*

'Bessie . . .' Eliza and Judith breathed the word at the same time.

There was silence for a time in the vast space peopled by the past, before Jude broke it by saying, 'If Prudence left of her own accord, wouldn't she have taken the locket with her?'

'You'd think so.'

If Eliza possessed a miniature of her mother, she would wear it next to her heart every day. She would never leave it behind.

'And if she subsequently met with an accident and disappeared, the locket would have disappeared with her. So—'

'So how does Bessie come to be wearing it in this portrait?' Eliza finished Jude's thought. That locket meant so much to Prudence.

All trains of thought led in one direction only – to perfidy. Somebody had killed Prudence but kept the locket. Presumably so that her body would be difficult to identify if it were found.

And that somebody was most likely to have been her husband. The man she had initially rejected. The man entrusted with her estate. The man who had the most to gain if she met with foul play, Eliza's great-great-something-or-other-grand-father – Edward Ambrose.

'Well,' Jude said with a slow shake of her head, 'it seems Edward did something to deserve the curse, after all.'

But more to the point, what had Prudence done to deserve her fate? What had Prudence done to merit a violent death, other than hankering after a life less ordinary?

29

Samoa

1833

Lupelele paddled alone. There was a second paddle in the canoe but her passenger caused so much havoc with it that Lupe decided it was safer to paddle alone. The pālagi woman had flipped the outrigger and capsized the canoe when trying to board, so that Lupe had to haul her aboard like a wriggling eel. Then, despite clear directions and an excellent demonstration, she paddled as if she were trying to shift the water rather than the canoe, causing a great deal of splashing and making little headway. Lupe wondered how a grown woman could be so lacking in sense.

Finally, they were skimming across the water and she hoped there would be no more mishaps. By waving her hands about and shaking her head vehemently, she had given her passenger strict instructions not to move about. If the canoe capsized in deep water she wasn't confident she could save her from drowning. Lupe had learned to swim as soon as she could walk, but she could not be sure about this woman from far away who did not have the sense to protect her pale face from the sun, and thought it was a good idea to chase chickens down cliffs. Not only that, she seemed to be attached to the chicken and had insisted on bringing it with them in the canoe. Perhaps the papālagi worshipped chickens.

The return journey seemed much longer than the trip out to the island, with the woman sitting in the bow, her hands gripping the sides of the canoe. If Lupe had any doubt that she was a woman, and not an aitu, her wet garment cleared the matter up once and for all, clinging like damp seaweed to every part of her body. And although the afternoon sun was hot, she shivered, glancing over her shoulder every now and again as if to check what Lupe was up to. Lupe was tempted to surprise her with a scary face – the one she usually reserved for her cousins – but decided that would be too childish. She needed to be grown-up in this situation, especially when her charge needed so much guidance. Instead, she frowned sternly the next time the pink-cheeked woman turned in her direction, indicating with her chin that she should face forward. Strangely enough, she complied and they completed the journey without further incident.

By the time they reached her village, Lupe's arms were aching and her head was pounding. Whether from thirst and the hot sun or from worrying over how she would explain the pālagi's existence to her father and the other matai, she didn't know. Or, for that matter, the borrowed canoe. She was also beginning to wonder whether she might have acted rashly. Whether it had been such a good idea to take off for the island alone. Whether she might have found another way to keep the yellow garment. A way that did not involve shouting at her aunt, borrowing a canoe, leaving the lagoon, talking to a strange pālagi, and bringing her back to the village without permission from her family or any of the matai.

She could deal with her aunt's scolding, for that was nothing out of the ordinary. She could even grit her teeth and bear it if Masina decided to beat her. But her sins did seem to be mounting, and her father would surely have something to say about it. He might even do more than talk. He rarely shouted, for self-control was paramount, as Lupe was constantly reminded. But he might make an exception in such extreme circumstances. And five misdemeanours in one day were exceptional, even for Lupe.

She didn't have to ponder the problem of her aunt for very long. As she dragged both canoe and guest up the beach, she found Masina waiting. Her aunt loomed larger and more forbidding than ever, standing sentinel upon the sand beneath the coconut palms, almost as if she had predicted Lupe's arrival. Or more likely, someone had spotted the approach of her errant niece and informed her.

'Are you feeling happy now, Lupelele? Are you content with the trouble you have wrought?' her aunt asked, as girl and woman gained the high-tide mark. Masina's voice was mild but her arms were folded across her chest, and her face was very fierce indeed. She did not comment upon the pālagi woman at all, although her sideways eyes followed her intently.

Lupe bit back the fighting words that trembled upon the tip of her tongue. Angry words had placed her in this situation in the first place. Better to be as mild as her aunt and hope her father would look upon her kindly; her aunt was a lost cause.

'I'm sorry if I've caused trouble,' she said, lowering her eyes to the sand.

'Half the village is looking for you. Your father is worried for this wilful girl who thinks she knows more than her elders,' Masina chided, while pointedly ignoring the very obvious presence of the pālagi.

Lupe wasn't so sure about such a search. The sun still floated above the horizon and the older girls often disappeared for hours at a time, foraging for shellfish or fooling about in the lagoon. No one was likely to begin searching for Lupe until later. Besides, at least half the villagers had now emerged from their houses and gardens and were gathering around Masina, their attention focused on the newcomer. She scanned the faces, young and old, most of whom she saw every day of her life. Some of those faces were scowling, some were laughing, but all were twitching with curiosity. And all except her aunt were gawking at the newcomer.

Lupe was relieved to see To'oa amongst the crowd and she almost smiled, bolstered by her friend's presence. She took a deep breath and pulled back her shoulders, telling herself, *you have not returned in shame. You have returned with an important visitor.*

'Who is that, Lupe?' one of her cousins called from high up in a coconut palm.

A difficult question to answer. She had found her clinging to a cliff on an uninhabited island but in truth she did not know how the woman had arrived there or where she had come from. She could only guess.

'This is P . . . P . . .'

She hesitated over the word, trying to remember how to say the strange name the woman had spoken. Glancing around her, she scanned the foreshore, beach and lagoon, trying to summon the name to her tongue. But it would not come, for the sounds were unfamiliar and the word held no meaning. She did not know how to introduce their visitor. Then, in a flash of inspiration, her gaze swooped upon a long-legged grey bird stalking the lagoon. The grey birds were local residents, hunting fish in the reef shallows. But occasionally a white one appeared amongst the grey, a visitor arriving from a far island. A rarely seen oddity. Lupe had discovered another oddity, a visitor from another land. And she would give her a new name. A suitable name that all would remember.

'Matu'u,' she announced. She gestured in the direction of the visitor, only to discover that she had disappeared behind her long yellow skirt.

She took her by the hand to coax her forward with an encouraging smile. 'This is Matu'u,' she said once more. 'I found her. She fell from a canoe in the storm.'

She did not tell how she had come to find the strange woman. She did not say that she had disrespected her aunt, disobeyed her family and ventured alone beyond the lagoon. That tale could wait for another day. Or perhaps not ever, if luck were with her and everyone forgot about her many transgressions in the excitement aroused by their visitor.

Earlier that day, Prudence had stood at the top of the ridge gazing at a village upon a distant shore and longed for rescue. Now that rescue had been attained and she waited at the sandy doorstep of that same village. Only a swathe of lawn and scattered coconut trees stood between her and the neatly spaced oval houses where she hoped to find refuge. On closer inspection, these houses resembled beehives with their steeply pitched roofs of thatch; open-sided beehives without walls or windows. And in front of each house sat a terrace of sand or pebbles, opening to a grassy lawn that seemed quite welcoming. All except for the largest house in the village; that was surrounded by a palisade of stakes driven into the ground.

The people appeared taller than she had imagined too – strongly built and not a little frightening. Prudence huddled instinctively behind her rescuer, almost wishing herself back upon that tiny islet with no one but Madame for company. For who were these people of the Navigator Isles, where even a child might paddle the ocean in a frail canoe? All she knew of them were the words of the *Kangaroo*'s captain, who had described their warriors as fearsome. And indeed they did look fearsome to her eyes.

Male and female alike were tall, with a breadth of shoulder born of physical activity. The men wore leafy skirts of a most indecent length. At first glance, she assumed they wore a kind of short dark trouser beneath these skirts, only realising upon closer inspection that the trousers were in fact tattooed decorations covering their thighs. The men also wore their hair long – left unbound or wound into a topknot – while the women cut their hair short and dressed it with a kind of brown pomade. Some of the younger girls, like her rescuer, had a single curling lock dangling from their left temple. She was relieved to see that although the ladies went as bare-chested as the men, the skirts of grass or woven mats they wrapped about their waists were more seemly, covering their legs to the knees. Both men and women adorned their bodies with armlets and necklets of shells, or placed flowers in their hair.

The flowers heartened her, for surely a people who wore flowers in their hair could not mean her too great a harm.

As they reached the outskirts of the village, a crowd of people gathered around them, some with eyebrows raised and smiling, others standing back frowning. Two adolescent boys scampered up the trunk of a nearby coconut palm to gain a better view, while small children hung upon their parents' legs.

Her rescuer took her hand and drew her forward. 'Ma-tu-u,' she announced, and the word echoed amongst the crowd of villagers. Prudence gathered there had been an introduction. Seemingly, the girl was christening her with a new name. Later, she would learn that Lupe named her for the long-legged herons that frequented the lagoon, but at the time she could only guess at the meaning. For all she knew, she might have named her 'devil'.

One face in particular did not appear pleased at her arrival. A tall woman who first spoke to Lupe glared at Prudence through narrowed eyes. From the stiff way she held her shoulders and her upraised chin, Prudence surmised she would not be hosting a tea party in her guest's honour any time soon. Although how her arrival caused offence, she could not discern. Nevertheless, she decided to give the woman a wide berth and hope the waters could be smoothed at some future time. She was far from everyone and everything she had ever known. She had cast herself out from England and now fate had cast her out from society, as she knew it. But she was alive, as Bessie was not. As the crew of the *Kangaroo* were not. And despite her fear, despite her deep regret, she wanted to stay that way.

She was finding in herself a hunger for life.

And so, clasping the hand of her young rescuer, she allowed herself to be led forward into her new life as a castaway amongst the denizens of these Navigator Isles, an uninvited and perhaps unwanted guest. For how long she would rest here, she could not know – so she had best make a good first impression.

'How do you do?' She nodded companionably to one part-icularly ferocious-looking young man with a row of shark's teeth encircling his throat and a club gripped in his hand, as she attempted to disguise her fear with courtesy.

Prudence had no weapon. Nor did she desire one, for a weapon would surely be a provocation. Prudence had nothing but the contents of her pockets, the shift she stood up in and the locket hung about her neck. All the comforts she had once taken for granted had gone down with the *Kangaroo* or rested thousands of miles distant in Somerset, never to be relied upon again.

All the people she once knew were never to be seen again: her father, who had departed this earth the year before; her mother, who had departed three decades before; Bessie, who had been gone these two days. And then there were those who remained so far distant that she would not see them again.

An image of Edward's face came to her, his hair as pale as these sandy shores, his eyes as clear as these unclouded skies. She had always trusted in those clear, untroubled eyes. Until she hadn't. Until she began to doubt him. She thought of his puzzled expression, that day by the river, when she had refused his offer of marriage. At the time, she believed it was injured pride she saw in his eyes, but perhaps it was disappointment. Except had he been disappointed in love, or out of avarice? Did he desire her money or her person? Now she would never know.

The thought that he was gone from her life forever jolted her with an unexpected sadness, so that a film of tears wet her dry, red eyes. Edward had been part of her life for as long as she could remember. She had trailed after him as a child when he spoke with the men about their estate. As a young woman she had followed him with her eyes as he chatted with her father's guests at table. And then, as a woman finally given her freedom, she had rejected his proposal.

Well, she could not dwell on the past or the future now. If she were to survive, she must contemplate the present. With trembling hand she patted the pockets tied beneath her shift, momentarily regretting the loss of her petticoats and gown, a loss that had almost certainly saved her life. A flimsy shift offered protection to neither body nor modesty. Her burgundy silk day dress with the gigot sleeves, bell skirt and three petticoats would have proved much more suitable armour. The future remained unknown, but at least she had her pocket book and her pencil. Its contents might prove small use in this new life yet it was consolation, nonetheless. Keeping a record of events helped keep her thoughts from disarray. And her steel penknife might prove of value to her new acquaintance. Her hand strayed to the necklace encircling her throat, the locket cradling her only memento of her beloved mother. Perhaps in adversity it was her mother who had kept her safe all this while.

She scanned the unfamiliar faces regarding her inquisitively. Yes, someone must have kept her safe. How else to explain her improbable survival?

'Matu'u,' the girl said once more, directing Prudence's attention with a slight tug to the hand she still clasped.

Prudence may have lost almost everything but she retained her will to survive. And so, despite her fear, she responded obligingly, for what else could a lone castaway do when arriving unexpectedly on someone's doorstep begging hospitality?

'Such a beautiful day,' she observed to her hosts as she bobbed a curtsy. 'So kind of you to invite me.' Then, with a swift glance to ensure that Madame strutted behind, she followed the girl into the village.

Friday: Welcome to Navigator Isles. Almost died chasing chicken. Saved by child.

30

Somerset

2022

By the time Eliza had walked the length of the drive and skirted around the side of the hall to the rear entry, she was feeling slightly wilted. Her lilac silk dress was limp rather than floaty and her underarms were damp. But that could not deter her mission to share the news from Taunton with her co-conspirator. Those unlocked gates had proved too potent a temptation to resist when she dropped Jude home after their expedition to the heritage centre. As she made her way up the drive she told herself that Daniel would be eager to hear what she and Jude had discovered about the locket. Of course, she could have called or texted but she banished that thought as being too perfunctory for such important news. It wasn't simply that she wanted to see him. Nor that she wanted to hear his voice as they stood, shoulder to shoulder, comparing the two portraits on her phone.

No, nothing as silly as that. Nothing as self-defeating or self-delusional as that.

As expected, the rear door to the hall was unlocked, and she followed sounds of activity through the house and up the stairs to the first floor. The creaking and banging noises seemed to be emanating from the room she thought of as Prudence's, but when she reached it there was no sign of Daniel in the empty room. Only scuffed floors, cobwebs and faded lavender wallpaper.

'Shit!'

Well, except for expletives.

'Crap.'

She followed the sound of swearing into Prudence's former dressing room, to find Daniel kneeling on the floor, crowbar in hand and a rueful expression upon his face.

'Daniel?'

'Eliza. Hi.'

'Are you all right?' She could see no signs of blood, but crowbars and hammers made her uneasy, having been on the receiving end of several minor miscalculations of her own.

'Yeah. I'm fine. It's the panelling that's not,' he said, glaring at the oak-lined wall as if in personal affront. 'I noticed some soft spots in this section of wall a while ago and thought I'd take a closer look.'

At his words she became conscious of an earthy, mushroom-like odour pervading the dressing room and the discarded splinters of wood scattered around him.

'Anyway, now I know why this wall looks newer than the others. At some point it's been replaced. There must be water leaking in from the roof. And we're not even on the top floor. God, I hate tracing leaks. Might as well be tracking the Loch Ness monster.'

'You're busy. I can come back.'

'Nah. Time to call it a day.'

'You look dangerous with a crowbar in your hand,' she said, a tiny smile twitching the corners of her lips. He didn't need a crowbar to be dangerous around her.

'Do I?' He stood up, brushed the dirt from his jeans and turned to her with a wide, open smile. 'I'm a pussy cat really.'

'Some people might even believe you,' she said, raising an eyebrow.

'So, what can I do for you, young Eliza? Or are you just missing me?' he asked, grinning.

'Always.' She grinned in return, trying to remember that the conversation held nothing more meaningful than banter. 'But I do have something to share with you. Something Jude and I discovered at the heritage centre in Taunton.'

'I'm all ears. But let's get away from this awful smell. How about a walk in the garden?'

'Perfect.'

The heady scent of lavender hit her as soon as they stepped on to the terraced lawn. The garden might be in disarray but nature had a mind of her own. The hardier roses were still blooming amongst overgrown shrubs, and the sun-loving lavender border had defied the worst weeds to flower year after year. As they strolled across the lawn towards the river she turned back to gaze at the sprawling silhouette of Westcott Hall. It had survived almost three centuries; the Palladian style retaining its elegance despite the decay of neglect. And soon that neglect would be repaired and the house turned into a luxury hotel.

Like the hall and its environs, the Ambrose family had fallen into decline, both financial and reputational. And they too had survived. What did it matter if one of her ancestors turned out to be a murderer?

'I'm beginning to believe that Edward Ambrose may have been the murderer that legend paints him.' Her words emerged on a sigh. In her own mind, if not in the public sphere, she had secretly wanted to exonerate him. Exonerate them all.

'Have you been thinking more about the bell pits?'

'Dwelling on the bell pits would be more accurate,' she said, flicking another glance over her shoulder to the wooded rise behind the house. 'But that's not the only thing. Jude and I had lunch in Taunton today and then went on to an appointment at the heritage centre . . .' She paused to search her phone for the evidence. 'Look. What do you see?' She showed him the photograph she had taken of Prudence's portrait.

'May I?' he asked.

She handed him her phone so that he could zoom in closer on the portrait.

'"Prudence Ambrose née Merryfield",' he read aloud from the tiny plaque at the bottom of the painting.

'Now slide to the next shot.' She watched his face as he inspected the second photograph, clearly wondering what connected the two.

'That's my great-great-something-or-other-grandmother, Elizabeth Pike. Bessie Pike. Prudence's one-time maid.'

He flicked from one photograph to the other, clearly wondering what he was supposed to be seeing. Like a 'spot the difference' puzzle.

'The locket,' he said, after a minute or two. 'They're both wearing the same locket.'

'Yes! And it's the same locket that Prudence sketched in her pocket book, the locket that belonged to her mother. Here, see . . .' Eliza rummaged in her plastic tote for the pocket book, before opening it carefully to a page she had earlier marked with a Post-it note, and handing it to Daniel.

He returned her phone so that he could handle the antique book with care. 'It looks like the same locket,' he said, catching Eliza's eye. 'In which case, Prudence wouldn't have lost it. And if she met with an accident and her body was never found, the locket would have disappeared with her. Am I right?'

'Jude and I think so.'

'So how does Bessie Pike come to be wearing it openly in her portrait?'

'Exactly.'

They both stared at the portrait of Bessie, perhaps looking for clues to the mystery in her wide-spaced blue eyes and the centre-parted auburn ringlets framing her face. She looked too young to be the ancestor of all the Ambroses who followed. Almost childlike, despite her twenty-eight years.

'Edward must have given it to her,' Daniel said eventually. 'Except why would he take that risk? I mean, if I were a murderer, I wouldn't be advertising the fact by giving my new wife my dead wife's jewellery.'

His words reminded her that Daniel too had a previous wife. She wondered, not for the first time, how that mystery woman could bear to let him go.

'Did you give your wife jewellery?' she had blurted out before she realised what she was saying.

He blinked twice, caught momentarily off guard, before saying, 'Not as much as she would have liked.'

'I see.'

'I doubt you do, Eliza,' he said, and she wondered what he meant by it. 'Unfortunately, there were a lot of things Julia would have liked that I couldn't give her. Both material and . . . emotional. At the time, I thought it was some lack in me and I redoubled my efforts to please. But whatever I did, it was never enough. *I* was never enough . . .' He trailed off, his eyes clouded by the past.

She stared at him, finding it difficult to believe that he wouldn't be enough for any woman. Thoughtful, kind, funny, not to mention very hot . . .

'Maybe the lack was in her,' she suggested quietly.

'Mmm. Or maybe we were both blinded by lust and forgot to take that second look. Maybe we just wanted different things,' he said with a shrug.

She liked that shrug. It suggested that his wounds, whatever they were once, had healed. Not that any of it should matter to her. They were just friends, weren't they?

'Julia found her Mr Right,' he added, looking at her thoughtfully. 'They even invited me to the wedding. Luckily, I happened to be in Portugal that weekend.'

Despite her stern self-talk, Eliza's heart lifted at this news. Julia was out of the picture then. 'Portugal is nice.'

'Portugal was nice. Anyway, I digress,' he said, handing back the pocket book. 'The big question is . . . why would Edward do something so incriminating?'

She returned the book to her tote, shaking herself mentally to banish any lingering recalcitrant thoughts. Of beaches in Portugal. Of walking hand in hand along a sandy shore. Of her and Daniel. She cleared her throat. 'Before we left the heritage centre, Jude and I visited the archives to access a document from the family papers. Specifically, the marriage settlement between Edward and Bessie.'

'Anything interesting?' Daniel asked.

'The marriage settlement specifically mentions the inclusion of a "gold locket with miniature portrait from the Merryfield collection".' Eliza clasped the pocket book to her chest, as if it might somehow shed more light on the mystery. 'I don't know what to make of it,' she added with a shake of her head. 'Edward and Prudence are friends. Bessie is Prudence's maid. Bessie and Prudence are shipwrecked. Bessie and Prudence are both rescued. Edward and Prudence marry. Prudence disappears. Seven years later, Edward and Bessie marry.' These were the bare facts. Yet there were so many gaps between these facts. And the real story lay in the gaps.

'One thing seems clear. For the locket to be mentioned in the marriage settlement, both Edward and Bessie must have known it remained at Westcott Hall after Prudence disappeared,' Daniel said. 'So she left it behind, or either Edward or Bessie – perhaps both – knew what happened to her.'

The past was a trickster; when you looked for certainty it only gave you more puzzles. Perhaps Eliza's search for the truth was pointless.

'Didn't Edward meet up with Bessie in Sydney during his journey in search of Prudence?' Daniel asked, prodding her from her thoughts.

'Uh-huh.'

'Well, maybe Prudence and Bessie weren't the only ones who formed a lasting bond during a long sea voyage,' he said. 'Huddled against the wind and waves. Edward comforting Bessie after her ordeal.'

As if on cue, the breeze freshened, setting the leaves on the chestnut trees to whispering. Eliza shivered. Perhaps she would never know what really happened to Prudence. Maybe Edward or Bessie had kept the locket in remembrance.

Or atonement.

'You're cold again. Underdressed as usual.' Daniel reached out an arm as if to encircle her shoulders, before dropping it to his side once more. Empty.

'Fashionably dressed, not underdressed, if you please.'

'Anyway, let's get you back inside.'

They turned and headed back towards the hall. The evening sun cast a mellow glow on the stone, hiding the decay. Yes, Eliza was cold in her beautiful silk finery. She was cold and lonely. She had given herself willingly to her parents' legacy, but in doing so she had somehow closed her heart to new love and new adventures. And now, when her heart was telling her it was ready to beat again, love wasn't an option.

'I had a thought,' Daniel said, as she suddenly found herself holding back tears. 'If you like, I can help you look for new premises. Give you an idea on renovation costs, that sort of thing.'

'That's okay. You're busy. Thanks for the offer, though. I'm planning one last foray in asking for a renewed lease.'

'Oh . . . what's that?'

'Well, negotiating through third parties doesn't seem to be working. So far, I've left it up to my solicitor. So I thought I'd go straight to the horse's mouth, so to speak. I can trace the owner through Companies House. I don't know why I didn't think of it before. Maybe we can work something out.'

Daniel stopped in his tracks and turned to face her. His face was half in shadow, half in light. His hazel eyes were dark in the almost dusk. He frowned, crossing his arms and putting a hand to his chin, as if pondering something.

'What is it? Bad plan?'

He drew an audible breath. 'There's something I've been meaning to tell you.' He removed the hand from his chin to tap at his arm. He seemed jumpy. Not his usual cool self.

'Should I be worried?'

He looked worried. What had he found out that she didn't know?

He cleared his throat. 'I should have told you earlier. But . . .'

'But . . . ?' She had always distrusted 'buts'. A 'but' with a pause following usually lead to disappointment. Like when a dealer said he had just the early nineteenth-century mirror you'd been searching for but . . . he sold it yesterday. Or a lover said he enjoyed your company but . . . he wasn't looking for anything serious. Or a paramedic told you your mother was in good hands but . . . she died minutes later. But.

'But . . .' He looked up into the darkening sky for inspiration. 'I . . . ah . . . didn't want to see exactly that look of disappointment on your face. Not caused by me. I suppose I wanted . . . I wanted to . . .'

It was the first time she had seen him lost for words. He always seemed so sure of himself. What on earth was going on? What could he possibly have done to merit this nervousness?

'I wanted to be the good guy.' He shrugged. 'Nobody wants to be the bad guy.'

When she looked back on this moment in the days following, she would tell herself that she was an idiot not to have caught his meaning. Anyone with half a brain should have worked it out by then. Except she was an idiot, wasn't she, where Daniel was concerned.

'What are you trying to tell me? It's not still that kiss the other week, is it? Because I thought we'd moved on from there. I mean, it was just a moment, wasn't it?'

'No. Not that,' he said, and she thought she caught a hint of regret in his eyes. 'Never that.'

At least that was something. 'Then what?'

'I'm the owner of your shop, Eliza. I'm the name behind True South Enterprises.'

Her first instinct should have been to walk away without a word. That would have been the smart thing to do. The brave thing to do, to cut him off and cauterise the wound before it could fester. But she didn't. She couldn't. His words knocked the breath from her body. She just stared at him.

'What?'

'I bought it years ago as an investment. And looking to the future, when my business was established enough that I didn't need an office in a town centre, I planned to relocate. So when I won the contract for the hotel development, and the lease on the shop came due at the same time, relocating became the logical thing to do.'

'But you didn't tell me.' Did she really sound as plaintive as her ears suggested?

'No, I didn't. Big mistake. I'm sorry.'

'I was always going to find out. Like when you opened your office, for example.'

'I know. I know. I kept putting it off. At first you were just a name on a lease. The compensation was fair. And then we met. And that day in your shop I saw how distressed you were about it.' He tried to hold her gaze but she looked away. She didn't want him to see the hurt in her eyes.

'And you thought you could salve your conscience by offering me a commission?'

'Not my conscience, no. Because I didn't do anything wrong. We had a fair contract. It was more that I ... I wanted time to ...'

She held up her palm to his face and shook her head. She did not wait to hear more excuses. That would only lead to more pain. She was off, her legs moving at a brisk march. Across the acres of lawn, crunching along the drive, hastening between the gathering shadows, through the rusting gates to her car. Back to the life she had been entrusted with.

Back to safety, or so she had once thought.

But maybe the notion of safety was just that – a notion. A fancy. And you could become lost in the storm, no matter how hard you clung to the mast.

Maybe sometimes you just needed to let go.

31

New South Wales, Australia

1834

Bessie woke to a room that rocked. Yet she did not appear to be aboard ship, despite the pitching room. She was lying in a simple bed with a headboard so low it could scarce own that name. Above her, wooden beams supported a shingled roof, while the floor was flagged in light-coloured stone. If it weren't for the swaying of the plastered walls she might have believed herself back in her grandparents' cottage in Somerset. Except that could not be so, for surely they were long dead. Her heart knocked at her ribs like some small cornered creature and she tried to calm it, but the swaying room and her confusion would not be quieted. She had been so long at sea, so far from home, that fear had become her natural state.

She clutched at the timber headboard as she tried to make sense of her surroundings. A second bed, currently unoccupied, a small table and an old sofa frame with fraying upholstery completed the furnishings. As to her dress, she was clothed in a simple cotton shift, while an unfamiliar garment in a style of twenty years before hung from a hook on the back of the door.

A knock sounded and for a moment she wondered if it were Wills come to berate her for sleeping late and forgetting to set

Miss Merryfield's fire. But Miss Merryfield was dead, wasn't she? Swept from the deck of the *Kangaroo* by a giant wave. Lost to the storm that had taken the captain and most of the crew. Even now, her mistress would be lying on the floor of the ocean, her flesh nibbled by sea creatures, while she, Bessie . . .

'Mistress Pike, may I come in?'

She did not recognise the voice at first, and since no one had ever asked her permission for anything, she hesitated before answering with a quavering, 'Yes.'

The woman who entered was garbed in a similarly old-fashioned dress to that which hung upon Bessie's door, her hair covered by a mob cap with a ruffled brim. Her brown and weathered face was ancient; her figure so stooped that Bessie's grip on the headboard relaxed in the knowledge that such an ancient personage could do her little harm.

'There's a gentleman to see you. The Governor says to show you to the morning room,' the old woman croaked. When Bessie stared at her in mute incomprehension, she added, 'Here, let me help you into your clothes, poor lass. You must be all at sixes and sevens. Shipwrecked and lost at sea in a wee boat as you were.'

'Yes. I was lost at sea. In a wee boat.'

'All alone with those rough sailors. Months living amongst the natives of Feejee. Then another sea voyage to Sydney Cove. And nought but a lass yourself.' The woman chattered as she helped Bessie into the faded blue dress and hunted out some worn leather slippers beneath the bed for her feet. 'It's ancient history now but I still remember my first days here as a convict. You probably don't remember where you are half the time. But you're safe now, at Government House at Parramatta. And Governor Bourke will likely find you a position when you're recovered.'

As the old woman chattered companionably, the room gradually stilled and Bessie's heart slowed as her memory scrabbled to return. Always it led back to the ship. Every night, she returned there in her dreams, the pitching and rolling in heavy seas, her mouth and eyes filling with water as she sank beneath the waves. Then she would wake to a new morning on dry land – in another alien land.

'Have I been here long, Mrs . . . ?'

'Eccles, Mrs Betty Eccles. Bird as was. 'Tis a week since the Governor had you brought to Parramatta to recover from your ordeal. We put you in this wee room by the kitchen since it wouldn't do to house you with the convicts in the servants' quarters. P'raps you'll remember when you're properly awake.'

'Yes, it begins to come back to me now. I'm sorry, thank you, Mrs Eccles.'

'Poor wee lass. But 'tis a fine gentleman come to call on you. P'raps he brings news of your family back home.'

'I have no family back home.'

She had no family anywhere. She had lost them all. Her mother, her grandparents, even Miss Merryfield who could not properly be called family and yet had been the closest thing Bessie knew to such a thing. And now even she was gone.

'Come along then. I'll show you to the morning room. Would not do to keep the gentleman waiting.'

Mrs Eccles led her along a corridor with windows looking out to a wide brown field on one side, and a series of small rooms opening upon the other. As they passed through the main wing of the house, Bessie spied several larger rooms through open doorways, before they continued along another windowed corridor until her guide paused to knock at the entrance to a sunlit room with windows on two sides.

'Mistress Pike, sir,' the old woman announced to a man standing in the middle of the room. He had his back to them, staring out at the bone-dry grass and strange trees with ghostly trunks and drooping grey leaves.

'Thank you, Mrs Eccles,' he replied as he turned to face them. 'Bessie. It *is* you. I hardly dared hope.'

'Mr Ambrose . . .' This time it wasn't the room that swayed, it was Bessie. She reached out an arm, seeking something to hold on to, and found it grasped by this man she had thought never to see again.

'Here, take a seat before you fall,' he said, leading her to a cane-bottomed armchair and setting her down.

She had never sat in a gentleman like Mr Ambrose's presence before and perched nervously on the edge of the seat, ready to spring up at his slightest word. It occurred to her that perhaps she was about to be blamed for her mistress's death. That she had failed somehow in her duties as lady's maid and was to be punished. Then again, surely it was the good Lord to blame for the wild weather and angry seas that had taken Miss Merryfield. Bessie couldn't be held responsible for those. 'The Lord's ways were ever mysterious,' as Mr Custard was wont to say. Look how he had spared Bessie when he could have taken her thrice now. That were mysterious, indeed.

'I'm very happy to find you alive,' Mr Ambrose said, taking a chair opposite.

He looked thinner than when she had seen him last. A year and a half at least since her mistress had quit the hall and taken Bessie with her. His dress was not so neat and tidy as she had known it either, and beneath his shipboard tan his complexion had a greyish look to it. Perhaps that's what came of chasing after a lady when you weren't wanted. Although she had never quite understood what had set her mistress against him so. He, who had always had a kind word for a simple servant girl like Bessie.

'I set sail as soon as I had word of the *Kangaroo*'s disappearance and your mistress's presence aboard. Once I arrived in Sydney, I found to my great relief that several crew had managed to sail a ship's boat south to one of the Feejee Islands and from there were rescued and brought to Sydney. It gives me hope, Bessie. Something I have been short on for a good long time now.' He clasped his hands to give weight to his words.

She did not see why her survival should give him hope. There was little enough in this world to hope for, she found. Every time she gathered together a few scraps of that sentiment, they were soon torn from her grasp. And yet . . . his beaming smile and bouncing tone tempted her. He was happy to see her. She clasped her own hands in her lap, staring down at the rich Turkey rug beneath her feet and determined not to trust any such slippery feelings.

'For if you survived, Prudence may well have survived too,' he pronounced.

Prudence. Of course his hopes were all for her employer. He who was Miss Merryfield's friend, who pined for a lady who did not love him, a lady who had run from him. Bessie would not have run from a man such as Mr Ambrose, not in a thousand years.

'She be gone, sir,' she said. 'I were there when the sea took her.'

'But you survived. How can we be sure that she did not? Perhaps she was washed overboard and managed to find some object to which she could cling. A boom, a ship's hatch, perhaps even a large barrel. I have read newspaper accounts of shipwreck survivors floating upon such objects . . .' He paused to give her time to agree with him. 'The current may have taken her to a nearby isle. We can't be sure she drowned. We can't be certain.' He leaned forward, his hands planted on his knees now, as if he could will it to be so.

'If you say so, sir.'

'I hope so, Bessie. Indeed I do. And I'm determined to do everything in my power to discover the truth of it.'

From everything that sailor Williams had told her, and from

the maps she had seen in her employer's books, the Pacific Ocean was speckled with tiny islands. Finding her employer in that watery vastness would be less likely than finding a needle in a haystack. Finding the woman who had been kind to Bessie in her offhand way, kinder than any other since her grandmother passed from this earth, would be a miracle.

'Good luck to you, Mr Ambrose. Good luck finding Miss Merryfield.'

'I shall need luck. But I shall also need you, Bessie. For you best know her state of mind, her manner of thinking.' He shook his head with a frown, adding, 'For I surely do not.'

'I don't know as to how I can help, sir.' Looking at his handsome, worried face, she wasn't sure that she wanted to help him find some other woman, even if it were Miss Merryfield.

'You can sail with me to the Navigator Isles. The nearest land to where the *Kangaroo* was wrecked, as far as I can ascertain from the surviving crew. The captain, unfortunately, did not survive.' His eyes fixed upon Bessie's so that she found it difficult to look away.

They were kind eyes, but not so kind that they would accept a servant girl's reluctance without protest, without pressure brought to bear.

'If we find her, she will need you. She may be . . . ah . . . traumatised. You wish to help your mistress, don't you?'

She supposed that she did. Miss Merryfield had treated her kindly. She had saved her from the workhouse. She had taught her to read. She had trained her as a lady's maid. She rarely shouted and never threw things. She had even emptied the slop bucket when Bessie was so sick from their voyage that she could not stand upright. She had comforted her with fine pale hands.

She supposed that she owed her that allegiance. Even so . . . Miss Merryfield wasn't the only one who had been terrified by her ordeal. She, Bessie, had endured days . . . weeks . . .

months . . . she could no longer remember, on that tiny boat . . . and many more weeks in a lean-to made of palm leaves in the Feejees. She did not wish to return to that.

'I don't see as to how she could be living, sir,' she persisted, tearing her eyes from his to stare out of the window at the hard light burnishing the trees, the sky so bright it hurt her eyes. This land might be foreign to her, hot and dry, and peopled with ramshackle buildings and rough convicts, but at least she was on solid ground. At least she wasn't rolling in mountainous seas with the wind whipping her skirts and the rain soaking her to the skin. At least she wasn't in danger of being dragged to the bottom of the ocean to join her unlucky mistress amongst the fish and the weed and the sharp-toothed sea monsters. At least she was alive.

'I need you, Bessie.'

Why did he have to go and say such a thing, standing there with his sad, kind eyes? She knew in her bones he only needed her for her mistress, and yet . . . if she were to sail with him on this foolhardy expedition they would be thrown into each other's company for weeks, nay months. And even then they might never find Miss Merryfield, for surely she was dead and gone by now. He might come to need Bessie for herself then. He might come to see her goodness, her cleverness.

'And once we have her safe, we can all sail home,' he said with a smile, as if the matter had already been settled to his satisfaction. The wreck of the *Kangaroo* and the loss of its crew and passengers were simply a temporary inconvenience.

'I suppose we can, sir.'

If the sea did not get them first.

32

Samoa

1834

Some days the lagoon seemed like an old, if somewhat tempestuous, friend. Prudence had made her peace with the ocean after it almost drowned her. After almost a year on the island, she had come to know it well. She enjoyed its sparkling wit on those days when the light skipped across the lagoon, while avoiding its darker moods when the wind whipped up the waves and the heavens emptied. And although Lupelele wasn't always the most patient of teachers (to the delight of the small children who Prudence sometimes caught giggling behind their hands at her clumsiness), at least she now knew the rudiments of constructing a small fish trap or weaving a basket to carry home her quarry. She had learned enough language to understand others and make herself understood. Indeed, given enough time, she might one day own enough skill to be let loose on the lagoon alone.

But this morning it was the time of the new moon and the women and girls of Lupe's āiga were foraging in the shallow waters of the lagoon at low tide. Each carried a long stick, a short stick and a basket as they waded waist deep along the reef, searching for small fish and shellfish. Prudence was about to join Lupe and the other girls as they moved closer to the shore in their foraging, when Masina hailed the group.

'Is Matu'u a girl?' she asked, rather tersely even for her.

Lupe and her friends stopped in their tracks and glanced at each other beneath lowered lashes. Prudence remained silent, unsure where the conversation was leading. She had grown accustomed to the meandering nature of her hosts' discussions, learning that it was wise to taste before partaking.

'Matu'u is a woman. She has breasts,' one girl volunteered.

'Big round breasts under her tiputa,' giggled another, for despite the constant teasing, Prudence insisted on wearing an upper garment of finely woven pandanus leaves to cover her breasts, a garment that the other women only donned on the rare occasions that the weather turned cold. She might wear a grass skirt that showed glimpses of her thighs but she stopped short of baring her breasts for the world to see.

'Then why does she fish with girls?' Masina asked, directing her question to her niece.

Lupe looked out to sea in silence. After almost a year in the girl's company, Prudence could guess at her feelings, having herself lived under Masina's 'guidance' in the fale of the aualuma. Dissent was always lurking beneath Lupe's forbearance, yet she appeared to hold her tongue and heed her elders – most of the time. An entire moon of confinement to the village, ordered by the council of matai after she returned to the village with Prudence in tow, had taught the girl that lesson.

'I have much to learn. Lupe is kind to teach me,' Prudence said, hoping to forestall any disagreement.

'There's no need. Lupe has caused enough trouble to her family. You will learn better by following the grown women,' Masina pronounced.

Her niece opened her mouth as if she might argue but Prudence signalled with her eyes to let the matter rest. After a moment, the girl dropped her eyes in assent and Prudence watched as the younger girls drifted through the shallow water in silence until they were far enough distant to chatter quietly amongst themselves. Meanwhile, she followed the older women as they waded deeper on to the reef. There was nothing more to be done about the situation, least of all by someone who almost everyone in the village secretly considered a child.

'Lupe is not your mother,' Masina said before they had gone very far.

The words were uttered mildly so that Prudence wasn't sure at first of their intent. Indeed, she thought she might have misunderstood entirely.

'You let her order you like a mother, yet you are not a child.'

'That is true,' Prudence replied, while thinking that neither was this woman *her* mother to tell her what to do. She had never had a mother to guide her, not since she was a small child.

'And you are not her mother,' Masina added.

Prudence did not know what to say to this, for as a statement of fact it was self-evident, yet she knew much more than fact lay behind these words.

'You cannot take her mother's place. You do not know how to guide her,' Masina said, her eyes scanning the lagoon for a likely fishing ground.

Prudence opened her mouth to reply but no words issued forth, for what could she say? Masina's words were true. She knew little of use in Lupe's world. She may have the contents of her pocket book by heart, but its repository of useful facts was superfluous in her present situation. Lupe had no use for a calendar of the births and marriages of the sovereign princes of Europe or a list of the baronets of England. An intimate knowledge of dining table etiquette couldn't help her make bedding of bark cloth or prepare ava for her father and his friends to drink. Prudence herself had no need for such knowledge, since the likelihood of her returning home was small.

'You do not belong with her.'

'I have nowhere else to go,' she said after a while. But Masina and the other women were already wading deeper into the lagoon, so Prudence followed behind, feeling not a little superfluous. She did not know what to make of this conversation, but there was little more she could do standing waist deep in the sea. She would worry about it later.

'Matu'u fishes with me,' Masina said when the group reached a place where the sandy bottom of the reef showed between outcrops of coral. A few moments later, her head disappeared beneath the surface as she laid her first trap.

Prudence watched Masina's wavering form as she placed a dark grey stone in the trap as a lure, before resurfacing.

'Be still while we wait for the tu'u'u to come. If you move he may bite you,' she instructed, before dipping her head underwater once more.

Prudence had discovered this fact one day when she reached out to touch these small pretty fish that lived amongst the branching coral, and received a nip on the hand for her trouble. So she waited several feet distant from her teacher, trying not to flinch as unseen creatures brushed against her legs. Periodically, Masina raised her head to take a breath but apart from this she remained motionless until, in a sudden flash of movement, she pounced upon the fish trap. She covered the trap's mouth with her hand to prevent her prey's escape. When she had it secure, she raised the trap to the surface and deposited the unlucky fish in her basket, before dipping her head beneath the sea once again.

They continued fishing in this fashion for perhaps an hour until Masina deemed it time to move onwards to a scattering of rocks and loose coral in shallower waters. 'You may help now. Use your long stick to lift the rock,' she instructed Prudence. 'Prop it up with your short stick and search beneath. Call me if you are not sure.'

Prudence had often foraged in this way with Lupe and had learned to recognise many of the creatures destined for the cooking pot or oven. She had even come to enjoy eating the odd-looking octopus she would have spurned as a curiosity fit for a museum not so long ago. Its flesh was unexpectedly tender when it emerged, steaming and flavoured with coconut, from the earth ovens tended by the men of the village. When she had first seen Lupe's father labouring over the cooking in this way she was surprised, but soon discovered that the work of heating and handling the hot volcanic rocks that fired the ovens was con-sidered men's work. Too heavy for a woman. Just as tilling the soil and fishing from canoes beyond the breakers was also deemed the labour of men.

Now, shadowed by Masina and armed with her two sticks, Prudence began to search beneath the coral rubble, stepping lightly around the delicate living reef. At first she did not have much luck, frightening away several crabs that scuttled out from under rocks and frightening herself when she disturbed a small brown eel with rather large and pointed teeth. Every now and then, she glanced over to note that Masina's basket was already brimming with creatures, while hers held but a solitary fugafuga, a spotted sea cucumber she had caught moving ponderously along the sand, too slow to escape even her clutches.

She was feeling quite despondent – certain that Masina would find words to shame her when they returned to the village – when a creature crawling slowly along the sand caught her eye. It was almost as long as her hand, with a cone-shaped shell in a swirling pattern of reddish brown and white. She had never seen such a creature before but it was beautiful, and she experienced an urge to have it regardless of any potential culinary uses. It would look so pretty in a necklace draped about Lupe's shoulders. Surely the girl would like it.

Bending low so that she was submerged to chest height, she

dipped her head below the surface and stretched out an arm to scoop it up. But before her hand could close around the shell she felt a whoosh of water buffet her and a long stick was thrust into the sand beside the creature, narrowly missing her hand. She reeled back in surprise, turning to face the woman alongside her in anger. Prudence had learned to hold her emotions in check during her sojourn in the village, never sure if she might transgress some unspoken rule or custom. But the spear thrust had thrown her off balance, and she rounded on the other woman in a fury.

'You speared me!'

'I only thrust my stick in the sand near your hand, Matu'u,' Masina said, as she withdrew her stick from the sand. 'If I had wanted to spear you, you would be crying out in pain, not anger.'

'Why would you do such a thing? What have I done to offend you so?'

The woman truly puzzled her. She could not fathom the reason for her dislike. Masina was a woman of standing in her community, the leader of the society of girls and single women, the aualuma, while Prudence was . . . Prudence was . . . what was she?

'You have done much to offend me, but that is no matter. I thrust my stick into the sand to save you.'

'Save me from what? A snail?'

Masina gestured with her chin towards the pretty creature, even now creeping along the sand near Prudence's foot. 'This one, this one will poison you. It will send out its harpoon to spear you. First you will feel pain. Then your hand will fall asleep, then your arm, and then if you are unlucky you will die.'

Prudence jerked her foot from the creature's path in horror.

'You do not belong here,' Masina murmured in a low voice.

'I have nowhere else to go,' she said, risking a glance at

Masina's disapproving face. Instead of the expected disapproval she saw only sorrow, a sad frown wrinkling the other woman's brow.

'And you do not belong with Lupe's father.'

Was this the reason for Masina's distrust? That she believed Prudence had designs upon Kisona? If so, she could soon set her mind at rest. She barely had anything to do with the man, and could not fathom why Masina would think that.

'Kisona does not want me,' she told the other woman. From the little she knew of Lupe's father he was a fine, strong man, the leader of his extended family. He was respected by the other matai of the village and his words held weight in the village council. But despite the fact that his āiga had adopted her, he had shown little interest of this kind in Prudence – little interest in her of any kind, in fact.

'And I do not want him. I do not need a man. I am content to live in the fale of the aualuma and contribute to the good of the āiga.'

If she had wanted a man she wouldn't have rejected Edward, who she had once loved in the way only a young girl can love. Desperately. Blindly. No, she did not need a man. She needed to be free to be herself . . . whoever that may turn out to be. She wasn't sure she knew any more.

Masina laughed but the sound held no mirth. 'You are young enough to get children. For a while.'

Prudence laughed. 'Kisona spends more time sitting by his wife's grave than he does with me.' Several times she had seen him sitting cross-legged there as if in deep conversation.

Masina drew back as if Prudence had speared *her*. Despite the bright sunlight reflected from the water, her eyes were shaded in misery as she said, 'It matters not what Kisona wants. His daughter wants you. And Kisona loves his daughter.'

Her father wasn't the only person who loved the girl, Prudence saw. Despite her harsh words, her aunt did too. And Prudence stood in her path, or so she believed.

'Don't worry. I can't take the place of Lupe's mother. Not with Kisona or Lupe. Nor can you,' she said with a shrug of acceptance.

For like her father, the child did not want another woman in her mother's place. But perhaps she did want someone to mother – someone like Prudence, who was as lost as she was. Perhaps she wanted the closeness, without the threat of someone usurping her mother's place.

And perhaps Prudence did too. Perhaps being a Lady Adventuress wasn't enough.

'Let her be and she will come to you,' she said to Masina.

But the other woman had already turned away.

Tuesday: Almost poisoned by snail. ~~Speared~~ Saved by Masina. Sea cucumber for dinner.

33

Somerset, England

2022

Sunday tea was accompanied by the rustle of leaves falling from trees in Jude's garden. The temperature remained mild enough to sit outside but summer was definitely over. A leaf dropped from a branch of the alder tree that shaded the terrace, drifting on a breath of wind to land in Eliza's cup. It floated there like a bright gold coin on the surface of Jude's preferred Darjeeling blend. She fished it out and placed it on her saucer, registering for the first time the thick drifts of leaves blanketing the garden paths. Summer had come and gone in a blink of the eye.

'Can I give you a hand raking leaves?' she said to her aunt.

'Not to worry, they'll be tramped down sooner or later. Besides, Bobby seems to be enjoying himself.'

Bobby raised his head at the mention of his name but when nothing of interest eventuated, he returned to rolling in a pile of leaves in various stages of decay. Rain or shine, the weather never seemed to bother him. He let the water run off his back, always rustled up a shady spot in the heat, and relished a romp in the snow.

'I've always thought a dog's life wouldn't be so bad. They're very forgiving, aren't they?' Jude gave her niece a sideways glance over the rim of her teacup.

'As opposed to?' Eliza asked, knowing full well what her aunt was hinting at, but Jude only shrugged and took a bite of macaroon. 'You're not very subtle.'

'You tend to ignore subtle, pet.'

She watched as another leaf dropped on to the table. Before she knew it the alder's branches would be bare.

'The days are going by so quickly,' Eliza said softly. And all she seemed to do was work. Except work might not be an option any more, if she couldn't find just the right new home for the business. She would have to close the store and find something else to do.

The idea should have induced panic but instead she felt a confusing sense of lightness at the prospect.

'You don't need to remind me,' Jude said. 'The years are just slipping through this old woman's fingers. All the more reason to make the most of them. Travel a bit. Try new directions. Meet new people?'

'Good idea, except I don't have time.'

If she relaxed for even a moment, took a weekend off, God forbid a holiday abroad, everything might come crashing down around her. Her parents' life's work would have been for nothing. And yet . . . it was a tantalising prospect, the idea of being free to do something else. Free to do her own thing, whatever that might turn out to be.

No . . . she wouldn't countenance the thought. Look what happened the last time she ventured down that road – her world had been completely upended.

'Well, I have time on my hands so I've been doing a bit more detective work in the archives,' Jude said, bringing out her phone. 'I decided to make a search for Edward Ambrose's will. We didn't get time to look for it on our last visit.'

'Anything juicy?'

'Only in what it didn't say.'

Eliza's ears pricked up. She may have put aside her quest to solve Prudence's disappearance for the moment, but she hadn't abandoned it. That would be like relinquishing some inner kernel of Eliza-ness that she had inadvertently mislaid. She had abandoned her first love, journalism, to help her parents – and she would never regret that – but Prudence's story had become a part of her story now. Her history, in fact. Even if she didn't succeed in solving the mystery, at least she would have tried. At least the search meant something to her.

'Edward left nothing to his third wife in his will,' Jude said, opening her phone to a photograph she had taken of the old document.

This was strange. Usually, the widow would be remembered in some way in the husband's will. After all, Shakespeare bequeathed Anne Hathaway his 'second-best bed with the furniture'.

'As you know, the marriage settlement granted her the right to live here in Gatehouse Lodge for the remainder of her life should Edward predecease her,' Jude explained. 'It also provided for a small widow's portion of the interest on two thousand pounds. But the will gave her nothing further. Everything went to their son. Not a single personal bequest, a painting or his mother's jewellery. Not even his favourite hound, which was actually bequeathed to one Samuel Bobbett. Not a thing for the mother of his only child.' Jude's face was a picture of horror at this ancestral injustice. 'After she gave him his precious son and cared for him in his dotage.'

That was another point though, wasn't it? The pair had only produced one child.

Eliza patted her aunt on the arm. She appeared to be taking it so personally, these misdeeds of their long-ago ancestor. 'I wonder what she did to offend him,' she mused. 'Or maybe he was just generally a bad lot. His reputation for murder would suggest that.'

'The greater the love, the worse the betrayal, I suppose,' her aunt suggested.

Eliza's head jerked up suspiciously at this but Jude was busy selecting another macaroon. 'These are delicious. Where did you get them?' her aunt asked.

A diversionary tactic if Eliza ever heard one. Her aunt was an expert in that regard. It seemed the conversation was over for the moment. Except, all through the clearing and washing of dishes that followed, she could not banish thoughts of Jude's comment about betrayal, even when her aunt flicked her with a tea towel for inattention. What was betrayal anyway? Did it count if it was only in thought? Did it count if it was in retrospect? And who suffered its consequences longest – the betrayed, who had to live with their hurt, or the betrayer who must live with their guilt? She was still wrestling with these thoughts when she bid her aunt goodbye.

'I'll see you next week,' she said as her aunt saw her to the gate.

'I suppose you haven't seen Daniel lately,' Jude said, pecking her on the cheek.

The comment caught her off guard, as if honing in on her own preoccupation with the man and his secrets. 'Did he tell you that?' Eliza snapped. 'Have you been talking about me behind my back?'

'What? No.' Her aunt's face was all wide-eyed innocence peeking out from amongst the wrinkles, but Eliza wasn't fooled. 'But he did drop in the other day to say hello and have a spot of tea. He happened to mention that you haven't answered his calls. Or his messages.'

'Sorry. I didn't mean to snap. Like I said, I've been busy. And Daniel hasn't been top of my list,' she said with a studied shrug.

'I see,' her aunt said, but her face said that she didn't see at all. She didn't see why her niece was ignoring the attentions of a man to whom she was clearly attracted.

And despite her pretence at nonchalance, Eliza's professional courtesy was outraged by her own behaviour. Was she or was she not a dealer in fine antiques? Did she or did she not desire to save her parents' business? After all, she had undertaken to help the man source antiques for the hotel, purely a business decision. If he had broken her trust in not telling her that he owned her premises, that was a personal betrayal.

Despite her common-sense self-talk, she could not bring herself to answer his calls. Not yet. Her wounds were still too raw. Because of him, she was about to lose the place her parents had loved, the place where they had lived and worked for decades. The last place she had seen her mother alive. The Cabinet of Wonders held so many of her memories, so much of her past, and she wasn't ready to let it go.

'You know, Daniel probably wanted to tell you about the shop a while ago. I suppose he was afraid of—'

'How do you know that?' Eliza interrupted her. 'Did you know already?'

'No, of course not, pet. I didn't know anything about it until you told me. Only he was so *mopey*, I suppose is the best word for it, when he dropped by yesterday, like a dog with his tail between his legs. I could tell that . . .' She paused, staring across the fields towards the hall for inspiration. 'I could tell that he was missing you.'

None of this mattered, though. Even if Eliza was missing him too, missing those excited calls whenever he made a new discovery, missing the way his warm hazel eyes scrunched in concentration when he was poring over old photographs, or the way he had of driving with one arm draped over the back of the passenger seat, even then it wouldn't matter. Even if she could find it in her heart to forgive him – and she suspected she probably could – it didn't matter. Because it was friendship he wanted, nothing more. And friends didn't betray each other.

Just like family didn't betray each other. Didn't make secret plans behind each other's backs. Didn't run when the going got tough.

'Couldn't you . . .'

'No, I couldn't, Jude. Not yet, anyway.' She knew she was being harsh. She knew that other people, reasonable people, might say that she was hard hearted. But it hurt too much. And she knew it shouldn't.

Bobby was panting by the time they reached the river. Eliza had set a brisk pace on the walk from Jude's cottage, as if she could escape her thoughts if she walked far and fast enough. They had cut across country, damp to the ankles from wet grass, a sheen of perspiration to Eliza's forehead and Bobby's circle work growing smaller and smaller as they trekked on. At the riverbank the pair paused to catch their breath, Eliza settling upon a fallen log with the dog hunkered down beside her, the late afternoon sun retreating behind clouds.

From where she sat, she could see the roof of Westcott Hall rising above the alder trees that shaded the riverbank. Without any conscious decision on her part she had set out upriver from her aunt's cottage, the route taking her towards the hall. Of late it was always the hall. Jude had lived just outside its gates Eliza's entire life; her father had grown up there. Yet, for most of those decades, the hall had existed on the periphery of her consciousness. She knew about the family connection, she knew her ancestors had once owned and then lost the estate, but it had seemed irrelevant to her real life. A conversational curiosity she might mention in passing to an acquaintance, Prudence's disappearance reduced to a quirky story to enliven conversation at a party. Now, somehow, she had become obsessed by the hall – and the man who intended to rebuild it.

She was still thinking about the conversation with her aunt when she heard barking from the direction in which she had come. A minute later, a familiar shape emerged galloping through the trees to worry at her knees and demand a pat.

'Ruby, girl, what are you doing here?' she asked, hugging the dog to her and nuzzling Ruby's shaggy face with hers.

The dog's owner soon emerged, his long, jeans-clad legs striding purposefully towards her. He bent to stroke Bobby's ears before offering Eliza a rueful smile and a tentative, 'Hey.'

'Are you stalking me?' she asked, not entirely jokingly. Except she had taken to wandering too, hadn't she?

'I think Ruby can answer for that. She must have caught Bobby's scent. Not that I haven't been trying to reach out to you,' he said, regarding her so intently that she had to look away. 'I really wish you'd give me a chance to redeem myself,' he said with a sigh. 'I hoped we were friends.'

'As you said, you've done nothing wrong.' She refused to look at him, concentrating instead on a knot in Ruby's hair. That was simpler to untangle.

'Not intentionally, no, except by not telling you everything in the beginning, I've hurt you. And that's the last thing I wanted. I should have owned up when we first met.'

'Yes. You should have,' she murmured into Ruby's fur.

'But I wimped out.'

His admission was so pathetic that she had to look up. He had that gleam in his eyes – the one that grown men get when they've been caught doing something naughty – and one of his feet was idly toeing a stick.

'The truth is,' he sighed, 'I have an aversion to letting people down.'

'Well, you're not alone in that.'

'Yeah, I know that. It's no excuse, really. Except it's become a bit pathological with me. I got so used to my ex telling me I'd let her down that I developed a bit of a phobia,' he said. 'Spiders . . . catch and put outside. Snakes . . . go around. Sharks . . . if large, stay out of the water. If small, ignore. Letting people down . . . run for the hills.'

Eliza laughed despite herself. 'Why *did* she think you'd let her down?' He didn't look the irresponsible type. He looked solid, dependable and sometimes, despite her better judgement, even cuddly.

'Truthfully? I think she had an idea of me in her head and when the real Daniel turned out to be someone quite different, wanting different things, enjoying simpler things maybe, she felt . . . well . . . disappointed.'

He had stopped toeing the stick and his eyes studied her in earnest. 'In the end, I grew tired of being a disappointment.'

It was Eliza's turn to sigh. This conversation wasn't turning out at all how she might have intended. Stand-offish was a difficult attitude to maintain in the face of his contrition. His confidences. Not to mention his cuteness.

'What do you want from me, Daniel?'

'Ah . . . dinner would be a promising start,' he said, grinning at her hopefully.

She almost snorted in reply. As if you could mend a broken heart with a curry and a Tempranillo. There . . . she had admitted it.

'Let me help you sort out new premises, at least. You've got several months left on the lease, and I don't have to take over immediately . . . please. You never know, we might be able to find the perfect solution.'

She knew in her heart that he was genuine. He might not be perfect but he was sincere. She could see that he wanted to help her. Except she wasn't sure what help she wanted or needed. Nor that he wouldn't be more of a hindrance than help to her heart.

But how could she tell him this without betraying all her secrets?

'Okay,' she said, finally.

'Okay then!' He was suddenly bouncing with enthusiasm. 'Friends again,' he said, holding out his hand.

That was the problem, though; being friends might prove to be the most difficult thing of all.

34

Samoa

1834

Her task that morning was to strip the coarse serrated leaves of the paongo, a variety of pandanus palm the women cultivated for making mats. She discarded the sandals she wore about the village while she worked in the sand where the pandanus grew. Unlike the other women, who only donned shoes to protect their feet from the sharp corals of the lagoon, she wore hers almost everywhere. Of necessity, stripping and plaiting hibiscus bark to make sandals had been one of the first skills she learned upon her arrival in the village. And although her feet had grown hardier, she clung to them through habit.

She tied her hair in a topknot like the men, for despite much teasing she still resisted the custom of cutting her hair short and dressing it with pomade as did the other matrons. Like her sandals and the pocket book she guarded so zealously, her long red hair was a vestige of her previous life she could not quite bring herself to relinquish. In her vanity, she would rather endure the teasing than be shorn of it. Sometimes, when she lay sleepless on her mat at night, listening to the sounds of the ocean with the breeze wafting through the fale, she wondered if she would ever return to that former life. Strangely, the thought no longer bothered her. Masina had once told her she did not belong here, but neither did she belong in Somerset, filling her days with paying calls, taking walks, painting and drawing. In truth, she no longer knew where she belonged.

The pandanus leaves caught the morning light, each leaf glistening like a shining green streamer after the overnight rain. The palms sprouted from the sandy soil on stilt-like roots, scattered amongst the coconuts by the beach. Her task earned her numerous cuts and scrapes from the sharp spines marching along the length of the paongo leaves. They had the longest and broadest leaves of all the pandanus palms cultivated by the village, each leaf taller than her body and wider than her palm. The women used these coarse leaves to make floor mats, a never ending supply of which was needed as the mats were replaced regularly. And Prudence was deemed too unskilled yet to be let loose on the slender leaves used for making sleeping mats, or the more delicate leaves used to plait the finest mats of all.

She had cut dozens of the leaves, trimming them along the central rib to remove the sharp spines and spreading them on the nearby lawn to dry in the sun, when she heard Lupe calling her name. The girl came running through the clump of palms, words flying so fast from her mouth that Prudence was hard put to make sense of them. She came to a halt, breathing hard and regarding Prudence expectantly.

'I cannot follow when you speak so quickly,' she said. She was still learning to wrap her tongue around the abundance of vowels in the Samoan language.

'The papālagi have come! Two pālagi have sailed into the lagoon on a travelling canoe with some Samoans from Manono. One of the pālagi visitors is a woman!' she announced, bouncing with excitement.

Prudence felt a ripple of apprehension lift the hairs on her arms. Visitors were a frequent occurrence, with a guest house set aside for their use. But this was the first time she had encountered any from Manono, the home of the high chief of all Samoa. She also knew that several Europeans had settled in the islands in recent years – but they were castaways, deserters and runaway convicts from Australia, or so she had heard. None were eager to return to their former homes. And none were rumoured to be women.

'The chief bids you come and talk with them.'

Who were these people? And whence had they come? Most particularly, what would they do when they discovered the presence of an Englishwoman in this village? Perhaps they might be prevailed upon to return her to England. The ripple of apprehension grew to a wave of trepidation that set her to breathing harder, for somehow this thought did not cause her to leap with joy, as it should.

She set her feet in her sandals, then turned to follow Lupe, carrying with her a last bunch of long trailing leaves. If a travelling canoe had arrived, they might have guests for many days and would need to renew the supply of floor mats. She could not allow herself to think further than that.

Bessie's legs were as weak as flummery by the time they sailed into the lagoon, where a scattering of tall round houses with thatched roofs resembling beehives were situated adjacent to the beach. The houses were built upon neat gravel terraces surrounded by lawns and shaded by coconut palms. Like the houses on the island of Manono, from where they had embarked upon this latest voyage, they were built upon low platforms that appeared to be made of rocks. Their roofs were supported by poles, with no walls to speak of, only blinds or curtains of woven grasses. Here was the village where the Tahitian missionaries in Manono had heard rumour of the presence of a European woman. Mr Ambrose was convinced the mystery woman must be Miss Merryfield but Bessie wasn't so sure.

Now he was tapping impatiently at his thigh, eager to disembark. 'Come along, Bessie,' he urged, 'I believe we will soon be standing before your mistress and bidding her return home with us to Westcott Hall. What say you to that?'

She could muster little enthusiasm for the charade that was sure to follow but he was so intent on his mission that there was nothing to do but play along with the fairy tale. He would soon discover the truth of the matter.

'Very good, sir,' she answered, forcing a smile.

Miss Merryfield was dead. She had drowned in the terrible seas that sank the *Kangaroo*. Bessie had watched as she was washed over the side into wild seas. If he sought that lady's fortune, as her employer had once believed, he was doomed to be disappointed. The hall and its estates would go to her distant cousins. If he sought her love, as Bessie believed, then he must look elsewhere. And elsewhere was not so very far away.

'You must be pleased to reach dry land once more.'

Despite his urgings, she could not put a toe to the water to wade ashore when it came to it. The shimmering white sands and friendly palms might well have been miles distant rather than a stone's throw away. The turquoise shallows might have been the ocean's inkiest depths for all she cared. She was still recovering from the previous day's voyage aboard the great double-hulled craft with its sail of woven grass matting. She wouldn't have thought it possible to fit so many souls aboard a single canoe – even one such as this, with a deck. She had promised Mr Ambrose to aid him on his wild quest but she had not promised to suffer in silence. It wasn't her fault they had been forced to carry her aboard screaming like a banshee, when she had barely survived one shipwreck already.

She hadn't slept a wink overnight either. While Mr Ambrose and the native crew took turns sleeping she had huddled on deck, too frightened to close her eyes lest she be cast into the ocean like a bit of flotsam by the first rogue wave. She vowed then that if she ever returned home to England, she would never set sail again, not even if she were ordered by royal command.

'You will need to let go of the mast first . . .' Mr Ambrose nodded encouragingly.

The thought of entering the water so terrified her that she could not release her hold on the mast, the only safety to be had on this flimsy vessel.

'The water be too deep, sir.'

'Let me help you,' he said, prising loose her hands and lifting her from the vessel to carry her ashore, cradled in his arms. 'I beg your pardon, Bessie,' he excused himself as he set her feet upon the sand.

Yet *she* could not be sorry.

There was a great deal of hallooing amongst the villagers who appeared on the beach amidst the new arrivals. Hallooing and pressing of noses to other noses or hands, which she thought a most unusual form of greeting and hoped she would not be expected to replicate. A curtsy or handshake was to be preferred. Soon, a gathering of many people surrounded their party, talking excitedly. The talk was a blur of sound; she understood only that they were to be welcomed, and she followed obediently as they were led towards a large round house and bade to enter. Some of their party stayed outside on the terrace while she, Mr Ambrose and the more senior members of their party were each led to a place adjacent to one of the roof poles. Amidst some discussion, the village members also took their places. Strangely, many of the men untied their hair in the process so that it hung long and loose over their shoulders.

Once all were assembled, they were gestured to sit upon woven mats that were newly placed upon the ground for their seats. One of their party proceeded to lay before the person she presumed to be the chief some lengths of cloth, a parcel of fish hooks and some tin cups. These appeared to be received with thanks, and soon an older gentleman sitting adjacent to the chief rose to his feet. Unlike most other men, who Bessie blushed to note wore nothing but a short girdle of leaves that revealed bodies tattooed from waist to knees, his lower body was wrapped in a length of patterned cloth and he held a tall wooden staff in one hand and a strange implement like a giant whisk balanced upon his other shoulder.

He proceeded to speak to the assembly in a courteous tone to which all listened politely for some minutes. It seemed to Bessie he was just hitting his stride when there was a commotion nearby and one and all turned to look to the outside. A woman appeared, standing tentatively on the platform at the edge of the house. She was smaller than the women Bessie had seen thus far, brown of skin, yet not so brown as others, and no longer young. She wore the girdle of leaves common to most of the women but had covered her nakedness in a length of matting with a hole cut for her head. Her hair was adorned with flowers and tied in a knot atop her head, which she now proceeded to loosen like the men so that it wound down her back in shiny ringlets, red as Bessie's own.

Bessie leaned back against the pole, not trusting herself to stay upright, and closed her eyes. Perhaps she was dreaming. Perhaps this native orator with the musical voice and the theatrical manner had lulled her into a trance. That must be it. The heat, her exhaustion and the man's dulcet tones had set her to dreaming. For how else could a dead woman appear in their midst? How else could a drowned woman rise from the deep to haunt her? To taunt her with Mr Ambrose's love.

'Edward,' the dead woman murmured.

'Prudence.' He uttered the word with such a note of wonder in his voice, such a ring of gladness, that Bessie felt it as a sharp pain in her womb. 'Prudence. I have found you. I knew you couldn't be dead. I knew I hadn't lost you.'

'Yet I thought I had lost you for good,' Miss Merryfield's ghost replied, as Bessie's poor tired body slipped from its resting place against the pole and toppled to the mat.

Her last thought as she fell into a swoon was that everything would now return to the way it once had been.

35

She waited until the feasting and dancing were done to venture alone on to the beach, the last sounds of revelry fading into the distance. Any excuse for a celebration was a good one in Samoa, and all had donned their finest mats and ie tōga, ornamented their bodies with shells, adorned their hair with flowers, brought out their log drums and fired up their ovens to feast the party from Manono. Lupe's friend To'oa wore the exquisite ornamental headdress of the village maiden, and even Lupe had combed her hair and decorated it with a pink hibiscus flower. Once it was discovered that the two pālagi arrivals were friends to Matu'u, nothing would do but that Prudence should join the women in dancing.

Finally, she escaped the celebration to seek some quiet place in which to collect her thoughts. She left her leaf sandals at the high-tide mark to wander along the beach, the crescent moon casting a shining path across the sea. In the recesses of her mind, the thought had always lurked that one day other papālagi would come, and with them the possibility of returning to England, or at the very least the possibility of sailing to some other settlement where she might order her affairs and continue her travels. She knew from talk amongst her new friends that absconding sailors and convicts sometimes washed up on Samoan shores, and she had even heard tell of strangers bringing a new religion. Except in the hurly-burly of fitting in and finding her place in the village, she had put these thoughts aside.

Now she was forced to face this new reality when all she wanted to do was dig a hole in the sand and bury her cares. For the truth was, Prudence did not know what she wanted. She did not know if she desired to return home. And she certainly did not know if she desired to return home with Edward.

And yet . . . she could not deny that her heart had skipped a beat when she saw him sitting there in the fale tele, surrounded by her friends and the visiting Samoans. And beside him Bessie, the girl she had thought dead. That discovery, at least, was unequivocally welcome, for she had carried the guilt of Bessie's death since she watched the *Kangaroo* sink beneath the waves. Seeing her had lifted a great burden, so that she trod lighter and smiled easier than she had this entire last year. When Bessie fainted, Prudence had been the first to her side.

But Edward, what did he do here? For all his assertions of joy at finding her, she could not quite quash the thought that it was her estates he sought to secure, not her person. If she were to marry here on this island, far from his reach – a visiting sea captain, a missionary or perhaps a Samoan man – then he would lose control of not only her person but her estate. And if it were indeed true that he had travelled half the world at no small danger to himself – not least in voyaging to the Navigator Isles where welcome was far from assured – for love of her . . . well, did that not mean he would guard her person all the more zealously in the future? She could welcome neither of these possibilities.

She fumbled for the locket beneath her tiputa, drawing it forth so that her mother's face glowed in the moonlight. 'What shall I do?' she whispered to the woman she barely remembered. For who else was there to guide her?

'Should I return to England with this man who professes to love me, a man I've known my whole life? Or should I stay here where I have begun to find some purpose, where I can contribute to the lives of those around me?'

An image of Lupelele's face came to mind, the determined set to her mouth when she longed to disregard her elders, the hint of sadness in her eyes when she thought no one was watching. Could Prudence be the person to help her find her way? And then there was Bessie. That poor child, ripped from the safe haven she had found at Westcott Hall and dragged across the oceans, almost to her doom. Prudence remembered the day she had first met the ragged urchin daubed with grime, hiding behind Mr Custard's coat-tails. She had offered the child a place in such a thoughtless manner and then treated her more like a favourite filly than a person, handled kindly but firmly and put to good use. Did she not owe her more, especially now, when Bessie had put aside all her fears in order to help Edward in his dangerous quest to find her?

Ah, her thoughts were more muddied than a taro patch.

She heard the sound of shoes kicking up sand and turned, knowing exactly who would be following her. His hair was longer than when she had last seen him in Somerset, and quite unkempt. And, despite the warm evening, he wore a rumpled brown frock coat and vest.

'Are you not hot in that coat, Edward?' she asked as he approached, conscious that her legs were naked to the knee. Once upon a time she would have blushed at exposing more than an ankle.

'It's no matter. I hoped to speak with you alone,' he said, taking one of her hands in his, a hand grown coarse from gathering shellfish and pounding bark to make siapo, a hand marred by dark spots from the sun. A working woman's hand.

'I expect I've grown ugly and haggard, with my skin as crisp as brown paper and lines engraved upon my face.'

'You could never be ugly in my eyes,' he said, lifting her hand to his kiss as if they attended the Bath Assembly.

This wasn't what she had been expecting. Edward had never been known for his flattery or his kisses.

'But what of me, how do I seem to your eyes?' he asked.

In the moonlight, his eyes were as dark as midnight, beseeching her for words of encouragement. But how to answer such a question – that he was familiar yet at the same time a stranger, that he set her pulse to racing, but whether from gladness or fear she could not say? The two prospects were irreconcilable and yet alike.

'You look . . . you look like yourself,' she said after a moment.

'And yet you don't appear pleased to see me, Prudence. In fact, you don't appear to desire rescue. Strangely, you seem quite at home here,' he said earnestly, yet disappointment lurked in his eyes.

She still wasn't sure what to say so she let silence speak for her. It was true that she had begun to feel part of this place, as odd as that might seem to Edward. It was equally true that Masina had told her she would never belong, that although she had been accepted into the aualuma and adopted by Lupelele's family, she would remain a visitor at heart. But hadn't that always been true? Lately, she had come to realise that she had never quite belonged in her father's house either. She had always felt like a visitor, abiding by another's rules. She had set her life by an almanac of her father's design, and then Edward had sought to impose an order of his making when she longed to write her life in her own words.

At this moment all she knew was confusion.

Edward filled the silence for her. 'When I learned the fate of the *Kangaroo* I was overcome with dread that you were lost to me forever. I felt an emptiness in my soul that no one and nothing but *you* could fill. I thought that if I had courted you more passionately, wooed you with deeds not mere words, you might not have fled. You might not have believed I colluded with your father.'

'And yet you did. You agreed to act as trustee of my life.'

'I never meant to cage you, Prudence, not even with my love . . .' He paused to take a breath as Prudence attempted to calm the maelstrom of her thoughts. 'Then when I learned that Bessie had survived, against all odds, I vowed that whatever it took I would find you. And, when I did, I would woo you as you deserve.'

This was the longest speech she had ever heard from Edward's lips, but still she struggled to find an answer.

'I don't wish to order your life, Prudence. I wish to share it. And I hope that you will share mine.'

She thought back to the day when he had crossed a fallen log to kneel and ask for her hand in marriage. Now he had crossed three oceans to find her. And still, she hesitated. Had he not proved his love?

Or was love not enough?

'Will you let me woo you?' he asked, pulling her towards him and folding her in his arms. Without waiting for her answer, he bent his head and touched his lips to hers.

To her surprise, in her loneliness, and in a hunger for an intimacy she had never dared acknowledge, she did not pull away. Indeed, she found herself leaning into him, pressing her lips harder to his. Without knowing how it came about, she crushed her body against him so that her thighs pressed his, her chest moulded to his. She felt the rough fabric of his frock coat against her skin where the leaves of her skirt parted, and unfamiliar warmth coursed through her body. For the first time in her almost thirty-seven years, she found herself trembling with what she presumed to be desire, for a man she knew well yet it appeared did not know at all.

Perhaps she owed them both a chance to find out.

'Let me prove my love to you,' he said, as he covered her face with his kisses.

'We shall see,' she whispered, almost believing him, this ghost from her past. 'We shall see.'

The turtle was small enough to fit in the palm of Lupe's hand. She watched as it flapped awkwardly over the sand towards the waters of the lagoon. Somewhere up the beach it had burrowed from a nest, along with its many brothers and sisters. Several of its siblings were already splashing into the shallows ahead of it. Soon it too would enter the water, where it would swim far out into the ocean alone, for its mother had laid her eggs then left her hatchlings to fend for themselves. Lupe wondered how it knew where to go, how it would survive the dangers that threatened such a small creature alone in the vastness of the world.

She had left the feast before the dancing and wandered along the beach almost as far as the next village, before turning for home. Matu'u would be gone soon; she knew that in her bones. She would return to her home with the man who had sailed the oceans in search of her. And when she was gone, there would be no one for Lupe to teach, no one for her to guide and no one who needed her. She would be surrounded by friends in the house of girls, safe in the arms of her āiga – and yet she would have no one who belonged to her. Family surrounded her, yet she often felt like that hatchling, swimming out to sea alone. Her mother was gone. Her father's grief had stranded him like a fish in its net. There was only her aunt telling her what to do, watching over her, guiding her, along with Masina's many other young charges in the aualuma.

Halfway to her village, she became aware of two people standing locked together at the water's edge. By their silhouettes, she knew one for the pālagi man who had come in search of Matu'u. She could guess who the other would be. They did not notice her approach, too caught up in their love business, a business that was unseemly between unmarried persons. Her aunt would have plenty to say about it if she caught them, despite their advanced age. Perhaps she should have left them to it, but for the first time she was angry with this woman who had come into her life and would now depart as abruptly as she had arrived.

'We've prepared no fine mats for your marriage,' she said loudly, surprising the couple so that they jumped apart. 'How many pigs and canoes does this man offer? As head of our āiga my father will want to know.'

Even in the moonlight she saw the puzzled expression on the man's face.

'I haven't agreed to any marriage,' Matu'u said. 'I haven't decided what to do.'

'But you will. I see this. You will leave Samoa, you will leave me, and you will never return.'

The man in the foolish brown clothes spoke a few words to Matu'u. When she replied he bowed briefly to both women and began heading in the direction of the village. She wished that he would get in his big canoe and disappear forever.

'You don't need me,' Matu'u said, reaching for her hand. 'You have your father to love and protect you. You have your aunt to love and protect you. You have your āiga to love and protect you.'

'But I must share my father with my mother who is dead. I must share my aunt with the other girls of the aualuma and with my cousins. I must share everyone and everything with others. The only person I have to myself is you.' Her throat was burning now.

Matu'u was silent for a few moments, as if searching for the right words, except there were none. 'We all share our loves,' she said after a time. 'That's what being part of a family, part of a village, means.'

She squeezed Lupe's hand as if to prove the truth of her words, saying, 'You will be grown in the blink of an eye and then you will have children of your own to share your love. You're not alone, Lupe. You've never been alone.'

She thought about Matu'u's words. She might not like them, she might not want to admit it, but perhaps it was true that her aunt told her what to do out of love. Perhaps it was also true that one day her father would emerge from his grief. And that her āiga would always be there when she needed them. That she wasn't truly alone. But it was also true that she might never see Matu'u again. The odd-looking bird who had arrived on their shores and made a home amongst them. *Her friend.*

'Promise you will return one day,' she said. 'Promise you will return to see my children.'

Lupe did not truly know how far away the papālagi lived. It must be far for them to sail such large canoes. Further than Tonga. Further even than distant Aotearoa. But somehow she knew that Matu'u would make that promise.

'I promise,' said her friend from a faraway island. 'I promise that one day I will return.'

36

Somerset, England

2022

Eliza took a last glance around the shop before she locked up for the day and headed upstairs to her flat. The Cabinet of Wonders was looking rather bare of wonders, these days. For instance, what was going on with that empty space over by the Welsh farmhouse dresser, a spot that had been occupied for months by a nineteenth-century reproduction Louis XIII ebonised wood side table with the adorable barley-twist base? Why hadn't she filled it yet? And why hadn't she replaced the 'sold' hat blocks on the French elm dresser with something equally quirky? It was almost as if her brain had embarked on its very own closing-down sale long before the need arose. She continued to attend estate sales, but increasingly she returned home with little to show for her time. And her Internet forays had gone off-piste too. Instead of searching for antique furniture, she found herself lost in the woods of Etsy, Preloved and Rebelle, dreaming of vintage clothes and how she might style them, or roaming the no-man's-land of Prudence Merryfield's disappearance.

Anything to avoid commitment. And all the while she was stalked by the spectre of self-recrimination. She had made a promise to her mother and now she would be hard pressed to keep it. Worse, she wasn't sure whether she wanted to keep it. Did that make her a terrible daughter?

She shot and locked the bolts with a sigh. Then she trudged upstairs to her flat, taking with her that day's mail. Perhaps she would have time to go through it before Daniel arrived to take her to dinner, his make-it-up-to-Eliza dinner. An invitation she was already regretting before she had even showered and changed into the pair of vintage Pleats Please chartreuse wide-legged trousers and black baby-doll tee she planned to wear that evening. Or perhaps this was simply another example of stalling her life. The truth was that thoughts of Daniel set her stomach churning one moment and her pulse quickening the next.

She wanted him.

He was the last person she should want.

For myriad reasons . . . not least that he didn't want her.

Showered, dressed and looking not half bad, she had ten minutes before Daniel was due to arrive in which to find her shoes = which had disappeared somewhere under the bed = and transfer her essentials from a capacious tote to a modest clutch. So naturally she decided to flip through the mail lying on the coffee table. As usual, it was mostly bills, except for one envelope that elicited a shriek just as she was rudely interrupted by the doorbell. Five minutes early.

'Letter from Harold,' she said by way of explanation, as she practically towed him upstairs to the living room.

'I must try writing next time, if it generates this level of excitement,' he said, 'since the phone doesn't work so well.'

'I didn't have time to open it until now. Do you mind?'

'No worries,' he said, man-spreading on her delicate empire-style sofa.

If she wanted to reach Harold's letter on the coffee table she had to squeeze in next to him. She wondered idly if this was deliberate but cast off the thought as wishful thinking. He was only being a man and taking up space.

'I was talking to him yesterday about organising trial prints of the Merryfield watercolours,' Daniel said.

Indelibly aware of his elbow brushing hers, she leaned forward to retrieve the letter and tear it open while he peered over her shoulder, so near that for a moment she thought he might rest his chin there. Why was he always worming his way in close when she was determined to keep a safe distance?

'You're no respecter of personal space, are you?' she said tetchily, then immediately wished she hadn't when he moved the offending chin and elbow.

'Sorry,' he said, 'I grew up with three older sisters, not conducive to personal space.'

'You never said.'

'You never asked.'

'I often wished I had sisters,' she said wistfully.

'I often wished I had brothers. My sisters used to practise their hair and make-up skills on me until I grew old enough to outrun them. Sometimes I forget that not every woman wants to paint my lips purple.'

She laughed. So that was the story behind his casual intimacy. Sisters. A tribe of them. In a way it was nice that he obviously liked women and felt comfortable around them, except she wasn't his sister. Nor did she want to be. And now, all through dinner, she would be imagining him with purple lips.

'Fuchsia is definitely more your colour.'

'I know. That's what I kept telling them. So, what does Harold have to say?'

'Let's see.' She pulled a letter from the envelope, as well as several photographs. Harold hadn't gone digital yet, it seemed. 'I think this must be a photograph of the headpiece he was talking about. The one he returned to Samoa. And another that appears to be some kind of matting,' she said.

The mat was a light straw colour, decorated with a row of vibrant red feathers, while the headpiece appeared to be made of shells. There was also a photograph of what she now knew to be siapo or tapa – the bark textile of Polynesia. She passed the photographs to Daniel as she scanned Harold's letter, which also enclosed a sheet of more official-looking correspondence.

'Harold has found those photographs of the artefacts he repatriated to Samoa. Plus he's sent a copy of correspondence he received from the museum at the time.'

She scanned the next paragraphs. 'The museum thanks him and includes a brief description of the artefacts donated. According to the curator, the mat is most likely early nineteenth century. Here's what he says about them. "Ie tōga are fine mats intended to be worn as a skirt but also used as a form of currency. They are made from the leaves of the pandanus plant, scraped thin, cut into narrow strips and plaited. This particular mat is decorated with the feathers of the Fijian parakeet (*Lorius solitarius*). Fine mats were arguably the most important component of a young woman's dowry, sometimes taking many years to complete. The border of red feathers is thought to have represented the virginity of high-status young women. Both women and men might wear these mats at major celebrations, the mat being doubled over and held in place by a girdle of bark cloth. They were sometimes also given to important guests at weddings and funerals."

'He goes on to say that the headpiece is "fashioned from pieces of nautilus shell strung together" and that "such headpieces were a popular form of adornment at important celebrations such as weddings and births".'

Daniel looked up from the photographs. 'The mat is certainly beautiful, such intricate plaiting. I wonder whether Prudence brought the mat and headpiece back to England with her, or if they were sent to her later. Except who could have sent them all the way from Samoa?'

'By the time of her second disappearance, there were English missionaries in Samoa, and quite a bit of trade, so it's not inconceivable that someone might have arranged for them to be sent. Perhaps someone about to be married,' she said.

A friend perhaps. The girl in the watercolours. Eliza thought of the girl Prudence had painted with such exuberance. That girl would have been of an age to marry by 1838. Prudence had lived in Samoa for more than a year, time enough to learn the language and make friends. Time enough to become someone to be missed.

Well, they would never know for certain now, but the idea that a person in far-off Samoa cared enough about Prudence to send these gifts was comforting. If she had indeed died at the hands of her husband, at least she would have died knowing that someone, somewhere, would miss her. That's what Eliza wanted to believe, anyway.

'I suppose we'd better head off for dinner then,' she said, blinking back a tear.

'Aren't you forgetting something?' Daniel nodded with a smile towards her bare feet under the coffee table. 'Although my sisters would approve the choice of colour.'

The toenails in question were painted a purple so dark it appeared black in certain lights. 'Do you always notice everything?' she asked.

'Everything about you.'

He said this with such a straight face that she didn't know what to make of it. Was he flirting or teasing? She didn't trust herself to know the difference any longer.

'I'll get my shoes and bag and then we can go.'

'Good plan, Eliza,' he said, as she decamped from the sofa in a rush, knocking her shin against the edge of the table so that she had to bite her lip to hold back a cry of pain.

'Let's not get too comfortable,' he added, with what might have been a sigh. 'That could prove dangerous.'

His words echoed in her head as she wriggled under the bed to retrieve her shoes. He was wrong, though. Being comfortable wasn't dangerous; being comfortable was about keeping things the way they were. It was change that brought danger, Daniel who brought change. And her world had changed so much in recent years that, for the moment, she would rather stay in her comfort zone. There was safety there at least.

37

Somerset, England

1838

Despite a fire burning merrily in the fireplace, Prudence's bed-chamber was so icy that she shivered in her wrapper of pink silk brocade. Edward had ordered it from France as a Christmas gift, declaring that the pink and silver roses became her admirably. Although, in truth, she had never regained the pale complexion of her youth, her freckles having taken on a life of their own after her sojourn in the South Seas. But it was kind of him to think it, for that was him, kind to a fault. She could make no complaint of her husband in that respect.

Her writing table was situated beneath the window so that she could look out over the grounds to the river. The trees and the sinuous green curve of the river comforted her. But this morning, the river shone silver; snow blanketed the lawns, and the trees stood stark and bare against the dull grey day. She shivered once again; from the cold and the thought that warmer climes were so distant she might never see them again.

A light tread and swish of skirts heralded the arrival of Bessie, who entered accompanied by Thomas, the hall boy, carrying between them a large wooden box with rope handles.

'You'll never guess! A delivery has arrived via the Singapore packet.' The younger woman and the boy promptly deposited the rough wooden crate upon Prudence's mahogany writing desk, before Bessie flung herself down in Prudence's favourite chair, saying, 'I offered to bring it up since you've lingered so late at your toilette.'

Prudence could never resent the familiarity that flourished between herself and her former maid, now companion, since their perilous adventures in the South Seas, for they had endured so much together. Nevertheless, she sometimes longed for those days when she had no companion but her own thoughts.

'Thank you, Bessie. Such a cold day.'

'Shall I have Tom bring more coal?'

'No. Perhaps it's just me. I was dreaming of warmer days. You may go, Tom.'

The two women exchanged a brief glance of mutual under-standing, before Prudence cleared her throat, saying, 'I expect I should open it then. From Singapore, you say?'

Upon her return to Somerset she had embarked upon an occasional correspondence with her former hosts in Singapore, assuring them of her safe delivery from the wreck of the *Kangaroo* and her continued well-being. 'Perhaps the mysterious delivery might be from our friends in Singapore,' she said, sniffing the crate suspiciously.

'Carp had Bobbett remove the nails,' Bessie informed her.

Someone was always at hand to anticipate Prudence's smallest need at Westcott Hall, so that she was rarely obliged to lift a finger. She wondered if Carp had also tested the opened crate, for the butler did like to supervise all matters pertaining to his domain, and a mysterious box from Singapore would have proven a formidable temptation. She removed the lid and set it upon the floor before peering into the crate. She discovered that it contained a roughly woven basket of coconut leaves – the like of which she immediately recognised, having plaited similar baskets with her own hands – and beneath it a fine mat rolled to fit the crate. And whatever the contents of the basket, they were wrapped in a length of siapo.

'What is it?' Bessie asked, not quite daring to pre-empt Prudence by peering inside.

'I think the more pertinent question is, "Where is it from?"'

In the years since their return from the South Seas, Bessie's perpetual expression of worry had gradually mellowed and with it she had grown more confident and, indeed, prettier. Her speech too had become more refined – aping Prudence somewhat, she had not failed to notice – so that one would never guess at the wretchedness of her origins. Now her face held only mild curiosity, her eyes widening and her lips parting in enquiry.

'I believe the crate has been sent to me from Samoa. And if I'm not mistaken, probably from the village where I was cast away.' She spoke the words 'cast away' ironically, for this is how the newspapers had described her sojourn in Samoa. She herself had never spoken publically of her time as the guest of Lupelele's village. And she had ceased thinking of herself as a castaway some few weeks after being welcomed to the village and given a place in the fale where the adolescent girls and single women lived. For a time, that village had been her home. She was part of the community. And then she was not.

'But who could have sent it all the way to Somerset? Are they not without such resources as post offices and shipping agents in Samoa?'

Prudence did not answer, being occupied in removing the basket to the floor, setting the contents upon her desk and removing the siapo wrapping to reveal an exquisite headpiece of nautilus shell . . . and an envelope. She paused to take a deep breath before bending to examine the rolled mat, with its border of parakeet feathers and fringed edges, which had been stowed beneath the basket. The mat wasn't as soft or intricate as those she had seen Masina make. The strips of pandanus leaf weren't

311

so thin, the plaiting looser. And yet, it was beautiful in its own way. In fact, she thought she recognised it as one she had watched Lupe plaiting with many a muttered complaint, intending it for her future dowry.

By the time she directed her attention to the envelope, her hands were trembling. Since her return to Somerset, and the notoriety that surrounded her adventures, she had tried to put thoughts of Samoa aside. The memories of her time there and the terror of the shipwreck still brought confusion. Only by burying those memories could she marry Edward and resume her former life. Now those questions were being resurrected, and with them the memory of her promise – a promise she had schooled herself to forget. She withdrew the single sheet of paper and began to read.

Tālofa Matu'u,

Mrs Lilias Mills, a lady missionary in Apia, sends these words for me. I write to say that I have married a young man from a nearby village. He is called Tuala and I like him very much. My father was also pleased because Tuala's family presented him with the gift of a new canoe, several pigs and a very fine club that Tuala carved for him. I am glad that my aunt helped assemble enough fine mats and siapo to give in return because, as you know, my work is far from fine.

We stay with my father until after the feast but soon we will return to Tuala's village. My father's fale is overflowing and very noisy. He and my aunt Masina have a new baby, and my cousin Fata has brought his wife to stay with us too. Tuna stays in his family's house with his new bride. My friend To'oa has married the son of a chief. Her wedding was a much grander affair than mine and there were many fine mats given and received.

She has moved away now, although secretly I hope she may return one day.

Do you remember that day we taught you to paddle a canoe? You capsized so many times that our stomachs hurt from laughing. But still you kept going, with your paddle chopping at the water. You didn't give up. I miss her, as I miss you, Matu'u.

Now my aunt helps me prepare for the birth of our first child. She and the other women of our āiga have plaited many fine mats for the occasion, and by the time this letter reaches you my child will be born. One day I hope you will meet her. One day I hope you will return. I will not give up either.

    Your friend,

    Lupelele

Bessie rose from her chair to peer at the gifts that had crossed three oceans to reach them. 'This looks like one of the mats the natives wore tied about their waists. What does the letter say?' she asked.

For several moments, Prudence could not speak. Her throat felt swollen, her mouth dry with memories. She remembered that day on the lagoon. At first, the two girls had been so patient with her clumsiness, demonstrating many times how to hold the paddle and dip it in the water. They smothered their laughter when she steered the canoe on to rocks. They bit their lips when she was flipped unceremoniously into the sea. But despite their good intentions, by the third time she capsized they could hold back the laughter no longer. She could see them now, two tall girls grinning behind their hands, trying to be polite in the face of her ineptitude.

Memories of Lupelele overwhelmed her. She didn't need the many watercolours she painted in order to picture her. She could

313

see her as clearly as if she stood in this room in her titi of leaves, with flowers in her hair. Now Lupelele was herself a mother, as Prudence would never be.

'Prudence?' Bessie's voice was tinged with concern.

'I . . . it is a letter from Lupelele. Transcribed by a missionary from the London Missionary Society. She . . . she writes to say that she expects her first child.' She turned her face from Bessie to brush away a tear.

'Oh. She is younger than me, I think.'

'Yes, she would be eighteen now.' Prudence faced the young woman once again with a smile. 'I am happy for her. And you too will marry and produce children one day, I'm sure. Then I will be as an aunt to them.'

She had been remiss in her attentions to Bessie, she realised. The girl was of an age to marry now. She should have discussed her companion's future with Edward – perhaps facilitated a marriage to a likely young man from the district. Instead, she had selfishly kept Bessie to herself.

'Perhaps, one day . . . yet I cannot imagine leaving Westcott Hall. Leaving you and Mr Ambrose . . . Edward.'

Prudence touched her young friend's hand. 'That's understandable. It's your home. But one day you'll meet someone suitable and desire children of your own. I've seen you playing at blind man's bluff with Mrs Bobbett's children, and you are made to be a mother, Bessie.'

'I should like to marry one day, if I could remain here.'

'They say home is where the heart is.'

'Perhaps, but my heart is here at Westcott Hall now.'

Prudence wasn't sure where her heart was, but she suspected she had left a little piece of it in Samoa.

Lupe's children would be rascals, if they were anything like their mother. Racing each other across the village green to the beach, competing to see who could climb the highest coconut palm or spear the biggest fish. She could picture them now, lithe and brown, running along the beach, kicking up sand with their heels. The boys would be helping their father in the taro patch and wrestling with their cousins. The girls would be wading in the lagoon with their mother, seeking out a hidden octopus for their dinner. But she would never see them. Despite her vow to return, that world was too far away and she was a different person now. She was Mrs Prudence Ambrose, mistress of Westcott Hall and Queens Knoll.

Matu'u existed only in memory.

That night, she wrote the following words in her pocket book.

Thursday: Frost bit magnolia buds. Package arrived from Lupelele. She is with child.

For decades, she had recorded her life in the fewest words, the tiniest hand, she could contrive. She had reduced her history to fit the palm of her hand. So many years of her life had been spent in a parade of afternoon calls, card parties and moderately good works, that her greatest adventure seemed so distant as to be a dream. For here she was, back where she began, and here she was likely to stay, here where life persisted with little required of her. Indeed, if she were to die tomorrow, life at the hall would scarcely miss a beat. Her friends would sigh into their handkerchiefs for a week. Bessie would mourn her for a time. And Edward . . . Edward loved her, in his way, but he had loved before and he was not yet so old that he could not love again, perhaps even produce children. He would welcome that, she was sure.

For the most part, Prudence was superfluous.

She opened the desk drawer where she housed the collection of pocket books she had amassed over almost two decades, reaching instinctively for the most tattered of the collection.

Worn and salt-stained, some words were illegible, others her ageing eyes struggled to read. But she knew them by heart, for the events they described were engraved upon her memory. She released the clasp to disclose this relic from her past. From constant use, the pages fell open to the middle where once she had jotted a record of expenditure on hats, gloves and seamstresses. Now a minute account of her life on the island stood recorded. Written in pencil in a cramped hand was the tale of 1833, the true *Narrative of the Shipwreck, Privations and Miraculous Rescue of Miss Prudence Merryfield*. A record which no one but she was ever likely to see.

"'Matu'u I am called. The heron,'" she read aloud. "'Speared a fish. Lupe laughed at size,'" she continued, flipping through the pages. "'Almost poisoned by snail. Saved by Masina.'" She could picture the lagoon even now. She did not need the watercolours she painted, over and over again, to remember its vivid brightness. She could see the tall girl with the ready laugh who had welcomed her to the village. She could see that girl's father, her aunt and her cousins. She saw them all.

"'Worked at siapo all day. New blisters.'" The words of the pocket book were like a chant that reverberated long after the melody had faded. "'Forgot – sandals. Feet bleeding,'" she whispered to the empty room.

'I see you have returned to the island again.' Edward hailed her from the doorway in a dull voice.

'Edward, I didn't hear you enter.'

'No. You usually don't.'

'Did you need something, my dear?' she asked, tearing her gaze from the page.

'I wondered if I might see this gift from Samoa,' he said, approaching her desk. The light from her candle threw his reflection on to the darkened window so that he appeared to loom over her.

'Of course. Lupelele made the mat herself, I believe. As part of her trousseau.' She glanced towards the chiffonier where she had draped Lupe's mat, crowned by the shell headpiece. In the process she must have knocked over the portrait of her father that formerly held pride of place. His face was now hidden beneath the mat.

'And she writes of impending motherhood?'

'Yes.' Prudence was surprised at his enquiry. Although Bessie had spoken excitedly of the gift and the letter at dinner, Edward seemed to pay little heed to her chatter, his attention reserved for the joint.

'It's strange. I remember her as a child. And now she welcomes a child of her own.' She dropped her eyes to the page, seeking solace in her memories.

'And is this why you dwell in the past so, Prudence? Because I couldn't give you a child?' he said, the hurt apparent in his voice. 'Is this why you're always so far from me?'

'What? No. I don't blame you for our lack of a child.' It wasn't a child she missed – or that was only part of her malaise.

'Perhaps you wish I had left you there. A castaway from all civilisation. Playing mother to that girl, playing wife to her father,' he said, his voice growing louder and more bitter as he spoke.

She looked up, surprised at his anger. He was the most phlegmatic man she knew. Usually only heedless cruelty to animals roused his ire.

'I had no desire to be Kisona's wife. I had no desire to be a wife at all, Edward, if you recall.'

'How could I forget? How could I forget that you did not choose me, Prudence – that you resigned yourself to me.' The hurt on his face was palpable in his sunken eyes and drawn mouth.

She considered his words. Were they true? Had she married

317

him, not from love but resignation? He had been her friend before he became her husband. And she had grown to love him, in her way; shared his bed at times, joyfully; enjoyed their intermittent conversation.

'Perhaps it is you who mourns our lack of a child,' she sighed. 'That *I* failed to give *you*.'

'If only you loved me, everything would be different. Everything.' He clenched his hands at his sides, as if to hold them back from what . . . she could not say.

'Would it?' She doubted it, for she would not be different. And nor would he. 'It's all in the past, anyway,' she said, bowing her head to the page once more.

'Is it?'

In one swift movement he lunged towards her so that she flinched from him. But it was the pocket book he swooped upon, grasping it and gripping it by the covers of its red Moroccan case so that the pages hung limply downwards.

'What are you doing?' she protested.

Ignoring her, he seized a handful of the flimsy pages and ripped them from their binding to hold them aloft. 'And yet you cannot let go of the past!' he shouted.

She half rose from her chair, grasping wildly for the stolen pages. But she was too slow, for he had crossed the room and tossed them into the fireplace before she could escape her chair.

'Please don't,' she pleaded, fearing that the pocket book would surely follow the lost pages into the flames.

'What would be the point?' he said, as she fumbled for the comfort of her mother's locket resting against her collarbone. 'I fear the words are engraved upon your heart.'

He dropped the pocket book on to the bed and let his hands hang loose at his sides. Then he exited the room without a backward glance. As soon as he was gone, Prudence scrambled to pick up the tiny book, clutching it to her breast. She had never seen such anger upon his face. For a moment she had thought he meant to strike her.

When his footsteps no longer echoed in the hallway, she hastened to find somewhere to hide the sacred book before he changed his mind and returned to complete its destruction. She needed to find somewhere he wouldn't think to look, and she knew exactly where that might be. A hatbox. No man would think to look amongst the frippery of her bonnets, turbans and caps.

It could rest in peace amongst her hats for as long as required.

38

In her grandfather's day, the finest assembly of horseflesh in the parish had occupied the stable's eleven loose boxes. But Sir Roderick had not been one for hunting, and neither was Edward, so now they kept only a pair of carriage horses and several for riding. That left a number of empty loose boxes alongside the tack room. Prudence always slipped an apple or two into her pockets when visiting the stables, and today was no exception. Several ripe, juicy apples jostled her pocket book as she crossed the cobbled quadrangle in search of her husband. Naturally, Carp was able to inform her of his whereabouts.

The stables were situated to one side of the hall in a red-brick building with a slate roof burdened with a fall of snow from the previous night. She expected to find Edward saddling his mare, Flash, for his morning ride or discussing the merits of a carriage he was thinking of buying with Bobbett. Since their marriage, the Bobbetts had moved from the stable master's quarters above the tack room to a larger cottage adjacent to the stables. But when she arrived, there was no sign of Edward or the stable master, only a very restless Flash, complaining noisily in her loose box, and the stable lad who was busy cleaning tack.

'Have you seen Mr Ambrose, William?' she asked.

'No, miss. And Mr Bobbett be exercising Tilly.'

'Ah . . . well, perhaps he has walked to the home farm to consult with Mr Piggot,' she said with a smile.

She couldn't help feeling disappointed. She had determined to make amends with her husband after their argument of the previous evening. She hoped to calm the waters of their marriage, even forgoing a card party later that day in order to spend the afternoon in his company. And now it appeared that she had braced herself for nothing. He had broken his fast early and gone about his business as usual, the argument of little matter to him, it seemed. How like Edward that would be.

Throughout their marriage thus far, he had proved himself a considerate spouse and an excellent guardian of her inheritance. She supposed she should be satisfied – and yet, she could not find the happiness she longed for. Perhaps the fault lay within her. Perhaps she should have remained a spinster, an ape-leader, an old maid – performing charitable works and doting upon other people's children. Then Edward could have married a woman more suited to him. But she had allowed herself to be wooed and, despite the outward trappings of felicity, she had still been a woman in mourning when they married. She was mourning a life she would never again lead.

She made offerings to the horses, which were received with thanks, and was preparing to return to the house when she heard the sound of children's laughter in the parkland behind the stables. She retraced her steps across the cobbles, passed beneath the gabled entry and followed the sounds of laughter, thinking to bid good morning to Wills while she was there. After turning the outside corner of the stables, she came upon the swathe of open grassland that formed the estate's park. The fields were white with snow and the scattered trees stark in the morning light. Yet, despite the wintry weather, hanging from the sturdy branch of an old oak was a rope swing where the Bobbett children were currently at play.

'Push faster, Mr Edward!' screamed the eldest as the younger laughed from behind her mother's skirts.

'That's Mr Ambrose to you, Alfie,' Mrs Bobbett said, drawing her shawl closer.

'Me next, Mr Ambrose!'

'What about you, Mrs Bobbett? Shall you take a turn?' Edward said as he gave Alfie a great push and sent him soaring high, the lad's winter jacket flipping up behind him.

'Me? I do not think so, sir. I shall keep my feet on the ground where they belong. But I thank you for putting up the swing for the children. It will do them no end of good to take some exercise in this cold snap.'

'Oh, I only supervised,' Edward said with a laugh. 'Young William the stable lad climbed the tree to tie the ropes, and your husband fashioned the swing from an oak board he found lying about.' As he spoke, he continued to push the boy, saying, 'Stretch out your legs and lean back as you go up, Alfie, then bend your knees as you come down, and soon you will be swinging like an expert.'

Prudence watched from afar as the lesson progressed, marvelling at the ease with which her husband played with the children. He would have made a good father, but while they remained married he would not have that chance. The only way he could father a legitimate child would be if she were dead. And she was very much alive.

At one point Edward swapped places with Alfie to demonstrate the fine art of swinging, which sent little Elsie into a gale of giggles when he swung so high that the swing wobbled dangerously, almost toppling him to the ground. He dismounted, staggering theatrically over to the children.

'Who is next?'

'My turn! My turn!' Elsie screamed, forgetting herself so far as to run from her mother's skirts and tug at Edward's trouser leg, which luckily was strapped beneath his instep or she would have exposed his ankle to the frigid air.

The sight of the diminutive child tugging so enthusiastically at her husband's tweed trousers was too much for Prudence, who promptly burst into giggles of her own, causing both her husband and her former maid to become aware of her presence, standing alone against the wall of the stables.

'Prudence!' Edward called. 'It's cold out. What are you doing over there?'

'Miss Merr . . . Mrs Ambrose,' her former maid said, dipping a curtsy, 'how nice to see you.'

'I was looking for you, Edward,' she said, 'but I'm fortunate to find Mrs Bobbett and the children too.'

Once discovered, she joined the party beneath the oak tree, stepping cautiously across the snow to shake hands with her old friend and promise her children she would bring more cake and fewer carrots next time she visited the cottage.

'Mr Ambrose has put up a swing for us,' declared Alfie. 'I'm an expert swinger, am I not, Mama?'

'I'm a better expert!' said Elsie, releasing the trouser leg to skip excitedly towards Prudence. 'Come and see!'

'I can see you're both experts but I'm not so sure about Mr Ambrose,' she said, taking the child's hand. 'He could do with more practice, don't you think?' she added, setting both children to laughing once more.

'Is there something you wished to speak with me about, my dear?' Edward asked, stepping back from the still-swinging Alfie.

There were many things she wished to speak with him about but suddenly her tongue was tied. There was so much she could say and yet so little point in saying it. Unobserved, he had looked happy only a moment ago. Now his face had lost all animation

323

as he regarded her with a coolness bordering upon indifference.

'Do you need me for something?' he continued.

'It's of no importance,' she said, backing away. 'Cook was asking about the week's menus and I wondered whether you would prefer mackerel or bream on Friday.'

'Ah . . . I see. Well, I'm sure you know best, my dear. One is much the same as another to me,' he said, taking up his post at the swing once more and beckoning towards the little girl with a smile.

'Mackerel then, I think. With fennel sauce. That should do nicely. Good day then, Mrs Bobbett. Good day, Edward.'

'Fare thee well, Mrs Ambrose. Fare thee well.'

'Thank you, I hope I shall.'

39

Somerset, England

2022

Daniel met her at the front door to Westcott Hall, wearing a secretive smile and a pair of jeans that hugged him so expertly that she had to tear her eyes away. Their dinner the previous week had been torture, with his laughing eyes teasing her over the crockery, and now here he was preparing to torment her again. Well, she wouldn't be caught twice by that trick. She took a step backwards, out of range of his matey affection, and almost toppled off the portico and into the rose bushes.

'Keeping your distance again, are you?' he asked, his eyes alight with silent laughter.

'It's not funny.'

'No, I suppose it's not much fun keeping other people at a distance.' He offered his hand to steady her but she waved him away.

It was her heart that needed steadying.

'I hope you haven't dragged me over here just to laugh at me. I have better things to do, you know, than provide your amusement for the day.' Although nothing as compelling as Prudence's story, or this infuriating Australian, she had to admit. Despite all good intentions, she kept getting dragged back to the scene of the crime.

'Oh, I think it will be worth it, if you'll just follow me to the boudoir,' he said with a wink and a nod.

It was her turn to stifle a laugh as she followed him through the open door, up the barley-twist staircase and along the corridor to Prudence's bedroom. He was funny, even if she was the butt of the joke. The room was just as she remembered it: faded lavender wallpaper, scuffed floors and mullioned windows looking out over the terrace to the river, the avenue of ancient chestnuts glittering gold in the autumn sunlight. Prudence would have gazed at this same view, as would her own ancestor, the former Bessie Pike, later Elizabeth Ambrose. Perhaps Prudence had sat at a desk right here beneath the window, writing her tiny words in her pocket-sized book.

'This way,' he said, leading her towards the wood-panelled dressing room. 'I think I may have mentioned that I was getting the plumbers in to trace a leak this week. Well, we started here where I first noticed rotting wood.'

The hint of damp she had smelled last time she was in this room was even more potent now. She caught a whiff, as if a troop of mushrooms pushed up through moist woodland soil. Daniel knelt by a perfect circle that had been cut in the slightly newer section of panelling. He reached in and felt around for a few moments, coming away with a small bundle clutched in his hand.

'A re-enactment for your benefit,' he grinned. 'We actually found the bundle this morning. We think there may have been a leak here long ago and after it was repaired new panelling was installed to replace the damaged wood. We'll be doing the same thing, reproducing the panelling to repair the wall. During the earlier repairs, someone must have secreted this bundle away before the work was completed.'

Settling on the floor with his back against the wall, he patted a spot next to him. Once she was seated, he set the bundle on his outstretched thighs – long and muscular in his jeans – and asked, 'Shall we?'

The bundle was shaped like a book or a box, and wrapped in brown oilcloth. Apparently, someone had wanted to hide it but they had also wanted to protect it from the elements. 'I wonder if whoever hid it intended to return for it, one day,' she said.

'Maybe. Or maybe they meant to inter it.'

She glanced at him questioningly.

'Like in a tomb . . . but without a body,' he said.

To preserve the bundle's secrets until the house fell down around it, taking all its secrets with it.

'You already opened it,' she said.

'I have. Sorry, couldn't resist.' He made a wry face.

'That's all right. I would have done the same. But stop faffing about and unwrap it, or I will.'

'Be my guest.'

Of course, to unwrap it she had to move even closer to him, to inadvertently graze his thigh with her hand as she folded back the cloth, to feel his breath upon her bent cheek . . . and all in close proximity to the business end of town.

'Sorry,' she said, conscious that her breathing had quickened and hoping he hadn't noticed. She was becoming adept at disguising desire. But all desire was trumped by curiosity when she saw what the oilcloth had been hiding – a Moroccan leather case with a brass clasp, small enough to fit in a pocket – a twin to the one residing in her bag.

'Open it,' he said.

The clasp resisted her at first, stiff with disuse. Then with a click it released and she opened the case to reveal the 1838 edition of *Peacock's Polite Repository* – the same publisher as Prudence's pocket companion. She flipped through the front matter and almanac, her fingers fumbling as she turned the pages, and went straight to the diary. And there on that first page spread for January she found the now familiar hand, confined and restrained by the limited space.

Monday: Custard called. Complimented sermon. Halibut again. Must visit Bobbetts.

She read the words, scanning the page excitedly.

Thursday: Frost bit magnolia buds. Package arrived from . . .

The next word was difficult to read, for it did not make sense at first. A name, presumably, but not one she recognised, which made it difficult to predict the tiny cramped letters. *Lu-pe-le-le* it appeared to read.

'Lu-pe-le-le.' She tried out the word on her tongue, tripping over the syllables but enjoying their musical rhythm.

And then . . . *She is with child . . .*

So this . . . *Lupelele* was with child. The unusual name suggested she might not have been a native of Somerset.

Friday: Samoa so far. Bobbett resoled boots. Scotland??? Post-chaise?

And then on another page: *Sent to Abercrombie to make arrangements. Jewellery?*

Eliza turned the next page in a flutter of anticipation, to find only empty space. The entries stopped abruptly on 13th February. She flipped through March, April, May, searching, hoping for more, yet all the time knowing that February had been the month of Prudence's disappearance. February was when she was reported missing, later to be presumed dead. She turned back to the very last week of entries and reread these words:

Saturday: Edward still brooding. Pockets brimming. My heart divided.

She was puzzling over the cryptic entry, so unlike Prudence's usual prosaic record, when Daniel said, 'Look inside the pocket.'

At his words, she became aware that there was indeed something bulging inside the pocket book's secret pocket. She slid a finger beneath the flap and gently withdrew what felt like a metallic object, irregularly shaped and trailing a chain.

'The locket,' she whispered. 'Prudence's locket.'

She turned the locket over to study the miniature portrait with its crystal cover. The face framed by gold could easily be the same face pictured in the portraits at Taunton. The face in the locket. Heart-shaped, pearl-skinned, with an artful arrangement of auburn curls. The face of Prudence's mother.

'Uh-huh. And I don't think she would have left it behind intentionally, do you?' he said.

'No. I mean, the entries in the pocket book hint she may have been planning to leave,' she said. 'Scotland, post-chaises and arrangements suggest something of the sort.'

'Maybe she even planned a return to Samoa. But not without her pocket book . . . and not without her locket,' he said.

She risked a glance at his face. He was so near, near enough that she could smell the spice of his cologne and the coffee he had drunk that morning, and yet . . . he was so far from her in every meaningful way.

'Here, let me.' He took the locket from her hands and draped it about her neck so that she felt it cold against her skin.

She was all too conscious of the contrast of his warm hand on the back of her cold neck. 'Stop flirting with me,' she suddenly ordered, 'It's really annoying.'

'It's the only way I know how to get your full attention,' he

329

said, in a provokingly reasonable voice. 'Otherwise you're all business.'

'But it's not fair. It's . . . it's . . . harassment. And besides, you only want to be friends.' He was so exasperating.

'Who said that?'

'You did! You very firmly friend-zoned me. You said, and I quote, "I'm sorry, Eliza. I shouldn't have done that. It was unprofessional."'

'Wow. You have it verbatim.'

'Why can't you be matey in a blokey way, like everyone else? You know, share a pint at the pub with me, or something. What's with the nice wine and tablecloths all of a sudden? What's with all the touchy-feely stuff and the . . . you know . . . the sexy looks?'

'The touchy-feely stuff is because I can hardly keep my hands off you, in a respectful way, of course. And the sexy looks . . . well . . . do I have sexy looks?' He inclined his head as if seriously interested in her answer.

'But you said . . . you said . . .' She couldn't get the words out.

'For a smart woman you can be very obtuse.' He leaned even closer so that his lips hovered only inches from hers.

She resisted the urge to back away, although every nerve in her body was saying, *Get out, Eliza, while you still can. Get out before you fall so far you'll never be able to crawl out.*

He took a deep breath. 'I said, way back then, that we should keep it professional because I was feeling like an imposter. I needed to explain that I owned your store, and at the same time I knew that if I did, I might lose you – before I even had you. I'm human. I chickened out. But I have an idea now about how we might fix things . . . I...'

Most of what he said passed in a blur of sound. She was still fixated on the 'couldn't keep his hands off her' part. She gulped. Had she heard him correctly?

'I think you can kiss me now,' she managed, finally. 'If you want to, that is.' Maybe she could deal with the other stuff, whatever it turned out to be, later. Much later. Plans and stuff like that. There were more important matters to be dealt with first.

'In an unprofessional manner?'

'Yes, please.'

And, obliging man that he was, he did.

At first, his mouth on hers was tentative, a fairy's wing against her lips. Then, as she felt something inside her beginning to melt, his touch became firmer, warm and hard and questioning. One hand came up to cup her face, while the other pulled her closer. She forgot the book in her lap, the locket about her neck. She forgot the past. Every fibre of her being became focused on her lips as an electric charge coursed through her entire body. And when he finally released her lips and drew back to gaze at her, with a look of certainty in his eyes, she could only nod and take a first tentative step into her future.

40

Somerset, England

1838

Fresh snow crunched beneath their feet and the clouds hung dull and grey overhead as Prudence and Bessie picked their way through the woods behind the hall. At one point, Bessie's boots slipped upon an icy patch and Prudence gripped her elbow to prevent her falling. It was not the brightest morning for a walk but it was bracing. And she needed to brace herself for what she was about to do.

'Perhaps we should return to the house,' Bessie said, brushing wet snow from her clothing. 'It looks to snow again.'

'I have something to ask you . . . away from prying eyes and flapping ears,' Prudence began, searching for the right words to tell the other woman of her plan. 'I wish to take you into my confidence.'

'You can always trust me, you know that.' Bessie withdrew her attention from the fur trim of her mantle to consider her friend. 'We've endured much together.'

More than most, it was true.

'You've been a good friend to me,' Prudence said, removing a hand from her muff to clasp the younger woman's gloved hand.

'And without you I would be living in the workhouse,' Bessie

332

answered, so vehemently that Prudence felt the shudder through their clasped hands.

'You are a clever, able girl. You would have found your place in the world without me. And your life wouldn't have been endangered as it was when I dragged you halfway across the world.'

As long as she lived she would not forget how carelessly she had treated the other woman's life, how thoughtlessly she had torn a young girl from all she knew to satisfy her own desires, her own fears. She would not risk Bessie's life again.

'Well, we are safe now, here in Somerset. And you have given me a home and a future,' Bessie said, releasing her hand from Prudence's to tuck a stray ringlet beneath her bonnet.

'Except I don't intend to remain in Somerset.'

At this announcement her friend stared, a perplexed frown between her brows. 'Are you planning to travel again?' she asked, taking a half-step backwards.

'Yes, but don't worry, my dear. I shall be travelling alone this time.'

'But where will you go?' Bessie gasped. 'And for how long?'

Tears welled as she gazed at her young friend, the ragged urchin she had adopted without realising it, six short years ago. Never would she have predicted this future.

'I plan to disappear,' she said. 'I know not where, as yet. But it will be permanent. I shall not be returning.'

'You cannot mean to leave forever.' As she spoke, Bessie wound her fur tippet about her hands as if she would strangle it, more distressed by this news than Prudence had anticipated.

'You don't need me any longer. You're ready to make your own way in the world. And I . . . I find I am not a woman satisfied to be mere adornment. I . . . I need to do something with my life, travel to other lands, explore the world,' she said, an icy wind drying her tears before they could fall.

'But what of Edward?'

'We have no children to tie me. And Edward has become the true custodian of Westcott Hall. I need to become a Lady Adventuress once more.'

'But what shall you do for money?'

Prudence laughed. 'I'm not so fond of new gowns and bonnets that I haven't salted away some funds,' she said, thinking of the reliable and inventive Mr Abercrombie of Alexander and Company who had been most helpful in this regard. And Edward had replaced the jewellery lost with the *Kangaroo*. That was safely hidden also. She hadn't thought about it before, but perhaps she had been unconsciously preparing for this from the moment she returned to Somerset. 'My needs aren't great. If I can travel, I will be content. Do not be concerned for me.'

Yes, she would become a Lady Adventuress once more. And if her travels one day took her to a certain island in the South Seas, which they surely would, then she would fulfil her promise at last.

The other woman was silent, thoughts flitting busy as a wren across her face while she digested these words. 'And what of me?' she said, after a time. 'What shall *I* do without you?'

'You're grown now. And you've educated yourself with some small assistance from me. Edward will provide for you. He thinks of you as a daughter, as do I. And he will need you when I am gone.' She did not delude herself that Edward would not miss her, but in time he would forget . . . and, she hoped, forgive.

'But Bessie, you must make him believe that there is no point searching for me. And in time, when seven or more years have passed and there is no word of me, I can be declared dead and Edward will be released from his vows. He can marry again, free to have the children he deserves.'

She unwound the length of fur wrapped about the girl's hands and encircled her in her arms. Even garbed in a woollen dress and swathed in a mantle, Bessie was slender. Then, drawing away, she slid an envelope from her ermine muff and pressed the letter into her friend's hands.

'Will you give him this letter for me? He must believe that I have left of my own accord.' For if he did not believe she meant to desert him, he would never stop looking for her.

'Of course I will, if that is your dearest wish. How could I refuse?'

The library fire was banked low, the house was quiet and she had bid the last servant good night. Bessie did not require a maid's services to put her to bed. Now she paced the library floor to the ticking of the French ormolu clock and the whisper of her silk slippers upon the carpet. Since the walk that morning, her thoughts had been in feverish turmoil. At first, she had feared for her future without Prudence as her benefactress, feared that she would be left adrift to sink or swim by her wits, to struggle for survival in a cold, cruel world. She had gasped as if water were filling her mouth and nose again. Then when Prudence revealed her true intentions, she could barely contain her glee.

She was to be left alone with Edward. Once more, he would have need of her. Once more, she would stand at his side as his helpmeet.

She looked to the mantlepiece as a single chime announced the midnight hour. From above the mantle, old Sir Roderick glared down at her and she thought back to the day she had met Prudence and Edward coming down the road the day after his funeral, black shadows against the afternoon sun. She had never told Prudence that in her naivety she imagined them to be the ghosts of her dead grandparents. She had never told her the truth of her drowning mother either. Perhaps she wanted to keep a part of herself secret. She did not own much else.

A youthful Prudence looked out from her portrait alongside

that of her father, casting a benevolent smile over her domain, the precious locket a flash of gold against her pale skin. *She* had never dressed in rags. *She* had never dressed in another's cast-off finery, as had Bessie. *She* could laugh at the idea of needing money.

'But where would you be without her?' Bessie whispered to the empty room. 'Who else would have a care for an illiterate girl with dirt beneath her nails?' A girl who did not know enough to blow her nose upon a handkerchief, or pen her own name.

A tear trembled on her lower lid and she blinked it away. Hadn't she repaid her former mistress with her years of service? For everyone knew that a companion was but a servant in finer clothes, fetching her embroidery basket and reading aloud rather than fetching tea and cleaning fireplaces. Hadn't she paid her dues when she almost drowned at her employer's side on the far side of the world? When her life was almost taken for a second time in this woman's service?

Bessie belonged at Westcott Hall. And Westcott Hall belonged with her. Now Prudence would have a chance to repay that little orphan girl.

She reached for the book resting on a side table beside the mistress of Westcott Hall's favourite chair. It was a copy of *Mansfield Park*, and Bessie had secreted Prudence's letter to Edward in its pages. Now she removed the letter and slipped the single leaf of paper from its envelope. Her lips moved as she read its contents, her whisper barely audible. One day she would be practised enough at her reading that she could read without moving her lips. One day she would read as easily as her employer.

'"Do not search for me, dearest Edward. For you shall never find me,"' she read, scoffing silently. Prudence might as well have told him not to breathe for all the good it would do.

'"We were not meant to be."' But who could tell what was meant to be and what wasn't? Bessie had escaped her fate beneath the waters thrice. She had learned that her will was stronger than fate. She had learned that, given the chance, she could make it so. And now she was being handed a chance.

She carried the letter to the fireplace, tipped the fire screen forward and dropped both letter and envelope into the coals, watching with interest as the paper curled into flames.

If she gave it to him, Edward would pay no heed to its contents. He was loyal; if he knew his wife to be alive, he would not rest until he found her. He would scour the globe to reach her. Only time and a conviction of her death would resign him to a new life.

Their new life, she hoped. He with his new wife. She with her new husband.

She understood him better than Prudence ever could. And when that woman was gone, Bessie would finally have her chance to love him better too.

41

Somerset, England

2023

'It seems like only yesterday we were celebrating your last birthday.' Jude watched as Eliza blew out the candles on her cake, only to see them flare into life again despite the afternoon breeze. They both glanced over at Daniel, to find him smothering a laugh. He almost looked like a boy, with his wind-tousled hair and faded jeans. He certainly acted like one sometimes.

'I can guess who bought the candles,' Eliza said, rolling her eyes.

'Sorry. I was tossing up between the pink glitter number thirty-six or the sparklers, but then I spotted these beauties and couldn't resist.'

'You're so lame,' she laughed.

'Just don't get those stinky ones,' Jude said. 'They start out smelling of apples or roses and then turn into something truly putrid. The ladies and I had to abandon our last poker night at my place because I succumbed to temptation at the gift store and bought one.'

They both turned to stare at her.

'It's true. I didn't read the label properly and . . .' she shrugged. 'Anyway, how is the book coming along?'

'I'm still puzzling over how to finish it,' Eliza said, cutting her aunt a slice of fluffy sponge cake and depositing it on a picnic plate. The detritus of her birthday lunch surrounded them on the lawn in front of the hall, while the smell of lavender filled the air and the distant sounds of hammering drifted towards them from the house.

'But I do have a title,' she added. '*A Lady's Voyage to the South Seas: the Remarkable Story of Prudence Merryfield*. What do you think? Not too long?'

'I'd read it,' Jude said, inadvertently spraying cake crumbs in her direction.

Eliza smiled at her aunt. 'You'd read a roll of toilet paper if I wrote it. I don't think that counts.'

'Well, it's a remarkable story, and who better placed to write it than her not-quite descendant? After all, we've had to live with rumours of evil-doing by our family for almost two hundred years.'

'Yes, except I think the rumours may have been right. One of our ancestors probably did do away with Prudence. If not Edward, then Bessie. We may never know exactly how she died,' Eliza said, 'only that she almost certainly didn't die of natural causes. All the rest is conjecture.'

'I'm sure you'll find the ending you're looking for,' Jude said.

'Maybe . . . but it's difficult finding time to work on it with the shop and everything,' Eliza said with a fatalistic shrug.

Daniel and Jude shared a look of exasperation over the birthday cake.

'What?' She paused mid-slice, the knife hovering menacingly above the cake.

The pair were silent for a few seconds – not without some frantic eye signals, she noted – but then Jude put up her hand, waggled her fingers and volunteered, 'You know you don't really want to keep up the shop, pet.'

'Yes I do! I love old things. You know that. And I have a level of expertise now, and a diary full of contacts, so why would I waste them?'

'They wouldn't be wasted,' Jude persisted.

'Anyhow, now that Daniel's decided to put his office upstairs where the flat is, there's no problem.'

'Just because you have the space, doesn't mean you—'

Daniel didn't finish what he was intending to say, quite possibly because she warned him off with her 'this is about to turn into an argument' look. He was a pragmatic man, she had come to realise. He didn't bother with arguments where there was no winner, only losers.

'How about that salad, hey? Ancient grains . . . who knew? I grew up on iceberg lettuce, tomato and a bit of cucumber if you were lucky. Now a salad isn't a salad without something ancient or deconstructed involved.'

He stretched out on the picnic rug, his arms behind his head as if he didn't have a care in the world. She supposed that was one way to win an argument – pretend it didn't exist. She had noticed this about him before. So different to her head-on-confront-all-opposition approach to conflict.

The conversation moved to the safer ground of holiday plans, and once Daniel was napping on the picnic rug in the sun, his stomach placated, Eliza and Jude decided to take the dogs for a walk in the woods while he slept. The dogs roamed ahead, while every so often she called their names to keep them in sight. She was still wary of Bobby nosing about indiscriminately. Recently, at the park, he had got a chicken bone wedged in the roof of his mouth and she had to undertake a major excavation with her fingers. Neither of them had been pleased.

'Daniel thinks Prudence was probably murdered and her body buried somewhere in these woods. The old bell pits would have been the perfect burial place before they were all filled in or fell in,' she said, as they wandered through the last of the fallen leaves.

'I'm glad I don't believe in ghosts then,' Jude said, glancing around as the trees closed in on them. 'What do you think?'

'I think he may be right. I really don't want to believe that one of our ancestors was a murderer, but the locket and the pocket book we found walled up in the dressing room certainly suggest foul play. Otherwise, why hide them?'

'Why indeed.'

'And the woods would have made the perfect hiding place. The bell pit's a ready-made burial plot.' She turned her head to regard the house, jutting above the trees behind them. It was beginning to look spruce, readying itself for a new era.

'Perhaps Edward and Bessie fell in love,' she continued, 'and one of them decided to remove Prudence from the picture permanently.'

'Money and love, both powerful motivations.' Jude considered her niece thoughtfully.

'Except the diary entries hint that Prudence was planning to leave Westcott Hall. Why else the mention of Scotland? Perhaps she even planned to return to the South Pacific. Why murder her if she was leaving anyway?'

'To make sure she didn't change her mind and return. People are allowed to change their mind you know, pet.'

Her aunt threw her a meaningful look, which she ignored. But Jude could be like a terrier when she wanted to make a point, and she wasn't about to let her niece get away that easily. After thirty-six years of aunthood, she obviously felt she had a proprietary claim over Eliza's life, and perhaps she did. She was the closest thing Eliza had to a mother now. She knew her story better than Eliza knew Prudence's. Still, there were always secrets.

'I don't understand why you're so determined to continue operating the Cabinet of Wonders when it's obvious you don't have a passion for it any more, if you ever did. There are so many other things you could do with your life,' Jude persisted.

Eliza covered her face with her hands and gave a sigh. Clearly, her aunt wasn't about to let the subject lie.

'I *was* about to do something else,' she said, after a few moments to gather her thoughts. 'Before Mum died.' She stared down at the ground as tears threatened to spill over. She really didn't want to talk about this, didn't want to bring it all back. And yet, in a way, it would be a relief. A confession of sorts.

'So why didn't you?'

'Just before Mum had her heart attack I accepted a job as a writer and digital marketer for an online antiques magazine. I was really excited to be going back to writing. But I hadn't found the courage to tell her that I was on the verge of leaving her to run the business without me. And then look what happened.'

There, she had said it. She had admitted her treachery aloud. She had been about to desert her mother, to leave her to fend for herself at the store. Then Eleanor had gone and died, bequeathing the store to her. So how could she abandon her mother's last gift? And how could she renege on the last promise she had made to her?

'Oh, pet, you can't put two and two together and make five. You know that. Your mother didn't die because you accepted another job.'

'I know that. But I promised her.'

'Your mother was a sensible woman. She wouldn't expect you to keep a promise to a dead person. How could she know if your situation had changed? How could she know that the whole world had changed?' Jude said in her voice of reason. 'And anyway, how do you know she wasn't waiting for you to find another job so that she could retire?'

Eliza could see her aunt's logic, but promises had nothing to do with logic.

'*I* would know,' she said, her voice catching in her throat. 'I promised her I'd mind the store when she was gone. That was the last thing she asked of me. Her last words to me.' She was blubbering the words through tears now. 'How could I break a last promise?'

She couldn't live with herself if she did. She was expecting her aunt to argue, to tell her that it was okay to break even a last promise. That's why she was taken aback when Jude didn't argue. In fact, she smiled. She smiled and pulled her niece into an embrace. Then she held her at arm's length and said, 'I was there when the paramedics put Eleanor into the ambulance, remember? I heard her last words to you.'

Her aunt was right. She had been there, standing by Eliza's side in the Cabinet of Wonders when the paramedics lifted her mother on to the gurney and strapped her in. She was there as the paramedics wheeled her mother through the store, knocking the corner of a Regency dining table as they negotiated the obstacle course of antique furniture. Eliza and Jude had followed the officers as they wheeled the gurney through the door and out into the street. Her mother had lain there with her arms resting over her stomach and no inkling of what was to come. None of them knew how their world was about to change. Eleanor had been smiling behind her oxygen mask, her soft white hair spread about her, the pain showing white on her face. And just as the paramedics were about to hoist her into the open rear of the ambulance, her mother lifted a hand and beckoned her daughter close.

'Mind the shop when I'm gone, love.'

Eliza quoted her mother's last words to her aunt. 'That's what she said to me as they took her away.' That's what she had asked of her daughter as she gasped for air behind that plastic mask.

Her aunt was still smiling gently. 'That's not what she said, pet. You heard it wrongly. Or remembered it wrongly. Your

343

mother didn't say, "Mind the shop *when* I'm gone." She said, "Mind the shop *while* I'm gone." She thought she was coming back. She had no idea she was going to die. She would never have laid that burden on you.'

Jude squeezed Eliza's hands so hard that they hurt.

'She said . . . what . . . ?' No, it couldn't be true. She had been there. She had heard.

'Of course she thought she was coming back. We all did.'

It was true that Eliza had thought her mother would be home in a few days. When she saw her taken away on the gurney she never contemplated the idea that she wouldn't see her again. She thought the doctors would save her. That they would fix her heart and send her home.

Could her aunt be right?

'Oh, sweetheart, you've been living with that memory all this time.'

'I felt like I'd let her down,' Eliza whispered, to herself as much as her aunt. 'I wanted to make it up to her somehow. And keeping the shop going seemed the only way.'

Her aunt was still holding her hands. 'Perhaps living your best life is the only way.'

42

Somerset, England

1846

Bessie took a step back and surveyed her easel with a sigh. The snow-covered ground of her sketch was a muddy grey and her winter-stark trees dripped blackly down the page. Instead of tripping lightly through the woods, the central figure of her painting resembled a wooden doll, and the sky was blanketed in runny white paint. She sighed and put her brush aside, contemplating starting anew with a fresh sheet of paper. Little good that it might do. Her art never seemed to improve, regardless of how many hours she devoted to it. All she knew was that she was compelled to repeat the same sketch, over and over, no matter how much wet snow soaked her shoulders or cold wind cut through her worsted jacket. This scene she painted had become a purgatory of her own making.

She picked up her smallest brush, dipped it on to a block of green and touched it to the featureless face. The eyes seemed to stare back at her accusingly, like angry green blots, while the hair capped the figure in a blob of red. She had inherited the mahogany paint box from Prudence, having always coveted its porcelain mixing pans and washbowls, its tray for brushes and scrapers, its blocks of inks and watercolours. Now it belonged to her. Yet no matter how many hours she spent at her easel, she could not capture her subjects with the same ease her friend once had. The colours were invariably muddied, and a heavy-handed brush obliterated the detail with which she took such pains.

Nevertheless, that afternoon she was determined to make the most of a brief spell of fine weather, for soon her body would be too cumbersome to paint *en plein air*. Her maid, Bevan, had already loosened her stays considerably, and it would not do at all to be seen waddling across the countryside big with child. There was tattle enough to keep the village blatherskites busy dissecting the goings on at Westcott Hall, without more gossip about the new Mrs Ambrose. Even old Custard had taken to sermonising about wolves in sheep's clothing and the like.

'You're at the same painting again, I see,' Edward called out as he approached through a thicket of bare trees, a voluminous figure in black against a ground filmed with dirty snow. His coat sleeves were crossed about his belly as if he carried some hidden object. For a moment she wondered what it could be, shrouded as it was by his greatcoat. Then as he drew closer, she recognised his favourite hound cradled in his arms, a fox terrier by the name of Sully. Once, when he had taken one too many cups of claret at dinner, he confided that he had named the bitch after a much-loved nurse from his childhood. And Bessie wondered what he might name after her, if she were gone.

'What ails Sully?' she asked, putting aside her brush. The poor creature poked its head up and barked at the mention of its name, resting its chin upon its master's sleeve.

Edward did not answer at first, striding towards her in silence with the wings of his coat flapping about him like a crow. 'There's some small resemblance,' he said instead when he reached her, staring down at the sketch upon her easel. 'But I've wondered . . . where does she go to, this woman fleeing through the snow?'

'I don't know, Edward. No one knows. That's the pity of it.'

'Yes. It is a great pity.'

'I thought we might hang the sketch in the library . . . if only I can do her justice with my brush.'

'Justice you say?' The harshness of his tone surprised her. He was usually so patient. So kind.

'I meant only that . . .' she began, thinking to make amends.

She had forgotten that Edward had little faith in justice any longer. Some in the parish had been braying for justice these past seven years. The London newspapers brayed even louder. They could not let matters lie; not after the constable found no evidence of foul play, nor after the coroner declined to hold an inquest without a body. Even after Edward had the servants comb the grounds for weeks. Still they muttered behind cottage walls, that of course the magistrate would bring an open ruling, since he dined at the hall at least once a month. And the newspapers continued to rake up the story of the adventuress who survived a shipwreck only to meet with foul play in the gentle vales of Somerset.

'But what of Sully?' she asked, to distract him from this line of thought.

'Oh, I found her . . . didn't I, girl?' He ruffled the fur between the dog's ears and was rewarded with a whimper.

'Did she tackle a badger again?'

'No. No. She fell down one of the ancient bell pits, poor girl. There are several in the woods, you know, from the days when the local people mined their own coal. Some pits have collapsed in on themselves, but a couple can still prove dangerous to the unwary.'

'I've seen several shallow dips in the ground when out walking,' she said, striving for a carefree tone, 'and wondered what they might be.'

'Well you might wonder, my dear. I heard the sound of a dog whimpering and followed the cries,' he said, stroking the old dog's quivering flank. 'Otherwise I might never have found her.

She might have lain at the bottom of that pit, moaning in pain, suffering thirst, cowering in fear, until at last she died alone. Knowing that none would come to save her, no matter how pitifully she cried out.'

Bessie felt a chill strike her body, despite her ermine-trimmed walking dress and worsted jacket. She busied herself cleaning her brushes. If she pretended not to understand, perhaps her husband might not persist in his tale.

'Yes, well may you shiver. Poor Sully shivered at the bottom of that pit. So I had Bobbett fetch our tallest ladder and climb down to rescue the old girl myself. What do you think of that, my dear?' His voice crackled as frostily as the snow beneath her feet.

'I know you're very attached to her.' She dare not look at him, for fear of what she might see on his face. She already heard the icy mettle in his voice.

'Should you like to guess what I found there?'

'Well, I am glad you found her only a little the worse for wear,' she ventured.

'There was a fall of unmelted snow, a covering of rotting leaves and branches, and beneath that a pile of earth and rocks. But once Sully knew she was rescued she scrambled to her feet and became even more agitated as she sniffed and pawed at the ground.'

'Perhaps some other animal met its end at the bottom of the pit,' she murmured, 'and Sully could smell it.'

'Found its corpse, you mean. Indeed. I prodded the ground with my cane – you recall the one with the engraved gold knob given to me by my former wife – and discovered the decaying remains of what I thought to be a dead beast. Except, on examining it more carefully, I realised that it was the fur of no animal that lived in this vicinity. In fact, it looked to be the remnants of an ermine trim of some kind. Of course, along with the fur I also encountered the decaying remnants of what I presumed to be a woman . . .'

He paused to allow for a response, but Bessie could find nothing to say. Her face tingled with the cold and her breathing grew shallower with each new revelation. He described his discovery in such a dispassionate voice, as if he spoke of a dead rabbit or fox. But beneath his calm and stolid tones she sensed an unspoken fury or grief – she could not determine which – or perhaps a combination.

'I'm sure you know of what I speak, don't you, my dear?'

Bessie could do nothing but shake her head in response. She did not wish to know. She did not wish to hear. She did not wish to remember. She had consigned the memory to her nightmares, along with her other fractured memories. The recurring images of a drowning mother, of her own struggle to find air, all the things that should not be contemplated in this world. Things that did not need to have happened, if only she could block them from her thoughts.

'And although it was an unpleasant task, particularly since my heart quickened and my throat choked with a most fearful anticipation, as I know you'll understand, I searched the corpse for further clues to its identity,' he said, compelling her attention with his eyes. 'And what should I find but the remains of a Brussels carpet bag, containing an oilskin bag with bone-handled brushes, a mirror and some rusting pins. I suspect at one time it may have also held a shawl, a nightdress and change of petticoat. But the fabrics were rotten and fell to pieces at my touch.'

He drew a few heavy, sighing breaths in the cold air before continuing. 'I forced myself to search further, seeking irrefutable evidence, and knowing that a lady contemplating a trip would not go far without the aid of her almanac. Would she, my dear?'

'No. I suppose she wouldn't.'

'And thus when I lifted the tatters of the cloak, gown and

petticoats with my cane, I discovered amongst them an oilcloth-wrapped parcel. And upon unwrapping that parcel I found that it contained a lady's pocket book. Here it is, my dear.' He supported the dog with one arm as he reached into the pocket of his greatcoat and produced a small bundle. 'The poor dead woman must have had it in her pockets. Here it is.'

She tried not to see the parcel he held out to her. Tried not to sniff the odour of death that emanated from it.

'It pertains to belong to Prudence Merryfield, don't you know. Our dear Prudence's journal of 1838. You know how attached she was to her pocket books. Here, take a look, my dear.'

She took the parcel with a shaking hand but did not open it, did not dare to explore its contents, despite his urging. She could only hold it in her hand as if it might poison her with a hidden sting.

'The most puzzling aspect of my discovery is that I should have known my late wife, my dearest Prudence, would never have left home without her mother's locket. She would never have run from us without that comfort. And yet . . . you wear that very locket about your neck.'

Although she shivered in the cold wintry air, beneath the protection of her gown and jacket, the locket nestled between her breasts warmed by her skin, protected by the drumbeat of her heart. It depicted a tiny image of a woman with hair as red and curling as her own. Why had she insisted upon keeping it? Why had she told Edward that Prudence planned to repair its broken chain?

Why did she not leave it with Prudence?

'It was an accident, Edward,' she began, her voice hoarse from the cold and from fear. 'I . . . I . . . did not know how to tell you.'

'Tell me what?'

'I did not want you to think Prudence intended to leave you. I did not want to hurt you so.'

'You thought it better that all these years I was never sure what happened to her? That the entire parish believed I murdered my wife.'

'I'm sorry. I'm so very sorry. I should have told you,' she cried.

'Told me what, my dear?'

'That Prudence planned to leave. That she confided in me.'

'I see,' he said, although from the way he glared at her she saw that he didn't. Didn't understand how it had been for her. How could he?

'I followed her . . . to see if I could dissuade her from leaving, from hurting you . . . us,' she said, searching for the words to make her admission. Her confession. She closed her eyes, shutting out her husband's stern face and cold words that brought the memories flooding back.

The snow had been hard-packed and slippery that day as Bessie followed Prudence through the woods. Her friend walked to her meeting place on a quiet lane with the post-chaise that would spirit her away to Scotland. Bessie had to tread carefully as she picked her way over the icy ground and through the woods. And when she finally caught up, Prudence had been surprised, even annoyed, to see her. 'What are you doing here?' she had said and ordered her to be gone. Bessie had begged her to stay, reminded her of Edward's love, of her own love. But Prudence would not be swayed. She was adamant that there was nothing at the hall for her any more. Nothing left between her and Edward. And when Bessie would have held her in an embrace, Prudence backed away in anger, tripping on a branch and stumbling backwards on the frozen ground.

'I reached out to save her, Edward,' Bessie said when she had finished her tale. 'I clutched for the only thing I could catch hold of – her locket. But the chain broke and she . . . she toppled backwards . . . falling down and down into the pit.'

351

She closed her eyes tight to shut out the image that always hovered on the periphery of her memory.

'I . . . I heard the sound of her head striking something, a rock perhaps. And when I looked down over the edge I saw that she was completely still, her body lying at a most unnatural angle. She was dead and I could not save her,' she whimpered. 'I could not save my friend.'

There had been no cries of distress, no pleas for help. Prudence was dead as soon as her head struck the rock. And Bessie had to live with that death forever more. Her memories were her punishment.

'Well, that is an inventive story, I'll give you that, my dear,' Edward said, a cruel smile pulling at one corner of his mouth.

Oh, why had she not thrown the locket into the pit after Prudence? Why had she not returned this memento to its owner before she covered her with rocks and scattered her with earth and branches. She should have thrown the locket into the pit before she scrabbled so hard in the snow that her gloves tore and her fingers bled. Instead, she had been tempted by this paltry thing.

This precious, precious thing that Prudence had from her mother.

'She . . . she gave me a letter for you,' she said, rising to her feet and clawing at his coat. 'She wrote telling you not to look for her. That she intended to take up travelling again. And in time you would be free to marry and have children. That you weren't to search for her, as she had taken great pains that you would never find her. She wanted you to find happiness.'

'And I suppose you have that letter still.'

'No. I saw no point in hurting you further. I . . . *please*,' she begged, clutching at air, for he turned his back on her.

'*Please* . . . you *must* believe me.'

But Edward did not relent. He was already striding down the

snow-covered path towards the vast empty rooms of the hall.

'Don't worry, my dear. I shall have some men fill in the pit,' he called, his voice reaching her like a thin echo as he strode away. 'We wouldn't want anyone else to meet with such an accident.'

'Please! Forgive me!' she called, but he did not look back. He would never look back again. And Bessie would never reach him again.

Prudence had been the closest thing to a mother she had ever known. She had guided and watched over her, she had petted and made a fuss of her. She had turned an urchin into a lady. And yet . . . at heart Bessie would always be that urchin, sleeping beneath hedgerows and foraging the woods for mushrooms. She would always live in fear for her future while she had no roof of her own and the morsels she ate came from another woman's kitchen. That roof and those morsels could be taken from her at a whim. Her life could be stolen from her at any moment and she would find herself drowning once more.

'Forgive me,' she sobbed, cradling her swollen belly. 'Forgive me,' she pleaded as she stared at the misshapen, doll-like figure on her easel, fleeing through that snowy landscape.

One day she would make amends, even if she had to paint the same scene, over and over again, every day of her life, until she made things right. One day Prudence would forgive her.

43

Somerset, England

2024

It was apparent from the crush of people spilling out into the entry that Eliza may have invited a few too many guests to the opening. She had asked everyone she knew and everyone on her mailing list, but never for a moment thought so many of them would turn up. Luckily, the off-licence was just down the road, and in case of emergencies there was always Deliveroo if the catering ran out. Meanwhile, she sipped her prosecco and nibbled her empanada as she surveyed her domain, hoping she would remember everyone's names. She had kept a couple of sofas and dressers on which to drape clothes but gone were the artfully arranged vignettes of eighteenth- and nineteenth-century life, and in their place were racks of pristine garments hailing from the eighties and nineties.

A few of her guests wandered out into the cobbled lane to inspect the front window, which she had arranged like a very untidy bedroom (a twin to her messy bedroom, let's be honest). A double-breasted Moschino Cheap and Chic jacket hung from an open wardrobe door, a shagpile rug was littered with cast-off combat boots and ballerina slippers, while a long red vinyl trench from Marc Jacob's 1993 collection for Perry Ellis featured on a hat stand. The display might seem at odds with the wood-framed

354

Georgian shop window and the tessellated black-and-white tiled entry – but that was the point.

Daniel was on duty behind the bar, while Jude exclaimed to sundry acquaintances that she would buy everything in the store if only it came in a size sixteen. Yes, Eliza could breathe easy for a moment.

In honour of the occasion, she had abandoned her usual oversized tote in favour of a mini crocheted yellow shoulder bag. It had left her feeling somewhat vulnerable. She felt like an expectant mother, except instead of a child she was birthing a business and soon a book. What if both her babies failed? What if no one liked them? It was all too terrible to contemplate. All she could do was take a step and then another step and see how far she could go. She would count on the prosecco to deal with tonight's butterflies.

Amidst a huddle of designer-clad female guests gathered alongside a rack of shirts and blouses, she spotted something incongruous; a short older gentleman in what appeared to be a natty Savile Row suit. Ah, it appeared that Harold Hobbs had arrived and was chatting amiably with her friend Sarah, of the braided hair and Pucci trousers. She had invited him but doubted he would brave the alien territory of women's vintage clothing. Then again, Harold was full of surprises. She raised her glass high to hail him and ventured forth into the fray.

'Harold,' she said, kissing him on both cheeks. 'You came.'

'I wouldn't have missed it for the world. Especially not when I claim a familial connection to the proprietress.' He glanced around the store beaming. 'It appears to be a wild success.'

'Free food and drink are always a wild success. But I'm hopeful. The online store is up and running and getting a lot of look-sees, so we'll see what happens.'

'And Daniel is manning the bar, I see.'

'Mm-hm. He thinks he's at a barbecue in Bondi. He's very liberal with the booze,' she said, turning to smile at the man behind the bar, who was laughing at something one of his customers said. He looked so handsome in his open-necked shirt and denim shorts. She'd had to gently dissuade him from adding a straw Fedora. 'Let's get you a drink.'

'I wouldn't say no, but I have something to give you first. Is there somewhere quiet we can go?'

'You do? Now I'm curious. Let's go into the back office.'

Harold followed in her wake as she forged a path through the crowd to her office, where it was marginally quieter. She hadn't been able to part with her mother's old table, on which Harold now set down a flat rectangular parcel wrapped in brown paper.

'I finished reading the draft of your book and I thought you might like to have this. A store opening and pre-book launch gift in one.'

'That's so kind of you. You shouldn't have bothered. But I hope you have notes for me. I'm still puzzling over how to end it, and I could use some insights,' she said as she put her glass to one side. She didn't know whether she was more nervous about her business baby or her book baby. She wanted constructive help – but then again, she didn't know how she would handle harsh criticism. They were her babies, after all.

'I believe this might prove more useful than notes,' Harold said quietly.

She glanced up but he merely nodded significantly towards the package. Even more curious now, she almost ripped off the sticky tape. Harold was a master of the mysterious, she decided; wondering, not for the first time, about the exact nature of his former profession.

'You weren't a spy in another life, were you?' she asked, as she tore open the paper wrapping.

'What a strange thing to ask, although I'm quite flattered. I never fancied myself as the James Bond type, though,' he said, blinking behind his bifocals.

She noticed that he didn't actually answer her question, but when no further comment was forthcoming, she redirected her attention to the package, which opened to reveal a framed watercolour. She immediately recognised it as one she had seen hanging on his library wall.

'One of Prudence's,' she said contemplatively. 'That's so generous. I'm really touched.'

The watercolour wasn't one of her best; the colours were muddy and the figure lacked the whimsy of her Samoan sketches. Yet the artist had imbued it with a degree of movement and naive detail, always interesting in historical works, and winter was palpable in the bare trees and suggestion of an icy wind. Eliza felt a shiver of déjà vu, as if she knew the exact spot depicted. The sketch showed a lone woman in a full-skirted dark maroon gown hurrying through a snow-blanketed wood. She clutched a carpet bag in one hand and a hooded mantle billowed behind her in the wind. The hood had fallen back to reveal dishevelled red hair, and she stared out from the sketch with a piercing green-eyed stare.

'It's my pleasure. Although I think you should take a closer look. She has something clutched to her chest.'

She eyed him questioningly, before taking up a loupe she kept at hand on her work table. She began with the object the woman held against her breast, noting that it was actually a small wine-coloured book of some kind. Further inspection revealed that a very fine brush indeed had been used to paint the face, the book, and the detail of the dress bodice where a gold locket rested between the points of a pelerine collar. She held her breath momentarily, realising what she was seeing. The locket was too tiny to show any detail, a mere blob of gold, but she knew immediately what it was meant to be.

'It's Prudence. Running through the woods,' she said at last. And if she was not mistaken, she clutched a pocket book in her hand and was wearing her mother's locket.

'I thought of this sketch when I read the draft of your book where you conjecture that she may have met with foul play in the woods behind the hall. So I had a closer look. I'd never given it much thought before. Just assumed it was some kind of self-portrait. And not a very good one at that.'

'Do you think she was painting her plan of escape?'

Eliza continued to explore the painting with her loupe, noticing a dip in the snow-covered ground near the horizon, a dip that may have been the remains of a bell pit. Roving further, she noted a familiar roofline glowering above the trees to one side of the painting, while the suggestion of a path wound towards the distant pit on the other. She then turned her attention to the signature at the bottom of the scene. As expected, it had been signed: *P Ambrose*. But no, wait a moment, that wasn't a 'P'; it was an 'E' . . . and it wasn't written in the same cramped tiny hand she knew so well from the pocket book.

She had been too quick, too presumptuous. She had assumed that, like the other sketches in Harold's collection, this too had been painted by Prudence.

'Have you examined the signature, Harold?'

'No, I was more concerned with the woman in the picture and where she was going.'

'Well, this wasn't signed by Prudence. I think it may be the work of our mutual ancestor, Elizabeth aka Bessie Ambrose, née Pike.'

Harold regarded her gravely. 'I see . . . well, you don't need to be a spy to work that one out then.'

Bessie had painted her one-time mistress fleeing the hall, for what lady would take a stroll in the woods carrying a travelling bag? And she certainly would not stroll in the woods alone in winter. If that weren't enough of a hint, the artist had also painted that lady wearing a gold locket – possibly the same locket Bessie later paraded in her own portrait at Taunton. The fleeing figure clutched a book that might have revealed her secrets, and the painting also revealed to an astute viewer the very location where Prudence may have met her death – all hidden in plain sight.

That poor woman.

What if it were true that she had died alone at the bottom of a pit. Screaming for help until her throat grew hoarse, moaning with the agony of broken limbs. Waiting hopelessly for someone, anyone, to hear her. Even now, many long years later, Eliza could imagine the fear and pain she would have known. She could only hope that it had not endured long.

She could not help wondering why Bessie would have revealed these secrets in a painting for all to see.

'Why would she suggest to anyone who cared to look that Prudence met with foul play?' she asked, meeting Harold's eyes.

'Perhaps this was her admission of guilt,' he suggested.

'Or her plea for forgiveness.' Perhaps in painting her sin for all to see, she had found a way of expiating it – a confession of sorts.

Or rather than being a confession . . . she might have been picking at the scab left by gossip and innuendo. Scratching the old wound of scandal that had plagued her marriage and tormented a poor maid whose only crime was to become mistress of Westcott Hall.

Was Bessie the perpetrator here or the victim? She had painted her pain – but whether from guilt or grief, Eliza would probably never know. Eliza studied the watercolour, feeling the loneliness of that figure fleeing through the icy landscape, but also sensing the loneliness of the artist who had painted it.

Is that what *she* had been doing? Painting her pain, over and over. Picking at the scab of her grief. Expiating her guilt and her sorrow each time she bought or sold a table, a dresser or an old jug. Is this why she had become so fascinated by Prudence's story?

She had become fixated on the past when she could have been looking to the future.

44

Somerset, England

1838

The woods were silent except for the sound of trees creaking in the wind and snow cracking beneath her boots. A rapid twittering in an overhead branch startled her, but it was only a wren surprised by her sudden appearance in its territory. She drew her mantle with the ermine trim closer to shut out the wind needling through her woollen dress, momentarily regretting that she had not brought her muff. To avoid detection, she must travel light, but the hand gripping her carpet bag had already grown numb through her glove.

Prudence was fond of walking but this season was the coldest she could recall for many a year, and she still had a long trudge through the woods before she gained the road where she had arranged to meet the post-chaise hired to take her to Scotland. She trusted that Edward would not think to look for her there, and in time she could travel onwards. He would assume she headed for London or some nearer port where she might board a ship for distant climes. He would not imagine she travelled with only a post boy for company all the way to Scotland. But she was a Lady Adventuress – although sadly out of practice – and she had been shipwrecked and cast away on a deserted island. Scotland was not nearly so daunting as the South Seas.

She lost sight of the last of Westcott's chimneys behind the trees and the path through the woods was obscured by snow so that she must periodically halt and search out the way forward. Once or twice, when she wandered too far from the path, she narrowly avoided the sudden appearance of a disused bell pit, a trap for any unwary wanderer in these woods. But now the slope became even steeper and her travelling bag seemed to grow heavier the further she walked, so that she laboured to catch her breath in the chill winter air. She thought of the last time she had fought her way uphill alone – on that tiny island in the Pacific – and how she had struggled to breathe in the hot humid air of the tropics. Then the sweat had trickled between her breasts and hot sun burned her skin. Then she had been searching for refuge, now she was running from it.

She thought of that last night on the beach by the lagoon she had called home for a brief moment in time. And she remembered her words to Lupelele.

'We all share our loves. That's what being part of a family, part of a village means.'

She thought of her promise to return, a promise she had conveniently set aside. She was so lulled by the habit of her life here in Somerset, a life cossetted and cocooned by her husband, her companion and a small army of servants. Now, she was leaving safety behind to once again set out on a long and circuitous journey to the other side of the world. A journey to fulfil a promise.

And yet, hadn't she also made a promise to her husband, vowing to love and honour him in sickness and in health? She had made an unspoken promise to love and protect Bessie too. And what of the Bobbetts and the other staff and tenants, did she not owe them . . . something?

Was Lupelele not the only one she had betrayed?

Prudence halted beneath the timid shelter of a wintry oak. She set down her bag and leaned her back against the gnarled trunk, staring up at the dull sky. She pictured Edward's face, usually a picture of restraint, when she did not appear in the dining room that evening. At first, he would be annoyed that the mutton was overcooked, for he was most particular about waste. Then he would be concerned that she had sent no footman with a message. Then, when she did not return at all, he would worry that she had met with an accident on the wet and boggy lanes. And when it finally became apparent that Prudence was nowhere to be found, his worry would turn to despair.

Shivering, she huddled beneath her mantle. She could shut out the cold but she couldn't shut out the thoughts that rained down as relentlessly as the falling snow. She had demanded love of Edward, but she hadn't given it. She had expected loyalty, but she hadn't returned it. For in offering up her love and loyalty she would also be gifting her freedom. And that she hadn't been willing or able to do.

She closed her eyes, trying to conjure images of fresh vistas, of faraway cities and foreign shores. She tried to recall the pleasure of setting foot in strange lands, of meeting different peoples and hearing foreign tongues spoken around her. She tried to conjure the smell of a godown in Singapore, the taste of ripe mango in Bangalore or the sea-salt scent of the village in Samoa that had once made her welcome. But all she could see was Edward's face, his eyes alight with hope on the morning when she finally agreed to be his wife. All she could hear was the laughter in his voice as he swung young Alfie high. And despite the snowflakes falling cold on her cheeks, all she could feel was the touch of his skin against hers.

This last thought scorched her with its intensity, for she hadn't felt his skin warm against hers for months. Hadn't been cradled in his embrace for so long. Their love – if indeed it had ever been more than kindly affection – had withered and grown cold. Or so she had thought. Once, years ago, she had felt it flicker there on a beach in the tropics. Yet somehow she had quenched it. Now, poised here in the woods in mid-flight, in bleakest winter, she felt a warmth trickle through her body at the thought of Edward's touch. It began in her most intimate of places and coursed through her belly and her chest to tremble down her arms into her fingers, which twitched as if blood returned them to life after a cold numbness. And in that moment she realised that she wanted him. That she had always wanted him, even as she had denied that need. He was her husband but he was also her lover. And she was his.

She was searching for freedom, but without Edward what would it be worth? Without Edward there would always be a hollow place in her heart. Without Edward she would be shackled by loss.

She had thought her path to freedom lay outside in the world but perhaps it lay inside her heart, after all.

If only she could find her way back.

The snow was falling even heavier than before but her path through the woods was clearer now that she was retracing her steps. All she had to do was follow the tracks of her previous flight through the snowy landscape and they would lead her safely home. And although the snow continued to fall, she hoped to reach the hall before it obliterated her tracks altogether. She walked with her head bowed, her hood raised, to keep the sting of cold from her reddening cheeks and chapped lips. Even so, from beneath the hood she glimpsed a shrouded figure approaching her through the falling snow. For a moment she flinched, for whom but a miscreant would venture forth in this weather? Then as the figure drew closer she recognised the voluminous silhouette and forest-green hue as that belonging to a merino cloak with double pelerine cape that she had not worn these three winters past.

The figure picked up its pace = for here the terrain dipped slightly as the path wound around one of the disused pits = so that Prudence heard the loud creak of boots treading upon the packed snow. She knew who had come to meet her now and waited, wondering what had led Bessie to follow her. She smiled beneath the protection of her hood, for if her friend had come to beg her to return, her mission was about to be happily rewarded.

'What brings you out in this weather?' she asked, setting down her carpet bag with relief. The tips of her fingers were numb now, and were she to remove her gloves they would surely be white and stiff with cold.

The younger woman did not answer immediately, inspecting Prudence from head to foot with a puzzled expression. 'You said you were leaving. You said that you would not return.'

'I have made a terrible mistake, Bessie. I thought that Edward would be free without me, and I without him. But the truth is we are bound to each other, just as I am bound to you in friendship, and to our neighbours and tenants in mutual trust. I did not understand before this.' She reached out a hand to her friend but Bessie hid her hands from the cold in her sleeves.

'You gave me a letter to give to Edward once you were out of reach,' Bessie said flatly. Perhaps she had not heard her above the whistle of the wind.

'I'm returning, so there's no need for him to know that I intended to leave.' And perhaps one day soon, he might be prevailed upon to accompany her on another voyage, a journey to fulfil her earlier promise. For she still carried Lupelele in her heart.

'No. It can't be,' Bessie moaned.

The expression of horror on her friend's face caught at Prudence's heart. The poor dear girl's grandparents had abandoned her by dying. And who could know what had happened to her mother, or indeed her father, if she had ever known them. She had been left alone once too often.

'I'm so sorry that I ever thought to abandon you,' Prudence said, stepping forward to envelope the girl in her embrace. Beneath the folds of the cloak she could sense the tension in Bessie's stance. 'I cared only for myself.'

'You have always cared only for yourself!' Bessie cried. 'And now, when finally I have the opportunity to find my true place . . . to find my true home . . . you would take it from me!'

Prudence felt the girl tremble in her arms. 'You have a home with me, with Edward,' she reassured her. She had forgotten how vulnerable Bessie could be, how thin her veneer of strength, how brittle her maturity. Beneath that tough exterior a waif yet lurked.

'You don't love Edward!' Bessie shrieked. 'But I do! And once you're gone I will show him that, unlike you, he can depend upon my love. You shan't take him away from me again. I won't let you steal my future.'

Prudence stepped back, her arms dropping to her sides. This wasn't what she expected at all. Had the girl lost her reason?

'You're overwrought, dear. Let me lead you back to the hall,' she suggested gently.

Bessie met her words with such a look of hatred that she froze where she stood, shocked and not a little angered by the girl's ingratitude. Prudence had provided for her material comfort, even if she had fallen short in other ways. She may have been an imperfect friend to Bessie but at least she had been a friend.

'What would you have me do, Bessie?'

'Go away as planned. Disappear from our lives for good.'

'I find that I cannot do that, after all. I find that I have a life here. I have people who need me here . . . Edward needs me.' And she needed him.

She was about to walk on, to continue her journey towards

her home, when she felt a sudden violent thrust to her chest, almost as if her heart were failing her. Unprepared for the jolt, she flailed backwards, losing her footing on the slippery ground. For a moment she hovered, arms outstretched like wings to keep her afloat, but the momentum caused by the thrust could not be denied and she began falling backwards, her heels sliding downwards.

In a flash of movement she saw Bessie reach out, as if to save her, but the hand only snatched at her bodice, clutching at the fragile chain around her neck. It held Prudence there for a second, held her to this earth, before the chain snapped and she resumed her fall. Toppling down the slope, her feet scrabbling futilely against the perilous snow, borne away by the force of another woman's hatred.

'Prudence!'

She heard the faint cry as if from afar, for she was already tumbling haphazardly through the air to land with a thud in the darkness below. She did not know how many minutes her body lay in a muddle on the hard ground before she opened her eyes. Dimly, she became aware of the crooked angle of a leg, the unnatural bend of an arm, a sharp stabbing in her chest. She tried to move, to raise herself up, but her limbs refused to obey. She was broken, it seemed, her body battered and beaten by her fall, but for the most part she did not feel pain. There was only the hammering of her head and a fuzziness of thought as she looked up to a circle of dull grey sky above.

She thought of Edward and how he would search the estate for her, wondering if he would eventually find her lying here at the bottom of this pit of darkness. Edward, who had sailed oceans to find her. Edward, who she had believed her jailer when he would have been her lover.

She wondered if she would ever see him again.

She stared up at the circle of sky. For a fleeting moment, she thought she glimpsed her mother hovering above her, tendrils of curling red hair framing her face beneath her hood. The same face that she carried next to her heart. Then the face was gone and there was only a frail ring of light. Soon that would fade too.

The last thing Prudence Merryfield saw, as she lay broken at the bottom of that ancient pit, was a flock of tiny finches flitting across the winter sky in search of refuge.

45

Somerset, England

2024

Daniel halted at the top of the rise and studied the map again, a frown of concentration etching his forehead. Then he compared it with the print of Bessie's watercolour in his other hand, and grimaced. Funny man, he had such inordinate faith in the power of hard data. If he had a detailed-enough topographic map to compare with the landscape depicted in Bessie's painting, then presumably he would be able to find the exact location of Prudence's demise. The problem was, the trees kept getting in the way.

'Maybe we could get a surveyor in to help find it,' he said, rolling both papers up in disgust.

'I don't think we need to go to those lengths yet.'

'I know a few.'

'I'm sure you do. But maybe we could just follow the main path and see where it takes us. Surely Prudence wouldn't have wandered far in the snow if she could help it,' Eliza said with a shrug. It wasn't that she didn't care. It was more that she could feel Prudence's presence throughout these woods, as if she had been waiting for them all these years.

'We could do that, but it's a very imprecise way of going about things.' He shook his head in dismay at her folly.

Eliza edged closer and tipped her head up for a kiss. 'I can be very foolish about some things, you told me that once.'

'Did I?'

'Mm-hmm.'

'Lucky you learned the error of your ways about us then,' he said, hugging her close.

'So lucky.'

'All right, have it your way then. We'll play it by ear. But just so you know . . . my mate Brendan's a surveyor.'

'Good to know.'

He handed her the rolled documents and pulled the shovel from the ground where he had dug it in. Then he whistled for the two dogs, saying, 'Maybe we could find a forked stick to help.'

'Very funny,' she said, biting her lip not to smile.

They set off along the path, basking in the sun filtering through the new spring growth. A pair of marsh tits flitted through the lower branches of a nearby oak, darting just above their heads, and scolding them half-heartedly. The birds weren't the only ones who would be nesting soon, she thought, snuggling closer to Daniel. In a way, Prudence had brought them together. And now she wanted to repay the favour.

The path wound through a grove of elderly oaks before dipping downwards once more. Their passage through the cushion of leaf mould was almost silent as they searched the trees for clues. She and Bobby had come to know these woods well but they had changed in the two centuries since Bessie painted them. And although she had come across a number of bell pit remains in the past, this was her first attempt at sleuthing out one in particular.

'I seem to remember there's another pit over this next rise,' she said, hopefully.

'I know the one you mean. It's just a slight hollow filled with leaf litter now. But who knows . . .'

They climbed a slight knoll, the dogs galloping ahead as usual, until Daniel halted, pointing to the shallow remains of a pit where a patch of celandines turned their heads to catch the sun.

'What do you think?' he said.

They stood looking down at the bowl of bright yellow flowers and shiny heart-shaped leaves. Could this be the spot where Prudence lay? Buried beneath a carpet of flowers? Perhaps it didn't matter exactly where she lay. Prudence was gone, whereas Eliza and Daniel were here and now. And their descendants would be the future. All they could do was remember her in their own way.

'My head says maybe. My back says this will do.' She squeezed his hand and nodded. Her back seemed to be protesting a lot lately. All those hormones.

'Okay then. Let's get to it,' he said, more enthusiastic than most people about the prospect of digging. 'You choose a spot and I'll shovel.'

Bobby and Ruby seemed to know something was afoot because they turned up just as Daniel and Eliza picked their way through the wildflowers, trying not to crush them.

'Stay!' Daniel commanded, before the pair could romp through the flowers after them.

'Here,' she said. She pointed to a patch bare of wildflowers, and Daniel got to work with his shovel. She quite enjoyed watching him.

Twenty minutes later, when he had a neat hole two feet deep and a mound of earth alongside, he stopped digging, smearing his forehead with dirt as he wiped away beads of sweat. 'The soil's quite soft here,' he said, happily.

'Thanks, my turn now,' she said. She set the rolled documents on the ground and reached for the satchel slung across her body. Her hand brushed comfortingly against her rounded belly as she delved inside. Keys, cards, phone, pocket book, lip balm. Okay,

371

pen knife and tape measure too. A leopard couldn't change its spots overnight. Plus a hot-off-the-press copy of *A Lady's Voyage* wrapped in clear plastic. And nestled in a soft cloth bag – the locket.

'Should we say something?' she asked.

'I think your book says it all.'

She supposed it did. She had put everything into the writing of Prudence's book. Everything she knew, or thought she knew, about her not-quite ancestor. And in the gaps between the words – everything she had learned about herself.

'Here, you do the locket,' she said, handing him the jewellery bag.

He knelt beside the hole and leaned in so far that the earth swallowed his arm to the shoulder. Then it was her turn. Kneeling beside him, she reached into her satchel and drew out the plastic-shrouded book, which she dropped into the hole with a flourish.

'And?' he said, searching her face.

She dug around in the satchel, feeling for the pocket book inscribed in her own hand by Prudence Jane Merryfield. But when her hand met worn leather she couldn't quite bring herself to let the book go. The hand simply refused to do her bidding.

'I knew you couldn't do it,' Daniel said gently. 'You take that book with you everywhere. I think it might have sprouted roots.'

'I wanted to.'

'I know. Prudence won't mind. She has her locket back.'

Yes, Prudence had her locket back now.

'And I have you,' she said, beaming at the man who had careened into her life and knocked her for six.

But, all the same, she would keep the pocket book.

Acknowledgements

The Samoan and Somerset villages where my novel is set are figments of my imagination. However, both are based on extensive reading and viewing of other people's research and knowledge. Planned visits were cancelled when borders closed during the pandemic, so I am even more thankful for that information. For pointing me in the right direction I would like to thank Professor Malama Meleisea of the Centre for Samoan Studies at the National University of Samoa. And for reading the Samoan sections of the manuscript, alerting me to any misunderstandings, and suggesting further reading I am deeply grateful to Associate Professor Penelope Schoeffel of the Centre for Samoan Studies. Any errors are very much my own.

I would also like to acknowledge the amazing resources I was able to access online from universities, libraries and archives, for the most part in Australia, New Zealand and the United Kingdom. Unable to travel (or indeed leave my suburb for much of the writing of this book), they were invaluable. Thank you to The New Zealand Electronic Text Collection at Victoria University of Wellington, Museum of New Zealand Te Papa Tongarewa, Auckland Museum, National Library of New Zealand, University of Adelaide's Pacific Collection, Trove — National Library of

Australia's digital collection, Museum Victoria, Australian National Maritime Museum, the State Libraries of New South Wales and Victoria, The Journal of the Polynesian Society, English Heritage, South West Heritage Trust, Historic England, for making your collections freely accessible.

No matter how diligent or talented an author may think herself, any book is a team effort. I would like to thank my very diligent and talented agent, Judith Murdoch, for keeping me on the straight and narrow and promoting my interests. To the team at Headline UK, who have turned my words into this lovely book: my excellent editor Kate Byrne, Yeti Lambregts, Emily Patience and Tina Paul, I offer my heartfelt thanks. And at Hachette Australia, a big thankyou goes to Meg Kennedy and Anna Egelstaff.

Thank you to my wonderful family, Vincent, Ru, Kit and Joice, who listened to the initial garbled ideas that eventually became an actual novel, and sympathised with the moaning whenever I was lost in the writing woods.

Lastly, I would like to acknowledge the unique beauty of the Pacific Island nations and the genuine friendliness of their citizens. I've travelled to many islands over the years and cannot wait to return. I recommend a visit.